STRANGE

COUNTRY

ALSO BY DEBORAH COATES

Deep Down

Wide Open

What Makes a River (e-original)

STRANGE COUNTRY

DEBORAH COATES

A TOM DOHERTY ASSOCIATES BOOK NEW YORK

TOR®

STRANGE COUNTRY

Copyright © 2014 by Deborah Coates

A Tor Book
Published by Tom Doherty Associates, LLC
175 Fifth Avenue
New York, NY 10010

www.tor-forge.com

Tor® is a registered trademark of Tom Doherty Associates, LLC.

The Library of Congress Cataloging-in-Publication Data is available upon request.

ISBN 978-0-7653-2902-8 (hardcover)
ISBN 978-1-4299-4847-0 (e-book)

Tor books may be purchased for educational, business, or promotional use. For information on bulk purchases, please contact Macmillan Corporate and Premium Sales Department at 1-800-221-7945, extension 5442, or write specialmarkets@ macmillan.com.

First Edition: May 2014

Printed in the United States of America

0 9 8 7 6 5 4 3 2 1

To Sarah, Jenn, and Greg. Your friendship means the world to me.

ACKNOWLEDGMENTS

There are a great many people who have been there throughout the writing of each of my books offering encouragement and insight. Without them, these books would not have been conceived, would not have been written, and you would not be reading them now.

To Stacy Hill, my terrific editor, who provides exactly the right amount of feedback and whose critical analysis has made every one of these books better. To Caitlin Blasdell, my agent, who continues to offer me good advice about my books and my writing and my career. To Marco Palmieri, who kept this book and me on track. To Eliani Torres for "sharp" and helpful copyediting. To Irene Gallo and the Tor production team, who have produced a great-looking book.

To Charlie Finlay and the rest of the writers at Blue Heaven for many conversations and critiques and all-around support.

Sarah Prineas, Jenn Reese, and Greg van Eekhout, not just for being supportive and encouraging but also for being critical and honest. I hope my books get better with each one I write, but if they do, it's because I have good friends who insist on it.

And, as always, to my family, to my dogs, to the farm I grew up on, to Iowa and South Dakota and the land.

Thank you.

STRANGE

COUNTRY

1

It was three o'clock in the morning and the car had been parked in the same spot since the night before, had been there long enough that it iced over; the ice had half-melted and it iced over again so that it now looked permanent, like brittle armor. A Toyota, twenty years old, maybe a bit more, a nice car when it was new and it still looked pretty good, with nothing more than a little rust along the wheel wells. There was a web of spidering cracks in the back window on the passenger side, from a kicked-up stone or a hard stab with something pointed, not much yet, but as warm days and cold nights heated and cooled the glass, the cracks would spread.

Boyd Davies left his patrol car running, light from the open driver's door spilling out, frost-white exhaust puffing out the rear. He shrugged his jacket up close and shone a flashlight at the car, the yellow beam bouncing off the icy windows. West Prairie City was quiet as a tomb. That's what people said—quiet as a tomb, because no one else was around, because there was that peculiar sense of emptiness that came with early morning and loneliness and cold. Boyd checked the license plate, had to scrape ice and old dirt away to read it. South Dakota plates, but not local. He went back to his car and called it in, sat in the driver's seat with the door still open.

It was cold and clear, but there wasn't much wind. Boyd liked it, liked this time of year when winter was still heavy in the clouds and in the pale sun, when the temperature still hovered down in frostbite territory. He liked the way the grass lay over, the way the trees looked, stark and forbidding, liked the faint hint of a promise of warmth underneath all of it, something changing in the wind and the slant of the sun in the afternoons. It was mid-March and it felt like it had been winter forever, but spring would come.

It always came.

Dispatch came back and asked him to repeat the license plate, which he did. A coyote trotted down the middle of the street, stopped in the wash of his headlights, its eyes gleaming. A moment passed, watched and watching; then the radio crackled and the coyote slipped sideways into the shadows.

"Go ahead," Boyd said when the dispatcher, Chelly Sweet, who was new, asked if he was available.

"That plate belongs to a 1987 Toyota Corolla, light blue, registered to a Tommy Ulrich. You want the address?"

"Yes."

She read off an address in Rapid City, on the west side, Boyd thought, though he'd have to look it up to be sure. "Phone number?"

"Hold on," she said. He could hear papers and the soft sound of computer keys.

"Yeah, looks like he called in earlier," Chelly said. "Said he was in town yesterday evening—not, yesterday, like eight hours ago. The night *before* that. His car broke down and he's getting someone to tow it." She made an irritated noise. "Somebody just wrote it down on a scrap of paper. There's no call record." She sighed. "Probably the new dispatcher." Like the extra two weeks' experience she had made all the difference between sloppiness and proficiency. "Sorry."

"Thanks," Boyd said. "It's fine."

He fastened his seat belt and closed the door. Templeton had its own two-person police force, but the rest of the county was his—the sheriff's department. Nights like this when it was just him, the central dispatcher, and the overnight cashier down at the Gas 'Em Up on CR54, he felt as if it had all been created just for him, as if the wide-open prairie and the distant smattering of lights at scattered ranches and mobile homes and crossroads were a separate world, his world.

He drove out of West Prairie City and headed south. He'd swing down past the ranch, though he'd already been that way earlier. It pulled at him, that ranch, so that he always knew where it was in relation to where he was, like magnetic north or homing pigeons.

Three cars passed him on the long loop, enough traffic so at this hour—three in the morning in the middle of the week—he watched them close. A cold dry wind blew out of the northwest. A tumbleweed bounced onto the road, hit the side of the car with a hollow scratch, and was gone somewhere behind him. A half mile later, he slowed to turn back onto the county road, no lights out here other than the stars and his own headlights. There was something ahead, a shadow in the twilight at the edge of his high beams. He slowed. Coyote. Another one. He tapped the brakes. Light from the coyote's eyes reflected straight back at him, sharp and otherworldly. It trotted toward him along the road. When it drew parallel to the car, it turned its head and seemed to look directly at him before it angled across the old pavement and disappeared back into the night and the prairie.

Boyd idled his car. A vast nothingness surrounded him. Darkness and grass, wind and cold. He put his foot back on the gas, put a hand up to check the set of his collar, smooth the flap of his shirt pocket, brush nonexistent dust from the yoke of the steering wheel—so automatic, he barely noticed that he did it.

He felt a familiar tug as he passed the end of the drive up to Hallie's ranch, like something real, like a wire. He didn't answer it. It was past three, he was on duty, and he wasn't that guy. The one who signed in, picked up his car, then drove home to sleep a few hours when he was supposed to be on patrol. He would never be that guy. Though he'd met guys like that—one or two—in the five years he'd been a police officer, met them at out-of-town trainings where they bragged in the bar after class. He didn't understand—understood the pull, but didn't understand—couldn't—the dereliction. Because it was a promise, not to the job, but to the people in the towns and on the ranches. A promise that he would be where he said he was and that he would be ready. People said he was a Boy Scout, all honor and duty and service.

And he was.

So, there wasn't any question when he passed Hallie's drive that he would drive past. No question that patrolling an empty road was more important than to see her, hear her say—as she did—"Jesus, Boyd, it's three o'clock in the morning." More important than her lips against his, the clean soap scent of her hair, the soft exhale of her breath against his neck.

Lately there'd been an on-again, off-again feel to their relationship, not on his side, but on hers. He liked her, liked her a lot, maybe loved her, though it wasn't a word he said quickly and when he did say it, he meant it honestly and deeply. But like her? Love parts of her like coming home? Yes. He liked the way she thought and even the way she acted, impulsively but worried about the consequences. Or acknowledging them but going ahead anyway. And he liked *her*, liked the way they fit together, opposite and yet the same.

After Hollowell, after the walls between the living world and the under had rebuilt themselves, after Hallie had told him what happened at the end—because he didn't, had never remembered on his own. After all that, she'd been different. Maybe no one else noticed. He'd figured it was the result of everything that happened, not just killing Travis Hollowell the way she had, but also the way her sister, Dell, had died, the way Hallie herself had been forced out of the army, the way Pabby'd died and Beth had disappeared and Death, especially Death who had asked her to take his place in the under, to control the reapers, the harbingers, and the unmakers. It was as if she'd decided, why commit to anything? And that would weigh on her, he knew, because whether she recognized it or not, it was what she did—commit—to everything she did.

Whatever it was that bothered her, it was evident in their relationship these days, three steps forward, two steps back.

The radio crackled, almost startling him.

"Are you there?" Chelly Sweet's voice sounded thin like old wire, like she thought maybe the world had disappeared in the last thirty minutes, like if she looked outside, there would be nothing but flat and dark and empty, which the prairie wasn't, not empty, and not as flat as people thought it was.

"Go ahead," he said. Precise as he was, he didn't bother to identify himself. This time of night he was the only one answering.

"Got a call from a woman over on Cemetery. Says she thinks she has a prowler." She gave him the address, which he punched into the GPS even though he didn't need it, knew pretty much where every occupied house in the county was. He flipped on the lights and did a quick U-turn.

No siren.

No one would hear it anyway.

Twenty minutes later he pulled to a stop in front of the address Chelly had given him. It was an ordinary house, vaguely Victorian, but with no extra flourishes—no shingle siding or fancy paint, the porch had been enclosed years ago so that it faced the street white and stark and blockish, seeming to glow in the early morning darkness. Boyd turned off the engine and climbed out of the car. He zipped his jacket against the cold, slipped the hem up over his holster so he could reach his gun if he had to, and stood for a moment, assessing. The narrow front sidewalk had a crack running lengthwise and jagged through the middle of three separate sections. There was no yard light, no porch light, though a dim glow shone through the closed curtains of the inside porch window.

Boyd checked up and down the street. Wind burned across his cheekbones, cold and dry. Cemetery Road was on the north edge of West Prairie City. The cemetery for which the road was named occupied two lots directly across the street with an open field gone to grass and the county road beyond it. To the east of the cemetery sat a two-story-and-attic Queen Anne; to the west, a three-bedroom, no-frills ranch house built nearly a hundred years later. Three houses down, there was a light on in a second-floor bedroom, a garage light on in the house across, but otherwise the entire neighborhood was dark and quiet.

He skirted the house once: straggly shrubs underneath the porch windows in front, a single car garage down a narrow drive, a long row of overgrown privet along the garage, a big old maple tree in the center of the backyard with a few clusters of dried leaves rattling in the wind. There was a small back porch, enclosed like the front one, and in the east side yard, a row of paving stones, like someone had once intended a garden, but had run out of steam. No sign of a prowler, but the ground was frozen hard and there was no snow to leave tracks.

His knock on the rattly porch door sounded like a trio of gun-shots, too loud for three o'clock in the morning. He waited. There was no movement behind the curtained windows where he presumed the living room was, no sound of footsteps approaching the door. He knocked again.

Finally the inside door opened and he saw, framed against the hall light, who it was who'd called—Prue Stalking Horse, who worked as a bartender down at Cleary's and who always seemed to know things, whether she was willing to talk about those things or not. Boyd dropped a step down and waited for her to open the porch door and let him in.

She was tall, though not as tall as he was, with long white-blond hair, high cheekbones, and light blue eyes. There was a certain age-lessness about her, but he'd never been able to figure out if that was because she really did look young or because she so rarely smiled or showed any sort of intense emotion.

He'd dreamed about her once.

Not—yeah, not in *that* way.

Boyd's dreams were, or at least had always been, about events that were going to happen. He'd dreamed about Prue maybe four months ago, just after Hallie came back to Taylor County, after Martin and Pete died, after the end of Uku-Weber, but before the rest of it. It had been a short dream, barren landscape, gray skies—not cloudy skies, but a flat gray, like old primer or warships. There'd been three people in the dream, all of them so far away, they'd seemed to him like nothing more than dark silhouettes, and yet he'd known just from their dark profiles who two of them were—Prue Stalking Horse and Hallie Michaels. The third figure wasn't someone he knew, or at least not someone he recognized within the context of the dream. He'd known it was that person, the unrecognizable one, who was important, who could have answered his questions, if he'd known which questions to ask. Of all of them, that third person was the one, in the dream, who knew exactly what was coming.

Tonight, Prue's hair was smoothed back flat and tight, caught up in a neat knot at the nape of her neck. She wore an oversized denim shirt with old paint stains and black leggings to her ankles. Her feet were bare despite the late hour and the freezing temperatures.

Boyd held the door as he entered, then let it close slowly behind

him. Prue still hadn't turned on a porch light, so they stood in a sort
of gray twilight illuminated only by the streetlights out along the road
and the light inside in the hallway. The enclosed porch was a clutter
of mismatched furniture, old rag rugs, and cardboard boxes stacked
three high. "You reported a prowler," Boyd said, his inflection set-
tling the sentence somewhere between a statement and a question.

She turned away without answering him and walked back into the
house. Boyd took a last look at the porch and the yard just beyond the
windows and followed her inside. He wondered if this was one of
those calls that came in the middle of the night sometimes, when sun-
rise seemed infinitely far and loneliness crowded in. People called
because they couldn't admit the real problem, that there was no sound
in the house except their own breath moving in and out of their lungs.
They called with whispered voices—something outside, they'd say,
please come. Prue Stalking Horse had never struck Boyd as that sort
of person. But then, people weren't always who you thought they
were.

The living room was dark, shades pulled tight over double windows
north and east. Like the porch, it was full of mismatched furniture,
mostly overstuffed chairs upholstered in faded chintz and small side
tables with delicately turned legs, everything looking like it was bought
at church sales and auctions after people died. The room smelled
like lemon polish and carpet shampoo, though dust danced along
a stray shaft of gray light from the floor lamp by the north windows.

"I heard a sound," she said.

"In the house or outside?" he asked.

"Out . . . outside." She stumbled over the word and it was the first
sign Boyd had seen that she was even a little nervous. She didn't
wring her hands or tug at her clothes. She didn't stare uncomfortably
at his face as if looking for a sign that he believed her or understood,
that he could stop whatever it was that had frightened her. She swal-

lowed and continued, her voice smoothing out as she spoke. "We close at midnight on weeknights," she said. "I usually get home around twelve forty or so, after I let the cleaning crew in and cash out. It's not far. A mile, maybe?" Like it was a question. Like he would know the answer. "Sometimes in summer, I walk," she said.

"But you drove tonight."

Boyd could be patient. It annoyed Hallie, when he was patient. Hallie acted. Even when they didn't know anything, even when there were important questions still to be answered, she preferred to do something. But patience worked. In this job, sometimes patience was all he had.

2

After a moment that was mostly silent, Boyd unzipped his jacket halfway, unbuttoned the flap on his shirt pocket, and pulled out a small notebook and a ballpoint pen. He clicked the top of the pen and flipped the notebook open to an empty page. He did it all slowly and deliberately, wanted to give her time to see him do it, to take a breath, to get what she wanted to tell him straight in her head.

She blinked when he clicked his pen, looked at the notebook in his left hand, at the pen in his right, then looked at him. "Yes," she said. Another brief pause. "Well, yes." She made a gesture toward the hall. "Let's go back to the kitchen, Deputy . . ." She paused again.

"Davies."

"Davies," she repeated. The word sounded rich, the way she said it, as if it described azure skies, mountain meadows, the faint sweet scent of clover in late spring, and the lazy hum of bumblebees. Boyd looked at her more closely. "I'll make coffee," she said. As if this were a social call, as if whatever the danger was, whoever the prowler was, it was over.

Or she wanted to believe it was.

The kitchen was a sharp contrast to the living room, bright and warm, the walls pale yellow, the trim bright white, accessorized in sage green and brick red with stainless-steel appliances, granite countertops, and a stone tile floor. Boyd removed his jacket, hung it on a chair, and sat.

One of the lights over the stove buzzed. The room smelled of nutmeg and freshly turned soil. The door to the cellar was wide open, though Prue had to walk awkwardly around it when she went to the counter. The back door was closed and locked, chained. There were locked dead bolts below and above the doorknob. Both looked brand-new. Not a usual thing—triple locks—for West Prairie City, South Dakota.

Prue's next words seemed to echo Boyd's thoughts. "I don't lock my doors. Usually. No one does around here. But lately, there's been . . . well, it's seemed like a good idea. When I got home tonight, the light was on by the garage. I didn't think a lot of it. It comes on when there's a storm, when the wind is strong, or a raccoon wanders through." She put the filter in the coffeemaker, added water from the tap, and turned it on. She took two white cups with a chased silver design and matching saucers from the cupboard. When she set the cups and saucers on the table, her right hand shook and one of the cups jumped sideways. Boyd caught it before it fell and set it back on the saucer. "Thank you," Prue said. For a moment, there was just the sound of the coffeemaker and the sharp odor of brewing coffee.

Prue sat down across from Boyd. She took hold of one of the cups by the handle and moved it back and forth as if to watch the silver catch the light. Boyd's radio crackled. When the coffee finished brewing, Prue retrieved the pot. She poured coffee into each of the cups and slid one toward Boyd. She didn't ask if he wanted cream or sugar, and he didn't know if it didn't occur to her or if she already knew he didn't.

Boyd put his arm on the table and looked at her, though she wasn't looking at him. "The prowler," he said.

"I came in the back door," she said, as if she'd simply been waiting for him to ask before she continued. "It was closed, but I realized when I grasped the doorknob that it wasn't latched. That was the first thing. The light over the sink was on, as I'd left it. Nothing seemed to be disturbed. Then I heard it. A noise from upstairs." She looked at him then, which she hadn't done since she'd sat down, had told him the story while looking down at the coffee in her cup, like secrets had been written there. Or she was writing them as she spoke. "That's when I called you."

Boyd didn't say, Why didn't you tell me you heard a noise upstairs when I walked in the door? Why did you tell me the prowler was outside when you already knew he wasn't? Because she hadn't and they couldn't go back and do it over.

Instead, he crossed to the back door and checked that it really was locked even though there were three locks and it was obvious that it was. "Stay here," he said.

Prue raised the coffee cup to her lips and took a sip as she watched him. He couldn't get a gauge on her and that bothered him, alternately relaxed and nervous and he couldn't understand what caused one reaction or the other. Hallie had told him once that everything Prue did was calculated. If so, she was good, each action or reaction seeming genuine in itself, just that it made no sense when it was all put together.

He moved lightly down the hall, unsnapping his holster and removing his pistol as he did so. There had been no sounds from upstairs since he arrived; if there had been an intruder inside the house, he or she was probably gone. But the gap between probability and certainty was wide. And dangerous. He thought again about Prue at the table watching him. She was playing a game, had probably been playing one since the moment she called the station. But he didn't know what her game was, and if there was even the slimmest possibility that there really was a prowler, he had to check it out.

At the top of the stairs was a narrow landing with four doors that led to what Boyd guessed were three bedrooms and a bathroom. He paused. Nothing. He opened the first door to his left—the bathroom, long and narrow—checked behind the door and the shower curtain. Nothing. The next room was filled with boxes, a long table and two armoires on opposite walls. Moonlight filtered in through the uncurtained window, and the room felt cold. There was an acrid smell, like burnt motor oil, and a low hum that Boyd felt more in his chest than actually heard. He flipped the switch, but the single overhead light didn't come on, so he worked his way along the wall, checking the corners before he moved on to the furniture. The first armoire was locked; the second was empty.

The third room, visible by a night-light in an outlet by the bed, looked like a guest room—bed, nightstand, narrow painted dresser, wooden rocking chair. Boyd checked behind the door, checked the closet. No other sounds than his own footsteps as he moved though the rooms. Still, he checked.

The last room was the largest, clearly Prue's own bedroom, with a night-light in the outlet near the door, and a second one to the left of the nightstand by the bed. Boyd checked behind the door and in the closet. He could see all the corners and he'd already lowered his pistol when he noticed that the window on the far side of the bed had been raised approximately six inches.

He approached with his hand on his gun.

There was a three-foot drop to the porch roof. The window and the storm window were both open, but not far enough for anyone to squeeze through. Cold from outside barely penetrated the warmth of the room, stymied by insulated curtains and the general stillness of the night. He tried the window himself. It lowered, but it wouldn't open any farther than the six inches it had already been raised.

After studying both the window and the porch roof below for several minutes, Boyd returned to the closet, turned on the light, and looked up. He saw a trapdoor with a pull rope attached. When he stood to the side and pulled, steps unfolded into the narrow closet space. He waited, didn't hear anything, and went carefully up the stairs. He could have called another deputy out, gotten them out of bed, and waited while they drove across town or ten miles in from a trailer on CR54, but even then, one of them still would have had to be the first one up the ladder.

He went up fast, pistol ready, and found what he'd expected— boxes, some dust. No intruder, but he could see that dust had been disturbed on a couple of boxes and a shelf on the near wall where there appeared to be something missing, a clear spot left behind in the shape of a small rectangle.

He refolded the attic stairs, reholstered his pistol, brushed nonexistent dust off his pants leg, and went back downstairs.

Chelly checked in on the way down, which meant he'd been there half an hour. "Five minutes," he told her.

He went back to the kitchen, where he found Prue still in the same spot at the table, looking at the cooling coffee in her cup, her cell phone laid on the table as if she'd just made a call or was waiting for one. She didn't look up until he approached the table. "Nothing," he said as he crossed behind her and retrieved his jacket. "The window was open in your bedroom," he said. "I don't think anyone could have come through or gone out that way." He shrugged into his jacket and zipped it. "There's no one up there now. Have you been in the attic lately?" he asked.

She looked startled for maybe half a second; then she smiled, looked at the open cellar door, and said, "Yes. Last week, maybe?"

Like it was a question he could answer. She added, "Cleaning, you know. Always something to put away."

"To put something up there or take something out?" he asked.

"There's nothing valuable in the attic," she said, not actually answering his question. "There's nothing up there to take."

"Maybe." He paused. "This is an old house. Are you sure you heard something inside the house?" He found it difficult to believe she'd imagined the whole thing. Mostly because he didn't think of people that way. But also because Prue Stalking Horse didn't jump at shadows or mistake the sound of a creaking door for an intruder. And then, there was the question he didn't ask, the one that hung between them—why did you stay in the house if you thought there was someone upstairs?

Prue rose in a single fluid motion.

"When you were upstairs, did you notice anything . . . odd?" she asked. The way she looked as she said it was unsettling, like it was at least partly for this, this question, that she'd made the call to central dispatch in the first place.

"Odd in what way, ma'am?" he asked her. It wasn't that he minded wasting his time—and this increasingly seemed like a waste of time—it was that it seemed like she did want something. She just wasn't going to come right out and ask.

She seemed relaxed and cool once again. She tilted her head. "You have certain . . . talents, don't you?" she asked.

For a horrible moment he thought she was actually propositioning him. Which had happened more than once. Women seemed to like him—until they figured out how much of a Boy Scout he really was.

"I mean"—she looked amused—"psychic talents. So I hear."

"I've had . . . dealings," he said. Hallie was the only person he'd ever talked to about his prescient dreams. Prue Stalking Horse wasn't going to become the second.

"This house has a certain . . . aura," she said. "I thought you might sense it. And if you did, there might be something you could help me with."

"Ma'am," Boyd said. "It is not appropriate to make nonemergency calls to emergency dispatch. People depend on me being where I'm supposed to be."

"Well, I do think there was someone," Prue said, though Boyd wasn't sure he believed her. "Just not . . . problematic."

"I'll make another circuit outside," he said, "before I leave." He was tempted to issue her a written warning about the emergency call, but she'd just say she really did think there was a prowler and it wouldn't go anywhere or make any difference to her anyway.

She walked back up the hall with him. "I'm sure it's fine," she said. "Maybe it was a raccoon." She opened the front door and walked out onto the porch with him, flipping on the porch light as she came.

Something poked at him, like the undercurrent of an approaching storm, something not right that he couldn't articulate, about the way she was acting, about one of the rooms upstairs, about something he'd seen that didn't entirely register. Prue opened the porch door and a blast of icy winter air rushed in. "Thank you for coming," she said.

He walked down the three porch steps, then stopped and turned back. He meant to tell her it was no trouble to come out, that it was his job.

He meant to tell her to be careful.

The crack of a rifle shot and the burst of blood on Prue's forehead happened simultaneously. In one swift motion, Boyd grabbed her around the waist and threw her to the porch floor. He scrambled for the light switch and plunged them both into darkness. His breath came quick and sharp, puffing out in bands of silver. It was the only sound in the room other than the soft hiss of the storm door closing slowly on its pneumatics. He slid back to Prue and took her wrist. She had no pulse.

He hadn't expected one.

"Chelly," he said quietly into his radio. "Shots fired." He gave her Prue's address.

"What?"

Whatever she'd trained for, prepared herself for, thought she knew how to handle, it hadn't been those words. She probably hadn't heard anything remotely like them since she started working night dispatch for Taylor County or probably ever in her life. "Oh. Jesus."

"Chelly," Boyd said. His voice was still quiet, but insistent. Steady too, and he appreciated that, because his heart was thumping so loud, he was having trouble hearing. "Call the sheriff. Wake him up. Tell him Prue Stalking Horse has been shot and give him this address."

He heard her take a deep shuddering breath. "Okay. Yes. Okay. Jesus." Then she was gone.

Boyd figured it would be at least fifteen minutes before anyone arrived. He sat tight up against the inside wall with his pistol drawn as Prue's body turned cold beside him and waited.

3

The phone woke Hallie while it was still dark outside.

She blinked, sitting up before she was even awake, but disoriented because it was dark and she'd been having a dream that she didn't actually remember, except it was about escape and wanting and things that had never been promised, but could still be taken.

"Hello?" For a split second, she thought it was Death on the phone, thought he'd found a way to reach her through the hex ring.

"Hallie Michaels?"

She didn't recognize the voice, couldn't have recognized it, because it was mechanical, spoken through what she suspected was some sort of computerized voice synthesizer, deep and slow and flat like something ground from stone.

"Who the hell is this?"

"Hallie Michaels?"

The same two words a second time, like a recording, or like she should know who it was, which she didn't and which, she figured, she couldn't, given that it wasn't anyone's real voice; of that much she was certain.

She threw back the blankets, dropped her bare feet onto the cold wood floor, and started looking for jeans and a shirt. Nothing good was going to come from a computer-created voice calling her in the middle of the night, and she thought she'd want to be dressed before finding out what did come of it.

"Tell me who you are and what you want or I'm hanging up right now," she said. She said it slowly, like maybe the problem was the person on the other end of the line couldn't understand her.

There was a long silence and she almost did hang up, would have hung up except she was awake now and she wouldn't get back to sleep wondering who was calling her at whatever the hell time this was.

"What do you fear?"

"What?"

"Do you fear death?"

"Who *is* this?"

Static filled the line, a sound in the background like sparks and shorting electrical wires, then silence.

"Hello? Hello?"

Damn.

Hallie looked at her phone. Dead.

She sat on the edge of the bed, feeling like she hadn't slept and trying to figure out what had just happened—who that had been on the phone and why they were calling her. She wanted it to be nothing, to be a continuation of the dream she couldn't quite remember. But the part of her that accepted ghosts and black dogs and everything else that had happened in the last half year, the part that moved forward in the face of things she didn't want and didn't need and hadn't asked for knew that it hadn't been.

She pulled on her jeans and a gray T-shirt, scrubbed her hands through her hair, and stalked downstairs. She plugged her phone into a wall socket on the far counter, flipped on the overhead light, and looked at the clock—five o'clock. So, not quite the middle of the night, though it felt like it. She'd have been up in an hour anyway.

29

Since she and Boyd had come back from the under, Hallie'd been waking regularly at two or three in the morning from dark dreams she didn't really remember. They weren't like the dreams she had when she'd first come home, all blood and screaming and the explosive sound of gunfire. Or even the ones she'd had right after the whole thing with Martin, when ghosts cold as winter nights had drifted through her sleeping hours, each one wanting something and each time not able to tell her what that something was.

These dreams were different. She wasn't even certain they were dreams at all. She thought maybe it was Death, trying to talk to her again, come to repeat the question he had asked her once already— to take his place in the under. And even though she knew what her answer was, what it absolutely would be no matter what or how he asked, she didn't want him to ask, didn't want to answer. What if he didn't accept no? What if he took her anyway? He was Death. He'd spared her once, back in Afghanistan. He could change his mind.

And now, someone had called in the middle of the night to ask her what she feared. Why? Was it a joke? It had to be someone she knew. But if so, who? Almost no one knew about Hallie's encounters with Death. And most of them were dead.

She stood in the middle of the room for a minute, then let out a breath, like a horse's huff on a frost-sharpened morning. She moved to the kitchen table, sat in one of the battered straight chairs, and pulled on her boots. It felt like someone else's kitchen table, which it had been and technically still was until probate was settled. Hallie had permission to stay there, though, to take care of the property and the horses. Pabby—Delores Pabahar—had left the ranch and everything on it to Hallie in her will, which wasn't so much of a windfall as it sounded, or as Don Pabahar, Pabby's son, tried to make it sound. The ranch was small; it had water problems. No one had made a living on it in years.

She pulled on a hooded sweatshirt and her barn coat, grabbed a cap and gloves and an iron fireplace poker, and went outside. It was too early, really, to move hay to the racks for the horses and check that the water in their troughs hadn't frozen, but she was up and she needed something to do, so she did it anyway.

None of the chores she meant to do lay outside the iron hex ring, so she leaned the poker up against the side of the barn before she began. She carried it pretty much everywhere these days, because there might be a gap in the ring, because it paid to be prepared, because the world was a dangerous place. She grabbed two small square bales from a stack against the lee wall of the barn and crossed to the corral. A lean-to covered the near end where the horses could get shelter in bad weather and contained a long hayrack against the fence. She dumped both bales into the rack, hopped up on the railing, leaned over, and cut the strings of the first bale, pulling the twine from underneath the bale as it spilled sideways. Then she did the same with the second bale. The horses she'd inherited from Pabby approached quietly, almost like shadows themselves, and took what felt like their assigned places, four of them at one end of the rack and the fifth by itself at the other. She'd need to move one of the big round bales later in the week, but these would do for now.

Afterwards, she made a quick circuit of the perimeter. Pabby's mother had buried the giant hex ring around the house, the barn and part of the lower pasture almost fifty years ago. It kept out ghosts, black dogs, reapers, and, Hallie figured, pretty much any other supernatural creature, including, she hoped, Death. There was a break in the ring back when the walls to the under had been torn, though she'd repaired it since. Eventually she intended to dig up the whole thing in sections, inspect it, and repair it where necessary. Later, when she actually owned the place. For now, she settled for checking it regularly. Not that she could see anything or tell if there was a break, since it was buried six feet deep.

She checked it anyway.

It was still dark and her feet crunched on the frost-hard grass as she walked. She could see headlights way off to the south and she wondered if it was Boyd, knew that he was working nights, and that he drove past the ranch at least once each shift. Usually not more than that. He covered a big area. But it was enough, she thought, to know that he was out there.

It was while she was watching the lights curving along the road that something lighter than the shadows beyond the yard light caught her attention. Whatever it was, it fluttered like an old flag a dozen yards along the driveway. It hadn't been there when she came outside. Or she hadn't seen it. But it had been darker then and still. She looked around now, her back to the front porch—force of habit, because there was no one and she'd known there was no one, because she always looked. Always.

She grabbed the fireplace poker from where she'd left it earlier. The iron was cold even through her gloves, but the weight of it felt reassuring in her hand. She headed down the driveway and stopped when she reached the edge of the ring. She had only a few more feet to go, just six steps. Six steps outside the ring. She didn't have to do it. Not right now. She could wait until it was light, until she could see exactly what it was from inside the ring, until she could be absolutely 100 percent certain there were no reapers or anything else from the under waiting out there for her.

Yeah.

She pulled in a breath and let it out.

Damnit.

She lived here. This was her place. She would go where she needed to go. Had to. She closed her eyes. Opened them. Took another deep breath. Her hand gripped the poker like a lifeline.

She stepped out of the ring.

Something rustled in the tall grass to her right and she took an immediate step backwards, hand gripping the poker like it was a baseball bat. She stepped forward. Nothing. A frigid gust of wind heeled the brittle grass over with a long sigh. Then the wind died and it was quiet. When Hallie moved again, the scrape of her boots against the dirt seemed like the only sound in the universe.

Six steps.

It was a fence post, an old wooden one that she didn't remember being there before, not this far up the drive. Lashed to it with what looked like half-unwound baling twine was a piece of heavy paper with thick writing that she couldn't make out in the dark. She took the note and kicked at the post with her foot, hit it solid with the sole of her boot. It shattered, like it was a thousand years old, crumpling to dust. She could see what remained, in the weak light from the yard and the fading moonlight, ash and char. There was a smell too, something she couldn't identify, old and dry and brittle.

She didn't even look at the note until she was across the ring once more, because who knew what had brought the note and the post. Something old and dark, she bet. Something she didn't want and had never asked for.

Goddamn.

With a sound half like a growl, but mostly like frustration, she returned to the house, walking around to the side door into the kitchen. She stomped her boots on the mat and let the storm door swing shut behind her with a snap. She put the iron poker by the door, sorry she hadn't gotten to use it on something, pulled the lined leather work glove on her left hand off with her teeth and read the note.

IT IS TIME TO FACE YOUR FEAR, it said.

Followed by a set of coordinates— +43° 46' 22.85", −102° 0' 17.38".

No signature. The words—and it looked like they had been written with a black crayon rather than a marker—were in block letters.

What the hell?

Clearly it was related to the phone call. Equally clearly she had no idea what it meant.

She laid the note on the kitchen table.

It had been outside the hex ring, which meant supernatural. Probably. Well, pretty certainly.

Unless it was a joke.

She shed her other work glove and her jacket, but left the hooded sweatshirt and her boots on while she made coffee. As the coffee brewed, she went in the room at the back of the house that had once been a downstairs bedroom—technically, two downstairs bedrooms, so tiny, they made one normal-sized room when the wall between them had been removed several dozen years ago. She fired up the desktop computer she'd bought in Rapid City three weeks ago, and looked up the coordinates. Right in the middle of the Badlands.

It had to be a joke.

Except so many things had turned out not to be jokes or myths or fiction lately that she was pretty sure she couldn't count on that.

A ghost? It would be the first ghost who had ever brought her a note.

Death?

She'd expected him for months. Thought maybe she'd imagined the whole thing at the end, imagined him asking her to take his place, though she knew that she hadn't. He'd told her he couldn't exist in the world—in dreams, yes, she could see him there, but not in the physical world, not where others could see him. For a while, when the walls were thin between the living world and the under, when reapers pursued their own missions and people fell through to the other side, he'd existed as a black shadow.

But that was over. The walls were back. He wasn't here. He couldn't be.

Still, Death would come; it was inevitable.

Just not now, she thought. Not today.

"It is time to face your fear," the note said. But Hallie was good at that, at facing things. That was what she did. She'd been through Afghanistan, Martin Weber, Death, for hell's sake. It wasn't as if she felt like she was invulnerable or even like she could handle anything—that was the kind of thing that got you killed. But this—the note, the phone call before it, all of it—was so obviously set up to frighten her. Hallie didn't like doing the thing that was expected of her. Especially if what was expected was that she should be afraid.

The coffeemaker beeped and she crossed to the counter to pour herself a cup, then returned to the table to study the note. The writing was crude, like it had been written with someone's off hand. The paper the note had been written on was thick and rough. She could see fibers in it, like someone had made it themselves from wood pulp. There was charring around the edges as if it had been thrown into fire and then snatched back out. She had no idea if any of that meant anything, because she didn't know what the note itself meant or who it was from.

, She looked at the clock. Quarter after six. Boyd got off shift in forty-five minutes. She'd call him then, ask him to meet her for breakfast at the Dove in Old Prairie City. Between the two of them, they would figure this out.

She heard a sound outside, like a truck changing gears as it came up the drive—a big truck, not a pickup. Automatically, she looked out the kitchen window, but of course she couldn't see anything, because it was still dark outside and the lights were on in the kitchen. She went to the back door, shrugged into her barn coat, and grabbed her gloves. She briefly considered grabbing the shotgun in the hall closet, but whoever had left the note had done it silently. They hadn't driven a big old truck up her driveway—she'd have heard them. And they weren't going to come back with one now.

Once she was outside and around the corner of the house, she recognized the truck—Laddie Kennedy. Laddie and his brother had lost their own ranch several years ago when cattle prices were down and they couldn't pay off their bank loans. The one thing Laddie wanted was to ranch again, and the dozen head of cattle he ran on Hallie's pasture were the result of years of saving and scraping and making do. In exchange, Laddie gave her information. About the dead mostly, who talked to him. And sometimes about the future. Maybe. Laddie himself said he wasn't completely sure whether he could actually predict the future or was just a really good guesser.

Either way, Hallie found him useful. And she didn't mind the company. Which was something too. Still, she had no idea why he was coming up her drive at 6 A.M.

He pulled into the yard and parked beside Hallie's pickup truck. The sun was still below the horizon, the only indication that dawn was approaching an almost imperceptible lightening to the east. Thin clouds hung low, hazing the moon and blotting out the stars. Laddie's truck, parked slantwise in the yard, was nothing but a dark shape, like a three-dimensional shadow cast by the yard light. Laddie climbed out of the cab, followed by a rangy coonhound that circled Hallie once and Laddie twice and then disappeared into the shadows behind the barn.

Hallie waited, but Laddie didn't say anything right away. He looked pretty much as he always did, sheepskin-lined denim jacket, old jeans and broken-down boots, no gloves and a gimme cap with frayed brim pushed to the back of his head.

"Didn't know if you'd be up," he finally said.

And yet, you're here, Hallie wanted to say. Instead, she asked, "Do you need something?"

Laddie looked around, whistled up the dog, who came loping over with its tongue hanging out despite the crisp air. He let it back into the cab of the truck, then turned back to Hallie. "You got coffee?" he said.

Hallie led him around and into the kitchen. He looked at the note on the table, but didn't say anything as Hallie picked it up and set it on a shelf out of immediate view. She poured coffee, sat down at the kitchen table, and waited. She wasn't patient, but she'd been back in Taylor County long enough to remember this—no one talked until they were ready.

4

"L ately," Laddie began. He'd taken off his cap and hung it on the back of his chair. His hair, which was light brown, graying almost imperceptibly at the sides, spiked up in the front from the hat, and he ran his fingers through it briefly as he continued. "Lately, the dead have been talking to me all the time." He ran a hand along the rough stubble on his chin, more gray than brown, and looked at a spot on the kitchen wall where an old picture of Pabby's had once hung. "I mean, all the time. Day and night. Most of it doesn't make any sense. That's the way they are, you know. Most of the time they tell me things that are important to them—how they died or how they wished they'd died or who didn't come to their funeral. But usually it's just one at a time, maybe two. And it can go days that I don't hear them at all unless I ask a question."

He took a long draw of coffee, both hands gripping the chipped earthenware mug. "But things have been different for a while now. Maybe since whatever you did back in the fall." He held up a hand without looking directly at Hallie. "And I don't want to know the details about that. Don't even tell me. But it seems likely that it's since then. I don't know if it's something that can be fixed or should be fixed, because once you start messing with things like that, who's to say where it'll end or if you'll just make it worse.

"But—" He reached into the pocket of his shirt and pulled out a small stone, which he laid on the table between himself and Hallie. It was round and smooth, the size of a large marble, light gray shot through with veins of a deep blue that seemed to flash in the glow from the overhead fluorescent light. "I've been thinking maybe I could get rid of this."

The stone, Laddie had told Hallie when they'd first met, was the reason he could hear the dead talk. He'd always been able to maybe—kind of—predict the future, but then when he'd been in Belgium on leave from the army, a carnival fortune-teller had handed him the stone. Since then, he'd heard the voices.

"I thought you'd tried," Hallie said, because that's what he'd told her—when he gave it away, it always came back.

"But someone gave it to *me*, right?" He frowned at the stone as if he could will it to give up its secrets. "And if they could give it to me, then it stands to reason." He drained his mug, rose and brought the coffee carafe back to the table, filled both his mug and Hallie's, and sat back down.

"*Would* you give it to someone else?" Hallie asked.

Laddie rubbed a hand across his chin. "Maybe it— Maybe it wouldn't work the same for someone else," he said. He started to say something, then stopped and stared at a spot on the wall for a long time. "I kind of figured I owed it to the dead, you know, when I first got stuck with it. You're never a hundred percent sure that the enemy you kill is, well, your enemy. In Iraq, I mean. Sometimes you wished you knew, but you don't. When I first came back, I just wanted to understand, the dead and the stone, how it all worked. I thought maybe there was more to it than just talking, like maybe there were other things the stone could do or I could do."

He rolled the stone underneath his thumb. "But then, I . . . I figured what you were asking me—would I give it to someone else, would I risk that it would be the same or maybe worse for them. I mean, maybe it would give someone else some terrible power—kill people with a touch or something."

"Could it?" Hallie asked. "Could someone kill with a stone like this? Jesus."

"I—I don't know," Laddie said, though Hallie had the feeling he knew more than he wanted to tell her. "I know, or I think, that it's more powerful than what I get out of it. Once, a long time ago, I went to see someone who knew a thing or two, someone who studied magic, you know. I asked them if they'd ever seen anything like it, if they knew how it worked. They were real interested, of course. Which, I guess you would be because it is kind of amazing." He shifted in his chair, leaned forward. "You get used to it after a while, like it's just everyday life, but it kind of ain't."

"Yeah," Hallie said. She knew exactly what he meant.

"They said this stone, that it stored magic. They hadn't seen one before, but they'd read about them, I guess. They said, this person I went to said, the stones attract people with an affinity for magic. Like, you know, how I could always kind of tell the future. They told me it was a gift." He said the word "gift" like it left a bad taste in his mouth.

"Why didn't you give it to them?"

Laddie laughed without humor. "I did. Thought it was great. Everybody happy." He looked at the coffee in his mug. "Didn't work out."

"Do you want me to take it?" Hallie asked, because she could, she assumed. And she thought maybe that was why he'd come to talk to her.

Laddie didn't answer right away. "What I want—," he finally began.

Hallie's cell phone rang. It was still on the counter charging, and Hallie reached for it without thinking, unplugging it from the wall as she did so. "Hello?"

"Hallie?"

It was Brett Fowker. "Did I wake you?" she said, not waiting for Hallie to respond, like she didn't actually care one way or the other. "Well, I'm sorry, but I thought you'd want to know."

"Know?" Hallie sat up straight, like bracing for a blow. No one ever said those words if it was going to be good news.

"There's been—" Brett took a breath. She sounded calm, her voice even and clear, but Hallie knew her, had known Brett since before school.

"Oh, you better just tell me," she said.

"Prue Stalking Horse was shot last night," Brett said, said it in a rush, like the sudden release of pressure.

"Dead?"

"Yes, dead, Hallie!" Brett sounded exasperated, like Hallie should have anticipated this. "Dead. Someone shot her on the front steps of her house."

"Prue Stalking Horse?" She looked at Laddie. "That can't be—" This was Taylor County, South Dakota. People didn't get shot on the front steps of their houses. Well, once in a while—a family dispute or a twenty-year-old feud over deer hunting or property lines. But, Prue Stalking Horse? Prue wasn't like most people in Taylor County. It wasn't that she saw ghosts, or black dogs followed her around or anything. She didn't dream about Death—as far as Hallie knew. But she knew about those things, which most people didn't or didn't admit to. She knew about everything. She'd helped Hallie during recent events, though she claimed she was neutral about the supernatural. Prue was careful was the point. She was nothing if not careful every single day.

"What happened? How do you know?" Even about things like this, even about murder, sometimes people got it wrong.

"I was on call last night. For the ambulance. I heard it on the scanner."

"You saw her?" Hallie knew, in some vague intellectual way, that Brett had passed her EMT certification the previous month, that she was a member of the West Prairie City volunteer fire department's ambulance service while she finished her master's in Rapid City. In her head she pictured minor injuries from traffic accidents, broken legs from horses, drunken brawls at the Bob. Because she didn't want Brett to see the things she'd seen, wanted there to be a different life somewhere in the world, where people never got shot and if they did, no one had to see it.

Which was stupid. She knew it was stupid. She wanted it anyway.

"No," Brett's voice was low. "Because there wasn't any reason for us to go out."

Oh.

Laddie made a noise that Hallie couldn't quite interpret. Then he stood abruptly and walked out the kitchen door. The slap of the storm door marked his departure, and Hallie realized Brett had been talking the whole time. ". . . was apparently right there when it happened," she said.

"What? Who was there?"

"Boyd. Weren't you listening?"

Hallie bent forward like someone had kicked her in the gut. "Wait. What? Is he all right? What *happened*?"

A brief pause, then Brett said, "I'm trying to tell you what happened. Apparently, Prue called the sheriff's office last night. Technically this morning, I guess. Around three?" Like it was a question, though Hallie guessed that it wasn't. Hallie paced, couldn't have stood still if she'd wanted to. And the kitchen was too small—feet and yards and miles too small. She strode through the dining room into the living room, turned abruptly at the front door, and headed back.

"She called dispatch to report a prowler. And Boyd was on last night, which you probably knew. So he went. And he was there. I don't know a lot more. He went, he checked things out, I guess, and when he was leaving—they were on the porch or something—someone shot her." She paused, then continued, as if she knew that Hallie would want the details. Yes, Hallie thought, because it happened how it happened whether anyone told you the grim parts or not. "One shot," Brett said, her voice carefully devoid of emotion. "High-powered rifle."

"No one saw anything. I mean, Boyd didn't even see anything. The shot came from somewhere across the street. The cemetery's over there, an empty field beyond, then the county road. It could have been anyone," she added helpfully, in case Hallie had been thinking the shot was fired by a neighbor leaning out their upstairs window.

Hallie took a sharp breath and let it out. "Jesus."

"Yeah," Brett said.

"Jesus."

It wasn't that there weren't murders in Taylor County. Less than six months ago, Martin Weber had killed Hallie's sister, Dell. He'd killed Hallie and Brett's friend Lorie Bixby too and, as it turned out, at least four other women going back three years or more. And though Martin was unique in a lot of ways, he wasn't the only one who'd ever murdered anyone in Taylor County. When Hallie was in sixth grade, Sten Cofield, who was the sheriff before Ole, went home one day for lunch, shot his wife and then himself. No one had liked his wife, or Sten much either, which meant most people still felt guilty about their deaths twelve years later. There had been one other murder, back when Hallie was too young to remember, probably a few before she'd been born, and several deaths over the years that could be called "misadventure"—shooting accidents, drunk driving, a sucker punch in a brawl. Not so different than any place, and yet different, because you always knew who and sort of knew why or at least knew afterwards when it was too late to do anything.

Shot in the head with a high-powered rifle was different and other and not the kind of thing that happened in Taylor County.

"Do they know who? What are they doing? How do they even handle a murder in this town? Do they call in the state? Boyd's not on duty now, is he? They sent him home, didn't they?" Because Boyd would think he should finish his shift. Or maybe he already had finished his shift. And he hadn't called her. Why hadn't he called her?

"Hallie," Brett said.

She stopped.

"I don't know any of those things," Brett said patiently. "You know I don't. You should probably—"

"Yeah, okay, I know."

"Call me," Brett said. "After."

Hallie disconnected.

She had her hand on the back door when she stopped. Prue was dead. There was nothing Hallie could do for her. Someone had shot her. Not a reaper. Not Death, except in the abstract sense. Not Martin Weber.

She dialed Boyd's cell phone. It rolled to voice mail. She dialed it again. "Call me," she said when it rolled to voice mail a second time. He was alive. He hadn't been shot. Those were the important things. But he hadn't called. He might be writing reports. He might be answering questions. He might even be sleeping, though she doubted it.

Back in November after they'd rebuilt the walls between worlds, Hallie had told Boyd everything: how she'd watched Hollowell choke the life out of him, how she'd waited for the moment of his death—his actual death—because that moment, when a reaper took a soul, was the only moment the reaper himself was vulnerable. Boyd had said it was okay. He'd said she didn't have a choice. He said he understood.

But he didn't.

She could tell by the way he talked about it, by the way it sat so lightly on him. And yet, she wondered if he hadn't called her this morning because some subconscious part of him did understand and had pulled away.

She called her father.

"Yeah?" He answered on the fifth ring, which surprised her. He never picked up the phone if he could possibly help it. She'd been prepared to leave a message. "Brett called me," she began.

"About Prue?"

She should have known he would know. "Yeah," she said. "When did you hear?"

"I been over to the Dove." She could almost hear him shrug across the phone lines. Not that he didn't care or that he didn't think it was big—major—news. But because he didn't want her to ask what it meant to him or how he felt.

"You want to come over for supper?" she said instead. It wasn't like she hadn't known him for twenty-three years.

"Guess I gotta eat," he replied, which meant yes. Because if he came to supper, he still might not tell her how he felt that someone he'd known for a good twenty years was dead—and not just dead, but shot in the head with a bullet from a high-powered rifle—but at least he'd be doing something other than sitting in his kitchen with one light on or working on some old piece of farm equipment until his fingers were too cold to hold the tools.

"Be here at seven," she said. "Bring meat."

"You want steak?" he asked.

"Beef or bison?"

"It'll have to be beef," he said.

"Good," she said. "See you then."

She found Laddie leaning against his truck on the far side out of the wind, the brim of his cap tilted down over his eyes. Maker was there—Hallie's more or less personal harbinger of death—just outside the hex ring. It stared at Laddie, didn't even move its head when Hallie approached, like Laddie was the only thing it had ever been interested in.

"Laddie," Hallie said cautiously.

He was smoking, something Hallie hadn't seen before—his house didn't smell like smoke and neither did he. He looked over at her, straightened and flicked the butt away, then he gave a huffing half laugh, crossed the few feet between where he was standing and where the butt had landed, picked it up, snuffed it, and stuck it in his jacket pocket.

"I used to have a dog that loved cigarette butts," he said. "I probably smoked an extra two years before I gave it up because that dog got such joy out of the butts. Died of cancer, though," he said after a pause. "So . . . yeah."

Hallie waited and after a moment, Laddie said, "What happened?"

"I don't know," Hallie told him. "She was shot. Prue Stalking Horse." In case he hadn't gotten that part, though she was pretty sure he had. "Middle of the night. She'd called in about a prowler, I guess."

"I didn't like her," Laddie said. He took his hands out of his pockets, looked at them like he thought they ought to be holding a cigarette or something, then shoved them back into his pockets again. "I've told you before I didn't like her. I didn't trust her. There was a time—well, that's water under the bridge now, I guess."

Hallie turned up her collar, shoved her own hands in her pockets, and moved closer to Laddie so the truck could shield her from the wind too.

"I didn't talk to her much anymore," Laddie continued. "But we did have kind of a fight a few days ago over to Cleary's."

"Kind of?" Hallie knew that Laddie and Prue had some history, though she didn't exactly know what that history was. When she'd been looking for information on reapers, Laddie sent her to Prue, but he also said she couldn't be trusted.

"It was a little loud," Laddie said, still looking at some distant spot on the horizon. "She had this idea. She'd get ideas in her head and they were stupid, dangerous ideas."

"And that was the last time you saw her?"

A hawk landed on the peak of the barn roof, its feathers ruffling in the wind. Laddie's gaze was fixed hard on it, the hawk looking steadily back like it was gauging whether Laddie was too big for prey. "She called me last night, late."

"Why?"

Laddie shrugged. "Doesn't matter really. It's old news now."

"Ole will want to talk to you," Hallie said.

"Yeah." Laddie drew the word out long. A sharp breeze whistled around the corner of the truck and rattled the tailgate pins. He rubbed his hands down the front of his jeans. He didn't look at Hallie, staring past the barn and the horse corral at something in the middle distance. "It was just . . . she should have stopped," he said.

"Laddie . . ."

"Goddamnit!" Laddie pushed himself away from the truck with a quick sort of violence, walked ten yards to where the hex ring was marked out with tattered bits of cloth tied to tall stalks of dried grass, stood there looking across the open plain, then walked back. Maker watched him every step of the way.

47

"Look," Hallie said. She stamped her feet and wished they were having this conversation inside, back in the kitchen, drinking coffee. Except this was exactly the sort of conversation that took place in the open, where words could be misheard in the wind and denied an hour later, where things were brought back down to size by the arc of the sky and the weight of the winter clouds. "I have to go to town," she said, could feel the urgency like a drumbeat along the base of her skull. "But we can talk later. About Prue. About your stone if you want."

Laddie's jaw was set in as tight a line as Hallie had ever seen. He'd told her once that he'd stayed in Taylor County because this was his place, even if he didn't have land anymore, even if everyone believed, or wanted to believe, that it was the Kennedys' own fault they'd lost their ranch, not bad luck or bad weather or bad cattle prices. Because if it was Laddie's fault, or his brother Tom's, then maybe they wouldn't lose *their* cattle or land or livelihood. People said the Kennedys were bad luck. Tom had left afterwards for Seattle or Denver or someplace farther west with his wife and two kids. Laddie's wife had left too. Laddie himself made most of his living reading the future in tarot cards and conducting unconventional séances. People talked about him in coffee shops. Sometimes they laughed.

And still he stayed.

Because sometimes all you could do was go forward. Hallie'd served in Afghanistan, her sister had died five months ago, she'd had to go into the under to save Boyd. She knew a lot about going forward and getting through. More than she'd ever expected or wanted to.

"It'll be all right, Laddie," she told him.

He gave a funny little quirk of his head, like a shrug. "Well, if it ain't, it'll be here anyway," he said.

48

Then he climbed in his truck, started it up with a throaty whine, backed it around, and rattled down the rough drive.

Maker trotted after the truck for half a hundred yards, stopped, looked down the driveway, wagged its tail once, turned, and trotted slowly back to the edge of the hex ring. Then, with a brief look at Hallie, it turned around once and disappeared.

5

Twenty minutes later, after Hallie had showered, changed her clothes, and grabbed her other jacket off the hook by the back door, she was finally ready to leave for town. Boyd still hadn't returned her call. He was all right; she knew he was all right. She'd know—someone would call—if he weren't.

She didn't want to talk to him on the phone anyway; she wanted to see his face.

Outside once more, she crossed the yard to her pickup, started it up and backed it around, then paused as she always did these days when she reached the edge of the hex ring. The walls were back now. There were few spare moments these days when she didn't remind herself of that fact. Death wasn't in the living world. He couldn't be. She would not be coming face to face with him if she stepped outside the hex ring.

She looked for him anyway. She looked for everything, looked for signs of harbingers, of reapers, of things that didn't belong in the world but could be sent after her—or that she was afraid could be sent after her.

She hated to admit it, but with each week that passed and no sign of Death, she left the ranch less and less. She had excuses—too busy, too late, too early. Still.

Damnit.

Which pretty much summed up her feelings every time.

Well, it couldn't be helped. None of it. She stepped on the gas, let up on the clutch, and crossed the line with a jolt. In nearly the same instant, Maker jumped through the side of the truck and onto the passenger seat.

It almost didn't startle her.

"What was that before, with Laddie?" she asked.

She didn't say hello, or I haven't seen you in a few days. She particularly didn't say I missed you, though it was possible she had. Hallie'd thought, immediately after everything, that Maker would have been shoved permanently back into the under when the walls rebuilt, back under Death's thumb. But it still came. She liked having Maker around even though it worried her too. If Maker could cross over to the living world, what else could cross over? She told herself Maker was different. Harbingers had always left the under. Usually they left to do a job, not to hang out on an old broken-down ranch in western South Dakota with someone they found interesting, though.

"Shadows," Maker said in answer to her question.

Hallie looked sharply over. "Like Death shadows? Like Laddie's going to die shadows?"

"Not today," Maker said.

Well, that made it all fine, then. Hallie stopped at the end of the drive, checked both ways for traffic though there was never any traffic, and made a left turn onto the county road.

"Laddie's not going to die," she said.

Maker huffed out a breath, like it was laughing at her. "Everyone dies."

Which statement Hallie didn't really have an answer to.

They were a mile or so down the road when Maker said, "Something happened." It sat straight up on the seat and looked out the window, like the something was right out there where anyone could plainly see it, though all Hallie could see at that moment were two dead deer, one right after the other along the west side of the road.

"Prue Stalking Horse died," Hallie said.

Maker looked at her. It neither knew nor cared about names.

"The cheater," Hallie said.

"It's not her time," Maker said, like it made a difference.

"Yeah, I guess you're wrong," Hallie said.

Maker looked at her with its head tilted to one side as if it didn't understand what she was saying. It looked out across the open fields. "That's not it," it said.

"Not it? Not the something?" She thought about the note from earlier—It is time to face your fear. The note itself was bullshit. Because, frankly, that was all she did, face things. It was the why—why was it out there, who put it there—that was the mystery.

Maker didn't answer—it was possible it didn't know. It circled three times and lay down on the seat, nose to tail.

Four pickup trucks, each one more battered than the one before it, passed Hallie going south. One had a crack that ran almost the whole length of the windshield, and one had an open window on the driver's side. The driver, whom Hallie didn't recognize, had his elbow on the doorframe, fingers on the steering wheel despite the frigid twenty-degree temperature. The last of the four had barely gone past her when Hallie had to step hard on the brakes as a coyote crossed the road in front of her moving fast. It leaped across the shallow ditch on the far side, all four legs stretched nearly horizontal.

A few minutes farther on, Hallie asked Maker, "Is she a ghost? Prue?"

Maker huffed out another breath and curled in tighter.

Hallie didn't want Prue Stalking Horse following her around. Didn't want any of the ghosts who had already followed her or would follow her in the future, if the truth were told, but Prue . . . Hallie didn't want to solve Prue's problems, to take care of her unfinished business. And frankly, she didn't need to. This time the police were involved. It was clearly murder, with a high-powered rifle. Someone else could take care of it.

Right.

Though it was past seven, there was no one on the road other than the pickups she'd already passed. Entering West PC, Hallie drove past Cleary's, where the parking lot was nearly full. Cleary's didn't serve breakfast on either the bar or restaurant sides and wasn't usually even open until eleven. But people had clearly come when they heard. It was somewhere to be, to talk about Prue as they remembered her, to talk about what the hell kind of a thing this was.

She drove past the sheriff's office on Main Street—three patrol cars and a nondescript gray sedan parked outside. If she turned left at the next intersection, she'd come out on Cemetery, one block west of Prue's house. She had an urge to go there, though she was pretty sure there would be a police presence and they definitely wouldn't let her inside. She wouldn't be able to do anything more if she went now than sit on the road and stare at the front door. Which she was pretty sure a lot of people were already doing. Still, she'd go, sooner or later. Because it felt like a way to say good-bye.

A block farther down Main Street, Hallie thought she saw a shadow running across the granite front of the old bank. She slammed on the brakes so hard, a Suburban behind her honked its horn, and when she waved it past, a woman not much older than Hallie yelled at her, though Hallie couldn't hear her through the glass of both their closed windows.

Jesus Christ, she thought. A shadow. Not now. Not today. Because Death had been a shadow back in November.

She pulled into slant-street parking and turned off the engine. Maker didn't even raise its head. She took a steel prybar from behind the seat, one that had been primed with sacrament and dead man's blood—her blood—so it was as good as iron, and got out of the truck. She had trouble closing the door for some reason, her hand not gripping the handle properly, and she stood at the curb for a long few seconds. At the spot where she thought she'd seen the shadow, there was nothing. A flag above the courthouse across the street snapped in the brisk morning breeze. Maybe that, she thought, maybe that had been the shadow. She looked at the slanting sun, at the thick bank of clouds just below.

Maybe.

And maybe her heart was pounding hard in her chest because it had already been a long day.

Get a grip, she told herself.

She returned to the truck, threw the prybar behind the seat, and after a minute or two or maybe three, she backed out of the parking space and went on.

Boyd's brand-new steel blue Ford Escape sat in his driveway. Until a few months ago, he'd driven a red Jeep Cherokee, but he wrecked that down in Ames, Iowa, tracking down Travis Hollowell. In the wrong place at the wrong time, hit by a dump truck running a light. A coincidence that, given everything that had been going on at the time, seemed harder to believe than ghosts and harbingers, harder than the fact that there was an underworld and that Hallie and Boyd had been there. And yet, it had happened. Boyd had the new SUV to prove it.

Hallie pulled into the drive.

Maker sat up and sniffed the air. "Be careful," it said.

"Of Boyd?" A gust of wind rocked the little pickup. The rough dirt in Boyd's front yard looked colder than the brown grass lawns and bare-limbed trees of his neighbors' yards.

Maker sniffed again. "Something's in the world," it said. Then it disappeared.

"Thanks," Hallie said to the empty space Maker had left behind.

Outside, it felt as if the temperature had dropped at least ten degrees between the ranch and town, though it was probably just the wind grinding bitter and cold across the landscape. Hallie buttoned her jacket, turned up the collar, and shoved her hands deep into her pockets. She jogged across the churned-up yard, another legacy of November, knocked on the front door, and tucked her head low as she waited for Boyd to answer.

Nothing.

She knocked again.

After a minute, she stepped off the porch and circled the house. The damage from November had been repaired—windows, porch railing, everything except the front lawn and a blue tarp covering half the garage roof, tied down so expertly that there were no loose ends to flap in the rising wind. Hallie tapped lightly on the side door to the garage, then opened it and went inside.

There was an electric heater plugged in and running several feet from the door. It didn't make it warm inside, but it softened winter's bite. In the middle of the floor under two work lamps fastened to the joists above it was a Farmall M tractor, more primer gray than faded red, with rust and bare metal mixed in. The tires were off, propped against the far wall, the tractor itself sitting on low blocks. In a neat circle on the near side were a carburetor, spark plugs, a starter motor, oil filter, generator, and a battery that looked new.

Old tractors. Hallie wanted to laugh.

Boyd was on a stepladder bent over the engine, cranking at a stubborn bolt. He straightened at the rush of cold air from the open door and stepped down. As he walked across the garage, he picked up a rag from the workbench along the wall and wiped his hands.

"You didn't call," Hallie said, and hoped it didn't sound like an accusation. Because it wasn't, not really, though it was a question.

"You know what I like?" Boyd said. He had a streak of grease along the back of one hand, like someone had marked him out. "I knew that you would come, that I wouldn't have to call or tell you over the phone, because it doesn't . . ." He hesitated. "Because I could have told you about Prue over the phone. That's easy. Or, not easy, but . . . yeah, in a way, easy." He flipped over the rag he'd been wiping his hands on, folded it, and laid it on the workbench. He took the socket off the wrench and put it and the wrench back in their case. He closed the lid. Only after he'd finished all that did he say, "It's easy because it's just words. It's not as if your father died and I had to tell you. Or my father. Or even a good friend. So, telling you about Prue's death in the ordinary way would be sad and probably unpleasant, but ultimately pretty easy."

He moved closer. Something tightened in Hallie's chest, like her heart was beating too fast, though it wasn't. "But I was right next to her," Boyd said. "Right there. And I couldn't save her. I mean, no one could have saved her. I know that. I do. But today. This morning." He took a breath. "I was the one who didn't."

Afghanistan had been the sort of place where—whether it happened often or not—someone could shoot you, or the person next to you, anytime. The sort of place where there was always someone who wanted to shoot you. Hallie had lived in that place. She'd survived there—pretty nearly. But one of the reasons she was so good at separating Afghanistan from Taylor County, South Dakota, was because she didn't expect that here.

So, she knew, she did. And yet, what she wanted to say was—I'm sorry. I'm sorry I let you die. I'm sorry I made that choice. It colored everything, like she'd failed in some fundamental way she couldn't recover from and that, her failure, led inexorably to this, had made him unlucky in some way neither of them understood, cursed to be surrounded by events exactly like this one. That he didn't see it that way, that he probably would never see it, made it worse.

She heard the muffled thump of a car door slamming.

She put her hand on Boyd's chest. He wrapped his own hand around hers. "I'm sorry," she said. "I'm sorry she's dead. I'm sorry you were there. And I'm sorry that if you had to be there that there wasn't anything you could do." She meant all that. And she meant, I'm sorry it wasn't me instead of you.

He gave her a wry smile. "I'm not," he said. "I'm not sorry I was there, I mean. She would have died anyway, whether I was there or not. Someone would have shot her anyway. At least she didn't die alone."

She pulled away from him. "Don't," she said. "Be angry or something. Be pissed off. Be upset. Aren't you upset?"

"Would you feel better if I shouted? If I cried?"

"The question is, would *you* feel better?"

"No," he said, "the question is—"

"You don't even know," she said. "You don't even admit that you could have died. It could have been you."

There was something dark in his eyes, just a flicker, like the reverse flash from a camera. "This is not that kind of thing, Hallie. This is not Travis Hollowell or Death or any of it. That's over.

He's not coming for you. And this isn't something you have to be involved in."

"Boyd—," Hallie began.

Someone knocked hard on the garage door.

6

When Boyd opened the door, a man and a woman stood outside, stamping their feet in the cold and talking in low tones that sounded like an argument.

"Boyd Davies?" The man, who looked about Boyd's own age, maybe a few years older, turned to face him and flipped his badge open. "Special Agent Cross. And this is Special Agent Gerson. From the DCI," he added as if they were not the only special agents wandering around West Prairie City on a cold March morning.

"I wasn't expecting you before this afternoon," Boyd said. He'd known they'd come; the sheriff's office didn't have detectives, though they were perfectly capable of gathering the initial evidence.

Cross looked at Gerson, who said, "We'd like to get your statement about what happened at the victim's house this morning. We called."

Boyd actually had no idea where his phone was, which was unusual enough that it made him pause for half a second before he answered. "I could have come to the station," he said.

He meant what he'd said to Hallie, that he was glad he'd been there when Prue died, that he was glad she hadn't died alone, but since it happened he'd felt like he was half a step removed from the world, like the things he did weren't quite the right things or he wasn't doing them quite right.

He heard the scrape of a boot behind him and turned. He'd almost forgotten that Hallie was there. She stepped up into the doorway beside him, looked the two special agents over, like she could judge them completely with one swift glance. "I have some errands to run," she said, as if she'd just been leaving anyway. She grabbed his arm and leaned in close. "Come to supper tonight," she said. "Seven o'clock." Then she kissed him on the cheek, and even that felt off to him, both the way she did it, quick and light, and the way it felt, his jaw rough with unshaven stubble, which it almost never was. She stepped away, loosed his shirt at the last moment, left, and didn't look back.

Boyd could feel the warmth of her hand even after she was gone. He rolled down his shirtsleeves, buttoned the cuffs, turned off the heater, and locked the garage door before walking across the yard with the two special agents flanking him.

"Storm damage?" Gerson asked, taking a quick glance at the ravaged lawn, the blue tarp on the garage roof, and the new glass and framing in several of the windows.

"Something like that," Boyd said, letting them in the back door. There was a small table in the kitchen, but he invited them into the dining room and asked if they wanted any coffee. Cross nodded as he seated himself at the head of the dining room table. Gerson said, "Just water, thank you."

Boyd had made the coffee when he got home—he glanced at the clock—an hour ago. He'd thought he would come home and sleep, but as soon as he walked in the door, he'd known that wasn't going to happen. He'd made coffee, changed his clothes, and gone to the garage to work on the M, not quite mindless work, work that required some concentration, and maybe work that kept him from seeing Prue Stalking Horse fall over and over again.

In less than five minutes, Boyd was sitting at the table with Cross and Gerson, a white ironstone cup of black coffee in front of him that he knew he wasn't going to drink. He didn't feel numbed by what had happened at Prue Stalking Horse's last night. He didn't feel angry or frightened or shocked. Well, maybe shocked. Maybe this was shock. Because none of those words, anger or fear or shock, was right—exactly. He was angry that Prue was dead, blamed himself for not seeing something that he should have seen, because there must have been something. He was frightened that it was a random killing, the kind of killing that meant more people would die unless he— unless everyone involved—was smart and quick and made no more mistakes. And he was shocked that it had happened in the middle of the night on a quiet street while he stood there—and did nothing. He was all those things and too numb to really feel them.

He wondered if he was supposed to talk first, because neither Cross nor Gerson said anything. Any other day he wouldn't have wondered. Things would have simply proceeded as they were meant to proceed. Any other day he wouldn't be sitting in his own dining room with two special agents from the state Division of Criminal Investigation talking about a murder he'd witnessed, but not prevented.

"You have my report," he said, not quite a question. How long had they been in town? He checked his watch. 8:05. He wondered if they'd been to the crime scene yet.

Gerson looked at Cross, who was fiddling with his pen. It looked expensive, Cross's pen, though Boyd didn't know all that much about pens. He was particular about a great many things, how they appeared and whether they had places and were in them, but all he asked of a pen was that it have the right color ink and that it work. Cross's pen was silver, looked heavy, and had some sort of engraving in a spiral along the shaft. Crooks was twisting it apart and tightening it, twisting and tightening as if it were this task and no other that he had come to Boyd's house on a dry, cold day to do.

Finally, Gerson said, "Yes, we've read your statement. It's clear and concise, which I appreciate. You went to Ms. Stalking Horse's house on a prowler complaint, is that correct?"

Boyd wanted to say, It's in my report, everything's in my report. Instead, he said, "I received the call approximately three twenty-five A.M. I was at the southwest end of the county, so it took me approximately twenty minutes to reach the house."

"Is that unusual?" Cross had put his pen back together, but he didn't look at Boyd when he spoke.

Boyd frowned. "That it took twenty minutes or that I was in the southwest end of the county?"

Cross looked up then. "Your position when the call came in," he said, like Boyd should have known from the way he asked the question. It was clear to Boyd that Agent Cross wasn't from South Dakota. His accent was flatter, like St. Paul maybe or Chicago, though he could have been from anywhere, wasn't necessarily from a city. He wore a dark suit with a dark gray tie, a wool topcoat, and dress shoes. Gerson was dressed more practically in wool slacks, hiking boots, a fine-gauge turtleneck sweater, and a parka with a fur-lined hood.

"We have only one deputy on duty at night," Boyd said calmly, "except Saturday nights in good weather and a few days when we call people in. We cover the entire county. At any given time, I'm going to be somewhere."

"Your primary population points are West Prairie City and Prairie City, though, correct?"

"And Templeton," Boyd said.

"Which has its own police force?"

"That's correct," Boyd replied.

"Are you certain it was a high-powered rifle that killed her?" Cross asked. He hadn't taken any notes, like he already knew the answers, which he would, if he'd read Boyd's report.

"It must have been," Boyd said. Did they think he'd shot her himself? Or that someone had walked up behind him and shot her? Or that he had been sleeping in his car and woke at the sound of a gunshot? "And we have the bullet."

"Mm-hmm," Cross said, the sound strangely emphatic.

Gerson frowned and made a note in a small notebook.

"Everything's in my report," Boyd said.

Agent Gerson laid down her pen and looked at him. "You've had some unusual activity in Taylor County this winter," she said.

"Unusual?" Boyd asked. You have no idea, he thought.

"Mysterious explosions. For example," she added after a slight pause. There was something intent about her gaze. She seemed relaxed, her hands folded neatly over her notebook, her face calm. And yet, it felt as if she was waiting for him to say something or do something that she didn't entirely expect him to do or say, but hoped he would.

"This isn't—," Cross began, a brittle edge to his voice.

Gerson held up her right hand. "We agreed," she said. She looked at Boyd again. "Deputy Davies?"

"Are you asking if this could be related to what happened out at Uku-Weber?"

"Is it related?"

"I have no idea," he said honestly. He didn't see how it could be.

The landline in the kitchen rang. "Excuse me," Boyd said.

"Jesus, is your phone off?" Ole didn't bother to identify himself. But then, he almost never had to. He'd been the sheriff for nearly twelve years, and he'd told Boyd once that if people didn't know him by now, they weren't likely to.

"My cell phone?"

"Hell, yes, your cell phone. I've been trying to call you for ten minutes."

Boyd rubbed his eyes. He didn't precisely remember where his cell phone was. He might have left it in the car. "Has something happened?" he asked.

There was a pause; Boyd could hear Ole draw in a breath and let it out. "Tell the Division of Criminal Investigations that I need them over here at the Stalking Horse place pronto." He pronounced each syllable in "Division of Criminal Investigations" as it were an individual word. "You better come too," he added. Then, "Jesus."

Boyd went back into the dining room and told Gerson and Cross what Ole had said.

"No details?" Cross asked, like Boyd were responsible for the cryptic nature of the message.

"No," Boyd said.

Cross frowned. "All right," he said, as if Boyd had issued a challenge or told a tall tale that was about to be disproved. While the two agents donned their coats and gloves, Boyd collected the two coffee cups—his and Cross's—took them to the kitchen, emptied the undrunk coffee into the sink, and stacked the cups in the small dishwasher. He returned for Gerson's water glass. He put the water glass in the dishwasher, took his own coat, a pair of leather gloves, and a baseball cap from the closet by the back door. "I'll take my own car," he said.

Cross looked like he was going to argue, but Gerson said, "Fine, we'll meet you there."

He let them out the front, locked the door behind them, and left by the back door, locking that as well.

It took less than five minutes to drive from Boyd's house on the west side of town to Prue's on the north. Gray sunlight filtered through thin clouds, and the wind buffeted his SUV as he parked on the street. There was no sidewalk, just a shallow slope of yard to tarmac. The driveway was on the west side of the house, two narrow strips of concrete with brown grass down the center. Cross parked in the driveway behind two Taylor County sheriff's cars, the tires of his nondescript gray sedan missing the concrete strips by nearly six inches.

Despite the frozen ground, there were clear signs that heavy foot traffic had tramped across the yard, grass matted down hard, the frozen earth underneath showing through. Yellow tape crossed the porch entrance, the door open and fastened with an orange-striped bungee cord so it didn't bang against the side of the house in the wind. The yard itself, seen in daylight, was neat but utilitarian, old evergreen shrubs underneath the porch windows, one lone tree on the far side near the house, a narrow sidewalk from the street to the porch door. Maybe there would be tulips and daffodils in the spring, but otherwise there was nothing to soften the stark white edges of the enclosed front porch or the bland old siding. If he'd ever thought much about it, which he hadn't, Boyd wouldn't have expected this house for Prue Stalking Horse. He'd have expected modern—glass and steel and blond wood furniture. He'd also have expected her to live in St. Paul, to run a New Age herb shop or a yoga center or a retreat for busy executives who wanted to pretend a weekend of meditation and moderate exercise would give them compassion or calm their overstressed hearts.

But she hadn't. She'd lived here, in West Prairie City. And now she'd died here.

7

After she left Boyd's house, Hallie stopped at the grocery store on the edge of West Prairie City, then headed over to Templeton to the ag supply. Pabby's old Ford tractor, which Hallie thought she'd fixed last week when she replaced the battery, had failed to start again three days ago when she went out to move some of the big round bales closer to the barn. This time the fan belt had snapped in two. Maybe it was old, maybe it was the cold, most probably a combination of the two. The tractor was a 1974 model, and she'd had to order the part in, but Forest Buehl, who'd worked at the ag supply in Templeton since he was fifteen, could find any part for any tractor.

There was no snow on the ground. Everything looked flat and gray brown and empty, even in West Prairie City, even with cars and trucks slant-parked all along Main, it looked empty. As if the apocalypse had come several weeks ago, and Hallie and the few other people still around had just completely failed to notice.

She looked for shadows along the road, torn between annoyance that Death hadn't talked to her in weeks and something that felt an awful lot like relief. She wanted it over with, wanted her chance to say it flat out—no. No, she wasn't going to be, didn't want to be, would never be Death. Wanted to stop looking for him in every shadow on every road.

Maybe he hadn't been back because he'd changed his mind.

That thought pissed her off almost as much as his absence, because he'd brought her back. He'd asked the question. And they'd saved him, she and Boyd, saved the under—saved the world, to be clear. The least he could do was show up.

There were only three trucks in the parking lot when Hallie reached the ag supply. Tiny dry flakes of snow swirled in the air. On the ground, they clustered together, then swept across the parking lot in narrow white lines. A band of clouds sat low on the horizon, not moving closer or farther away, just sitting there, like foreboding.

The ag supply was so brightly lit in contrast to the gray day outside that Hallie had to stop just inside the doorway for a minute and blink. It was a big space—horse supplies and tack to the left, boots and denim to the right, the parts window clear in back. There were two women on the cash registers, one of them Jenny Vagts, who gave Hallie a half smile before she went back to ringing up three pairs of jeans, two rubber calf feeders, and a blue salt lick for a white-haired rancher in a sheepskin jacket and black hat.

By the time Hallie had walked the length of the store to the parts window, Forest Buehl had the fan belt sitting on the counter waiting for her.

"Thanks for getting it in so fast," she said. Hallie couldn't help studying Forest every time she saw him. He'd disappeared back in the fall, along with two dozen other people, dropped straight into the under when the walls had gone all thin. All of them, at least the ones Hallie'd talked to, claimed they didn't remember a thing from the moment they fell through until they were back in the world. Hallie found that hard to believe, that they didn't remember, figured even without conscious memory, the act itself had to have an effect. They'd gone to the land of the dead and come back. That ought to make a difference. So far, she couldn't see that it had.

"You want to pay for that here?" Forest asked her.

"Sure," Hallie said. "I don't need anything else."

Forest took the fan belt back from her and turned to the register. "You know we've still got slots open for Saturday-night bowling." He took her debit card and ran it through the slot. "It's pretty informal, not leagues or nothing. But, you know, if you're looking for something to do . . ." He shrugged, like the shrug was actually the punctuation.

"You know I'm kind of dating someone, right?" she said. More than kind of, actually, but she always said it like that, like it might change at any moment, like she didn't quite trust that it was a relationship, which she didn't.

Rather than looking embarrassed, as she'd expected, he looked at her with a grin and handed her card back to her. "Everybody knows that," he said. "You know how it is around here—everyone's business is everyone's business. But, I guess what I mean is, it's the same people every Saturday, and I like 'em and all, but you can get tired of the same people and the same topics and things turning out pretty much the same way all the time. Someone comes back who's around our age and done some different things, I like to ask. Most people don't come, but most people are just looking to leave town again as soon as they can. Hey, it can't hurt, right?"

"I'll think about it," Hallie said, and was surprised that she meant it.

He slid the fan belt into a paper bag with a stamped logo on it. "Yeah," he said, "that's all I'm saying."

Back out in the truck, Maker was watching two delivery trucks jockey for position at the loading dock on the side of the ag supply, focused on them like their maneuvering was the most interesting thing it had seen in days. Hallie tossed the bag with the fan belt onto the floor of the truck, started the engine, and turned on the heater.

"Is Death ever coming?" she asked without looking over at Maker.

"Death always comes," Maker said.

"To . . ." She was surprised it was hard to say, because usually nothing was that hard for her. Think of it and do it, all one thing, because anything else was too slow. "To *take* me." She had to bite down to get the word out, and she changed it as soon as she had. "To ask me again."

Maker turned to look at her and licked the tip of its nose. "Did you answer?" it asked.

"He didn't give me time to answer," she said.

"You can answer anytime," Maker said.

Hallie put the truck in gear, but she didn't pull out of her parking spot. "Really?" Because it didn't seem right. Or likely.

"Anytime," Maker repeated. "Anytime he can hear you," it added. Then it jumped through the window, disappearing before it reached the ground.

Hallie thought about it all the way home. As usual with Maker the question was, what exactly did it mean? Anytime Death could hear her? Saying it out loud? That didn't seem likely. In a dream? How would she convince her dream self to do it? Go into the under? She didn't know how and even if she did, would she? If she could do any of those things, would he just accept her answer? Why had he asked her at all, come to that? Couldn't he simply make her do it? Grab her and take her to the under and say—hey, it's all on you now?

There were too many questions and not enough answers and she still wanted to know what she'd wanted to know for months—what were the real choices, what could she really choose?

She stopped at her father's on the way back to Pabby's—hers, almost hers, but it felt disloyal or ungrateful to think of it that way. Pabby would have told her she was an idiot. *If I hadn't wanted you to have it, I wouldn't have left it to you,* she'd have said.

Of course, whether Hallie thought of it as hers or not, the neighbors would refer to it from now until eternity as the old Pabahar place, even if it had a hundred owners between now and then.

Her father was out somewhere when Hallie let herself into the house, the storm door ushering her into the familiar scents of old boots and straw and coffee. She went into the back room and pulled three packages of steaks from the freezer, since her father hadn't remembered to do it. Then she wrote a quick note—*Took the steaks, see you at 7*—and left.

It wasn't noon yet as she pulled back onto the state road, but so overcast that it felt like late afternoon with dusk approaching. A pickup with a dual rear axle and a light bar that looked brand-new passed her, and she could see the lights of another car maybe half a mile back, but otherwise the road was empty. She didn't pay much attention, couldn't stop the progression of thoughts—Prue and Death and the note she'd gotten that morning. Laddie too. None of it the same thing, but none of it a problem she could solve the way she liked to solve problems, by running straight at them.

As soon as she turned into the driveway, she saw it, something fluttering in the breeze like a trapped bird. Same spot—hell, the *exact* spot—where the note had been that morning. Same fence post—or, at least, another fence post that looked exactly like. She slowed, then stopped, sat with the engine idling and looked at the post, at the surrounding fields, all the way up to the house and the barn. Nothing moved. Nothing except that damned note on its post.

She left the truck running and got out, carrying the prybar from under the seat.

It was the same as before: heavy paper, note lashed to the fence post with baling twine. Despite the overcast, she could read this one fine right here.

FACE YOUR FEAR.

And then the coordinates. The same set as before—+43° 46' 22.85", −102° 0' 17.38".

What the hell? No, really, what the hell?

She hadn't decided if she was going to take it or if she was going to leave it right there and see what happened, when she heard a car slow on the road and turn up into the drive.

She grabbed the note off the post, watched the post crumple into dust again, stuffed the note in her jacket pocket, and kept hold of the prybar as she stepped to one side so she could see who was approaching.

The car, a thirty-year-old gold Buick with a vicious dent in the rear passenger door, stopped behind Hallie's pickup; the engine turned off, then dieseled for a moment, like it was trying to come back to life on its own. Which wouldn't surprise Hallie, because it turned out things did come back to life. Hell, she'd come back to life. But this was just a car. Probably. It was probably just a car. Sometimes things actually were just the ordinary things they appeared to be.

On the other hand, she'd just received a note that had come fastened to a post that no longer existed. And if she'd learned anything from Afghanistan, from Death, from Martin Weber, it was that it paid to be prepared.

The car door opened. Beth Hannah stepped out.

Beth Hannah, sister to Boyd's murdered wife, Lily.

Beth Hannah, Death's daughter.

Who'd been stalked by a reaper and who'd turned to Boyd for protection.

Hallie hadn't seen Beth in months, not since the reaper, Travis Hollowell, had come out of the under to find her, to convince her to marry him because marrying her would make him human again. And immortal. Because Beth, and Lily, who'd been married to Boyd before she'd died, were Death's daughters. Marrying one of them conferred immortality on their spouse—sort of.

Beth had disappeared after the final confrontation, after Hallie had stopped Travis Hollowell, after Lily and Pabby had rebuilt the wall between the worlds. Boyd looked for her, put out calls to sheriff and police departments all over the country. But he hadn't found any trace of her. Beth was maybe not precisely the last person Hallie had expected to see coming up her driveway on a dry, cold March afternoon, but she was pretty damned close.

She was recognizable and yet, she looked different from the last time Hallie had seen her—hair still curly but pulled back into a tight ponytail, black jeans, black T-shirt, hiking boots, and a black hooded Carhartt jacket. She had dark makeup around her eyes so that the irises looked darker and larger. She had a messenger bag slung across her chest and black biker's gloves on her hands.

"What are you—? Where have you been?" Hallie asked.

"I need your help," she said, just like that, no preamble, not hello or What have *you* been up to? or even, How did it all turn out, there, at the end?

8

They entered Prue Stalking Horse's house through the side door, which was a relief. Not that Boyd wouldn't have walked in the front, past the spot where Prue had lain on the hard porch floor and died. He'd have done it. He was a master at pushing things down and moving past. It was what he did.

Some days, though, pushing things down and moving past was exhausting.

The kitchen looked almost the same as it had the previous night. The gloomy winter sky outside cast shadows underneath the counters, but Boyd could see that on a sunny day, it would be warm and welcoming.

They heard heavy footsteps, and a moment later, Ole emerged from the cellar. He nodded at them in greeting and crossed to a short counter near the door where he retrieved a big steel thermos. He poured coffee, still hot enough that Boyd could see steam rising, into a collapsible cup, then offered coffee to each of them in turn by the simple expedient of holding the thermos toward one and then the next in his large hand. He drained his cup in one long swallow, wiped a hand across his mouth, and said, "You better take a look."

He gestured for Boyd to go first, like he wanted his impressions of the cellar and whatever was down there without Ole or Agents Cross and Gerson interfering.

The basement was really a cellar with dirt floors and stone walls, cold and damp even now as winter shifted over into spring. Light came from two naked bulbs, one directly at the bottom of the stairs and another just to the left of a big furnace that must have been at least fifty years old. The two bulbs cast weak yellow light on the dark walls and floor.

Past the furnace and a small stack of old cardboard boxes darkened by age and probably by the dampness in the cellar was a single work light clamped to a floor joist, the white cord running down the wall and across the cellar to an outlet attached to another floor joist near the stairs. Boyd approached, noting that the floor was uneven beneath his boots.

A pickax and a shovel were leaned up against the long wall. Someone had dug a shallow pit, maybe a foot deep at most. Inside, clearly though not completely exposed, were the remains of a human skeleton.

Boyd looked at Ole, who was standing just behind him at the bottom of the stairs, Cross two steps up, and Gerson halfway down.

"A body?"

Ole still didn't say anything, his mouth set in a grim line.

Boyd stepped forward and crouched by the pit, taking a moment to study the exposed parts of the skeleton carefully—half the skull, the arc of a collarbone, the upper portion of the rib cage, the left ulna, bits of both the right and left hand, and what he took for the right femur. In the dirt just to the left of the lowest exposed rib, but also in the dug-out pit, was a disturbed bit of earth and what looked like chunks of newly mined coal, gray and dark. He almost reached out to brush the dirt from the area, but stopped himself. Instead, he got up, unclipped the work light from the overhead floor joist, squatted back down in a slightly different location for a better view. He tilted the light to shine on the spot he wanted to inspect. Something shone back at him. Three somethings, he realized as the lamplight shifted, spaced like an equilateral triangle. Not clumps of dirt or even coal, but something that reflected light, like glass or gemstones.

"What—?" Before he could finish the sentence, there was a bright flash of light big enough to fill the cellar and momentarily blind him. As it faded, Boyd heard a rumble of thunder as if from a long way off. He stood, quick enough that he stumbled.

Ole put a hand under his elbow. "Okay?" he said.

Boyd blinked against the afterflash. His heart pounded like a roar in his ears. He wasn't sure why. He wasn't nervous. He wasn't even breathing hard and he didn't think his heart was beating too fast— just loud. It felt as if there was still something there, something unseeable in the cellar with them.

"What was that?" Boyd asked. No one answered.

Ole frowned at him, something resembling concern on his face. "What was what?" he asked.

Cross, intent on the bones, stepped past both of them and crouched in the same spot Boyd had been a few seconds earlier. Gerson had stepped back, against the stone wall, one hand on her chest. She looked at Boyd, looked back at the bones. She drew in a visible breath, reached into her bag, and retrieved a notepad and pen.

"We need an evidence team," she said. "I'm sure your people are good. . . ."

But they're not trained for this, Boyd thought. Or, they were trained for bones and bodies and even for small objects buried in dirt. But they weren't trained for things that appeared to be clumps of dirt but reflected light instead; they weren't trained for bright flashes of light everyone didn't see. Neither was he.

"Already called," Ole said. "But I wanted to make sure you saw this.

What the hell?" he said, to himself mostly, Boyd thought. "What the hell went on here?"

"They need to pay attention to those stones beside the body," Boyd said.

Ole frowned. "What stones?"

Boyd ducked his head to move past Cross, who looked up at him and then grudgingly rose and stepped around the bones to the darker side of the cellar.

Boyd crouched again and pointed. "Right there. What are those? At a glance they look like dirt clods, but they're not and there's something—" He stopped, not sure what to say about them. Ole had never said anything about any of the things that happened in Taylor County last fall—not about Martin Weber or his blood magic, not about Travis Hollowell, the reaper, who had killed Boyd's wife and, at the end, almost killed Boyd. He had never said anything about Uku-Weber and the destruction there, at least nothing beyond—yeah, hell of a gas leak. Nothing. About any of it. So what was Boyd going to say now? That he'd seen a flash of light, heard thunder while Ole and, he was pretty sure Cross, had seen and heard nothing?

He glanced toward Gerson. He wasn't sure about Gerson.

"Something in particular about them?" Ole asked. He appeared to be studying the bones, not looking at Boyd or even—at least on the surface—trying to figure out what the hell he was talking about.

"I don't know," Boyd admitted, because he really didn't.

"We'll bag 'em with the rest," Ole said.

"No," Gerson said.

"They could be evidence," Boyd said.

"I'm sure they will be," Gerson said evenly. "I'll take charge of them."

"What?" Cross moved back into the light. "No. This is a murder investigation. We agreed. There's a procedure."

"We've had this discussion before," Gerson said coolly. "Some things are outside the scope of regular procedures. I saw something a few minutes ago—a flash of light—as, I expect, did Deputy Davies here." She indicated Boyd with a brief nod. "You didn't see it. The sheriff didn't see it. I can't ignore that."

Cross made a sound like a snarl crossed with a groan, pushed past Boyd and Ole, and went back up the stairs. Near the top, he said without turning back, "I have nothing to do with it. I'll be upstairs."

"Becky knows a little something about this sort of thing," Ole said to Boyd after Cross was gone.

"Becky?"

"Special Agent Gerson."

Gerson smiled for the first time. "Not much," she said. "You hear things from other investigators or at a conference. Something happens on an investigation. You look into it. And sometimes, if you're open-minded, you learn something new. Ole's told me about the things that have happened here. He says you've been involved."

Boyd looked at Ole. He looked at the skeleton, at the small objects—he'd call them stones until he knew differently—nearly buried in the hard-packed earth of the cellar, tried to understand how this had suddenly become part of an actual police investigation. He'd always separated it in his mind—the dreams he had, the things that had happened to him and to Hallie, and police work. He needed them to be separate. He needed the daily routine of police work to counteract the unpredictable chaos of his dreams and Hallie's ghosts, of the under and blood magic. He needed something that was knowable.

But here they were.

"What will you do with them?" Boyd asked. "With these . . . stones or whatever they are?"

"I'm not entirely sure," Gerson admitted. "The sheriff says you're good with details, that you notice things. Would you be willing to take one? Tell me what you find? You saw and heard what I saw, correct?" Boyd nodded and Gerson continued. "There aren't many sources of information about this sort of thing, though I have access to a few. We need to use everything we've got, all avenues. Right now, you're one of those avenues. If you're willing, I'll sign one of the stones out to you. We'll have a paper trail. And I'm confident you'll bring it back."

It wouldn't be an official paper trail, Boyd thought, couldn't be. What he and Gerson were doing would interfere with the official chain of evidence. On the other hand, it was clear the bones had been in the cellar a long time. Maybe they were in the cellar before Prue had moved in. Maybe they had exactly nothing to do with her death. Or maybe they were the key to everything. Either way, Boyd wanted to know. It was a puzzle. Several puzzles. What were the stones? Why were they in the cellar? What did they have to do with Prue Stalking Horse? With the bones they'd been placed beside? With magic?

"All right," he said, thinking how much his view of the world and what was possible had changed over the last half year.

Gerson nodded again. "I'll get evidence bags. We'll want to get them out of here before the forensic team comes down."

Ole watched her go. Then he said to Boyd, "Look, I don't really understand this. And, frankly, I don't want to. But there's been a hell of a lot of strange stuff going on in this county for the last six, eight months or so."

"Longer than that," Boyd said.

Ole gave him a sour look. "Maybe," he conceded, as if it were a negotiation, "for longer than that. Maybe. You've been involved in it. That goddamned Hallie Michaels has been involved. There's always a big damn mess, and nobody tells me anything."

"Did you want to know?" Boyd asked him.

"No! Hell no, I didn't want to know!" Ole's voice boomed in the confined space. "I don't want to know now. But if it's going to affect my county and my people, if good people are going to start disappearing again or if someone's going to go around shooting people at three o'clock in the morning with a high-powered rifle? Well, I gotta tell you, I am not overlooking anything. Not anything," he said firmly.

They heard the quick sound of footsteps above them. A door squeaked on its hinges.

"You're going to be my guy," Ole said.

"What?" Though Boyd was pretty sure he knew what Ole was telling him, was somewhat nonplussed that it had come to this. It was a big change from the thing that only happened to him, the thing he never talked about, the dreams that couldn't be explained and that he'd never wanted.

"My guy who looks into stuff like this," Ole said. "You're going to liaise with Becky. She's going to tell you stuff. Though—" He reflected. "—I gotta tell you, I don't think she knows as much as you'd expect." He waved a hand at the skeleton. "And right now, you need to get those—whatever they are—out of here before the forensic guy gets here."

He clapped Boyd on the shoulder hard enough to make him take a half step forward, then turned and left, clumping up the stairs with a tread so heavy, dirt sifted from the stair tread onto the cellar floor each time his boot landed.

When Boyd finally reentered the kitchen after Gerson had brought down the evidence bags and they'd collected the stones, marked the bags, and she'd handed one of the bagged stones to him, he found Ole on the phone. He was taking notes in a spiral notebook that was half the size of his hand. "Hold on," he told the person on the phone when he saw Boyd. To Boyd he said, "Hold on a minute, would you?" He didn't wait for an answer, just turned back to his notebook, saying, "Yeah, give me the rest."

Boyd felt a cold draft against the back of his neck, like a puff of frosted breath. He looked at the kitchen door, but it was closed.

"Been looking at her phone," Ole said to Boyd as he stuck his own phone in his shirt pocket. "At her phone calls." He flipped back a page and shoved his notebook toward Boyd. Four numbers neatly written on the page. "Recognize any of them?" Ole asked.

Boyd was certain Ole already knew whose numbers they were. The fourth one was the sheriff's office, not 911, just the regular office number. "She called these numbers yesterday?"

"Uh-huh," Ole said.

"The Minnesota number?" It was the third number. St. Paul area code. She'd called it twice, once just before she'd called the sheriff's office.

Ole frowned. "It's a copier business. Asked them if they knew a Prue Stalking Horse and they said—we'll have to check our records. But she called at midnight. Who the hell was there at midnight?"

Boyd didn't have an answer, and he figured Ole didn't expect him to have one. "You want to know if I recognize either of the local numbers?" he said instead.

"Do you?"

"One of them's Laddie Kennedy's," he said.

"Huh," Ole said, though Boyd was certain he'd known before he asked. "The other one's the barn number out at Sigurdson's," he told Boyd.

"That could mean a lot of people. What time?"

Ole shrugged. "Seven. One-minute call. Which could mean a conversation. Could mean she left a message. Could mean anything. Foreman out there says Pat and Tel went to Pierre for some estate auction yesterday morning, won't be back for a few days. Says that phone's in Tel's office, but everyone uses it." He leaned back in his chair. "Hell. You going to see Laddie?" he asked.

"What?" Boyd was tired of feeling out of step.

"Laddie Kennedy," Ole said patiently. "You think you'll see him today? I been trying to call him, but he ain't home. He spends time out to Pabby's place, doesn't he?"

"I can ask Hallie if she's seen him," Boyd said.

"That's what I'm saying," Ole said, like it actually had been. He rose to his feet, graceful for a man his size, and clapped Boyd on the shoulder. "You need to get some sleep," he said. "Get out of here."

9

You better come up to the house," Hallie said. It had gotten dark while they stood there, a heavy cloud like spilled ink flowing over the sun.

Beth looked at her hard for a minute, then nodded. Hallie thought she saw something moving way out in the field to the east, dry grass folding over and then back. She couldn't be sure, but she knew she'd feel better—like they'd both be safer—back inside the hex ring.

Half a minute later, with both vehicles parked side by side in the yard, Hallie waited for Beth, then led her around to the kitchen, opening the door on a rush of warm air from inside. She shed coat and gloves, started another pot of coffee, washed her hands at the kitchen sink, then turned to Beth, leaning against the counter with her arms crossed. She'd asked the question—Where have you been?— now it was Beth's turn.

"Can I use your bathroom?" Beth asked.

"You know where it is," Hallie said.

It was almost five minutes before she returned. Hallie pulled the second note from her pocket, took the first note from the shelf where she'd put it, and compared them. They looked exactly the same to her. She'd put them both back on the shelf, poured coffee into two mugs, and was setting the mugs on the kitchen table when Beth returned.

They sat. Hallie waited.

Beth lifted the mug to her lips, took a taste, grimaced, and set it back down. She looked at the dishes stacked in the glass-front cupboards, at the old milk glass overhead light fixture, at the faded red café curtain on the window to the right of the back door. She tapped the side of her thumb against the table, quick, like there was so much tension stored just in that single digit that it couldn't stay still.

"I know where there's an entrance," she finally said. "Well, almost," she qualified. "I know *about* where there's an entrance."

"What are you talking about?" Hallie asked.

Beth shifted in her chair. She looked at her coffee without drinking from it. "I figured it would be better if I came, if I asked you face-to-face." She let out a long breath like a sigh, shifted the strap of the messenger bag she'd been carrying up and over her head, and set it on the floor with a thump. She pulled off her gloves. She said, "Look, there's no one—I mean I don't have any family anymore. And there's no one who *knows*. Except Boyd. And, I guess, you. See—"

Beth's mouth compressed in a thin line, and Hallie was surprised that she couldn't read Beth's emotions at all. When she'd met Beth— well, actually the entire time she'd known her—Beth had been mostly scared and occasionally angry. Hallie hadn't written her off, exactly, more figured she couldn't count on her, that Beth wasn't used to the kinds of things that were happening and wouldn't be much help. But this Beth, five months later, looked harder and determined, like she had a plan and she was carrying that plan out, no matter what.

"I figured," Beth said, like Hallie should already understand, "I figured you'd be able to open it."

"What are you talking about?"

"You wouldn't believe the people I've talked to since—well, since," Beth said. "Most of them won't even talk unless you offer them money or, you know, threaten them. I'm not very good at threatening, though I think I'm getting better. It's like—you know there aren't that many magic-users and you'd think it would be more of a community, like everyone would help everyone else, but it's not. Trust me. It's been really weird." She took another sip from her coffee, considered it, then took a larger swallow.

"You've been talking to magic-users?" Because Hallie would have thought after Travis Hollowell stalked her and threatened her and tried to take her into the under that Beth would have had enough of magic.

"He came to see me right before," she confided. "Right before you fixed everything."

"Hollowell?"

"Pabby and that other reaper had left about an hour before, told me to stay inside," Beth said, not answering Hallie's question directly. "I told them I wanted to help, but that reaper, the white one, said that I'd be a target. I guess they thought Hollowell would grab me or something, but he couldn't marry me without my consent, so what was the danger?" Beth blew on her fingertips and rubbed her arms.

Hallie could name at least a dozen dangers. But then, she'd actually been there at the end. Beth hadn't.

"It was a good thing I hadn't gone, as it turned out, because I might not have gotten to see him." She waved a hand like that would make everything clear. "You know, my father."

"Death?" So that was where he'd been. Maker had said at the time that he wasn't really there and Hallie'd thought it meant he disappeared deeper into the under or that he was damaged so much by the disappearing walls between the worlds that he'd been pretty much a ghost. Apparently, though, while the rest of them were trying to save the entire goddamned world, Death had been visiting his daughter.

"Yeah." Beth smiled. "It was kind of weird and awesome at the same time. I mean, he's Death. He's, like, in charge of all the reapers and harbingers. Basically everything in the under? He's in charge of it."

"I'm not sure that's right," Hallie said. "I don't think he's in charge of everything." She didn't think anyone or anything was in charge of unmakers, for instance. They were implacable, unstoppable. There wasn't much awesome about an unmaker, to Hallie's way of thinking. Though there wasn't much awesome about Death either.

"No, he is," Beth said. "He's in charge. And he loved my mother, you know. I mean really loved her. She should have, I don't know, she should have gone with him. She didn't have to stay with Odie. I don't know why she did."

"Beth—" Because Hallie wasn't sure any of that was right, wasn't sure Death had ever even asked Beth's mother to go into the under with him. She wasn't even really sure Death had loved Beth's mother, though she understood that he thought he had and Hallie believed that he'd appreciated her at least, which she guessed was something.

"No, I know. It's not important, really. She's gone now and beyond his reach, because I guess people move on? I don't really understand all that. Yet. I don't understand it yet." She shoved back her chair and rose, going to the kitchen window to stare out at the open field just beyond the backyard. "He told me he wanted to quit," she continued. "To stop being Death. To be human again, I guess. He told me you were going to take his place."

Now it was Hallie's turn to rise. "No, I'm not," she said. She hadn't actually told Death that, of course, but only because he hadn't given her the chance. It was why she didn't sleep well anymore, why she looked for shadows everywhere she went. Waiting for Death.

Sooner or later, he would come. Even Maker agreed. Because that's what Death did. "I'm not going to take his place."

Beth shrugged. "That's what he said."

She glanced over her shoulder at Hallie, but didn't move away from the window. Hallie wanted to tell her to leave, to just get out right now. She didn't want to talk about Death, about any of it. But Beth was here and she wanted something and Hallie figured it wouldn't hurt to find out what it was.

"I asked him where my mother was, where Lily was. He was Death, right? I thought he would know. But—" She shook her head. "—I'm not sure he really understood what I was asking. He told me this confusing story about fortune-tellers and magic-users and how you can tell if they know things or if they're just making something up. He said some of them did have real power, said once—and this was a long time ago, or at least it sounded like it from the way he talked about it. Said this fortune-teller—or magic-user, he seemed to get confused about which was which—anyway, this person, a real, live person, once walked into the under and came back out again. Which is really amazing when you think about it. I asked him what it meant, how they did it. He said no one's ever done it—like he hadn't just told me that story. Then he asked me who I was, like he'd forgotten." She tilted her head to one side as if she were considering the implications of that.

"He was—" Hallie thought about how to describe it. "He wasn't quite all there, then," she said. "Because the walls were disappearing, because everything was falling apart."

"Yeah," Beth said, though Hallie wasn't sure she cared all that much about the why of things. "He said, 'Look—' Then he disappeared. Just—" She snapped her fingers. "—disappeared. Like that. Right in the middle of whatever he'd been going to say."

Which must have been when she and Boyd and the others had

done it, stopped the walls from falling between the worlds, between the world of the living and the under.

"And that was unfair, you know," Beth continued. "It was *really* unfair. I lost my mom and my sister and even my stepfather. I mean he wasn't much, but he was my stepfather. I lost all of them, and then I got, like, five minutes with my real father. I had no one. I *have* no one. I decided there had to be a way to see him again, my father. I mean, you've seen him. And he's there. In the under. People can go there. You went there."

"That's not—," Hallie began, but Beth continued as if she hadn't even spoken.

"Maybe if there was a way to see him again, there'd be a way to see Lily too."

Hallie thought the obvious way would be to kill herself, but since she didn't actually want Beth to kill herself and she wasn't entirely sure she wouldn't do it if Hallie suggested it, she didn't say it.

"The first thing I thought of," Beth said, "was killing myself. But I didn't think that was fair either, that I'd have to kill myself to see my father. Plus, it might not work or I might not go to the under, just pass right through because you don't go to the under, I guess, unless you have unfinished business. I decided if it could be done, going into the under while I was still alive, I would find out how to do it. I was pretty sure you wouldn't tell me. Or Boyd. But someone else had to know."

"So you left? And didn't say anything? Boyd's been looking for you."

"When Pabby and that reaper left," Beth said, "they said things were falling apart. And I guess they were. The reaper said that people were falling through, that things were falling out. I didn't really know what she meant. But after my father, after he disappeared, there was, I don't even know how to describe it, something like a shadow that passed over everything—like an eclipse, except it wasn't an eclipse. It moved across the landscape. You could see it move. And when it passed, I could feel it, like something pushed at me, deep in my chest. It was weird, like everything was different afterwards even though nothing looked different. I heard someone yelling behind the barn. When I looked, I found two women and they were freaked out because they didn't know where they were or why they were there. I think they thought I kidnapped them.

"They finally calmed down and called someone who came to pick them up. By then it had probably been two hours since the weird shadow passed. I knew Pabby wouldn't be back. I don't know why, really, but I knew she was gone. And I didn't know what had happened to you or to Boyd. I figured I was on my own, so I got a ride with them. And I just kept going."

Hallie could hear a noise, like a low hum or maybe a vibration. In fact, she wasn't sure it was a noise at all; maybe it was something she could feel in her bones. Beth had crossed back to the table, though she hadn't sat down again. Hallie went to the window and looked outside, but she didn't see anything except acres of grass and the old windmill. Not even Maker.

"There had to be a way to find him again," Beth continued. "To find Death. And I was determined. Anything outside of that goal— well, I didn't care anymore. I found a fortune-teller. I found twenty fortune-tellers, and all of them were fake—he was right, it was pretty easy to tell. I went online, into libraries.

"Nothing."

And all this time, you could have called, Hallie thought but didn't say, because it was clear that it hadn't occurred to her that anyone might be worried.

"Then one day, I walked into this shop—you know the kind of place where they sell tarot cards and scented candles and crystals.

I'd been in dozens of shops just like it, but I knew the minute I walked through the door that this one was different, that there was something real there."

Hallie came back and sat at the table too. Of course there had to be other magic in the world. Other places where things happened. She'd started to see ghosts in Afghanistan. But it hadn't, somehow, occurred to her in any concrete way that there were people out there somewhere who could see the future like Laddie or had dreams like Boyd or who could wield magic without killing someone for the power it gave.

"What?" she asked.

"I didn't even know," Beth said. "The person who owned the store came out from the back and it wasn't them, because it feels different, people who can see things or have some kind of ability and regular people, you know?"

Hallie didn't know, but she nodded anyway.

"I told him I was looking for something and I'd know it when I saw it. He basically showed me everything in the store and it wasn't there, there was nothing. I could see he thought I'd lost my mind and he was getting exasperated besides. I mean, who could blame him? Then—" She stopped, got up from the table again, and refilled her coffee mug. She took a sip, grimaced, and said, "This old lady came out of the back, and I knew right then."

"She was magic?" Which felt weird even to say. But what was a better word? Did she see ghosts? Did she have dreams? Was she doing spells in the back for happiness and luck?

Beth shook her head. "I don't know. Is that the right word? Magic? Am I magic? Are you? It's all different with different people. I can just tell when people see things or know things not what they see or what they know.

"Anyway, she looked at me for a long time like she could see it too.

The man said, 'She doesn't know what she wants,' to the old lady. 'Yes, she does,' the lady said. Then she walked over and pulled something out of her pocket and put it in my hand."

Beth, who had dropped her messenger bag but hadn't taken off her jacket when she came inside, pulled something out of her pocket and put it on the table. It was a stone.

Hallie had seen Laddie's stone, the stone that let him talk to the dead, once. This one was bigger, though just as smooth and more oblong, whereas Laddie's was round. It was black like onyx and glistened as if it were wet in the light from overhead.

"So, what," Hallie said carefully. "You can talk to the dead now?"

"What? No?" Beth said it as if the suggestion were idiotic. "No. It's a key. Or, I guess, a map. Because as soon as I touched it, I knew." She stopped and looked at Hallie as if it should all be crystal clear.

It wasn't. "Knew what?"

"Where the entrances are," Beth said. "All of them."

"Entrances to what?"

"There are doors into the under," Beth said. "I want you to open one of them for me."

10

No. Jesus, *no*."

Hallie and Boyd and everyone else had worked too hard, sacrificed too much to open up the under again.

"You have to open it," Beth said. "I have to go through."

"Why?"

Beth stared at her as if she thought the answer were obvious. "Because I'm going to take his place."

There was one brief moment when Hallie felt a wave of relief. One less thing, one less burden dying and coming back had demanded of her. No more visits from Death, no more wondering when the hammer was going to drop. She could just live. Well, with ghosts and Maker and the occasional weird occurrence demanding her attention. But at least without demands from the afterlife. But no. This wasn't the answer. She couldn't claim a solution for herself at the expense of a nineteen-year-old who'd lost her entire family.

"You have no idea what it means," she told Beth.

"I think I do." Beth tilted her chin, as though defiance were the same as strength.

"You really don't," Hallie said. "It means death all the time. Dead people. The dying. It will mean you're all alone, that you can't come back here. Ever. It will mean you're dead."

"I think I can come back," Beth said, persisting. "I think Death used to come back. I think he forgot how."

Which Hallie admitted was a possibility, because he'd come to Beth's mother. In dreams, Beth had said, but there'd obviously been something physical or there wouldn't be Beth.

"Why?" Hallie asked.

"I want—" Beth stopped, thought for a moment. "I want to belong somewhere, for who I am to mean something."

"Beth—" Hallie stopped too, had to think about what she was going to say next. "You can make a home here if you want. In Taylor County, I mean. There's Boyd. And I would help you. Or finish college and then decide. But you don't want to be Death. You'd be alone forever."

"No, I wouldn't. I'd make sure I wasn't."

Less than five years separated Hallie and Beth, but it felt like a lifetime, like an abyss that couldn't be crossed.

"You think I don't understand about death," Beth said. "Not Death, my father, but dying. You think I have no idea."

"You don't have any idea," Hallie said.

"I watched my mother die. And Odie. I lived through my sister dying when I was twelve. People die, I get that."

"You, personally, have never been in danger of dying."

"I'm not afraid of it."

"Then you're an idiot," Hallie said.

Beth looked at her like she knew something Hallie didn't know, which pissed Hallie off. "Look, I'm not helping you," she said. "It's stupid and dangerous."

"Fine, I'll ask Boyd," Beth said. She bent to retrieve her messenger bag. "I just thought maybe . . ."

When she straightened, Hallie was standing between her and the door. "Don't," Hallie said, fighting to keep her voice steady. "Don't ever do that. Play me against him. Ever. Besides, he wouldn't do it."

Beth's shoulders slumped. "Yeah." She sounded tired. "I know. Or I would have asked him first. I figured you were more likely. Because it would help you out, you know? If I went instead. I thought it was worth a try."

Hallie leaned back against the door, resisting the urge just to throw Beth out and be done with it. "What makes you think either one of us could? Open a door to the under? What makes you think you can't just walk right in on your own? You're Death's daughter. If they're going to let anyone in, it's going to be you. Have you tried?"

Beth sank back down into the battered kitchen chair. "No," she said. "Because . . ." Her voice dropped, and Hallie couldn't hear the rest.

"What?"

"Because I don't know exactly where it is!"

Hallie heard the sound of a car coming up the driveway. Jesus. It was like she was Grand Central Station today. First, Laddie. Then, Beth. And now? Who knew.

"Hold that thought," she said to Beth, grabbed her coat, and went outside.

She rounded the corner of the house in time to see a blue and tan long-bed pickup with rusted-out rear wheel wells pulling up behind Beth's big old Buick.

Who the hell was this?

The temperature had dropped since she and Beth went into the house; the sky was still overcast, but it didn't feel like snow—they'd had plenty of snow in January and February, and Hallie hoped they were done with it, but she was pretty sure they weren't. Everything looked colder than it would have if there were snow on the ground— gray and hard and frozen.

Brett Fowker got out of the truck.

She was wearing her ever-present cowboy hat, though she'd exchanged the off-white felt one she wore for dress for a dark brown low-crowned model. Her hair was pulled back in a low ponytail and it swung slightly from side to side as she walked. She had on a flannel-lined denim jacket, leather gloves, and a red scarf. Hallie'd known Brett just about forever. "Just on my way back from the city," she said by way of greeting.

"Is this your truck?" Hallie asked. It was obvious it was, because who else would it belong to?

"Daddy's gone back down to Arizona for another few weeks," Brett said, looking at the truck like she barely recognized it herself. "Until the weather really gets good, I guess. He took the little pickup to trailer a couple of horses down, and you know what happened to the other one. I needed something to haul feed. It was cheap."

The "little pickup" was a three-quarter-ton Dodge with a special power train package and towing hardware. The other pickup, four doors with a dual-rear axle, had been totaled back in November when Brett had plowed it into a Humvee sitting in the middle of a road that had been completely empty a second earlier. It wasn't as if Brett couldn't afford something better than the rusty pickup sitting in Hallie's yard; it was that, for the most part, she didn't care.

"Are you busy?" Brett asked, nodding toward Beth's car. "I can go. I thought I'd stop to see how Boyd was doing. And your dad."

Hallie snugged the collar of her jacket up around her ears. "Come on inside," she said. She couldn't remember if Brett had ever met Beth or not. She was pretty sure Brett knew Lily had a sister and that neither Hallie nor Boyd had seen her since November.

"So how *is* Boyd doing?" Brett asked again as they headed toward the house.

"Fine, I guess," Hallie said. "He wouldn't tell me."

Brett looked at her sideways. "Yeah, I think he would," she said.

"Well, then I guess he doesn't know." Which was probably true.

"I didn't see him for more than a couple of minutes. Some state investigators came to talk to him."

"That's good, right?" Brett said. "That the state's called in?" She turned and walked backwards a couple of steps, turned back, scanning all the open land as she did it. "It's a weird feeling. A *bad* feeling. That someone shot her, that they could be anywhere. Could be out there right now. It's got to be settled. Quick."

Hallie didn't know if there was something wrong with her—though there probably was: dying and coming back, for one thing—that she hadn't considered the issue, how it would make other people in the county feel, that someone had been shot right on their own front doorstep. Taylor County was the kind of place people considered safe. Not that nothing happened. Martin Weber had happened, for one thing. People had mysteriously disappeared and reappeared just a few months ago. But those things felt different, felt like things that happened outside the regular rules of society. Shooting someone with a high-powered rifle felt like a broad strike at everyone and everything, because it could have been any of them, just going about their everyday business. It still could be.

She stamped her feet as she entered the kitchen, and behind her Brett did the same. There wasn't any mud or snow or anything to stamp onto the kitchen mat, but it was almost automatic, something you did when you came in from the cold. Beth wasn't there, but her bag was slumped against the chair she'd been sitting in. Hallie gestured toward the coffeepot and shrugged off her jacket on her way out of the kitchen.

She found Beth in the office with half a dozen maps pulled up on her computer and the stone clutched in her hand. She looked up when Hallie came in.

"Yeah, I'm not exactly sure, okay?" she said defiantly.

"You're not exactly sure?" Hallie repeated the words because she figured she hadn't heard right or Beth hadn't said them right. "I thought you said you knew where all the entrances were."

"I know generally where they are." She stressed the word "generally" like Hallie should have understood that from the beginning. "But the world's a big place. Knowing where a door is in relation to the whole world still leaves a big area. There's one somewhere in Custer National Park?" She said it like it was a question, like Hallie could say whether she was right or not. "Or the Badlands?" She turned back to the maps. "The Badlands is kind of big, isn't it?"

"Will you know it when you see it?" Hallie didn't bother to hide her sarcasm.

"Yes," Beth said. "Yes. I mean, I *see* them all. And some of the surrounding area. I'll know. I think. It can't be more than a hundred square mile area. It's not in Rapid City. And it's not across the river." She frowned over the maps.

Hallie left her and went back to the kitchen. If Beth couldn't actually find the door, then she, Hallie, didn't have much to worry about.

Brett had already started another pot of coffee when Hallie returned. She raised an eyebrow but didn't ask Hallie whose car was out in the yard or where they were. Questions like that were nosy, and in a place where everyone knew everyone's business just as a matter of course, it was bad form to ask directly.

"So, does your dad like Arizona?" Hallie asked. Like a neutral topic would make everything else easier to talk about.

"I think he has a girlfriend down there," Brett said.

Brett's mother had been from Minneapolis, had met her father at college. She'd married him and come to South Dakota, stayed ten years on the ranch, then left and moved back to the city. Brett had visited her at Christmas and spring breaks when she was in school. Hallie had no idea how often Brett saw her now. For several years, her father had had an on-again, off-again relationship with Molly Eckles, who cleaned houses and baked pies to order over in Old Prairie City. Back when Hallie and Brett were in high school, Molly had lived out at the ranch half the year and in town the rest. She and Brett's father had never married, and sometimes Hallie hadn't even been sure they'd liked each other. Two years ago, Molly had packed up and moved to North Carolina.

"Is he coming back?" Hallie asked.

"I don't even ask," Brett said. There was a pause. Hallie stretched her legs in front of her and crossed them, one over the other at the ankle. "Prue Stalking Horse," Brett said abruptly. "Jesus."

"I know," Hallie said. What else was there to say?

Brett took a cautious sip of coffee and said, "I'm on call a couple of nights a week right now. I usually stay at the fire station in West PC, though, honestly, unless the call is actually from someone in West PC, it's going to take upwards of a half hour or more to get there anyway. But I guess that's not the point," she added, like she was arguing with herself. "It was . . ." She tapped her index finger against the side of the mug. "They don't call us out if someone's already dead, you know. Sometimes they die before we get there. And a lot of times you can't tell from the call. I've seen car accidents where the car rolled over three or four times before it stopped. I've seen someone who had their arm ripped off by a power takeoff.

"So it's not like I'm a voyeur or anything. And it's not like this is the first time someone I know has died. But this—" She swallowed. "This was different."

Hallie nodded. It was the way Prue had been killed, with a bullet from a high-powered rifle. In Afghanistan, Hallie's squad and two others had been pinned down nearly the whole of one day by snipers on rooftops. Andy Rodriguez, whose squad was teamed with hers on almost every task they'd been assigned for two months, and a second soldier, who arrived less than three days earlier and whom she hadn't known at all, were been shot and killed that day. Hallie didn't know if that was what Brett meant. She might have only meant that it was violent. But it was more than that, Hallie knew, that kind of death. It was sudden, it was nearly silent, and it was completely faceless. It could happen again, any second. It could happen to you. And there was nothing you could do.

"I was sitting there in the fire station, and it's only about a five-minute walk." Brett drained her coffee, then sat with the mug in her hands. "I guess I thought maybe there was something I could do. Like someone might need something, though God knows what. So, I walked over.

"No one paid any attention to me. There were lights everywhere, of course, and one or two neighbors in their yards, not even talking to each other, just standing there looking at the house and the deputies going back and forth across the road. It looked like they'd already gotten all their pictures and taken all their measurements. They kept Boyd standing outside—or, at least, he kept standing outside—and Ole kept walking up to him every few minutes and poking him in the chest. Mostly he just stood there, though."

She paused.

Hallie wasn't sure where this conversation was going, whether Brett just wanted to lay it out for its own sake, which was fair enough, or whether she was building up to something, some point that had brought her to the ranch on this particular afternoon to tell this particular story.

Brett got up and grabbed the coffeepot and refilled both her mug and Hallie's, didn't ask if Hallie wanted more coffee, just did it. She returned the pot to the counter, but didn't sit back down. Instead, she leaned against the wall next to the living room doorway and said, "The coroner arrived and went in the house and I realized that I didn't want to be there when they brought Prue out. Not because it would have been awful; there wouldn't have been anything to see. But it would have been real, like I could pretend it was a dream, standing there at four in the morning in ten-degree weather because someone here, someone in West PC, for God's sake, because they'd been shot in the head in the middle of the night. It had to be a dream—how could something like that be real?

"I walked back the long way, not really thinking about much except Prue and what happened and wondering why, was it someone who hated her that much or just a random thing? And I didn't really think anything of it at first."

"What?" Hallie had been thinking about Prue too as they talked, thinking about that moment—had Prue even had time to know, to recognize what was happening to her? Probably not, because death would have been instantaneous, not even one minute to the next, just there then not. Blinked out.

"Past the actual cemetery, there's mostly empty fields to the north, streetlights just on the one side, and I was walking on the field side because I hadn't crossed back over yet. . . ." She paused, took a long sip of coffee. "And I was maybe halfway down the second block when Tel Sigurdson went by in that white pickup he has—or it could have been someone else's white pickup, because you know there's a ton of them around here. In any case, after it went past me, it stopped up the street and just sat there with its lights out for, like, two or three minutes. Not close enough for the deputies to notice it, I don't think, but whoever was inside could have definitely seen Prue's house and everything. That was when I started thinking maybe it wasn't Tel Sigurdson's truck at all. Maybe a little older?" She said the last like a question, more to indicate she wasn't sure herself than that Hallie might have an answer.

She downed a giant swig of coffee, then grimaced at the bitterness.

"When they turned around and came back down the street, they still didn't have their lights on, like they really didn't want anyone to notice them. I kind of stepped farther off the street into the field and the moon was down by then, so I don't think they saw me, at least not on their way back." She hesitated, leaned forward in her chair so that she was looking at Hallie with a sort of painful intensity that wasn't normal for Brett, who was usually laid-back and unflappable. "Do you think that was it? The killer?"

Hallie could tell that she was shaken by the idea, that a killer was there, that they'd come back, that she—Brett—might have seen them.

"It could have been," Hallie said cautiously. "But it could have been someone curious, someone who didn't want to talk to the deputies for whatever reason. You couldn't see who was driving?"

"No." Brett leaned back in her chair again as if saying it out loud— was I on the same street as a killer?—had helped in some way to make her feel safer again. "That was weird too, don't you think? I mean, Tel would have stopped. At least when he went by me the first time. So, maybe it wasn't Tel, because he didn't offer me a ride or anything either, and I know he saw me when he drove in."

"Did you talk to the sheriff?"

"Do you think I should? I mean, what am I really saying? That it might be Tel's truck? It might not be."

"It might have been the killer," Hallie said. "You need to tell someone. Boyd's coming to supper. Do you want to come? You could talk to him about it first."

Brett nodded. "Yeah. Okay." She gave a quick half laugh. "At least this time it doesn't seem like your kind of thing."

"My kind of thing?"

Brett waved a hand. "You know. Ghosts and devils and things."

Brett knew about Martin Weber and his blood magic, about the ghosts Hallie saw. She knew what had happened with Travis Hollowell and Boyd's wife, Lily. She chose not to believe it, to recon-struct reality so there wasn't any room for ghosts or blood magic, or anything else that wasn't concrete and knowable and everyday.

"Someday you're going to see something you won't be able to ex-plain," Hallie said. "And then what are you going to do?"

"Get you to take care of it for me," Brett said promptly. She got up, set her coffee mug in the sink, and crossed the room to retrieve her coat from its hook by the door.

"Supper'll be around seven," Hallie said.

"Can I bring Sally?"

Hallie wasn't sure who Sally was, but, "Bring anyone you want. Bring salad or something."

Brett settled her hat on her head, zipped up her coat, and left with just a quick wave of her hand to say good-bye.

She hadn't been gone five minutes when Beth came back into the kitchen in a rush, grabbed her messenger bag, and was out the kitchen door before Hallie could even say anything.

Jesus.

"Hey!" Hallie shouted out the back door, the wind cutting through her shirtsleeves like a knife. Beth stopped and turned, her hands shoved deep into the pockets of her jacket and her shoulders hunched, like that would keep her warmer. "Where are you going?"

"To check a couple things out," she said. "If I have to do this my-self, I'll do it." She shoved her chin forward, like a challenge.

Hallie sighed. "Tell me what you find."

Beth straightened, took a step back toward Hallie. "You'll help me?"

"No, I won't help you. I mean . . ." For once she didn't know what she meant. She let the door swing closed behind her. "I mean, tell me and we can talk about it." Which didn't mean she'd do it, because she wouldn't do it. Let Beth go into the under? Let *Beth* become

Death, some nineteen-year-old who didn't even know what she was thinking? No. But maybe it was a way for her, Hallie, to talk to Death. Maybe it was a way to figure this thing out, for both of them.

"Just . . . talk to me. Okay?"

"Yeah. Okay."

Then she was gone.

11

Boyd woke from the middle of a dream into the gray light of his own bedroom with the curtains half-drawn so that the dull light of early dusk softened the edges of the room and gave everything a timeless muted quality. He sat up, blinking against the abrupt transition. In his dream, the world had been split in two—darkness and light. And he'd been the one, the person who was going to have to choose—one or the other. It seemed like a simple choice, seemed like something anyone could choose. Light, of course, light. But in the dream, he'd been sure there was a trick, been sure it was particularly important that he understand, that he make the correct choice.

It had been impossible to see what lay in the light, and that seemed dangerous, everything sharp-edged and illuminated, no secrets in the light, but so bright that it all seemed to be one thing, one color, blended together forever. Darkness promised shadows, shades of gray, reflections in moonlight, and privacy.

He wouldn't choose, shouldn't have to choose, but the world would end, they told him. Who told him? He didn't know.

Choose, they said.

Then he woke.

He felt as if his heart were pounding in his chest, though he

103

checked his pulse with a finger on his wrist and it wasn't, felt like
he'd been running a marathon, but he wasn't even breathing hard. It
was just past four. He had another hour or so before he had to leave
for Hallie's. He needed more sleep, but he knew it would be impossible. He reached for the notebook he kept beside the bed, wrote
down his dream—dated and numbered. He flipped back through
the last three weeks of notes, but he couldn't see that this particular
dream related to anything that had preceded it. Maybe it did; maybe
he couldn't see the connections yet.

He got up, took a quick shower, shaved, and pulled on a clean
pair of jeans. Still barefoot, he cleaned the sink and the bathtub,
took the towels he'd used and put them in the laundry, laid out clean
towels, carried the laundry basket to the basement, and ran a quick
load of wash. Back upstairs, he added laundry detergent to the grocery list he kept on a small marker board on the refrigerator. He got
the mail, sorted it, filed three bills to be paid later, checked his email,
responded to a question from Ole from the day before about whether
he could pick up an extra shift on Saturday, and one from his mother
about whether he'd be home for Christmas. He shut down the computer, went back into the bedroom, put on a shirt, tucked it into his
jeans, took socks and a pair of boots back into the office, and sat back
down.

It wasn't until after all that, that he pulled the evidence bag with
the stone he'd taken from Prue's house off the shelf where he'd put it
earlier, and placed it on the desk. He still wasn't comfortable having
it in his possession. It was evidence in a murder investigation. And
yet, he understood Gerson's reasoning, even if he didn't understand
Gerson herself—what she knew and what she wanted. To investigate
the stones, regular police procedures wouldn't help. He and Gerson
had dusted the stones for fingerprints before the forensic team had
been allowed downstairs. Boyd had insisted and Gerson hadn't ar-

gued. There was nothing; he hadn't expected anything, but it was procedure and important. It was the way you got to the end.

From the center drawer of his desk, he pulled out a new notebook and a ballpoint pen. First, he noted down his observations from Prue's house. The cellar with the buried bones and the three stones. The stones had been separated from each other, as if the distance were important? He'd measured the space between them and made a sketch of the way they'd been placed. The three stones had been exactly twelve inches apart—twelve, twelve, twelve. They were buried, but both he and Gerson felt that they couldn't make any conclusions from that until they knew how long they'd been there. There had been the weird flash of light, light that only he and Gerson had seen. Light and thunder, like something had been asked and answered. Gerson had seen only the light. She hadn't heard the thunder. And that meant something too. It all meant something. The task was to figure out what.

He looked at the stone itself still in the evidence bag.

He'd used his cell phone camera to take a picture of all three stones, in position, but with the dirt wiped off. He pulled his phone out now and laid it, with the picture he'd taken earlier on-screen next to the bag. All three stones were oval in shape, though not identical, the two Gerson had kept smaller than the one in front of him. They looked smooth, like stones that had lain in a creek bed for years. He wanted to touch the stone on the desk in front of him, could almost feel the smooth coolness in his hand. But he was patient. He could wait.

All three stones were mostly gray, mostly granite he suspected, though he was no expert on rocks. Each of them had distinct undertones, though. The stone he'd kept looked more silver in the light; the two Gerson had were gold, not like precious metal, the colors warmer, like if you touched them, your hands would feel warm. He turned out the light in the room and pulled the shades. In the dimness, the stone glowed. It seemed to vibrate very, very slightly, though if Boyd touched the evidence bag, he couldn't feel the movement.

He wrote all these observations in the notebook, not just how the stone in front of him looked, but how he felt, the flash of light in the cellar, the positions of all three stones, the sense of energy or movement or something he couldn't quite grasp, but which seemed important. He made another sketch—the stones in relation to the bones, the furnace, and the cellar walls, all the measurements taken before he'd left the cellar. He recorded everything Gerson had said, which wasn't much. He wanted to know more about her, where she'd learned what she knew and what she knew that he did not. He wrote *Conclusions:* on a line by itself, stared at it, and realized he didn't have any. Not yet.

As he walked out of his office, his cell phone rang.

"Got a minute?" It was Ole. He almost never said hello, never introduced himself. His greetings varied—"Got a minute?", "Something you might be interested in," and "Where the hell are you?" among his favorites.

"I'm on my way out," Boyd said.

"Can you come by the office? Won't be more than five, ten minutes. I'll catch you up on where things are at."

In a reaction that surprised him, Boyd realized that there was nothing he wanted to do less than stop at the sheriff's office and talk about the investigation. "I'll be there in ten minutes," he said. That he didn't want to, didn't compete with duty and obligation. If Ole wanted to talk about the case, if he thought Boyd could help, Boyd would be there. It was simple. It was what he did.

The wind was hard out of the northeast when he left the house, locking the door behind him. No snow, though the ground was rock hard, like the surface of the moon.

It took him less than three minutes to drive from his house to the sheriff's office, but he let his SUV warm up a full minute before he put it in gear and backed out onto the street. He didn't do it because the car needed to warm up before he drove it or because he wanted it to already be warm inside when he got in; he did it because it was a habit formed years ago when his father had taught him to drive, when they'd sit in the car and his father explained every dial and button on the dashboard, how internal combustion engines worked, what a solar-powered car would look like. He didn't think he did it because it reminded him of his father, whom he could call on the phone and talk to anytime he wanted. And he didn't do it because he wanted to relive his high school years. He did it because it was winter and it was cold and it was what he did.

As he headed up Main, he noticed that Tommy Ulrich's Toyota was gone. Sometime during the day when Boyd had been at Prue's house or writing his report or sleeping, someone had come and towed it away. One thing, just one thing in a crappy day that had been cleaned up and taken care of. It wasn't enough and it didn't make up for anything, but it was something.

The glass doors of the main entrance to the sheriff's office were etched with ice like an abstract study in white and gray. The reception area was empty with half the overhead lights dimmed. Ole said it kept people from lingering or saved on the utility bill—one of those. He, Ole, was still deciding which sounded better. Boyd could hear voices farther back and walked around the front desk and down a short hall with photographs on one side depicting the three county sheriffs who'd served before Ole, all three photos in black-and-white, including the one from just ten years before.

Boyd could see a light on in Ole's office, the windowed door half-open. He knocked on the door before he entered.

"We'll look into it," Ole was saying into the phone. He waved at Boyd to close the door and take a seat. "We'll do whatever it takes, but my people aren't investigators. Frankly, that's your job. That's what we pay for, isn't it?" He was silent, presumably listening to someone on the other end of the line. "Yeah, well," he said with heavy sarcasm. "Budget? Manpower? We sure as hell don't have any of those problems here. Look, you give me a list of what you want done, and it'll get done." He banged the phone down so hard, Boyd was surprised it didn't crack the plastic.

"Bureaucrats," Ole said. "They're pulling Gerson and Cross back to Pierre until the lab work is done, and they want us to do all the leg work for 'em. Don't we pay taxes or something?"

"Everyone pays taxes," Boyd said.

Ole looked unimpressed. "Yeah, well, whatever we do, they'll manage to screw it up somehow back in Pierre and blame me for it later on. But—" He smacked his hands together, the sound loud and hollow in the enclosed space. "—we got a job to do and we're going to get 'er done. I figure you want to be involved."

It wasn't exactly a question, but Boyd answered anyway. "Absolutely," he said. Then added because he couldn't not say it, "I feel like—I know I couldn't have done anything different, I don't think I could have seen what was going to happen, but I feel like I should have."

"Yeah," Ole said. He scratched at something on the surface of his desk. "Yeah. I'm sorry about that."

He leaned back in his chair, put his hands behind his head. "Here's what we know: Stalking Horse didn't have any next of kin. She was originally from St. Paul or Minneapolis, one of those. She had a sister who apparently disappeared about twenty years ago. Eventually had her declared dead, but no one knows what really happened. Family name was Shortman—Stalking Horse changed it when she moved to South Dakota. Patty out front says she used to know the sister, long time ago, when Stalking Horse first moved out here. Used to visit all the time. No other family that we can find, though Teedt is looking.

"She didn't have any other jobs than the one at Cleary's, but she had a lot of money in the bank, over thirty thousand dollars, and we don't know if she had any other accounts that weren't local. DCI'll check into that."

"What about the skeleton?" Boyd asked. When their conversation began, he had leaned back in the battered vinyl chair he was sitting in, one of two that Ole kept for visitors, but as Ole talked, he leaned forward until he at the edge, his back muscles tensed as if for a punch. Something cold seemed to have settled along his spine, like there was a persistent breeze in the room even though the door and all the windows were closed.

"Cross and Gerson—or, I guess, the forensic team—took it back to Pierre. They'll try to identify it from dental records, that kind of thing. I told them if we knew about when they think it went into the cellar, we could turn up missing person reports. I mean how many people go missing in a place like this?"

More than anyone cared to think about, Boyd knew. He said, "She must have known the bones were there."

"Yeah." Ole drew the word out like a curse. "I think we can assume Prue Stalking Horse either put them there or knew they were there. Or knew who put 'em there." He studied Boyd for a minute. "How well did you know her?" he asked.

Boyd sat back. "How well?" He had to think. "We were acquainted," he finally said, not sure what Ole was actually asking. "I knew her from Cleary's, sure. And she called dispatch once in a while, but I never knew her on a personal level." He'd known her from people around the county talking about her, because people did, some odd thing she'd done or some place she'd been that someone hadn't expected her.

"Never thought I'd see her away from that bar," people would say, though it wasn't shocking, as far as he knew, any of the places people saw her. It was more that Prue convinced you to see her in a certain way and even if you saw her at, say, the grocery store on the edge of town, it seemed odd and out of place and a little bit uncertain. Hallie had talked to her several times in connection with Martin Weber and with dying and, probably, Death, but just to talk? To sit at her kitchen table and drink coffee? No. He'd never known her like that.

The cold along the back of his neck persisted.

Ole leaned forward in his chair, the springs creaking madly as they adjusted. "You'd hear things about her," he said. "You know, like she was a witch or something. But who the hell believes that? I mean, aside from that stuff I'm not talking about and don't believe in and shouldn't be happening."

"As far as I know," Boyd said, the tension in the room a fraction lighter than it had been a minute earlier, "aside from the Wiccan religion, there's no such thing as witches."

"Yeah, that's what you say," Ole grumbled. He reached sideways and opened one of the desk drawers, drawing out an evidence bag that looked like the one Boyd had. "Gerson left this for you."

Boyd recognized the bag. It was the one he and Gerson had used for the two other stones from Prue's house.

"Why?" This casual handling of evidence was a problem. A big problem that no one but Boyd seemed to recognize or be concerned about.

"She says they can't go into the regular evidence pool. Says it screws everything up. She wants you to handle that side of things since she's gone back to Pierre. She and Cross will take care of the lab and autopsies. And apparently, we're going to do all the goddamned legwork."

"She doesn't know me," Boyd said.

"I vouched for you," Ole told him, as if that were sufficient for anything. "I told you, you're my guy."

All his life, Boyd had resisted acknowledging the prescient dreams he had, had avoided admitting that they made him different or made the world stranger. But in the last five months, everything had become strange; strange had grown from dreams to encompass ghosts, reapers, black dogs, and blood magic. And he'd been in the middle of it all.

Apparently, he'd always been the guy.

He rose and picked up the evidence bag. It felt as if something hummed along his bones, like an extremely low-level electrical current.

"Who makes—?" He hesitated. "If she didn't have family, if Prue didn't have any family, who takes care of the arrangements?"

"Maybe us," Ole said. "We'll see if there's a will first, though. And go from there."

12

When Boyd left the sheriff's office through the double-glass main doors, two of the big lights in the lot were flickering, one of them making a noise like the snap of an electric fence. A cold north wind scattered loose dirt and pea gravel like dry leaves, then died as suddenly as it had arisen. It was already twenty to seven and he was running late, which he rarely did.

A car pulled out in front of him from the street just past the parking lot and sped up as soon as they passed the town limits. Three miles out of town, the only thing he could see of the car ahead of him was the dull red of its rear taillights. Two cars passed him going the other way before he turned. It was full dark, nearly seven o'clock now, a Wednesday night in early March.

He could see the headlights of a car down the long straight stretch of road coming toward him. They appeared, disappeared, appeared again as the road rose and fell so slightly that in the daytime it looked completely level, the only set of lights, other than his, on an empty road. It wasn't until the approaching vehicle came over the last shallow rise, maybe a quarter mile ahead of him, that he realized it was coming straight at him. He honked his horn. Nothing. Laid on the horn hard, the sound nearly deafening in the enclosed space of his SUV. The lights came faster. A blast of cold across his face like—

Ditch.

Thinking it and doing it at the same time. He was in the ditch, through, and out, as the car screamed past. One big thump, into the field, turning as he came, grass striking against the undercarriage of his SUV. Back through the shallow ditch, still turning, but the car was gone.

Boyd sat for a minute, SUV idling, foot hard on the brakes. The car had either turned off, gone into a ditch itself, or turned off its lights. He backed around, pulled the Escape to the side of the road, and got out. With the headlights angled to light the asphalt, he walked up the road in the direction the vehicle had come. No skid marks.

He got back in the SUV, turned again, and drove slowly back up the road. He didn't see a car in the ditch, though there were two gravel roads it could have turned off on. He reversed again, heading back toward Hallie's ranch.

He called it in.

"You didn't see the car?" Ole was running dispatch, which was unusual but not unprecedented. He filled in when there was no other substitute. "Keeps my hand in," he'd say if anyone asked. But everyone knew it was because his son and his daughter were both in college out of state and his wife worked in Rapid City during the week and was home only on the weekends. Mostly home on the weekends. Ole would never say it, but everyone knew he hated an empty house.

"Headlights only," Boyd said. "It was dark. Not big, judging from the height of the lights. Maybe a small SUV. But that's about all I can say."

"Think they were drunk?"

"Probably."

"I'll tell Mazzolo to keep an eye out," Ole said. "She's on tonight."

"Thanks." Boyd replaced his phone in his belt clip, drove on, and turned into Hallie's long driveway fifteen minutes later.

Ole was right. They'd probably been drinking. Or fell asleep at the wheel. Probably. The problem with that was how they'd disappeared. They hadn't ended up in a ditch or the middle of a field. Either the close encounter had sobered them, woken them up, or there was something going on that he didn't yet understand.

He parked in the yard next to a tan and blue pickup he didn't recognize. On the other side was Hallie's little pickup, a newer truck he thought might belong to Hallie's dad, and an old squarish Chevy Malibu with primer spots on the trunk and rear passenger door. He wasn't sure how he felt about a big group, had been thinking it would just be the two of them. Wanted that desperately, to relax, to spend a few minutes or hours not thinking about Prue Stalking Horse, about who shot her, about the sound of the bullet as it hit or the infinitely slow way that she'd fallen.

But maybe this was all right too.

Maybe this was better.

He reached across to the glove compartment and took out a flashlight. The porch light was on and it cast shadows across the yard, intersecting with the big yard light by the horse barn. Boyd walked down both sides of his SUV, looking for scratches or dents, ran the flashlight quick underneath, but figured he'd have to wait until daylight to look for damage there. When he was satisfied that there was nothing that couldn't be cleaned or touched up, he turned off the light, replaced it in the glove compartment, and went inside.

When he opened the front door, there was a rush of warm air, the smell of meat and potatoes, garlic and butter, underlaid with the smell of horses and wheat and old dirt.

Hallie came out of the kitchen. "Sorry I'm late. It's been a busy day," he said.

"Yeah," Hallie said dryly. "Here too."

* * *

There were six of them at the table. Laddie Kennedy had showed up around six thirty and Hallie'd invited him to stay. So, it was Hallie, Boyd, Hallie's father, Laddie, Brett, and Sally, whom Hallie had met, sort of, at a car wreck in November. It wasn't quite like being back in the army, where you were always eating with someone and sometimes with everyone, but it was the most people Hallie'd fixed dinner for since she came home.

It was kind of a big deal. Or it would have been a big deal, if there hadn't been so much else going on.

There was an almost-awkward moment when they all sat down because although Hallie knew everyone at the table, and some of the others had known each other for years, the rest had never met. After an odd quiet moment, Boyd reached across the table to Hallie's father, to Laddie, to Brett, and to Brett's friend Sally. "I'm Boyd. Boyd Davies," he said, shaking each one's hand by turns. He sat back down and started talking to Vance about rebuilding his big equipment shed while Hallie looked at him. Apparently he had social skills.

Brett sat next to Hallie with Sally across the table. As the food was passed around, Brett began to talk about Hallie's horses, which she'd finally gotten the chance to look at when she and Sally arrived earlier. Of the horses Pabby had left, two were at least fifteen years old, one was lame, and two—a two-year-old gelding and a six-year-old mare that threatened to bite anything that came near, including Hallie—hadn't had any training at all.

"So, it's like a horse retirement home," Hallie said.

"Well—" Brett paused to cut herself a bite of steak. "—the black has potential."

"The biter?"

Brett waved that off. "She wants something to do."

"Like bite me."

"Did you look at the way she moves?" Brett said, ignoring Hallie's objection. "She could be awesome. And the gelding, the young one, you can tell he wants to please. He just needs some training."

"But the others? They're basically hay-eaters, right?"

"The pinto could do easy rides if you get her back in condition. But the Appy needs a lot of rehab for that leg, and even then . . ." Her voice trailed off. Then, she said, "And the bay, uhm, I think she's got to be twenty years old."

"So, hay-eaters. Jesus."

Brett gave her a look, her head tipped sideways, like she was looking over the top of a pair of glasses. "If you were going to sell them," she said, "you would have sold them without asking me to look at them. So, you know you're not going to sell them."

"So, what? So don't bitch about it?" Hallie grinned at her. "You know me, first I bitch about it, then I fix it."

"Right," Brett said dryly. "You bitch about it the whole time."

Hallie wondered how long it had been since she and Brett had sat at a table and talked like this. They'd both changed in the meantime. Hallie had four years in the army, Afghanistan, and ghosts. Brett had most of a master's in psychology and was going off somewhere next year to get her doctorate. Different paths, but they still had ranching and the West River, horses and a past.

"Long-term," she said, "I'd like to put the older horses in a back pasture, build them shelter and water. There's a windmill back there, so there must be water. But the gelding and the biter, yeah, I'd like to work with them."

"It might help if you stopped calling her 'the biter,'" Brett said.

"Yeah, well, maybe she should stop trying to bite me."

Sally, who looked around the table, not like she wasn't enjoying herself or she wasn't comfortable, more like she didn't entirely un-derstand how she'd gotten there, said, "I don't know very much about horses. I'm learning—" She smiled at Brett, then looked back at Hallie. "—but, here's something to think about, her situation has changed recently. Her owner is gone and she doesn't trust you, her new owner. She might be afraid. And though I don't know horses, I do know what it's like to be afraid, to be afraid of change. Sometimes it makes us retreat or hide, but sometimes it makes us aggressive."

Hallie wished she could say she didn't know what it was like to be afraid. And it was true that she wasn't afraid in lots of situations that terrified other people. If she could act, if there were something to do, then she did it, didn't think much about whether it was stupid or whether she should do it or even if it might end badly. She did. It was situations where there was nothing to do or she was prevented from doing something or, worst of all, when she didn't know that whatever was happening was even happening, when she couldn't do or couldn't have done anything even if she'd wanted to. Those situations scared her to death.

Sally—and Hallie didn't know her last name, though Brett may have told her, had probably told her—was wearing a denim shirt that looked brand-new, or at least ironed within an inch of its life, a pair of jeans that even Hallie, who didn't notice things like that, figured cost more than the entire pile of jeans she had in her dresser upstairs. She wore two plain silver bracelets on her left hand, a silver ring with an intricate design Hallie didn't recognize, and a thin silver chain around her neck. Her hair was short and sharply angled to the chin; Hallie couldn't tell if it had been colored, but its honey brown shade seemed almost too perfect to be real. She was wearing just enough makeup to look like she wasn't wearing any.

She didn't look precise in the particular way Boyd did, but she did look as if she knew what looked good and how to achieve it. She had a friendly smile and she had seemed game earlier when Brett took her out to see the horses in her brand-new hiking boots and brand-new jeans. Hallie appreciated that, that willingness to try.

And she had a point. Hallie had seen it in Afghanistan, soldiers who'd been so scared, they did stupid-brave things. There hadn't been anything she could do about them. Couldn't tell someone not to be afraid of random mortar fire or stupid ways to die. Those things were still going to happen; Hallie couldn't stop them. And one thing Hallie did know, had learned it from Dell a long time ago—you could ruin a horse by being mean to it, but you couldn't ruin one by being too kind. Spoil it, maybe, but you could both recover from that.

"Sure," she said to Sally. "That makes some sense."

Sally sort of flinched, more like a flicker in her eyes, an antici-pated flinch, like she'd expected Hallie to say something else. Then she smiled, a tight smile that still might have actually been genuine, and took a tiny bite of steak, which she chewed hard on before she swallowed.

"Sally doesn't eat meat very often," Brett said in a low aside.

"Huh," Hallie said, because meat was pretty much a big deal around Taylor County, something you could raise or shoot or barter for and lay up extra for winter. Fruit and vegetables were expensive, things that had to be shipped in. The climate and soil made for a short growing season that often failed, so vegetables were mostly potatoes and several kinds of squash and at the brief end of the season a lot of tomatoes and cucumbers and zucchini.

"You want to help with the training?" she asked Brett.

"Sure," Brett said. "I mean, it's not like I don't have my own place to take care of or classes to study for or anything."

"It's not like you don't want to do it anyway," Hallie replied.

It felt good to talk about something normal, like other people on other ranches probably talked about all the time. Felt good to pretend that even here, life could sometimes be normal. Despite mysterious notes that might or might not be threats. Despite Beth's reappearance. Despite Prue's death.

Despite Prue.

Voices at the other end of the table made Hallie looked toward her father, who was talking to Boyd about . . . "Are you talking about *tractors*?" she asked.

Her father poked a finger at Boyd. "Farmalls," he said, like it was the worst thing he'd ever heard about the Boy Deputy.

"What?"

"I'm telling you," her father said. "Biggest piece of shit that was ever on the market."

Boyd laughed. "My dad has a Farmall my grandfather bought used in 1965. It's worked every day on our farm for the last forty years."

"On a dairy farm," her father said, implying somehow in just those few words that dairy farming, unlike ranching, was done by soft men with soft hands who mostly sat on porches and drank lemonade.

"Nah, come on, Vance." Laddie joined the conversation, reaching across the table for the potatoes. "We had a Farmall once. An H, I think. Pretty good little tractor. I almost bid on it at auction when we lost the ranch. But we were living in an apartment above the old Laundromat in Prairie City at the time and I didn't have any place to keep it. Or any land to use it on," he added.

Hallie's father looked at him, like he couldn't understand a fellow South Dakotan choosing to side with an upstart Iowan. But Hallie could see he was relaxed, that this was the kind of conversation he liked, and she could see a taste of normal was important to him right now.

"Maybe you should get a Farmall, Dad," Hallie said. "Fix it up." He'd lost his old Allis, the tractor he worked on all the time, but which had never actually run as long as Hallie could remember, in the equipment shed fire in September. He'd bought another Kubota and a small Ford, but he hadn't yet picked up anything to work on in the evenings when everything else was done.

"Nope," he said definitely. "Got my eye on a 1947 Ford pickup over to Lead. Been sitting out back of some guy's barn for fifty years. Going to give him two hundred bucks for it as soon as I can talk Tom into going over with me and towing it home."

13

Hallie made coffee in Pabby's old stovetop percolator, and as the smell drifted from the kitchen into the dining room, people began to rise from the table. Brett insisted that she and Sally would clean up, though she spent a few quiet minutes talking to Boyd first, who nodded and put a hand on her shoulder. Hallie's father took a steaming mug of coffee, put on his coat, and went out on the front porch, something he'd done after any big supper with lots of people since Hallie could remember.

Laddie followed Hallie to the kitchen, then back into the dining room. Boyd watched him and started to approach, but Hallie touched him on the arm and held up a finger—wait. He put his hand over hers and stepped out of the room, like they'd just had an entire conversation.

Hallie watched Laddie walk around the dining room, pick up a small metal figure—a cowboy on a bucking bronco—turn it over in his hands, then put it back down. He ran his hand along the edge of a small side table, straightened a chair, and then stopped, his hand still gripping the chair, not looking at Hallie or much of anything.

Hallie couldn't read him. He seemed to be wound just a little less tight than he'd been that morning, but there was still something there. She could see it in the way he fingered the third button on his denim shirt and every once in a while when he'd stick his hand in the watch pocket of his jeans like he was checking something was there.

After a long stretch of silence, he said, "You know Martin Weber, you know the kind of magic he did. Prue never did that, never messed with blood or sacrifice, and you gotta appreciate that, because it's always there, that way of getting power. But she studied it, everything about it. She was convinced that there was another path. Convinced she was going to find it. She could be pretty persuasive. Back when I first knew her."

"She's the one, isn't she?" Hallie asked. "The one you talked to about the stone, way back?"

Laddie pulled out the chair he'd been gripping the back of and sat down at the table. He reached into his shirt pocket and pulled out a pack of cards. He shuffled them, flipped the top card over, stuck it back in the pack, and said, looking at the cards more than at Hallie, "Yeah. She came from a family that had their own magical traditions and she definitely had an affinity. But still, you know, she could maybe start a fire with damp wood or unlock a padlock or something. Nothing big, nothing complicated. And it took a lot of effort, more effort than making a key from scratch or hunting up dry wood. That's the way small magics are a lot of times, a way to stay in touch with the land or with a way of life, but not big enough to make a difference in how things work. She came here, originally, because of the reservation, wanted to study another magic tradition, learn everything there was to know and how to use it.

"I come back from the army not long after she'd moved here, had the stone, and I did a lot of—well, I did a lot of drinking. We were in Cleary's one night and I showed it to her, or she asked me about it, like she could tell I had it before she'd even seen it."

Hallie remembered that Prue had been able to see a mark on her, had seen Maker or not actually seen, but seen the spot where Maker was sitting, like a dark smudge.

"So, we talked. About the stone, about the dead, and everything. And it was great, you know, someone who understood what had been happening to me." He paused, laid out a set of five cards, then straightened the edges so they aligned perfectly with each other. "She said I was lucky, that not many people had access to that kind of power. I said she was welcome to it."

"So, you gave it to her," Hallie said, because that seemed where things were going. But Laddie still had the stone. And Prue was dead.

"I . . . gave it to her, but—" He gathered up the cards he'd laid out, shuffled the deck again, and laid out one card, studied it, then laid out three more. "—I was a little bit sorry afterwards and I kind of wanted to know more about it and the other stuff and I started hanging out with Prue and her sister—she used to visit from St. Paul. I was young and stupid. I should have walked away. Just given her the stone and left it all behind." He gathered up the cards again, then laughed. "What am I saying? I did walk away, at the end when it was too late."

"What happened?"

He shook his head. "She got to liking the . . . the power of it. And, you know, she wanted this powerful magic that wasn't per-verted by death or sacrifice and all, but in the end, even her way, the magic perverted her. Her and her sister both. I tried to tell her, get her to see what was happening. But she wouldn't listen. I finally took it back, the stone. Stole it back, actually. I figured it was better I have it than her."

"And what? She just let you?" If the stone was power, why had Prue let it go? And how did a Prue who was hungry for power fit with a Prue who'd told Hallie she was neutral in all magical things, who'd refused to help even when the world was at stake?

"Her sister came to see me after I'd taken it back," Laddie said. "And she . . . laughed at me. Said they'd figured it all out and they didn't need me anymore. Which was, you know, fine. I just wanted to be left out of things. Though it was right after that, things went all to hell. Her sister left. With this guy, I think. In any case, I never saw her again. Prue never talked about any of it. Like it never happened.

"She came to me a few days ago and said she needed it back. The stone, I mean. Which, I don't have to tell you was tempting after all this time, no matter what had happened twenty years ago. I wouldn't give it to her, I'm smarter now than I was, but it got me thinking about it again, about giving it away. You know, though—" He dealt out twenty cards, like he was looking for something, for a particular card in the deck. "—it's never going to happen. I can talk about it, about getting rid of the stone, but it's like the ranch I haven't got anymore: It just is."

"You can give it to me," Hallie told him again. It wasn't that she wanted it. She didn't. But the dead already talked to her. Okay, not talk exactly, but they followed her around. She'd figure it out. She felt like someone ought to do something for Laddie, just once. This was something she could do.

Laddie shook his head again, gathered up his cards, and stuffed them back into his shirt pocket. "No," he said. "It's different now that the dead are talking all the time, but I'll get used to it. And I trust you, Hallie, I do, but I *know* I won't use it wrong. I don't even have the ability, I don't think. It's safer if it stays with me."

He got up to leave.

"You're going to talk to Boyd before you go," Hallie said, not like it was a question.

Laddie looked at her like he didn't know what she was talking about.

"About the fight you had with Prue, about the fact that she called you last night. Don't wait, Laddie. Don't make Ole come find you. Take care of it now."

Laddie sighed, then nodded. Hallie led him out into the living room, where Boyd was hanging a set of pictures Hallie'd brought over from her father's ranch the week before. Hallie heard an unfamiliar laugh from the kitchen—she assumed it was Sally—followed by a low-voiced response from Brett.

Boyd looked at Hallie, then at Laddie.

"I got something I need to say," Laddie said.

Boyd nodded. "Good, because as it happens, I have something to talk to you about too."

"I'll go—" Hallie pointed vaguely toward the doorway. "—out." She went to the kitchen and grabbed her barn coat. Sally and Brett were discussing a research paper one or the other of them had read recently. Hallie departed through the living room, pulling on her coat as she went, and stepped onto the front porch.

Her father stood on the edge of the porch, looking out toward the horse barn. It was maybe twenty degrees, but the wind had died completely. The sky was clear, and the air was crisp and dry. "Ole says the county will probably be making the funeral arrangements," Hallie's father said. "She didn't have anybody."

"Yeah," Hallie said.

They were both quiet. Somewhere down on the main road, Hallie could see the lights from a big truck, the entire cab outlined in red. "Did you ever—?" she finally said. "I mean, was she—?"

Her father laughed, like he'd been waiting all his life for Hallie to ask him awkward questions about his social life. "She was a friend. Nothing more. Never saw her much outside Cleary's. Few times at the Dove. Maybe at the Bob when I used to go there which was . . . was a long time ago."

125

"Will you miss her?" Hallie asked.

He looked at her, but he didn't answer.

Hallie leaned against one of the porch supports and studied him in profile. He didn't leave the ranch often, went to the Dove for breakfast once a week, the farm supply store in Templeton and the Viking in Box Elder when his friend Norman Henspaw bullied him into it. He'd taken Hallie and Dell on vacation once three years after their mother died to the Kennedy Space Center to watch a shuttle launch. He'd dropped the two of them off at Disney World while he went to look up a guy, had some new breed of cattle from Bavaria or someplace. The whole thing had actually been kind of fun, but it was the only vacation the three of them had ever taken together.

He didn't have many friends, though the ones he had were good ones.

"I mean," Hallie said, "you knew her a long time."

"Of course I'll miss her," her father said, looking out across the yard as he spoke. "Things happen. You get used to it."

Hallie was pretty sure that wasn't true, but she also knew that was what you said, how you dealt with things around here.

"Are you sure about this?" he asked, the question so abrupt that it was a minute before Hallie could even figure out what the question was.

"About talking to you?"

"About this," he said impatiently. "This ranch. This place. This.

"Your mother used to talk about living on the coast," he continued after a minute. "We'd had that one vacation back before you and Dell, and she loved it. I knew this was my place—that I belonged here. But I never knew about her. She said it was enough, that that vacation would be enough to last her. And, of course, we thought we'd go again. Maybe with you kids. Maybe a second honeymoon. But we never did."

They'd gotten a long way off the subject of Prue and her death. Or, maybe they hadn't.

"I'm not sorry to be here," Hallie said. "And this ranch is . . . I like fixing things," she said. Which wasn't quite the same as saying she was happy. She'd have liked, in a more perfect world, for it to have been an real choice, for the army to still be available to her, for the decision to reenlist or not to have belonged to her. But it was what it was. There were plenty of things she liked about the way things were right now—Boyd and the ranch, her father and Brett, maybe even the biter. But she wanted to know that it would mean something. That her life would mean something.

And, of course, Death, which had to be settled one way or another. But that wasn't something she was going to talk to her father about.

"You need to get that paddock fence fixed. Should have done it back in the fall," her father said, by which he meant, "Well, we're pretty well done with this topic, aren't we."

"It's just the gate," she said. "Not the whole fence. I picked up supplies last week."

"I'll come over Saturday," he said. "We can do it then." He handed her his coffee cup, pushed her right shoulder, which was almost, sort of like a hug, stepped off the porch, and crossed the yard. As if he'd said it out loud, she knew he was glad she'd stayed.

Laddie, Brett, and Sally came out, all of them together in a group. Laddie didn't say much, just thanks and got to go. Brett gave her a quick hug and said, "I'll be over next week. We can start working with that mare."

Sally said, "Nice to meet you."

Brett and Sally were already in Brett's old pickup and turning around when Laddie came back across the yard, his hands shoved deep into his jacket pockets, his face hunched against the cold. He handed her a card, which she couldn't see in the shallow light.

"Don't take him with you into the Badlands," he said.

"What are you talking about? I'm not going to the Badlands."

Laddie was already off the porch, heading back to his truck, but at her question, he turned and raised his hands, like, What are you going to do? "I'm just saying," he told her, like this was the sort of thing people said to each other all the time. Or at least Laddie, who might or might not be able to tell the future, who was sometimes right, though it might just be a coincidence, who probably did say that sort of thing all the time.

14

After Laddie started his car with a sharp engine whine, turned it around, and his red taillights disappeared down the drive, Hallie went back in the house. She hadn't known she was cold until she came inside.

Boyd came out of the kitchen with two mugs of coffee. "I hope you don't mind," he said.

"God, no," Hallie told him, because it was exactly what she wanted, though she took it back into the kitchen, shed her jacket, and sat at the kitchen table, which tipped slightly on one leg because she hadn't gotten around to fixing it yet. He sat with her, but he didn't say much.

"What did you say to Laddie?"

"That he should talk to Ole. Prue called him, you know, last night. And it's not as if everyone doesn't already know that he and Prue have been at odds for years."

"He wouldn't shoot her," Hallie said.

"You don't always know what people will do," he said. Like she didn't know. Like she hadn't been in Afghanistan.

"Yeah," was all she said. After a moment, she added, "He thinks she was after his stone."

"He could have done it, Hallie. Ole says he was a marksman when he was in the army."

"So that's what they think? That Prue called him and after he hung up, he got in his truck, drove over there at three in the morning, and shot her?" Hallie expected better police work than that. She expected it from Boyd, and she expected it from everyone else because Boyd would expect it of anyone he worked with.

"No." And for the first time that evening, he sounded tired. "Of course not. There's crime scene evidence to sift through, people to interview. Laddie wasn't the only person Prue called last night. There was also a call to the Sigurdson ranch and to a number in St. Paul. That one might have been a wrong number, but it's got to be checked out."

"She called Tel Sigurdson? Why?"

"She called the barn phone. So, it could have been for a lot of people. Foreman said Tel himself was out of town, but now Brett's saying she saw him in West PC."

"I can't believe it would be Tel," Hallie said. "I mean, why?"

"Why would anyone do it?" Boyd asked.

Why.

In some ways, Hallie didn't want to know why. Why made things complicated. Why made things gray. If all you knew was what happened and who'd done it, then you didn't have to worry about extenuating circumstances or complicated motivations. You could just take care of the problem.

"Are you staying?" she asked.

He shook his head. "I have to work in the morning."

"Really?" Because hadn't he worked last night? And after everything, she'd figured they'd give him a couple of days off at least. Or that Boyd would take them—which she should have known wouldn't happen.

"We've got a lot of work to do on this investigation, and Teedt's going to Omaha for his niece's wedding," he said. "So, I really—I have to get going." Though he didn't get up.

Hallie'd been carrying the card Laddie gave her since she'd come back in the house. She flipped it over onto the table. It was Death. A tarot card. Which didn't always mean literal death, if she remembered what Laddie had told her. It meant change. "Doesn't mean it's bad," he'd said. "Could be something good." Could be.

Though in Hallie's case, it probably wasn't.

"Do you think they'll find out who killed her?" she asked.

"Yes." Like there wasn't any other answer. "We have to."

"You don't have to," Hallie pointed out, noticing that he had shifted from "they"—the DCI—to "we."

"We will." Quiet emphasis, but still. After a brief pause, he added, "There's another thing. At the house, we found several stones."

"Stones like Laddie's?" That made a certain amount of sense, that Laddie's stone was not the only one of its kind and that Prue had managed to find others, especially as she'd been interested in them. Maybe that's what her sister had meant all those years ago, about not needing Laddie anymore, because they'd found others. But then, why had Prue tried to get Laddie's stone back, at the end?

Boyd seemed to be searching for the right words. "Are they like Laddie's? I don't know. They're not ordinary stones, I'm certain of that. There was a weird flash when I shone a light on them. A flash not everyone saw. And they were in Prue's cellar, next to some old bones."

"Old bones, like a *body*?"

"Yes."

"Jesus."

"Yes."

"There's a *body* in Prue Stalking Horse's cellar?"

"Old, like it's been there a long time. Maybe before Prue moved in. We're checking."

"She must have known about it, though. She must have known about the stones."

"That's what we need to figure out. Even if the bones have nothing to do with Prue's death, we need to know who it was and how they died. As for the stones, they asked me to see what I could figure out, actually."

"You? Why?" Wouldn't they bring in their own experts or take the stones to a lab?

"Ole says I'm his go-to guy for unexplained phenomena," Boyd said with a ghost of a smile.

"Ole? You've talked to Ole about this? I didn't think Ole talked about 'unexplained phenomena.'"

Boyd got up, crossed to the sink, and grabbed a paper towel from the roll. He came back and wiped the table underneath his coffee mug, wiped the bottom of the mug, threw the towel in the trash, and sat back down.

"He says he doesn't talk about it. He says, figure it out. You know Ole."

Hallie tapped a finger on the table. "What happens when you pick one of the stones up? Can you hear the dead? Or anything weird?" She remembered what Laddie had told her, that the stones affected different people differently.

"I have no idea," Boyd said. "I haven't touched them and neither, as far as I know, has anyone else. It just—" He paused as if he couldn't find the right words. "—it seemed like a bad idea."

"Yeah," Hallie agreed. It probably would be a bad idea. Probably. Someone ought to do it anyway. "Laddie says that Prue was interested in his stone," she told him. "He said the stones store magic."

He nodded. "That's what he told me too. Magic storage. I don't even know what that means. Where does the magic come from?"

"What does any of it mean?" Hallie got up and started pacing. "Prue was shot in front of her house at three o'clock in the morning when you were there." She stopped. "Do you think the fact that you were there is significant?"

He considered the question. "There's no way to know. If you were going to do it at night, this would be the way to do it. Get her to come to the front door, line up the shot and . . . shoot her."

"Couldn't you shoot her when she came home from work? When she was leaving Cleary's? Couldn't you break into her house and kill her just about any time you wanted?"

"Maybe it means something," Boyd said, "the timing, making sure someone was there when it happened."

"Maybe she had her house protected somehow, like the hex ring."

"Maybe. I don't know."

"And now you have these stones."

"Which may not have anything to do with Prue's death."

"Okay," Hallie conceded, unsatisfied.

Boyd frowned at her and Hallie realized again how tired he was, thought about how little sleep he'd probably had and that he'd just told her he was going to be working tomorrow. "I know," she said. "You don't know." Why was everything always so slow?

Boyd rubbed a hand across his face. "Look," he said, "there's really not much more we can do with this right now."

"I guess not," Hallie said. But there had to be something. "I think Laddie knows something he hasn't told me. I don't know if it's important."

He nodded. "Okay. I'll talk to him again tomorrow."

Hallie could see even that seemed like a lot of effort, thinking about tomorrow, about talking to people, about doing anything. She knew about that, about being that tired, when you couldn't stop thinking, but every thought seemed to carry the weight of a thousand years, too much and too hard and just . . .

"Or, I could talk to him," she said.

Boyd stood. "You need to be careful," he said. And Hallie hoped he would stop right there, but he didn't. "This is an official police investigation. You can't interfere."

She drew in her breath and held it. It didn't do any good; the words tumbled out anyway. "Really?" she said. "All of it? It's all official? What if this is about the stones? What if that's why she was killed? How are they going to figure that out? Did they 'officially' give you one of the stones? Like, you're the official expert in weird stones? They're not going to pursue that, they don't want to pursue it, they don't even want to know."

"It's an official police investigation," he repeated. Like, I can't do this now, can't come up with anything else to say.

"Yes," she said. "And we know how that goes."

Boyd looked at her for a minute. "Damnit, Hallie," he said wearily. "Just . . . damnit."

She couldn't tell if he was swearing in general or at her. She was sorry about not leaving it alone, about his lack of sleep, about Prue's death, about all the things they hadn't even touched on—Beth and Death and what would happen next, but she wasn't going to tell him she would leave it alone. Because she wouldn't. And she wanted him to know it. That was how they did things.

He didn't say anything more. He crossed the room, poured his undrunk coffee down the drain, rinsed the cup, and set it in the sink. Then he put his coat on and went outside. Hallie looked at the closed door after he left. Damnit. Was this what all men did when they didn't want to talk or just the men she knew? Her father, Laddie,

Boyd. Who *wouldn't* want to stand outside in the cold instead of inside somewhere where it was warm?

She waited a few more minutes, didn't hear the sound of his car starting up, so finally, she got up too, put her own coat on, and followed him.

She found him on the leeward side of the old barn with his hands shoved into his pockets and the collar of his jacket turned up against his neck. She went over and put her arms around him without saying anything. She laid her head against his chest. She could smell the clean scent of aftershave and soap. After a minute, he pulled his hands free from his jacket pockets and pulled her closer, resting his chin on the top of her head.

"Don't we ever get a break?" he said.

Hallie almost laughed. He had no idea. Which wasn't fair and she knew it wasn't fair. They'd spent the whole night talking about Prue's murder and who knew or had seen what and when, and still, he didn't know the half of what was going on.

She took a moment she didn't usually take, a moment where she didn't say—hey, I have something else to tell you or I saw Beth Hannah today, though she would, and before he left. But for a minute, for the length of a long breath and less than the time it took for the cold to penetrate to her bones, she stood with him like the world had finally left them space, even though it hadn't and probably never would.

She tilted her head up and kissed him, long and slow, like it wasn't ten degrees outside, like they hadn't both spent the day on things that shouldn't have happened and couldn't be believed. He tightened his arms around her waist and kissed her back.

She could feel the rough stubble of the short hairs on the back of his neck, could feel him tight up against her, couldn't feel the cold at all, because this was what mattered, this moment, right here. Reluctantly, she broke the kiss and stepped back.

"Beth Hannah was here today," she said.

Boyd stepped back too, almost as if he couldn't help himself.

"Why didn't you say something?" he asked.

She said, "I am saying something."

"Hallie." Like she was missing the point.

"Boyd." Like, no.

"She's been missing for months. I've been looking for her for months. I was worried about her."

"I left you a message."

"What?"

"On your phone, after she left, I called you."

"What did she want?"

"It's . . . complicated."

He moved so that he was backlit by the yard light and it threw the planes of his face into relief so that he looked older, or his actual age instead of like a kid who was barely out of high school. "Complicated like you don't want to tell me or complicated like it's actually complicated?"

"Are you *trying* to start an argument with me?" she asked.

She could see his breath in the stillness of the night air, spooling out in slow motion. "I just . . . ," he finally said. "I don't understand. Why did she come here? Why hasn't she called?"

Because she doesn't need you to lean on anymore, she thought. What she said was, "That's part of what's complicated."

"Is she okay?" he said.

"As far as I can tell," she said.

He didn't say more, didn't ask the dozen questions she thought he wanted to ask, which was good—it was good—because it *was* complicated. Not least because Boyd thought that Death wasn't coming back, thought that even if he did, Hallie would say no and it would be fine. Because there are rules, right, he'd asked her. The rules are back in place. Which, maybe. But the rules said that she owed Death. She'd been supposed to die and she hadn't. *She'd* already broken the rules. The question was whether what happened next was her choice or Death's.

She reached toward him, then let her hand fall because it would be easy, she could already see that. Kissing him again, wrapping her arms around him, taking him upstairs right now to her bedroom, those were all things that made sense of the world—or denied it— made her feel as if she were sufficiently weighted, as if nothing could free her of this place, this land, this earth. Not even Death.

But tonight—today—was not about easy.

"Boyd," she said. "I will always tell you. That's what I'm telling you. But Beth is okay. You have a lot on your plate. And the details can wait until tomorrow. I wanted you to know that she'd been here, but you don't need to know all the details now." She sounded cool and rational and not like herself at all.

The truth was, she wanted him to leave it, to concentrate on Prue's murder and leave this to her. She didn't want his advice, she didn't want his help, she didn't want to talk to him about it. And she didn't know why, like a wall had gone up that she couldn't see through or around and didn't even know why it was there. Just— *wham!*—barriers to the horizon. Or between her and Boyd, at least.

Finally, he nodded. He rubbed a hand across his chin. "All right," he said. "I understand."

Though he didn't. She could tell. She didn't even understand it herself.

He kissed her again and Hallie wanted to kiss him back like it was the last time, though she had no idea why. He got in his SUV. The engine started with a reluctant whine against the cold, and he was gone.

She watched him go, his taillights red against the darkness of the night. She'd been alone before—on the ranch, in the army. She'd vacationed once in a cabin in the mountains in North Carolina and hadn't talked to anyone for three days. All that had been fine.

But tonight she felt lonely and smaller than seemed fair.

15

It was dark when Boyd woke the next morning. The fleeting edge of a dream left a nagging sense of urgency and foreboding. He'd left the bedroom window open an inch the night before, and the early morning air was sharp and chill. Damp too. Damp the only promise that spring was coming, but at least it was a promise and there would be a spring. He turned onto his back and looked at the ceiling. He had a pretty clear idea of what to do today—go back to Prue's house and look around again, this time without a dozen police officers obscuring everything. He wanted to look more closely at the stones Gerson had given him. He wanted to know more about Gerson, what she knew and whether she could point him toward reference material, toward any information at all about magic, about reapers and black dogs, about prescient dreams, about any of it. Because if there was one thing Boyd had, it was questions.

Last night when he left the ranch, he'd been, not angry, but tired and unhappy and wanting something he couldn't quite name. Beth was back. And Hallie hadn't told him. That was how it felt, though it wasn't true. She did leave a message; he'd checked. But for some reason, in his head last night, in the way everything had come together—Prue's death, the stones, going for a day and a half on three hours' sleep—it seemed not enough. And as he drove, the moon rising slow in front of him, the night sky clear and cold and bowing deep to the distant horizon, he had realized that what Hallie had or hadn't said about Beth Hannah was not the problem.

When he first met Hallie—which hadn't been that long ago, but seemed like a lifetime, like he'd always known her or been waiting to meet her—it had been clear that she didn't need anyone. It had also been clear that she could use help, whether she knew it or not, and he'd done his best to deliver. She'd appreciated it, but she didn't look for it. Over the last few months, they'd achieved an understanding about whom to talk to and whom to look for in a crowd, and whom to call when something happened. In a way, last night felt like they were back where they'd begun. He was pretty sure that if a challenge came along, say, this afternoon, Hallie would do her damnedest to keep him away from it. Not because she didn't trust him or believe that he could help. Not even—he didn't think—because she wanted to protect him, though she probably did; he knew he wanted to protect her.

She wouldn't keep it from him because she didn't trust him. She'd do it because she didn't trust herself.

For the next three days he didn't see Hallie at all. He called a couple of times, got voice mail. She called him back. They talked briefly once and arranged to meet for breakfast at the Dove, but then canceled on each other in crossing voice mail messages.

He spent a day and a half tracking down the phone number in St. Paul that Prue had called on the evening before she died. Ole said that DCI should take care of it, but he expected they weren't going to get to it for a while. There'd been a triple murder in a parking lot in Rapid City, which everyone suspected was drug-related and which even the governor was demanding fast action on. Prue's death all the way out in Taylor County merited a half page in the local section of the paper, and no one outside Taylor County was all that worried about it. Even Gerson, when Boyd called her to ask about the lab and forensic results, acted like she hadn't thought much about the case since she'd left the day before.

"We're a little busy here," she said.

"We're a little busy here too," Boyd said. He wondered if Taylor County sat in some sort of psychic zone, something that made people forget what happened there once they'd left. Then he was sorry he'd thought it, because the way things had gone the last six months, it would probably turn out to be true.

The phone company didn't keep records back more than five years, and all that time the phone number in St. Paul had belonged to the copy shop. When he called the shop directly, they said for a year or so after they'd first opened, they'd gotten calls for a meat locker that had gone out of business.

"We did get a call once for—let me think," the owner told Boyd when he'd finally tracked her down. "Well, they called the franchise office, looking for old records, and the franchise office sent it to us. They couldn't be bothered, I guess," she said. "But, anyway, yeah, there was another name, because this person who called was looking for someone who had this number before the meat locker. Cheryl, maybe? Or Shannon? A woman's name anyway. I remember because the person who called laughed when I told her we didn't have any information back more than four years—never hurts to check, they said. Which struck me odd, you know. Check what?"

"Wasn't that Stalking Horse's sister's name?" Ole said when Boyd told him. He thumbed through a yellow notebook with a cheap cardboard cover bent in at the corners from wear. "Yup. Shannon Shortman. Funny Stalking Horse would call that number twenty years after her sister disappeared. Not like she didn't know."

The second morning when he'd been supposed to meet Hallie for breakfast, someone called to say that they'd heard shots fired out by the old Uku-Weber building. Normally, gunshots—particularly shotguns or rifles—were something people in Taylor County didn't pay much attention to, but, "After Prue Stalking Horse," the person on the phone had said, "well, I just don't know."

Boyd and Ole had driven out there, but all they'd found was debris from the stone fountain still scattered across the parking lot, and an empty building that looked like it had been standing unused for twenty years instead of just six months. There was a FOR SALE sign by the road with 24,000 SQUARE FEET and INDUSTRIAL in big red letters. There was a row of neat bullet holes around one of the zeros in 24,000, but when Boyd got out to look closer, it was clear they weren't new.

"Who do you think will buy this place?" Ole asked as Boyd turned the patrol car around and headed back to town.

"No one," Boyd said.

"Yeah." Ole looked at him closely, as if he were seeing more than Boyd was comfortable revealing. "You're probably right."

Boyd asked Ole for time to go back to Prue's house now that the investigation teams were finished and to figure out what he could about the stones. "Well, sure," Ole said. "I'll just send DCI a bill when you're done. Since we seem to be doing their jobs for them."

The house looked empty when Boyd parked on the street in front. The stark landscaping and blank white front giving the impression that it had been abandoned for years. Weedy grass grew along the corner of the garage, heeled over from months of winter snow and frost. He approached the house up the old sidewalk that ran from the street to the porch steps. He wondered if Prue had gotten many visitors, if she'd gotten any visitors. The house wasn't inviting, impossible to tell, day or night, if anyone was home.

He stepped around and let himself in with a key through the kitchen door. Everything looked disturbed, a film of dust on the counters and furniture, and yet it all looked just the same. He wasn't sure what he was looking for beyond a better sense of who Prue had been and what she'd done. He spent a little over two and a half hours going through closets and dresser drawers. In the attic he found a stack of old photo albums, dusted for fingerprints but still there. It looked as if half the pictures were missing. Most of the remaining photographs were of open prairie, mountains he didn't recognize, and oceans against gray-white skies. There was a series of photos, a total of five in all, shoved into a pocket in the front of one of the albums. He pulled them out to look at more closely because at first glance they reminded him in some way he couldn't identify of the dream he'd had the night before. Though he angled them toward the window and toward the dim overhead light, it was impossible to see clearly what they were actually photographs of.

He put all five of them in an envelope and put the envelope in his inside jacket pocket. He put everything else back the way he'd found it, walked through the house one more time, checking windows and locks and pausing briefly in the spare bedroom, but deciding that he'd have to come back again if he wanted to go through the dozen or so boxes stored there. The contents of each box had already been cataloged and he'd looked at the lists, but it didn't mean there wasn't something important to be found in them.

He left the same way he'd come in and locked the door with the key he'd signed out from the office. Up on the road, near his car, hunched against the wind, a woman stood watching the house. She was young, maybe his age, maybe younger. She was dressed warmly in a heavy coat, a knit cap and scarf, but there was something about the way she wore them—the scarf wrapped tight around her neck and chin, the knit cap pulled low, the coat buttoned up like armor—that made him think she wasn't accustomed to the weather, hadn't been anyplace cold for a long time. The coat and cap were black, but the scarf was a bright blue, like clear summer skies. It stood out, a stark contrast to the gloomy light and winter gray.

"Can I help you?" Boyd asked as he approached her.

"I lived in that house once—a long time ago," she said. "I heard there was a shooting."

"Yes, ma'am," Boyd said. "Do you know something that might be relevant?"

"She was a cheater," the woman said. Her eyes were a curious light blue, lighter than the scarf, like winter skies, the whites like old parchment. "Cheated all her life."

Hallie had described Prue as a cheater too. She'd gotten it from the harbinger, because, said Maker, Prue cheated Death. He wondered if she'd cheated at other things. Cheated someone who might want to kill her.

The woman raised her hand. She wasn't wearing gloves, and the faint thin lines of old scars crisscrossed her palm. "Will it be going on the market, you think?"

"The house?" Someone died here, he wanted to remind her. To most people, that meant something. He had reached inside his jacket for his notebook when his radio crackled. "Davies here," he said. It was the daytime dispatcher, Patty Littlejohn, asking him to call Ole on his cell. He pulled out his phone, said excuse me to the woman, and walked to the other side of his patrol car. When he turned around, he saw her getting into a late-model rental car. He noted the license plate, then called Ole. He didn't expect to see her again, but it paid to take note of things.

That night he studied the photographs he'd retrieved from Prue's house. He got out a magnifying glass and looked at them, but they were dark and they were nothing more than pictures of sky and floors and empty walls. In two of them, he could see nothing but a blank concrete wall like a cellar maybe, though both photographs included a window well with no actual window, not even the framing—an old foundation? The photos depicted two different sections of wall, one marked with an *X* and the other with a circle. Each photograph had the number *6* marked in the corner with white ink.

The third photograph was also of concrete, but for some reason—shadows or the slant of the light—Boyd was pretty sure it was a floor, not a wall. An arrow had been gouged out of the concrete, rough and obviously done in haste, but quite clear. The number *3* had been marked in the corner of the photograph, like the other two with white ink. The final two pictures were just dirt. That was it. They must have meant something to someone, but they didn't mean anything to him.

Finally he stacked them up and instead took the three stones from Prue's house out of the safe in the corner of his office. They were still in their separate evidence bags, and he'd stored them on two separate shelves in the safe. He noticed when he'd picked up the second bag, the one Gerson had left at the sheriff's office, that it vibrated, and now when he opened the bags and rolled all three stones onto his desk, he could see that all of them were vibrating, like self-powered baby rattles thrumming against the bare wood of the desk.

He was hesitant to touch them, but he couldn't see what the harm would be. Laddie had carried his stone around for years. Hallie said he'd tried to give it away, which meant other people had handled it, presumably without ill effects. But these were different stones, and he was a different person. What would happen to him if he picked up one of these stones?

He studied each one with a magnifying glass. Nothing he hadn't already seen. Nothing that made them seem any different from any other stone—smoother than some, smaller than some, possibly they were all a certain type. He could take them to the School of Mines in Rapid City. They could tell him where they'd come from and what had formed them into stone, though they wouldn't be able to tell him about storing magic or talking with the dead or how they'd come to be vessels for holding magic. Before he could think too much, think about how he was always the careful one, about how someone else ought to be present, about how Prue Stalking Horse had died right in front of him, he picked up the smallest stone and held it in the palm of his hand.

The vibrating slowed, then stopped altogether. He closed his hand around it. No voices, which was a relief. Nothing. Then he realized that there really was nothing. No sound at all. Not the steady push of the furnace fan, not the hum of his computer, nothing but his own breathing. He turned around, and the entire back wall of his office had disappeared. He could smell damp grass and woodsmoke, see a swath of prairie grass, but that was above him, not at his feet. The air was heavy and wet like August, though the height of the grass made it look more like late May or early June. Light came from what would have been over his left shoulder if he were actually standing wherever this was.

There were no people in the scene in front of him. There wasn't anything, except the prairie grass above him, a few weeds at his feet, and some broken timber framing. He was down in something, in a hole. Too big for a grave—thank God. Something moved, right across the periphery of his vision, a sound like a shout, though he couldn't make out words. A shovel clanged against a hard surface. He took a step closer, like he really was right there, like it would be clearer if he could just get closer, and it disappeared. It was his office, a wall of bookshelves, the smell of lemon cleaner and leather.

He blinked. He put the stone down on his desk. It vibrated quietly, like nothing had happened. He picked it up again. The same scene, like he'd turned on a television set or he'd just had one of his prescient dreams while he was standing in his office, wide awake.

He didn't know if it was the only thing the stone could do, the only thing it could do for him, or the only thing it would do right now. He didn't know whether what he'd seen was dangerous or could be dangerous. He didn't even know if the vision, or whatever it was, would come again at some time not so convenient.

He put all three stones back in the safe, placing them all on one shelf this time, just far enough apart from each other that they didn't rattle the papers he'd set them on. He closed the safe and locked it and studied the bookshelves in front of him as if the things he'd just seen were still visible there.

He didn't know what he would find or what any of it meant. He didn't obviously know the exact location of what he'd just seen. But he had an idea where he could start. He had the photographs from Prue's house in addition to the scene he'd just witnessed. He'd start looking first thing in the morning, and he hoped what he'd find would tell him either something about the stones or about who had killed Prue.

16

The morning after everyone came for supper, Hallie fixed the gate her father had been nagging her about for months. She put the fan belt on the tractor and moved the remaining big round bales up near the horse corral. She went back inside, tore the sheets off the bed, and spent half an hour dealing with the cranky washing machine in Pabby's utility room. She called Boyd twice, but left a message only once, and it was a stupid message—"Haven't heard from Beth. I'll let you know." Stupid because it had been only about fifteen hours since she last talked to him, not even twenty-four since she last saw Beth, and pretty soon she'd be up on the roof in a windstorm, fixing loose shingles just for something to do.

Boyd called her back around five, but she missed the call because she'd decided to see if she could saddle up the gelding, which she could, and she'd gone out to the back pasture to check on Laddie's cattle. It had warmed up to about twenty, which felt like a heat wave, and although she was outside the hex ring, the air was clear and the world stretched out empty to the horizon. Nothing would sneak up on her here. She hoped. She had an iron poker strapped slant along the left side of the saddle and a shotgun with primed iron shot in an improvised sling on the right, and things felt, if not safe, then at least like she might go on a little longer without having to decide or have things decided for her.

She got back to the house just as dark was closing in and discovered another note on another post down the drive. This one said—
TIME RUNS OUT.

Goddamnit.

Inside when she checked her phone, she found two voice mails. One from Boyd asking her to meet him for breakfast the next morning at the Dove, and one from the mechanical voice, which just said—"Soon."

Jesus.

The next morning, the right front tire on her truck was flat—or at least soft.

"All right," Boyd said when he called back, because she'd had to leave another phone message when she called him. He sounded like he didn't quite believe her.

"It's flat," she said.

"Do you need a ride?" he asked. "I can make time."

"You left me a message," she pointed out. "I saw it after I called you."

There was a long moment of nothing. "I'm sorry," he said, though he didn't offer an explanation.

"Me too." It felt like distance, the whole conversation, and though she wanted to tell herself that she couldn't understand how it had happened, that distance, she knew exactly how and when and why. She told him she hadn't heard anything from Beth—she hadn't tried to get in touch with her either, which she didn't say. She hoped Beth couldn't open the door, and she knew she should be doing something about it, but she wasn't. She told herself it was because she didn't know what to do, though she knew that wasn't it. Boyd told her he'd tracked down the phone number in St. Paul, the one Prue called that last night, and that he'd gone through Prue's house again, but he didn't tell her whom the number had belonged to or what he'd found. Hallie didn't ask him because . . . she didn't.

She changed the tire, glad she had a regular spare in pretty good shape, and spent the afternoon making iron shot primed with her own blood—dead man's blood—and sacrament. In case she needed them.

She hadn't seen Maker for a couple of days, which wasn't unusual. It was still a harbinger, still had obligations to Death, even if it seemed to go back and forth more or less as it pleased. She'd asked if it didn't mean other things could go back and forth. Maker had unhelpfully told her, "Yes, but they don't."

She spent the evening pacing from the living room to the office through the dining room and back. She put on her jacket and lined leather work gloves and went outside and walked the entire perimeter of the hex ring. She felt trapped. Boyd was busy with a murder investigation that might have a supernatural element; there was certainly magic at Prue's house in the shape of the stones they'd found. But what that meant and whether it had gotten Prue killed, wasn't at all clear. She told herself that she wanted to help Beth—hell, she'd told Beth she wanted to help—but she wasn't actually helping. Ghosts were no longer following her, or at least she hadn't seen one in weeks. She was more or less okay in the daytime, or at least she told herself she was, but at night the walls of the world seemed to close in and she was sure that would be when Death would appear, in the dark, or in her dreams.

Something had changed for her after the events of the last few months and especially after she'd watched Boyd die. The idea that if she moved forward fast enough, if she fought hard enough, things would be okay, didn't feel like enough anymore. Sure, Boyd was fine. Both of them were alive. That hadn't changed. And yet, it felt to Hallie as if it could change at any time.

She didn't sleep well that night, hardly slept at all, and in the morning she left the ranch as soon as she finished feeding and watering the horses, even though she wasn't entirely certain where she was going. Hiding wasn't the answer. Everyone who'd ever lived behind the hex ring had learned that sooner or later. The ring could keep you safe from reapers and black dogs and maybe even Death, but safety wasn't enough, not for a lifetime, not even for a few months.

She'd just pulled onto the county road when three deer ran across in front of her, fast, with their white tails flying. Hallie scanned the fields, but she couldn't see anything chasing them, nothing but a couple of distant trees and the dried brown grass that had snapped over as the deer passed.

She took the first turn onto the county road, away from West Prairie City, toward Old PC, but then turned onto a gravel road a quarter mile later. Thin clouds lay across the early morning sun, so the day looked flat, what little color there was in the landscape leached away.

Eventually, she came to the cemetery down past Thorsen and Bear Creek, where her sister, Dell, and her mother were buried. She'd been headed there the whole time, since she left the ranch, though she hadn't admitted it. She pulled into the gravel parking lot, the whole world empty as far as she could see, except her truck, the grave markers, and three bare trees. There was no wind, the temperature around fifteen, everything still like a collective intake of breath.

Hallie pulled on gloves and a baseball cap, pulled the collar of her jacket close up around her neck, and got out of the truck. Gravel crunched under her boots as she walked. At the edge of the lot she stopped, as if she'd just bumped up against an invisible fence. There was no way she could actually visit her sister's grave or her mother's, had never even seen her sister's grave marker. When she entered a cemetery, any cemetery, ghosts rose from their graves and surrounded her, leached the warmth from her bones until she could barely move. These graveyard ghosts were different from the ones that followed her, than Dell's ghost or Lily's or Eddie's. Dell and Lily and Eddie had wanted something, some unfinished business in the world, something that needed to be fixed or said or uncovered. The graveyard ghosts were more like old memories attracted to her warmth, to her ability to see them, to whatever attracted the dead to her. They were cold and they made her cold, though they'd once saved her life and, by extension, the world.

"I don't know what to do."

She said it out loud as if saying it would provide the answer. It wasn't strictly true. She did know what to do. All the world required was that she go forward. Not that she be right. Or do the right thing. Just move.

What she couldn't say, at least not out loud, was what she actually meant: I don't want to die. It didn't seem all that controversial. Most people, she assumed, didn't want to die. But it was new for her, unsettling. In the army, she hadn't thought about it one way or another, hadn't believed that it was possible for her, specifically, to die. She believed people died, of course. She'd seen people die. She just hadn't believed she would be one of them. Even dying and coming back hadn't changed anything, not really. She hadn't remembered dying. She hadn't remembered coming back.

Now it was like she kept dying over and over, kept reliving the moment when Hollowell had killed Boyd—the moment of death—though it had turned out fine, had been the *right* decision. She'd seen people die before that moment. People she liked. People who meant a lot to her. But not when she could help it. Not when she could have acted and didn't. Hallie acted. That was how she knew herself.

She had acted in the end. She'd let it go as far as it did only so she could kill Hollowell. She'd done the right thing. Boyd agreed she'd done the right thing.

So why did it feel like betrayal and failure?

Because it did.

Without warning, ghosts flew up in front of her, ghosts from every gravestone. Ghost upon ghost upon ghost, like a rush of frightened birds. Hallie stepped back, thinking she'd misjudged the line and entered the cemetery without knowing it. But the ghosts continued to rise, like battering against walls, hurling themselves against invisible barriers. She took two more steps back. The fireplace poker was in the truck behind the seat, five steps away. Might as well be half a world.

The ghosts split apart suddenly, straining away from their gravestones, which was when she saw it, a black shadow moving straight toward her.

No.

Her right hand shook. She ignored it. She was tired of being afraid, tired of pretending that Death wasn't coming, tired of wanting things to be different. If this was the time, right now, then it was. She stepped back anyway, involuntarily.

Blackness flowed over the ground like lava, thick and oily. Then it stopped at the edge of the cemetery, as if, like Hallie, it had encountered an invisible wall.

"Come on," Hallie said. "Let's do this." One hand clenched tightly into a fist.

The shadow rose, like gathering itself, forming itself into—what? A person? It didn't look like Death, but then it didn't look like anything yet. Hallie's heart thumped. She had a reckless urge to leap forward, to embrace it before it could embrace her, to just get whatever this was over and done.

But she still didn't want to die.

The loud blast of a car horn shattered the nearly silent morning. The ghosts stopped. The shadow stopped. Hallie's heart nearly stopped. Suddenly, everything was gone, all of it, the ghosts and the shadow both. It was a cemetery again, like any other cemetery, with grave markers both old and new, surrounded by fields of old grass and tangled multiflora rose.

Jesus.

Tires crunched on gravel as the car, an old Ford station wagon, parked at the edge of the lot. For a long moment the car sat there, engine idling, but no one got out. Hallie wondered if she'd traded one problem for another. But then, this one, at least, seemed human, and she figured after everything, she could handle people.

If her legs held her. If her heart stopped beating like a drum.

The hinges on the station wagon door shrieked in protest as it opened. To Hallie's astonishment, Beth Hannah climbed out. She was wearing a hooded down parka with a tear in one elbow patched with duct tape. Her hair was caught up on her head in a messy bun, and she was wearing a dingy pair of fleece earmuffs that curved around the nape of her neck.

"I've been all over the Badlands," she said with no preamble. "I'm pretty sure it's there. I can feel it. But it's a big place and it all looks kind of the same. And even if I'm within a couple of miles—I know I'm within a couple of miles, but still—it could take forever. And what does it look like, anyway—a door? A pile of rocks? At least you've seen a door. I figure you would know. I mean maybe I would know. But you would for sure. I think. You could . . . you should . . . you should do it. Okay?" She'd started out talking quick, but her voice fell off by the end, as if she didn't know what she wanted to say, just that she'd wanted to find Hallie and say it.

"What are you doing here?" Hallie asked. "How did you find me?"

"I always know where you are," Beth said, as if it ought to be obvious. "Well, within, like, a mile or two."

"What do you mean?"

"I *know*." She laughed. "I know how to find Boyd all the time too. You want to know where he is right now? It's kind of annoying."

"Really?"

"I think it's because you've been there, in the under. Like you've been dead. That would make sense because I've only known since, you know, then."

"Anyone else?" Yet another conversation she couldn't quite believe she was having. She was thinking Beth might know where Laddie was. Or Maker. Beth said, "Yeah, somebody. I don't know who it is. But they popped up here around the same time I did."

"Here, like here?" Hallie pointed at the gravel parking lot, though she meant here in Taylor County.

"Yeah, here. I mean, I *think*."

Hallie had to remember that no matter what Beth said about going to the under and living with her father—taking over the "family business," as it were—this was all new to Beth too.

"So there's someone else in Taylor County who's been to the under?"

"That's not really important right now." Beth waved her hand in a dismissive gesture. "What's important is opening that door."

"No," Hallie said. "You have no idea what that means. You'd be dead, Beth. You might as well kill yourself." Which she regretted as soon as she said it. She wasn't going to encourage suicide.

"I don't think that's right," Beth said.

"You don't want to think it's right."

"Did you die when you went to the under?" she asked.

"I would die if I took Death's place," Hallie said. "When you're Death, you're not in this world anymore. Ever."

Out of the corner of her eye, Hallie could see the ghosts in the cemetery rising again. "I have to go," she said, and she didn't like the sharp pitch of her voice as she said it. "Look, Beth, I will help you. Boyd will help you. You have a place here if you want it. But I'm not helping you die."

She'd already turned away when Beth said, "Do you want to go in?"

"What?"

Beth pointed toward the cemetery. "In there." She took Hallie's hand. "Come on."

Hallie could never remember being as dumbfounded as she was right then when Beth led her into the cemetery. The ghosts, those cold painful creatures, began to rise once more, then calmed as they passed, sinking slowly back into the ground.

"I could always do that, I *guess*," Beth said. "I didn't know it—well, I'd never been in a cemetery until a couple of months ago."

"Not even when your mother died?" Hallie couldn't help it; she looked from one side of the path to the other as ghost after ghost sank down and disappeared.

"She was cremated and we didn't . . . No."

They reached Dell's grave, and it was the first time Hallie had seen it with the marker in place. ADELLE TEMPLE MICHAELS. *LOVED, LOST, BUT NOT FORGOTTEN*. There were dried flowers in a vase sheltered from the wind by the marker itself. Her father must have brought them, she thought. She touched the smooth cold stone. This wasn't Dell, though her bones lay underneath. It was just a place, and Dell was gone from it.

She took Beth to the next row over, underneath the shade of the same tree Dell was also buried under, to visit her mother's grave. It shouldn't mean that much. Hallie of all people knew where the dead went, what happened to them. But it meant someone remembered,

meant it had meant something that they were here. Her mother's
marker was smoother, colder, worn down from more than ten South
Dakota winters. But there were flowers here too. And a plaque that
Hallie hadn't seen before, something her father must have added recently. She wondered if he'd saved for it, set aside wrinkled fives and
singles until he had enough. It was copper she thought, already turning green, backed on something solider and riveted right to the stone.

BECAUSE I COULD NOT STOP FOR DEATH . . .

"Thank you," she said to Beth back in the parking lot.

Beth shrugged. "I guess I have an affinity."

"I guess you do." Hallie'd thought she had an affinity, but maybe
it was just an attraction. "I'm not going to open that door for you,"
she said.

"I know," Beth said. "It doesn't mean I'll stop looking."

"Good luck," Hallie said.

"Yeah."

Yeah.

17

It was just after noon when Boyd drove out to Jasper, or to where Jasper had been before it was flattened by a tornado twenty years earlier. The sky had turned storm gray, and it was sleeting. The temperatures had been in the high twenties since before noon, and the old road he was on was slick, mostly frozen, with maybe a half inch of melt on top.

He parked on the old road, pulled a slicker, rain pants, and a waterproof baseball cap from the trunk. He donned the rain gear and walked the length of the former town—a hamlet, really, with twenty or thirty houses, a garage–post office–diner, a small church, an open area close to the road that had once been a small park with a freestanding metal pole barn (long gone), a wooden shelter (of which two broken poles and a stone fireplace remained), and a baseball diamond (which was little more than the suggestion of a baseball field in the way the vegetation had grown up over time).

The photographs Boyd had taken from Prue's house showed the inside of an old foundation, and he'd thought when he looked at them last night that the best place to start looking for the particular foundation pictured would be Jasper. It was one place where he knew there were lots of old foundations. But even overgrown and twenty years worn by winter and weather, it was still clear that none of them fit the photographs. Either the dimensions were wrong or the foundations were concrete block or brick rather than poured. There was one larger basement at the western edge of the old town that he thought might be it, but once he was down inside, he could see that the windows weren't in the right place and he tripped over a furnace pad that was three feet too close to the south wall.

He climbed out, the holds slippery in the continuing sleet and drizzle. He looked east then west, saw a vehicle sitting up on the main road, engine idling, but as he trotted back to his patrol car, the car—black, he thought, and not a sedan—pulled back onto the road and drove off, not in a hurry, more like they'd stopped for a minute for some reason and then gone on.

He considered his situation. He was wet and cold, his waterproof boots weren't as waterproof as advertised, and he wasn't even sure what he'd find if he did locate the source of the photographs. He walked back up toward the road, turned when he reached the old baseball field, and looked back. From here he could see all four streets. Could he have missed a foundation? Overgrown as they were, it would be easy enough to do, though the time of year helped, since the native grass and nonnative invasives had been beaten down all winter by wind and snow.

Of course, there were lots of old foundations scattered all over Taylor County. Some of them didn't have roads or drives or rutted muddy lanes leading to them anymore, places where someone had tried to make a serious go and failed—bankruptcy or fire or tornado had knocked them down and they'd stayed down. Aerial photos might help. And he could talk to old ranchers who not only knew where many of those abandoned places were, but also knew everyone who'd ever lived there and what had happened to drive them out.

He pulled the photographs out of an inner pocket and looked at them again. The poured foundation ought to be a clue. It wouldn't have been built somewhere too remote. It would be a place someone had spent money on. At least to build it. He returned to his patrol car, backed around, and was almost back out to the road when he remembered the old farmhouse. It wasn't in Jasper proper, but down a lane and close to the spot where Hallie's sister, Dell, had died. He reversed back up the old road, his tires slipping on the slick, half-frozen, half-melted surface, turned, and drove along the barely visible track.

Where the house had once stood, there were the remains of two old fireplaces, stacks of scattered bricks from the chimneys. Old timbers lay in the grass and Boyd could see immediately that the house had burned. It didn't mean that it hadn't first been hit by the tornado that leveled Jasper, but it had definitely burned, most of the old timber charcoaled and black. It was a deep foundation and definitely poured, weeds and grass growing up through cracks in the floor. Boyd pulled out the photographs. He walked around the opening, careful not to get too close to the edge. There was an *X*, not large, but visible underneath one of the windows on the west side. The second window on that side had a circle inscribed underneath it, both of them faded with the passage of time but clearly visible.

He went back to his car, pulled a spade, a rope, and a couple of tie-down straps out of the trunk. He radioed his location back to the office.

"Does Ole know where you are?" Patty Littlejohn asked.

"Tell him I'll fill him in when I get back," Boyd told her. "If I find anything," he added to himself after he signed off, though he was pretty sure he'd find something. Had already found something—the place where the photos had been taken, the symbols in them.

He fastened the rope to the base of a volunteer tree and used the tie-down straps to secure it, dropped the other end of the rope down the old wall, then lowered himself down through one of the old window wells. The floor was half dirt and half concrete, though it took

him a while to figure that out, all of it covered with dirt and vegetation from years of wind and winter.

He taped the photographs up underneath the symbols that they
matched, stood six steps away and halfway between them, scraped
away the dirt until he found an arrow carved into the concrete, faded
almost to nothing so that he had to feel it with his fingers. He took
three steps in the direction the arrow indicated, felt the change between concrete and dirt. The last two photographs had been pictures of the same thing—a small area of bare ground—like it was
never going to change.

He scanned the area. The sleet was coming harder now. It made a
sound as it hit his slicker, like the slap of a wire brush. To his left
there was a big crack in the upper wall—a tall bull thistle and some
dried lamb's-quarter, bursting through. He looked down, and just in
front of him but obscured by an old timber laid crossways, was a
patch of ground a foot or maybe a foot and a half square that was
green with foxtail actually starting to seed out, barnyard grass, and
chicory in flower—all of it growing in the hard-packed dirt of an old
cellar in March, when everything else was still brittle and brown. He
took off his glove and felt the ground—soft and muddy and definitely
not frozen, felt the dirt floor to the right of the green patch. It was
much colder, still frozen hard.

He wiped his hand, pulled his glove back on, and dug.

He had to go down nearly a foot and a half before he found it, and
by then he'd more or less guessed what would be there—another
stone. It was larger than the others and a deep purple that looked
almost black in the gray afternoon light. He picked it up with his
gloved hands and wiped the mud off. The sleet had lessened by the
time he finally climbed back out of the old cellar, though there was a
steady drizzle, like cold mist. He could hear cars up on the main
road, tires sounding loud on the wet pavement. He was careful—had

always been careful, it was how he knew himself—but after scanning the area to see if there was anyone or anything around, he took off the glove on his left hand and dropped the stone into it.

He didn't see anything right away, and had nearly decided that maybe what happened the last time had been a peculiar combination of a particular stone and a particular person, when he smelled the faint odor of sulfur and smoke, the scent of gunpowder, and then the sound of the shot, which came loud, like it had been fired right beside him. He dived sideways without even thinking about it, the stone gripped tight in his hand. After a moment—when there wasn't another shot and he didn't see anyone close enough to have fired the one he'd heard—he picked himself up. He kept the stone in his hand and snapped open the flap on his holster with his right. It was another vision, he was sure it was, but picking up the stone was enough risk, and he was going to be careful about this.

The sky overhead was the same as it had been all afternoon, but the ground in front of him—or the ground of the vision—looked like it had been cast in deep shadow. Night, maybe? A body lay there, the face turned away from him. His heart thumped hard once as he moved closer, then remembered that he couldn't. The body would never be any closer than it was or look any different than it did. He heard a siren, someone shouting. But what was important was the body, the blood that trickled slowly along the curve of the neck.

Because whether he could see her face or not, he knew that it was Hallie.

Something was following Hallie, had been following her since she left the cemetery. Her instinct was to run, to run forever, out of Taylor County and South Dakota and the world if she could pull it off, and that was wrong, so wrong because Hallie didn't run. She'd known that one thing about herself for years, got her through her mother's death, through basic training, through goddamned Afghanistan and dying, through Dell's death, through everything. She didn't run. She stood and she faced things.

She *did*.

She slammed on the brakes and pulled over to the side of the road, her truck slanting toward the ditch. She got out, grabbed the fireplace poker automatically, then deliberately put it back behind the seat, shut the driver's door, and crossed behind the truck. A semi hauling hay stacked five tiers high blasted past her on the road so fast, it rocked her truck. Maker appeared beside her.

"Is it Death?" she asked. Her voice sounded like it had when she talked to Beth, too high-pitched and thin. Damnit. She wasn't going to be afraid. Not anymore. She *wanted* this life. Here. The way it was all coming together. She couldn't have it if she ran, if she hid out on the ranch. It wasn't life then. It was just . . . living.

Grass heeled over way out in the field.

"Not Death," Maker said.

"What, then?" Hallie asked.

But Maker barked once, something Hallie had never heard it do before, spun around twice, and disappeared.

Her cell phone rang, rolled over to voice mail, then rang again almost immediately. Without taking her eyes off the open field and the spot where the grass lay flat, Hallie pushed it to vibrate. It vibrated twice in quick succession. The thing in the field didn't move.

Hallie took a deep breath and stepped off the shoulder into the grass, wet from sleet and a hard rain that was almost ice. She hadn't gone more than a dozen steps when she was soaked to her knees. Her phone vibrated again, then again. The thing in the field moved away from her—at least the grass heeled over like something was moving south, like it didn't know she was even there.

Hallie pulled her phone from her pocket. Three texts and two missed phone calls, all from Boyd. She looked at the texts without taking her eyes off the field.

Answer your phone!

All the texts said the same thing, even the exclamation point at the end. Boyd never spoke in exclamation points.

Hallie called him back.

He answered on the first ring, said her name—"Hallie"—then didn't say anything, though she could hear him breathing hard, like he'd run a race.

"Boyd?"

"I need to see you," he said. "Now."

"There's something—"

"No. Right now."

Not an order, but urgent all the same.

Hallie looked out into the field. The thing waited. It had been waiting months, hadn't it? *She'd* been waiting months. "All right," she said to Boyd.

"My house. Be careful."

He disconnected without saying anything more.

Hallie turned her back on the thing in the field. Let it come, she thought.

Boyd got home in record time, put the fourth stone in the safe with the others, and was outside in the rain, pacing when Hallie arrived. It had been night he told himself, the vision happened at night. But things could change, the dreams he had could be changed, so it stood to reason that the visions that came with holding the stones could be changed too. Hallie was fine. He'd just talked to her.

He forced himself to stop pacing. There was time. They could fix this. He didn't know where or why or how or when. He didn't know if the vision as he'd seen it was even a real thing or symbolic. Could Hallie be dying metaphorically? Because she'd stayed in Taylor County? Was that killing her? Staying with him? Staying at the ranch?

He saw her truck when it turned onto the street, and he just stopped himself from running to her as she pulled into the driveway. He felt like this almost every time he had one of his prescient dreams, like the world was going to end, like everything had gone horribly wrong, like there was nothing anyone could do, and for some mysterious reason, he was the only one who knew. When he was a kid, it had sent him racing through the house and into the barn, tracking down his brother and his parents. Once he'd called every single kid in his class, then couldn't figure out what to tell them or their parents. He'd made up a story about inviting them to a birthday party he wouldn't even have for seven more months. His parents grounded him for a week, and it had been the last time he said anything to anyone even remotely related to the dreams he had until he met Hallie.

"Jesus, Boyd, it's raining," Hallie said when she got out of the truck, and he almost laughed because it sounded so normal, so— Hallie.

"I just . . . wanted to see you," he said. He grabbed the front of her jacket, like he could physically hold her there forever.

"Really?"

"Well—" Before he could finish the sentence, before he even knew precisely what the sentence would be, there came a sound like a high-pitched whine, like an oversized angry insect or an overcranked engine.

Hallie grabbed him at the same time he grabbed her, and they dived for the ground as the sound and the concussion of an explosion hit like a thunderclap.

18

Sirens.

Boyd rolled over and spit dirt out of his mouth. He searched for Hallie, who was just sitting up next to him, shaking her head and wiping a hand across her face, streaking dirt in a dark smudge like war paint. She grinned at him. "Maybe you should move," she said.

Before Boyd could respond, a patrol car swung into Boyd's short driveway and almost hit them, slamming on the brakes so hard that the hood tilted sharply downward. Boyd rose, offered a hand to Hallie, and pulled her to her feet. Teedt got out of the car with his radio mike in one hand and the other on the butt of his gun.

"Fire truck's on its way," he said, which turned out to be unnecessary because the West Prairie City ladder truck and a pickup with a blue and red light panel on top pulled to a stop in front of the house before he'd finished talking.

"What the hell's going on?" Teedt asked.

Boyd didn't bother to answer, thinking both, What does it look like? and I have no idea. Hallie was already halfway across the front yard. Smoke poured around the corner of the house along with a thin flicker of flame. The volunteer firefighters moved quickly, pulling hose, and ran past Hallie and Boyd as if both were just in the way, which they probably were.

Maybe ten minutes after the fire trucks had arrived, Haxon Blake, the volunteer fire chief came over to talk to Boyd. "It doesn't look like much of a fire," he said.

What it looked like was an explosion, Boyd thought. He and Hallie had retreated to stand next to his patrol car while the firefighters worked, and he'd pulled a couple of towels from the trunk so they could wipe mud and dirt off their faces. Now, they walked over with Hack to inspect the damage. A hole maybe six feet by six feet had been punched in the outer wall of Boyd's house, right where his office was. The window and some shattered siding were ten feet away, twisted up against the hedgerow, insulation scattered like confetti along with slushy water from the fire hose, the framing from the window, and glass.

"This is your house, right?" Hack asked Boyd. "Dispatch said it was your house."

Boyd couldn't stop looking at the mess. "Yes," he said. "Yes, it's mine."

"Looks like something blew a hole in the side here," Hack said somewhat unnecessarily.

My house, Boyd thought. He had just repaired it. Just gotten the windows back in and the siding replaced, had just spent last weekend outside in the cold, sanding and refitting the south porch railing.

"—limited the damage to that one room."

"What?" he said.

Hack cocked his head sideways. "I said it's pretty well contained, never really much danger from it. Except to your house, of course. I think we can limit most of the damage to that one room and, well, some smoke. And some water probably." He added.

"What happened?" Boyd said. Hallie had left the two of them and was approaching the hole itself, waved back by one of the firefighters so she had to skirt to the other side, the smoke still too thick to see much, though it looked like they were pulling the hose back out, pulling away loose siding, and testing the rest of the side wall.

"Well, something blew up." Hack said it like he felt Boyd was being a little slow on the uptake. "Probably from the inside out." He waved a hand. "Well, you can see."

"Can I—?" Go in? Look around? He wasn't entirely sure what he wanted to ask, what he wanted to do.

"Give us half an hour," Hack said, "and you can get in the house, but stay out of that room. At least until tomorrow. I want to get someone in in the morning to test the joists. Make sure it's safe."

Boyd wanted to point out that there were people in the room right now, Kate Wannamaker climbing over the ragged gap to jump the short distance down to the lawn.

Someone—something—blew a hole in my wall.

It echoed through his brain, that single phrase, as if he couldn't quite get past it. Explosions; his house; and West Prairie City, South Dakota, didn't fit together. Or didn't seem like they ought to fit together, because lots of things were happening in West Prairie City that didn't fit these days.

"Davies!"

Boyd turned to see Teedt approaching. Behind him, Kate Wannamaker said, "Hey, Chief, you better come look at this."

"Ole wants to talk to you," Teedt said as he stepped over the fire hose. He looked Boyd up and down as if noticing for the first time that he was soaking wet with mud splattered up his pants leg to his knees and all down the front of his slicker. "What the hell happened to you?" he asked.

"My house exploded," Boyd said dryly.

"All over you?"

"It's a long story," Boyd said. One he was reasonably certain Teedt didn't want to hear.

"It's always a long story," Teedt complained. He looked at the hole in Boyd's house one more time and shook his head. "Come on. Ole's waiting."

As they crossed the lawn, Boyd could smell burnt wood and plastic, could practically taste it in the back of his throat, harsh and corrosive. He looked around for Hallie, but she had disappeared somewhere in the chaos, not just firefighters now, but Boyd's neighbors too, cars lining the street where people had stopped just to see what was going on. A white pickup followed closely by a small black SUV wound carefully down the street, the pickup pausing in front of the house before a honk from the SUV behind it got it moving again.

Ole stood by Boyd's back door. "This is surely a hell of a mess," he remarked.

"Yes, sir, it is," Boyd agreed. Teedt's radio crackled, and with a quick wave of his hand in Boyd's and Ole's direction, he strode away toward the street, one hand on his radio mike.

"I want to show you something," Ole said. He pushed open Boyd's back door.

"That was locked," Boyd said.

"Yeah, well, it's not a very good lock," Ole said. As they walked up the three steps into the kitchen, he asked over his shoulder, "You need a couple of days off?"

"I thought we were shorthanded," Boyd said.

Ole grimaced, like he had just bitten down on something unpleasant. "The wedding thing, it's apparently not happening." He held up his hands, like waving something aside. "Don't ask him about it. He'll say he doesn't want to talk about it, then he'll tell you his sister's entire life story, how many times she's been married, what the kid's father said to Teedt's sister and to Teedt. I mean, just . . . don't ask. But the thing of it is, I'm not shorthanded and you're going to need to take care of this, whatever this is."

A set of muddy tracks crossed the kitchen floor. Ole, Boyd guessed, checking things out while Boyd was still absorbing what had happened.

"I want to keep working," Boyd said. "I have some new information." New data, because he didn't know yet what it meant, whether it pointed to any suspects or was just something else that didn't make any sense.

"Take a look at this," Ole said.

The door to the office was open. It was a sloppy mess. Desk tipped sideways, water running down the wall, the rug on the floor flung up against the far wall and torn right through the middle, fraying threads dangling like a fractured curtain. Both shelves above the desk had been tipped, one of them falling to the floor, a single end tilting up like the spar from a shipwreck. He looked for the safe, which had been against the wall to his right, the one opposite the outside wall. It was no longer there, just a hole through to the dining room, pretty much exactly the size of the safe. Bits of plaster, shredded paper from the wallboard, a jagged bit of old lath made a trail from the hole across the dining room floor. Ole grabbed his arm and pointed at something underneath the table—the safe, metal curling outward as though it were nothing but tinfoil, and yet it still sat upright and square, as if it had always been there.

"What do you make of that?" Ole asked.

Before Boyd could answer, footsteps pounded up the back steps and Hack joined them, clapping Ole on the shoulder. He said to Boyd, "Things're looking pretty good. I'm going to leave the little truck here with Kate and Stu. It wasn't much of a fire, like I said, just smoke and debris from the explosion." He thought for a minute. "Or whatever. You want some help sealing things up?"

Boyd ran a hand along the back of his neck. "Thanks. I've got a roof tarp out in the garage. If we secure that, it should keep the weather out."

"That door any good?" Hack asked, nodding at the entrance to the office.

"Pretty good."

"It's the cold. You don't want to let the temperature in the house get too low. Freeze your pipes. And it plays hell on your drywall and plaster."

"It's a good door," Boyd repeated. "I can insulate it."

Hack repeated his recommendation that no one should walk on the office floor until a builder looked at it. "It'd be best if you could get a structural engineer," he said, "but it's easier to find a good construction guy. That'll probably do ya anyway."

"No," Boyd said. "I'll need to go in there. I've—"

Hack was shaking his head before Boyd could finish. "Nothing's going to change in there before morning," he said. "Trust me."

Which might have been true if the only danger were from wet flooring and damaged joists.

"It can't be that dangerous."

"It'll be less dangerous in the morning, after someone's checked the flooring."

Which was right, Boyd was sure, but not helpful. The stones—stones he'd put in his safe not that many minutes before Hallie arrived—were now pretty clearly no longer there. Also pretty clearly, at least to Boyd's thinking, the stones were the cause of the explosion. Where it had occurred, how it had occurred, and the results all pretty clear indications. He needed to find them—all of them—and make sure they were put away safe before anything else happened.

To Hack, he said, "It's my house, I'm going in."

Hack looked like he wanted to argue, but Ole turned him back

172

toward the kitchen, saying, as they moved away, "You've seen a lot of fires. This make you think of anything? Anything . . . suspicious?"

Boyd squatted down to look at the destroyed safe. He'd set all four stones together on top of the title search for his house and an inventory of his valuables. Three of them were just gone. The fourth was tangled in the ripped-open steel of the door. Boyd pried it out carefully, cutting his right index finger in the process, and put it in the left slant pocket of his rain slicker. He found two more of the stones in the office, one stuck underneath the shattered leg of his desk, probably what had shattered it, and one hard up against the baseboard on the outer wall. He shoved both of them into the right slant pocket of his rain slicker, where they vibrated against each other until he moved one of them up to his shirt pocket. The floor was spongy, and he realized that Hack had been right, he probably shouldn't have come in.

Hallie appeared in the doorway. "Jesus," she said as she took in the damage. She looked at him, her eyes that particular hard focus she got when things didn't make sense. "Do you know what happened?"

"Don't come in," Boyd said. "Meet me outside." He pointed through the gap. Hallie nodded and disappeared. Boyd pulled his gloves back on so he wouldn't cut his hands any worse than he already had and climbed through the hole in the outside wall using the same path he'd seen Kate Wannamaker take twenty minutes earlier.

When Hallie joined him, he motioned her over toward the hedgerow that separated his yard from his neighbor's.

"It's the stones," Boyd said.

Hallie looked skeptical. "Boyd, you've had those stones for days."

He shook his head. "I've had three of them. I found a fourth today. That's the difference." Hallie opened her mouth to speak, but he held up his hand. Wait. She had questions. Hallie always had questions, but he was figuring this out as he talked, and he needed to finish before she asked them. "I put all of them in the safe all together. Then I came outside to wait for you. I was here. That's part of the point. No one came into the house. I don't smell explosives or gunpowder or see any residue in the room. It's true I might not smell it or see it and we could ask Rapid City or the feds for a dog. But I don't think it was explosives."

"You think it was the stones." Her skepticism was clear. He didn't blame her. He would have trouble believing it himself, and Hallie liked to see things with her own eyes. He pulled one of the stones from his shirt pocket and put it in his gloved hand. "Look, I hold it in my hand, it doesn't do anything, right?"

"Right."

He pulled a second one from the left pocket of his rain slicker and put it with the first one. They vibrated against each other with a barely audible clatter. He separated them a little, and the vibration lessened but didn't stop. He pulled the third one out, placed it between the other two, and they knocked together so hard, his hand shook and he almost dropped them. He grabbed one of them out of his hand and stuffed it back into his shirt pocket.

"Yeah," Hallie said. "All right. So . . . what are you thinking? The fourth was critical mass?"

"Yes," he said.

"Where is it now?" she asked, because Hallie always went right to the heart.

"I would guess"—Boyd pointed into the hedges—"in there. It won't be dangerous. For most people. I hope," he couldn't help adding.

"Jesus," Hallie said. Which sentiment Boyd definitely agreed with. "I mean, you're right. Probably not dangerous. If they don't have any affinity for magic," Hallie said. "Or if there's not something else we don't know about them."

Boyd nodded grimly in agreement. He took two of the stones,

wrapped them in a clean white handkerchief from his pocket, and handed them to Hallie. "It's probably not a good idea to carry all four of them around," he told her.

Hallie slid the stones into the back pocket of her jeans, looked at the jagged six-foot hole in Boyd's house, and said, "Yeah, that would be a very bad idea."

"Hey!"

Boyd shoved the third stone back into his shirt pocket as Deputy Teedt approached them. "Mrs. Otis over there?" he asked it like it was a question, which it never was with Teedt. "Says she'd like to talk to you when you have a chance."

"Would you tell her I'll come over when I'm finished here?" Boyd asked Teedt.

Teedt's lips twisted in something that wasn't quite a frown. "Sure," he said. "What else have I got to do?"

"I can take care of this," Hallie said, waving at the big gaping hole in Boyd's house. "If you want to look for . . . the other thing."

19

It wasn't much past four in the afternoon, the sun was still at least two hours from setting, but the sky was so gray and the sun low enough on the horizon that long shadows made the ground under the hedges nearly impenetrable. There was a trail of broken branches that told him this was the spot, though he couldn't tell how far the stone might have traveled. He needed a flashlight before he could do anything.

Margaret Otis was waving frantically to him from the sidewalk. Nate, her eight-year-old son, was beside her wearing rubber boots, an orange rain slicker, and blue and yellow basketball shorts that went down past his knees. Boyd frowned, but went over there. He was aware of the stone in his pocket, of the other stone still missing, like lead weights to drag him down. But he could take a minute.

"Deputy Davies!"

Nate hopped up and down, like he was on springs. He'd turned eight three weeks earlier, Boyd knew, because in the summer, Nate came through the gap in the hedge to Boyd's house to watch him work on the Farmall in his garage and hand him tools. He'd crouch for an hour at a time, peering under the tractor, asking questions, and telling Boyd things about the Otis family that Boyd was pretty

176

sure his mother and father would rather he, or anyone else, didn't know.

"Aren't you cold?" he asked.

"You'll never get him to admit it," Margaret Otis said.

She was tall, large-boned and broad-shouldered, looked as if she could wrestle steers, though as far as Boyd knew, she'd grown up in Rapid City and had never even ridden a horse. She had long, thick light brown hair that usually hung down her back in a single braid, though tonight she had it pinned up in a messy bun at the nape of her neck. She was wearing jeans, a blue and yellow sweatshirt that said, SDSU JACKS on the front, and a fleece-and-canvas vest. "You want to come in the house?" she asked. "We've got coffee."

"We called the fire department," Nate announced. "They were fast! They had the siren and the lights and everything. It was loud!"

"The siren?"

"Your house exploded!" He made a noise and threw his hands wide to demonstrate.

"I know," Boyd said. "Was it scary?"

"It was a little scary," Nate admitted. "But there wasn't very much fire. Just smoke and stuff." Boyd thought he sounded disappointed. "Do you think someone was trying to kill you? Like in the movies?" Nate asked.

"No one's trying to kill me," Boyd said. "It was an accident." He'd pulled off his gloves as he crossed the yard and he looked at his hands, which were filthy, dirt and soot etched into the creases of his knuckles like he'd been cleaning battleships with toothbrushes. He'd given his handkerchief to Hallie, which left him nothing to wipe his hands on now except his khaki pants, which were already soaked and covered with mud.

"Accidents don't just happen," Nate said.

"What?" Boyd asked.

"I don't know," Nate said with an exaggerated shrug, "that's what my dad says."

Your dad's wrong, Boyd thought, though he didn't say it. Sometimes accidents were just accidents—not that this was, but he remembered when he'd wrecked his Jeep Cherokee down in Iowa. That had been an accident. Sometimes things actually did just happen.

"He misses his dad," Margaret Otis said in her blunt way. She tousled Nate's hair until he jerked his head away.

"I'm sorry if your sons were frightened," Boyd said. "They're not worried about your house, are they? Because what happened here won't happen to you."

"What did happen?" Meg asked. "And don't tell me it was a gas leak. Because I didn't believe that the last time, and it's completely unlikely that it was the cause this time. If it had been your kitchen or even the back bedroom, you might get me to believe the furnace was involved. But that wall?" She shook her head. "There's no way. There's no ductwork along there. There's no gas line on this side of the house either. Besides, whatever it was blew out not up."

She grinned. "I installed gas furnaces for a living before the kids."

"I can't really explain it," Boyd said.

"Mom." Nate tugged at his mother's sleeve. "I thought we were going to show him."

Meg Otis looked up the street, then across Boyd's yard to the gap in the side of his house, where Hallie had tarp and ladders and three people including Ole to help her seal things up. She looked all the way down the street the other way. "Nate wants to show you something. He found it," she said. "Afterwards."

Without seeming to, Boyd moved Meg and Nate and himself so the hedge that separated their yards was now between them and any few remaining onlookers.

"Nate says it talks to him." Meg said it apologetically, like—crazy kid—but also as if she couldn't help believing it a little, and it scared and angered her in approximately equal measure.

Boyd didn't ask what talked to Nate. He already knew. "Can you show it to me?" he asked. He squatted down so he could see the boy's face. It had started to rain again, gentle but cold, the drops making a pattering sound as they hit Boyd's slicker. Nate pulled the stone out of his pocket, the large dark one, and let it lie in the palm of his hand. "It told me where to find it," he confided.

"Where was that?" Boyd asked.

Nate pointed straight to the spot Boyd had planned to search, just inside the Otis yard in a straight line from his office.

"What else does it tell you?"

Nate shrugged. "Just stuff," he said.

"Different voices?" He didn't want to ask if they were the voices of dead people, because it sounded really crazy, not just a little, and because he didn't want to scare Nate or his mother any more than they possibly already were, but he did want to know. He hoped knowing would tell him more about the nature of the stones, about what sort of affinity Nate had. Whatever it was, was probably going to be hell for him someday, and Boyd was sorry the boy had been the one to pick the stone up.

"No"—Nate said it like Boyd was just being dumb—"not different voices. It's like another kid," he said. He looked at the stone, then sighed. "It tells me what people think. Like right now? My mom is thinking that her feet are cold and she hopes she turned off the stove before she came out here and Stevie my brother is probably jumping on the bed right now and it better not break. And you're thinking that it's cold and you think I must be cold but I'm not and how much is it going to cost to fix your house and what will the insurance say and how will it get done because Stalking Horse and it's important and what if the world ends or someone dies. And there's someone over there"—he didn't pause to give Boyd time to say anything, but waved vaguely across the street—"thinking that you better not go looking for any more things that aren't your business because you're not stupid or maybe you are stupid and if you don't watch out . . . Well, you better watch out," he finished with a half-startled look on his face.

Boyd stood and walked out to the sidewalk, looked up and down the street. There was no one on the sidewalk he didn't recognize. Two cars and a pickup drove past slow. The cars belonged to Mrs. Pierce from over on Main and Jed Klein, and he was pretty sure the pickup was Patty Littlejohn's. There were headlights at the end of the street, someone turning around in someone's driveway, and there could be other people he couldn't see or someone who'd turned away or driven by when he wasn't looking. He returned, put a hand on Nate's shoulder and said, "Who? Your mom and me and who else?"

"It doesn't tell me who," Nate said, shifting the stone from one hand to the other, "but I know what my mom sounds like. And you. And the other one is just . . . loud. Not like they're right here like you or my mom. Like they're yelling."

"I have to take it back," Boyd said.

"Yeah," Nate sighed. "Can I come look at it sometimes?"

"Maybe," Boyd said. Even without the stone, Nate had something—empathy? Sensitivity? The stones enhanced things that were already there, as far as Boyd could tell. It couldn't create abilities in someone who didn't already have them.

"Tel Sigurdson was here earlier," Meg said suddenly.

"Tel Sigurdson?"

"He was looking for you—knocked on your door, then came over to see if I'd seen you or knew when you'd be back. He seemed angry, which was why I mention it. Because of what Nate said about someone's—" She stumbled over the words. Hard to believe, what her son had just demonstrated, but she was practical and she knew what she'd been thinking and whether it matched what Nate had said. "—someone's thoughts. Maybe it was him."

"It doesn't sound like him," Boyd said doubtfully. Tel Sigurdson owned a majority of the land in Taylor County and was one of the few truly successful ranchers in the area.

Meg frowned. "No. In general, he's pretty easygoing. That's been my experience. Although . . . I heard he lost a bundle on that whole Uku-Weber disaster. Had to sell off a bunch of cattle. For bad prices too. You know he wanted to buy the Packer place, which I expect he thought he'd get for pretty much nothing. I heard he can't even scrape up the money for that."

"How do you know all this?" Boyd asked.

Meg grinned. "Tel's wife, Pat, and I did the lunch for Delores Pabahar's funeral. You know, over to the Lutheran church? Pat's mad as fire at Tel, even though she thought Uku-Weber was a good investment too, at the time. Or maybe because of that. Pat Sigurdson doesn't care all that much about jewelry or fancy cars, but she likes property. If it's for sale in Taylor County, she's interested in it. I don't think she cares that the ranch is struggling or that they have to pinch pennies, but I think she cares that they lost some land and some cattle over it."

"So you think Tel is looking for ways to make money?" Boyd asked.

Meg raised an eyebrow. "He's always looking for ways to make money," she said. "Why?"

"I'm just trying to figure out what's going on," Boyd told her. "Why he'd want to talk to me particularly."

"Seems like there's a lot going on," she said. "I'm home most days, and since that 'gas leak'"—Boyd could hear the skepticism in her voice—"I've paid particular attention to what goes on right on this street. Which, frankly, isn't all that much most of the time. Except your house. Lots happening there," she said.

"I'm sorry. I don't want you to worry."

Meg waved a hand toward Boyd's house. "I'm not worried about that," she said. "About our house exploding or anything." Her voice dropped. "What I'm worried about is Nate, about stones that talk to him, about what all that means. I'm worried that you know about things like that, that you're not even surprised. I'm worried about what it says about the world and what I always thought I knew."

"Yeah," Boyd said. "I know."

It was nearly ten o'clock when Hallie pulled back into the yard at the ranch. There were no notes on posts, no shadows in fields, and the rain had stopped, which was something. Boyd had said he'd be right behind her, but she couldn't see his lights down the road. She headed out to the corral to check the horses. The gelding came to the fence and she rubbed his neck. He pushed his nose against her shoulder.

She'd been thinking about Prue's ghost, about why it wasn't following her. She'd expected it. Had been waiting for it every time she left the ranch the last few days, but there had been nothing. Maybe Prue didn't think she had unfinished business. Maybe she didn't care who'd killed her. It was hard for Hallie to imagine, just drifting away as if none of it really mattered, as if your whole life came to nothing in the end. At least that's how it would have felt to her. Hallie sure wouldn't do it. She wasn't leaving this place or her life without a fight.

She heard a car down the road and she waited, leaning against the gate. Headlights illuminated the yard, reflected off the windshield of her pickup and an upstairs window on the house. A minute later, Boyd's SUV pulled in. His brake lights flashed. The engine idled for several seconds and then died. When the door opened and he got out, Hallie could see he was still wearing his yellow rain slicker, and even streaked with mud, it was like a beacon in the darkness.

"Boyd."

Hallie didn't say it very loudly, not much above her regular speaking voice, but he turned and looked in her direction. It made her heart jump, that he was attuned, that he would know, that there was someone in her life who listened, who knew what she knew, who was *so* not her type, and yet everything she'd ever wanted. She was wearing a black Carhartt vest, a blue and black buffalo plaid shirt, and was standing underneath the overhang of the corral lean-to. She didn't think he could see her, but he headed her way unerringly. He didn't say anything when he reached her, put his arms around her, and kissed her. She kissed him back, and though she'd already decided not to be afraid anymore, to face what came, there was a—she didn't know what to call it—peacefulness, maybe, from standing there with him. It wasn't even a new feeling, more one she forgot each time or couldn't let herself believe in when she was dealing with the world and Taylor County.

"Let's go inside," she finally said. "There's a lot to talk about."

She made coffee, had drunk enough coffee the last few days, she felt like she should be floating. Boyd shed his slicker and rain pants, went upstairs to wash, and came back down in jeans and a T-shirt, his hair spiked up, like he'd forgotten to comb it.

"I put one of the stones in the bedroom," he said. "One of them in your office. Where are the others?"

Hallie dug them out of her back pocket. Boyd unwrapped them. He put one of them in the dining room on a shelf and brought the other one back into the kitchen and placed it on the table.

Hallie looked at it. It was small and smooth and it looked, well, ordinary.

"Tomorrow I'll take one of them into town and put it in a safe deposit box," Boyd said. "That should keep things safe."

"Jesus, I hope Laddie doesn't show up before you go," Hallie said.

Boyd looked startled, like that scenario hadn't occurred to him yet. Without a word he took the stone off the kitchen table and headed out the back door. A minute later he was back. "I put it in my SUV," he said. He poured coffee for himself and Hallie before sitting in one of the kitchen chairs. "Maybe that's why they buried one of them," he said. "So there wouldn't be any mistakes."

"Yeah. And I suppose they wouldn't actually do anything here, inside the ring. But we're not testing it," she said firmly. She pulled out a chair and sat. "Who do you think 'they' are, anyway?"

"Prue Stalking Horse, for one," Boyd said. He ran a hand through his hair and spiked the front up even more. "Her sister? I don't know. I'd like to find out more about her, the sister. Though she couldn't have had anything to do with Prue's death. She's been gone twenty years. But maybe if we knew more about what happened then, we'd know more about what is going on now."

"The fourth stone," Hallie said. "You found it in Jasper?"

Boyd nodded. "You know where that old farmhouse was? It was buried in the cellar."

"Martin Weber's grandmother's house?" Hallie said.

"Yeah," Boyd said. "You wouldn't expect that to be a coincidence."

"So, Prue Stalking Horse had a body and three stones in her cellar. An old farmhouse that was destroyed twenty years ago had a fourth stone buried in that cellar. And it just happens that the woman who used to live in that house practiced perversion magic and had a grandson who tried to use that same magic and blood sacrifice to control the world."

"The world's weather, anyway. Do you know how it was destroyed? The Weber house?" Boyd asked.

"In the tornado, I'm assuming, when Jasper was destroyed. Are you hungry?" she asked. She didn't wait for an answer, but got up and opened the refrigerator.

"I don't think so," Boyd said. "It burned."

Hallie looked at him. "Really?" She took a plate of cold cuts, bread, cheese, and milk out of the refrigerator and a bag of chips off a shelf. She brought everything over to the table and grabbed plates and silverware and glasses.

"Besides, the stone was buried after the house was destroyed," Boyd added. "At least according to the photographs I found."

"That doesn't make sense," Hallie said. She went back to the refrigerator and got mustard and sliced tomatoes and lettuce.

"It makes sense," Boyd said. "It has to make sense. We just don't know what kind of sense it makes."

"Well, who?" Hallie asked. "Who wanted Prue dead? Who are your suspects?"

"Same as before. Laddie Kennedy. Tel Sigurdson. That's a long shot. But there's some connection there, I think. Random unknown killer. Someone we don't suspect and have no evidence for."

"So, not much progress," Hallie said. "Haven't you heard anything new from DCI?"

"No, they've had this other thing in Rapid City, which shouldn't involve them since Rapid City has its own detectives, but apparently does."

His cell phone rang and he answered it. Hallie got up while he was talking and went upstairs, having pretty much just that minute realized that she was cold, her jeans still damp from the rain and walking out into the field earlier in the day.

When she returned in an old pair of jeans and an oversized sweat-shirt, Boyd was putting his phone back in his pocket. "That was Gerson," he said. "She heard about the explosion and wanted to know if it was related to the investigation."

Hallie laughed. "What did you tell her?"

"Maybe? She's going to be in town tomorrow, says they think they've identified the body."

Hallie was putting together a sandwich, and she stopped with a piece of bread in her hand. "Who?"

"William Packer."

"Who?"

"I don't know." Boyd rubbed his eyes. "She's bringing more information tomorrow."

"Eat something," Hallie said.

Boyd laid a hand on Hallie's arm. "Tell me what's been going on here. Are you okay?" There was an underlying urgency in his voice that made Hallie lay down the sandwich she'd just finished making and face him.

"I'm fine," Hallie said. Better, at least. At least she thought she was better.

Boyd took a breath. "I had a dream about you. I dreamed that you died."

Hallie put her hand over his. "I did die," she said. "You've had that dream before."

He shook his head. "This was different. This was now. It was new."

"I'm not going to die," she said. "It's not going to happen."

She hoped like hell that it was true.

20

Hallie woke while it was still dark. She could feel Boyd beside her, hear him breathing. She liked that, liked that he was there. She shifted onto her elbow and looked at him. He still looked too young, too pretty—not handsome, not exactly, more like the lead singer in a boy band or the teenaged son on a bad sitcom.

"Are you looking at me?" he asked without opening his eyes.

"Yes." She kissed him.

He put a hand on the back of her neck and pulled her closer. The kiss deepened. She slipped the tip of her tongue into his mouth and moved so she was above him. There was time; for once there was time enough. Wind rattled against the window.

Hallie had always preferred her sex athletic and sweaty, but with Boyd she liked it slow, like holding back time, like if they were just tender and patient and slow enough, they would live forever in the moment they created.

Moonlight filtered through the uncurtained window. And Hallie thought that Boyd in the silver light of the moon looked amazing, his face not just planes and angles, but exactly the right planes and angles, the perfect definition of a man's face. It actually made her heart hurt to look at him. Like, what would happen if she lost him, if she didn't know that she could call him, could see him sitting across the table at the end of a long day. She touched his face, ran a finger down his cheekbone; he turned his head to kiss the palm of her hand.

"Jesus, Boyd," she breathed.

In a cool smooth movement, he switched places so he was above her, one arm underneath her. He kissed her and she could feel him hard against her and she wanted him more than she had ever wanted anything. This—this—was why she would stay, wanted to stay, would do anything to stay forever, but not just this, not just sex. Sex was just the feeling, a way to express what everything else, the quiet moments, the companionship, the conversations, and even the arguments meant. It meant "I want you." It meant "I love you." It meant . . . Oh God, it meant everything.

"Hallie?"

She realized that while she'd been thinking of the world and their place in it, he'd reached across, retrieved a condom, and put it on.

"Yes," she said. And, "Yes, oh yes."

He entered her and it was perfect, the way sex ought to be but often wasn't. Like this was where the witching hour came from, where magic came from, when they matched up and the world matched up and just, right then, when she came and he did, time actually stopped. It stopped. Until they had to breathe or die and both of them, at the same time, chose breath.

An hour later, the sun was up and the world and everything in it was back.

There were outside chores to do and more to talk about, things that they had been too tired to figure out the night before. Boyd was heading into town to meet with a contractor and possibly Agent Gerson, and Hallie planned to join him, at least for the contractor part, figured she could help throw and sort and make the temporary repairs from last night a little more permanent. She was heading upstairs to change out of her chore clothes when her cell phone rang.

"Beth?"

"It's Laddie. I heard about what happened. At Davies's house."

"Do you know what happened?" Hallie asked, standing in the doorway between the dining room and the kitchen. Boyd had gone outside to load an old tarp and some tools into his SUV. "Not the explosion, but how? The stones caused it. Somehow."

"Yeah. I had an idea," Laddie said. "From what people were saying."

"Did you know something like that would happen? *Could* happen?"

"We should talk," Laddie said. There was something in his voice, both sad and—Hallie couldn't quite identify it. Angry? Frightened? Hopeless. "There's something I haven't told you about the stones and Prue and all that back then."

"All right," Hallie said. "I'm on my way to town. I can come over."

"Nah," he said. "I don't think it's a good idea. Can you meet me . . . You know where'd be good? If you could meet me at that old church, you remember the one. St. Mary's. It's good and open."

"I know where it is," Hallie said. It was where Lorie Bixby had died back in the fall, where Martin Weber had killed her. Laddie was right, you could see a long way from there in every direction, though she wasn't sure why that was important. And she didn't like most of the reasons, from back when she was a soldier, why it had been important in the past.

She went outside to find Boyd and told him she'd meet him later. It was drier and colder than it had been. The thin layer of ice that had coated things the night before was gone, no match for a dry north wind.

"I'll come," Boyd said.

"Don't you have a contractor to meet?" Hallie asked.

"I'll call," he said.

"All right." Truthfully, she didn't mind. Prue's death was, after all, an official police investigation, so if Boyd wanted to come, well, it was probably a good idea.

It took them ten minutes from the time Laddie called to get on the road, Boyd driving because his car had a better heater than Hallie's old pickup, and they were five miles from the ranch, so maybe fifteen minutes altogether when Hallie's cell phone rang again. She pulled off one of her gloves and answered.

"Hallie . . ." The sound like a single breath puffed into the thinness of the dry, cold day.

"Who is this?"

"I need . . . listen . . ."

"Laddie?"

"I'm sorry. Shouldn't have—"

Hallie could feel the SUV slow, could feel Boyd's hand on her arm, though it felt like something distant, like someone else's hand or someone else's arm. "Laddie, where are you?" Hallie asked. "Are you at St. Mary's? We're coming, Laddie. Hang on. What's happened? Tell me what's happened."

The car stopped. Hallie felt more than saw Boyd reach for his own cell phone, heard his voice a soft murmur as he called the central dispatch. Laddie lived on the outskirts of Templeton, which had its own police force, though their calls went through the county dispatch anyway. If Laddie was at St. Mary's already or between there and his house, then it was Taylor County, the sheriff's office, who'd respond. The important thing, though, was to get someone.

"I made mistakes, you know, but . . . I never," Laddie said after a long pause, his voice so soft, Hallie could barely hear him. "Just . . . a guy's got to get by. Everybody's got to get by."

"Laddie, tell me where you are," Hallie said.

She was vaguely aware that Boyd had stopped talking, that the SUV was moving again—even if they didn't yet know exactly where they were moving to.

"It don't . . ." This time the pause was so long that Hallie wasn't sure Laddie was going to speak again. "It's cold," he finally said.

"St. Mary's or his house," Hallie said quietly to Boyd. "Or somewhere in between." Jesus.

"Templeton's sending a car to his house. A sheriff's car and the ambulance are going to St. Mary's," Boyd said equally quietly. "They'll call."

"Okay." She didn't even look at him, like all her concentration had to be on Laddie, like it was the only thing that might save him. To Laddie, she said, "Help is coming. Can you hold on?"

"I never hurt no one," Laddie said. His voice was softer, but seemed more steady. Or maybe Hallie just wanted it to be. "I mean, I wasn't always smart. I wasn't . . ."

"Laddie." Hallie gripped the phone so tightly, the edges bit into her hand. "What happened?" Not that she wouldn't know soon enough, but talking was good, right? If he kept talking, that would be good.

"I don't even know," he said.

Hallie was vaguely aware that Boyd had to be traveling at least eighty miles an hour, and she was glad it was daytime and the roads were dry. He was the most careful driver she knew and there was never much traffic, but—

"Deer." Spotted the almost invisible movement of brown coat against brown grass.

Boyd hit the brakes hard so that Hallie had to put her hand out quick, though she was wearing her seat belt. He slowed to under forty, but didn't stop, and they passed half a dozen deer right at the edge of the road; then he sped up again. In the outside rearview mirror, Hallie saw the deer step lightly onto the highway, then take off again, like hounds were chasing them.

"Thanks," he said.

"Yeah," Hallie said. It was something she did automatically, all the time, because deer and cars on roads that weren't heavily traveled were a tricky combination, even in the daytime, even if you were paying attention. Laddie had continued to talk, but Hallie had heard only a little bit.

"You need to know," he was saying now. "The stones. They don't just happen. It takes big magic. Big. You understand?"

"Yeah, Laddie, I understand," she said, though she didn't.

"Big magic," he repeated, like it was important. "Like . . ." His voice faded. ". . . Could have done it. But I been looking. Maybe because of the iron or the blood or the way it happened. I think it's all right."

"Okay," Hallie said. "Good. It's okay."

Silence. Then,

"All the trouble I've ever had," Laddie said. "That stone."

Hallie was pretty sure that wasn't actually true, but it probably wasn't a good time to say so.

"Lost the ranch. Lost my wife. Lost—"

"Laddie?"

Silence. Shit. Then—"Lost the best dog I ever had."

Hallie could hear a siren. Thank God. "Can you hear that, Laddie?" she said. "Help's coming. You hang on." Said the last like it was a command, like one of her soldiers.

There was no reply. "Laddie. Laddie!" Nothing. "Shit."

Hallie heard the siren again, louder now, then really loud, a final whoop, and silence.

Boyd slowed again for deer, two of them this time on his side of the road. There'd been a lot of deer lately, a lot of animals in roads.

Half a mile later, Boyd turned onto the gravel road to St. Mary's church.

"Hello? Still there?" A new voice on Hallie's phone.

"How is he?" Hallie asked.

The voice, a man and sounding very young, hesitated. "We'll do what we can," he said.

"Tell me." It wasn't a question. It even felt like she was back in Afghanistan. It was cold, thin sun in the sky, someone was injured, and she didn't know who the enemy was or where they were.

"He's been shot. He's lost a lot of blood. Thanks for getting us to him—now shut up and let me do my job."

Okay.

Hallie could appreciate someone who got on with things.

She disconnected.

Boyd slowed further. They could see the lights of the ambulance now, another mile, maybe two, farther up. The road they were on was narrow and badly maintained over the winter. The SUV jounced heavily along the rutted surface.

The EMTs were already loading Laddie into the ambulance when Boyd pulled in behind Laddie's old Malibu. Maker lay on the ground a few feet away. Hallie wanted to stand right between Maker and Laddie, wanted to tell the dog to get out of here. Go away. It couldn't have Laddie. She wouldn't let it have him.

"You the one who called?" one of the EMTs asked when Hallie reached the ambulance. He looked like he was no older than eighteen, which he probably wasn't. When she nodded, he said, "Thanks," slammed the back door shut and banged on it, then headed to the front of the ambulance.

Hallie paced him. "How is he?"

The EMT hesitated, pulling open the driver's door. Boyd, who had come up behind Hallie, flashed his badge, and the EMT said with a grimace, "We can't stabilize him here. We're going to the clinic in town. Hopefully, we can buy enough time to get to Rapid City."

"Bad, then."

"Yeah," he admitted, sounding both stressed and apologetic.

"Sheriff on the way?" Boyd asked as the EMT started up the engine.

"Ten minutes, they said." Then he was turning on the lights, shoving the ambulance into gear, quick whoop of the siren and he had turned and gone, throwing up gravel in a scattering of spray as they left. Hallie had barely seen Laddie, let alone talked to him, if he could even talk. Bad, the kid had said.

Goddamn.

What had happened? What the hell had happened? She strode to the middle of the parking lot where she could see in all directions at once. Nothing. The only things moving were grass and a loose shingle on the one section of roof that hadn't burned.

Hallie looked over at Laddie's car. Before she could move toward it, Boyd laid a hand on her arm. "Wait," he said.

For the Taylor County sheriff's car, he meant, for the official investigation. But she wanted to know. Wanted to know what had happened. How it had happened. Was it the same person who'd shot Prue? It had to be the same person. And what had Laddie tried to tell her? Big magic? What did that mean? Like flinging open the car door and riffling through Laddie's possessions would answer those questions, like destroying evidence would net her the information she craved.

She wanted to do it anyway. It was what she knew how to do.

Waiting was harder.

Five minutes later, Sally Mazzolo rolled slowly into the old gravel lot. She angled her car so it was headed back out again. She sat in the car for another minute, radioing in her location, then got out and looked from Boyd to Hallie with narrowed eyes.

"He called Hallie," Boyd said. "That's how we knew."

"Because if he'd just called 911, they wouldn't have been able to get here on their own," she said dryly.

"Well, he didn't call 911," Boyd said, not inclined to argue about something someone else did when he wasn't there. "Photographer coming?" he asked as Mazzolo continued to look at Hallie with suspicion.

"State's coming," she said. She walked around Laddie's car, bent to peer in the windows, but didn't open the doors. A mile or so up the road, approaching from the direction opposite the way Hallie and Boyd had come, they could see a gray sedan making its way slowly toward them. It stopped just past the turn-in. The three of them—Boyd, Hallie, and Deputy Mazzolo—waited as the engine turned off, the place suddenly agonizingly quiet again.

Finally, the woman Hallie had seen at Boyd's that first day—God, it seemed weeks ago—climbed out of the car. Boyd and Deputy Mazzolo both approached her, Mazzolo giving Boyd a look, like— step back.

Hallie moved closer so she could hear what they were saying. The state investigator looked exasperated. "Do you have a photographer, evidence bags?"

"I thought you'd be in charge, being from the state and all," Deputy Mazzolo said, standing back with her arms crossed, like just the presence of a state investigator was an affront to Taylor County, the sheriff's office, and her personally. There was a brief moment, something charged in the air between the two women; then the state investigator—hadn't Boyd said her name was Gerson—turned back to her car, popped the trunk, and took out two cases that she set on the hood of the car. She pulled out a camera, which she handed to

Mazzolo. "I want pictures of everything," she said. "Overlapping pictures. Not just the car, but everything around it."

"The ambulance was in here," Mazzolo said, as if that made pictures or even gathering evidence unnecessary.

"Just do it," Gerson said. "And don't touch the car until I tell you to."

With a deep sigh, Mazzolo took the camera. Gerson turned to Boyd. "What are you doing here?"

Hallie thought Gerson gave him an assessing air, and she couldn't really blame her. This was the second shooting Boyd had been present at in a week. She had to admit, she'd be suspicious too.

Boyd looked to his right; his gaze caught Hallie's and held it. "This is Hallie Michaels," he said to the investigator. "Laddie Kennedy, that's the man who was shot, called her."

"You knew this man?" the investigator said to Hallie. "The man who was shot here this morning?" Now that Hallie was close, she could see there was something taut about the way the woman held herself, her eyes boring into Hallie's face, like she was looking hard for something.

"The man who was shot, yes," Hallie said. "You don't know that he was shot here."

"Hallie," Boyd said to her, ignoring the agent's question, "this is Special Agent Gerson. She's investigating Prue Stalking Horse's death." It was as if Boyd had a way he thought the conversation should go and he was determined to hold up his end of that imaginary conversation, whether anyone else cooperated or not.

"Are you aware Laddie Kennedy is a suspect in an earlier shooting?" Gerson asked, as if she could keep the information about which particular shooting to herself, as if there were so many shootings in Taylor County in the past week that Hallie might not be able to figure out the specific one she was talking about. She took a step forward, aggressive, less than two feet separating them.

Behind her, Hallie could hear Sally Mazzolo swearing softly under her breath, the flash of her camera barely noticeable in the sunlight. "Prue Stalking Horse's shooting?" Hallie didn't play according to anyone else's rules, and she didn't care about aggressive. "Yeah, he didn't kill Prue Stalking Horse."

"Does he have a rifle? Would you say he's a marksman?"

Hallie wasn't sure why Gerson was asking these questions, and particularly why she was asking them of her. "I don't know," she said, like she'd told Boyd earlier. "He was in the army."

"And you don't know anything about what happened here or why anyone might want to shoot him?"

"*I* didn't shoot him. Is that what you're asking?"

Boyd put his hand on her arm, like, Take it easy.

"I'm asking," Gerson's tone was deliberate. Hallie thought she was trying to convey a patience she wasn't actually feeling, something in the undertone, edgy and a little strained. "If you know anyone who'd want to shoot him."

"He called me to say," Hallie spoke slowly, trying to keep her own strain from showing. Shouldn't they be worrying about Laddie, here? Wasn't he the one who'd been shot? "That he had some information, something he wanted me to know. But something happened before we could get here and before he could tell me."

Gerson looked at her long and hard. Finally, she gave a quick nod that was more like a jerk. "Okay," she said. "Thank you." Then, "Deputy," her voice was sharp. "Have you photographed the entire area?" She stepped between Hallie and Boyd and walked quickly over to Mazzolo and Laddie's car.

Boyd pulled Hallie back toward the road. "*Did* Laddie tell you something on the phone?" he asked.

"Yes. But I don't know what he meant. It's related. It's all related, that's the only thing I'm sure of. He called because of the explosion

197

last night and because of something that happened twenty years ago. Some connection between those two things. I think he knew what too many stones too close together would do. I should—I don't know—I should have forced him to tell me when we talked the first time, right after Prue died."

"Don't," Boyd said. "You can't change what's already happened."

"You don't actually even know if that's true, given what happens around here on a fairly regular basis. Maybe we *can* change what's happened. Maybe we just have to figure out how."

Boyd shook his head. "I don't think that's a road we want to go down."

"I didn't want to go down any road, not from the very beginning. I didn't ask for this. I didn't want it. And look how it's turned out."

"It's the hand we've got," Boyd said.

"Well, it's a pretty goddamned lousy hand."

21

eputy Davies!" Agent Gerson's voice sounded high-pitched and brittle. Boyd glanced at Hallie, but she was looking down the road, like she could see all the way to Templeton and Laddie in the clinic.

"Do you know who these people are?" Gerson asked Boyd when he approached her. She showed him a faded photograph, preserved in a plastic bag; one corner of the photograph had been bent up, and within the triangle of the bend, the picture contained what Boyd figured were the original colors, but the rest had gone sepia-toned. He took it from Gerson's outstretched hand and examined it carefully.

The photograph looked like it had been taken fifteen or maybe even twenty years earlier, judging by the haircuts, the clothes, and the car they were standing in front of. There were four men and two women in the picture, and though three out of the five looked different than, say, the way they'd look today, Boyd recognized Prue Stalking Horse, Tel Sigurdson, and Laddie. The two remaining—a woman with a thick braid pulled forward over her shoulder and a scarf worn like a cowboy's kerchief around her neck, her hair so light, it looked nearly white in the faded tones of the photograph; and a thickset man with dark hair in a severe crew cut, a heavy five-o'clock shadow, and his hands shoved deep into the pockets of his leather jacket,

Boyd didn't know either of them, although the woman looked familiar in some way he couldn't quite place. He couldn't tell where the picture had been taken. There was a building wall just visible at the right edge of the photograph—brick and the hint of a cornerstone, though he couldn't read the date.

He pointed at the three people he knew. "That's Prue Stalking Horse," he said. "Laddie Kennedy next to her, and Tel Sigurdson on the far left. He's the big rancher out northeast of Prairie City."

"What about the others?" Gerson asked him. "What about him?" She pointed to the third man.

Boyd shook his head. "No."

"You don't know him?" Gerson persisted.

"No."

"It's William Packer," Gerson said.

"The body in the cellar?"

"Yes." Gerson's response was clipped. "The woman?" she asked again before Boyd could ask more questions about William Packer, about who he was and why he was in a photograph with Laddie Kennedy and Prue Stalking Horse.

"I don't know. She looks familiar." He showed the photograph to Hallie, though Gerson made an aborted move to take it back from him before Hallie could look.

Holding the photo in one hand, Hallie said, "No, I've never seen either of them. That building, though. It's the old schoolhouse in West PC, I think." She flipped it over and looked at the back. "What does this mean?" she asked. In a thick hand, someone had written—
All the talents.

"Talents? What? Like they can play the piano or something?"

"Where did you find this?" Boyd asked Gerson. "On the seat? In the glove box? How do you think it's related?" Boyd thought the photograph was probably the reason Laddie had called Hallie. Or a piece of it. Right time frame—at least, twenty years ago seemed to come up over and over, and he'd sure be happy to know what had happened back then.

"You're certain you don't know the other two people in this photograph?" Gerson looked at him intently, like she suspected he knew something he wasn't telling her. She probably looked at everyone like that in the middle of an investigation, but it was a contrast to the last time they'd been together, and he wondered exactly what had happened between when he last saw her and now.

"Never seen them before," he said. "Do you have a theory?"

She didn't answer, but turned to Mazzolo and said, "Log everything and get someone out here to tow this car back to town." To Boyd, she said, "Tell me where to find the clinic in Templeton. I want to talk to this Mr. Kennedy as soon as possible, if it's possible." She grimaced. "I understand he spoke with our murder victim a few hours before she died. He should have been interviewed days ago."

"He was," Boyd said. "The sheriff was working on the follow-ups. He's sent you updates."

She frowned. "All right. Maybe I missed a message. In any case, we don't have much time to waste. Can you finish here?"

Behind them, Mazzolo cleared her throat. Boyd nodded. "I'll take care of it," he said.

"Tell me how to get to this clinic," Gerson said.

"Go back the way you came," Boyd began.

"I'll come with you," Hallie said.

Gerson looked like she wanted to say no, and Hallie added. "It'll be quicker. I can show you."

Hallie took hold of Boyd's arm by the sleeve, pulled him back a step, and said quietly, "Maker was here."

Maker was often around. Boyd wasn't sure why Hallie was pointing it out now.

"He was here and now he's gone," Hallie said. She paused. "I think it's Laddie."

"Harbinger," Boyd said quietly. He had seen Maker once, when he and Hallie were in the under. He remembered it like a particularly vivid dream. He remembered details from that time—what things looked like and even what they smelled like. He remembered that it had seemed so much like Iowa, like the home he grew up in, that it hadn't occurred to him to question it until Hallie showed up. He remembered, but it didn't feel like a memory, not like meeting Hallie for the first time, or getting married when he was nineteen. Not quite real and not exactly a dream, that was how the under—and Maker—felt to him.

"Yes," Hallie said, "Harbinger of death."

He touched her cheek. "Be careful," he said.

She didn't reply.

Gerson started back to her car, but Boyd stopped her. "What?" she said impatiently.

"The photograph." Boyd gestured toward the picture in her hand. "Don't you want to log it with the rest of the evidence?"

"No," she said. "I'll ask Kennedy about it, if I can. We'll log it later."

Boyd frowned, but let it go.

"I'll be there as soon as I can," he said to Hallie, a promise and a reminder.

Hallie hadn't realized how cold she was until she got into Gerson's car. The interior of the car itself was barely above freezing, even though it hadn't been parked long, and when Gerson started the engine, cold air came out of the vents with a muffled roar. No wind in the car and it still felt colder, or made Hallie feel colder than the air outside.

Gerson didn't talk and Hallie was fine with that. Halfway to Templeton, snow began to fall hard. Hallie didn't think it would last, but it was one more thing. The windshield wipers went back and forth, back and forth. All she could think was—Laddie. Jesus, Laddie. Why didn't you just let me help?

"You can't see him," Gerson said as she pulled into the clinic parking lot. "If he's awake, I need to question him."

"Oh, I can see him," Hallie said. She had her seat belt off and was out of the car as soon as Gerson stopped.

"Hey!" Gerson said, but she was still fumbling with her own seat belt, and Hallie was already inside the clinic. It was weirdly quiet, no one up front and she couldn't hear any sound from the back. The door closed behind her with the nearly silent whoosh of a pneumatic release. She rounded the front counter and headed down the hall. The first two rooms were empty, but she found them in the last door on the left.

No one moved. The young EMT looked at his hands. The other EMT, whom Hallie hadn't seen out at the church and who she thought now was Charlie Bishop, who ran the only shoe store in Templeton, sat on a stool with his head buried in his hands. A woman in a white lab coat, who Hallie presumed was the doctor, stood in the middle of the room with her hands at her side. Her coat was streaked with blood, and she was still wearing gloves.

Opposite the door, Laddie lay on a narrow hospital bed with a thin sheet pulled halfway up his chest. There was an impossible amount of blood, IVs still running into both arms, but the monitors were off and the room was silent.

The chill Hallie felt ran all the way up her spine and hit the back of her head like an arctic blast. She recognized this look, this attitude, this silence. She'd seen it before.

"Goddamnit," she said. No one even looked at her.

She crossed the room and took Laddie's hand in hers. It was already turning cold.

Oh, Laddie.

She wanted to cry, but she was too angry to cry. Wanted to hit something, wanted to punish the person who'd done this—why had they done this? To Laddie, who never hurt anyone, who never had any luck, who never *would* have any luck now.

"Who are you?"

The doctor's voice sounded shrill in the stark, sterile room.

Hallie ignored her. There was so much blood that she couldn't tell exactly where Laddie had been shot. Just above the heart, she finally decided.

"You can't just walk in here," the doctor said.

"I just did," Hallie told her.

Special Agent Gerson strode into the room. "What did you think—?" then stopped when she saw them all.

"Get out," Hallie said without turning away from Laddie. "All of you. Just get out of here right now." Her voice was low without much inflection, but it must have been effective because a moment later she heard the soft whoosh of air as the door closed.

She hadn't known Laddie long at all, had really known him only the last couple of months, but she'd liked him. He'd been quiet and not particularly comfortable with what life had handed him, his fortune-telling abilities, the dead talking to him. All he'd ever wanted as far as she could tell was a ranch to run his cattle on and to maybe do something that mattered.

Goddamnit.

She sat with him for a few more minutes, just because she didn't want him to be alone even though whatever made him Laddie was already gone. Then she grimaced and went through his pockets, his shirt and jacket, which had been cut off and thrown on the floor, already gone stiff with drying blood. She found the stone in his front shirt pocket. It was hot when she picked it up, like it had been in a coal fire, and she almost dropped it, but it cooled quickly, though it still glowed blue-white along several thin cracks. There was dried blood, like old paint across the flat top of the stone.

Hallie didn't care about the blood, thought it was right that it should be bloody, thought Laddie deserved for it not to be neat and clean and as if he hadn't died. She stuck it in her pocket, brushed the hair off Laddie's forehead, and kissed him gently on the cheek.

Then she walked across the room and opened the door.

22

The two EMTs, Charlie Bishop and the young man Hallie didn't know, stood behind the front counter, just stood there, like they'd been frozen. The doctor typed something on a keyboard attached to a wall-mounted monitor.

"Where's Agent Gerson?" Hallie asked. Her voice sounded so loud and unexpected that she startled herself. The two EMTs turned their heads almost in unison and stared at her as if they couldn't quite remember who she was. People must have died before, she thought, maybe not like this, but certainly in car crashes and farm implements. Messy deaths, because lots of deaths were messy.

But maybe they'd never gotten used to it.

Hallie never had.

"Who?" the doctor sounded angry, but Hallie didn't think she was angry at her.

"Special Agent Gerson. From the state." She cleared her throat, surprised at how rough she sounded. "She was just here."

The EMTs looked at the doctor, who scowled and said, "Oh, her. She went outside."

Hallie looked outside. It was still snowing. She pulled open the door and stepped out. She could see Gerson puffing furiously on a cigarette, talking on her phone and pacing. Hallie stepped back inside. "Did she say anything?" she asked.

"She said nobody leaves, nobody touches the body, and nobody goes back in that room," the doctor said, then gave an exasperated sigh, like all this had been designed to inconvenience her, slapped off the wall monitor, stalked down the hall to the first door on the right, went inside, and closed the door.

Hallie crossed to the far side of the room, to a bank of plastic chairs hooked together. She didn't sit down, didn't feel as if she could sit down, like her knees refused to bend. She pulled out her phone and called Boyd.

"Laddie's dead," she said when he answered. She didn't know another way to say it, just flat out, because nothing could soften or make it better.

Boyd swore.

"I'm sorry," he said. "I know he was your friend."

That was painful, like a blade to the heart, because you knew it, knew it all the way down, but you didn't say it. Saying it made it public, put it right out in front of people. Saying it made you want to actually cry.

"Yeah," she said. Like, don't talk about it anymore. "What the hell is happening?"

"I don't know," he said, and again, he sounded uncharacteristically tired.

"What are you doing?" she asked.

"Waiting for a tow truck," he said.

"Did you find anything? Any idea who did this? What they want? Why?"

"Hallie," Boyd said in that quiet way that made her feel both better and worse. "I don't know."

"Yeah," Hallie said. By which she meant, goddamnit.

She hung up. Charlie Bishop had gone outside, was standing right in front of the glass doors, smoking a cigarette and, Hallie judged by the direction of his gaze, watching Gerson pace and talk on the phone.

The younger of the two EMTs sat in one of the chairs near Hallie. Just sat there, with his elbows on his knees and his clasped hands between them.

Hallie went and sat beside him, leaving one empty chair between.

"What's your name?" Hallie asked him. He really did look as if he was about eighteen, which he probably was.

He cleared his throat, sniffed a couple of times, and said, "Gatsby Waters."

"Gatsby?"

He winced. "My dad, he grew up in Wyoming and he had this horse. Killed a mountain lion, he said. Saved his life. He named me after the horse."

"At least he didn't name you after the mountain lion."

"Yeah." Like he hadn't really heard her. "I go by Gats mostly. Or just Waters." He stared at the far wall, like something might appear there, something that would make the day, this particular run, make sense. But Hallie knew that would never happen. "I'm sorry," he said finally. "I'm sorry we couldn't save him."

"I'm not mad at you," Hallie said. "You didn't shoot him."

Maker trotted into the reception area, stopped and looked at Hallie; then it crossed the room and sat beside her. Maker didn't shoot Laddie either, she told herself. It was just there, like Death or reapers or the inevitability of time. No one killed Laddie but the person with the rifle. She put her hand on Maker's head, which she'd never done before. It was cold, but not uncomfortable. Maker lay down and rested its head on her boot.

"It isn't that I think I can save everyone," Gats was saying.

Yes, you do, Hallie thought. You do think that. Because that was the kind of thing you thought when you were eighteen. She knew, because she'd thought that way at eighteen herself. She still did.

"I mean . . . I just. I guess it nicked an artery because it looked bad, but it didn't look *that* bad. Maybe if we'd gotten there faster or gotten out of there faster or if we'd been closer to Rapid City. Maybe if . . ." He trailed off because none of those things mattered. He couldn't go back and do it over or find a way for Laddie to be shot right in front of the hospital. He couldn't change the way things had happened, though Hallie knew what it was like, that wish that you could try.

Special Agent Gerson came back inside in a swirl of cold air and tiny snowflakes, dry as dust. She crossed the room to where Hallie and the young Gatsby Waters were sitting. Maker stretched out its neck and sniffed at her pants leg.

"I'm sorry," Gerson said. "I understand he was a friend of yours."

"Thank you," Hallie said. "He didn't kill Prue Stalking Horse."

"No," said Gerson, considering. "If he had, he wouldn't be dead now."

Hallie winced, though she figured Gerson was right.

"Where's the doctor?" Gerson asked.

"In her office," Waters said, and pointed.

"Huh," Gerson said, and headed over.

Four hours later the coroner had come and taken Laddie's body away, the Templeton police under Gerson's direction, had bagged all of Laddie's clothes as evidence and taken those away as well. The EMTs had restocked their ambulance and left, called out to a car accident seven miles north. Gats came over and said good-bye and thanked her, though Hallie wasn't certain exactly what he was thanking her for. Gerson left after an hour and a half, sweeping through the reception area as if no one else were there.

Finally, there was just Hallie. She called Boyd.

"Are you okay?"

"Not really," Hallie admitted.

"I should be there in ten minutes," he said. "It took a while for the tow truck to get here. It wasn't Tom and they got lost twice. Plus the snow, I guess. Hang on."

That's what I do, Hallie thought. I hang on.

She saw his car as it pulled into the parking lot and was out the door and pulling the passenger door open as soon as he'd pulled into a parking space. She didn't want him to get out, to come inside the clinic, to touch her, especially she didn't want him to touch her. She didn't want him to say he was sorry, to ask her if she was okay, didn't want him even to look at her with sympathy.

"We have to stop at Laddie's house," she said.

"Hallie, you can't go there. It's an—"

"Don't say it, goddamnit. I know what it is."

"Well, they're going to have to search his house. It's all evidence now. Everything."

"He has dogs," Hallie said.

"Oh."

Hallie wasn't sure how many dogs there were, because Laddie had different dogs every time she saw him, but she knew she couldn't leave them there alone and she didn't want to hear about evidence and official investigations. Someone told her once that Laddie found stray dogs and took them in, fed them up, and found them homes. Dogs who never had anything until Laddie gave them something. They wouldn't understand. Wouldn't understand why Laddie wasn't coming back or why strangers were going through his things. They would probably hate her, dogs did, because of the ghosts. She'd do it anyway.

When Boyd pulled into Laddie's oversized front parking lot,

three motion lights snapped on, the day just dark enough with the snow and clouds overhead to activate them. Inside the yard, drifting underneath the light closest to the house, was Laddie's ghost.

"Shit," Hallie said.

"What?" asked Boyd.

"Never mind." The ghost looked younger than Laddie had looked in life, wearing a plaid shirt, jeans, and lacers. It wore a battered black cowboy hat tilted forward, and it pissed Hallie off because of course it had unfinished business, of course it was here, but she didn't need to be reminded.

She got out of the car, Boyd next to her. She wasn't even sure yet what she was going to do. Laddie's ghost hanging around in the yard wasn't going to help.

She'd expected the dogs to be hiding, but to her surprise, all three of them were right beside the ghost—a Jack Russell with a graying snout, a young fawn and white pit bull, and a slender Australian shepherd with an amazing blue merle coat. They huddled against each other for warmth, from the snow and the cold and the ghost. She could see three doghouses with blankets inside and electric running to them. But the dogs were here, with a ghost who'd once been a man who'd taken care of them.

If the person who'd shot Laddie were standing in front of her right then, Hallie would have ripped his heart out with her hands.

She opened the chain-link gate slowly, prepared to get out quick if the dogs made any aggressive moves. They didn't, though the pit bull watched her suspiciously as she approached. Laddie's stone felt warm in her pocket, growing warmer with each step she took.

She crouched beside the dogs and offered the back of her hand; the pit bull stretched its neck as far as it could without actually shifting its position and sniffed suspiciously. The other two dogs curled tighter into their balls. The Jack Russell shivered so hard, Hallie could see it shaking. The temperature was in the low twenties and damp, and the extra cold from the ghost just in front of her left Hallie feeling as if she were deep in the depths of arctic winter.

"You can't stay here," she said quietly to the dogs, like they would understand her. "Laddie wouldn't want you to."

At Laddie's name, the Jack Russell's ears twitched. Hallie studied them for a minute. They might let her carry each of them to the car, but she didn't think it was a good idea just to pick up strange dogs, and the pit bull weighed at least sixty pounds. She rose to her feet, trotted over to the side door into Laddie's garage, and went inside. There was a light switch just inside the door, and when she switched it on, she saw three lined trash containers that, when she opened them, held dog food, dog treats, and sawdust—she had no idea what the sawdust was for.

Above the food was a row of hooks with an assorted jumble of leashes and collars. Hallie picked out three collars that looked about the right size and three leashes, which all had brand-names for dog food manufacturers and looked like they'd come free with purchase. She stuffed the collars and leashes into the pocket of her jacket. She grabbed a handful of dog treats and put them in her other pocket. Then she gathered up the trash bag full of food, tied a knot in the top, and took it out to the car. She came back and took the pads and blankets out of three doghouses, surprised that they smelled as if they'd been freshly laundered, and put them in the backseat of Boyd's SUV. The pit bull stood when Hallie took the blankets, but it didn't move.

"Are you sure this is a good idea?" Boyd said. He had stayed outside the fence, but he dropped his hand for the pit bull to sniff. "There's a shelter in Templeton."

"It's a good idea," Hallie said. Boyd didn't argue.

Laddie's ghost had drifted a few feet away from where it had been, and all three dogs were on their feet watching Hallie approach. She hoped they wouldn't run, hoped she and Boyd wouldn't have to chase them down. Maybe they'd have been okay in their heated dog-houses. Maybe the shelter would be fine, better than taking them to the ranch, where there could be ghosts and Maker and god knew what else. Maybe she should leave them alone. But they hadn't been in their houses when she and Boyd had arrived; they'd been outside with Laddie's ghost, slowly freezing, and she couldn't bear, for reasons she didn't feel like examining too closely, for them to be hauled unceremoniously off to the shelter.

She didn't speak, didn't know what to say or why it would do any good, but when she'd fastened the collars and leashes on each of the dogs, they just came with her, like they knew. Laddie's ghost trailed behind. Once, the Jack Russell turned and looked back like it could see; then it turned back to Hallie and trotted alongside her with the others. She let all three dogs into the backseat, and after sniffing everything carefully at least three times, the dogs each curled up on a blanket, the Australian shepherd panting like it had just run a marathon. Hallie closed the door and walked back around to the front passenger door.

As she was opening the door, she heard, or thought she heard, *Thank you,* like a whisper.

She looked across the top of the car to where she'd last seen the ghost, but it was gone. Not for good, she was pretty sure. There would be a sound, then, and a scent of some sort, something unique to the person the ghost had once been. No, Laddie's ghost had just gone somewhere else for a while.

It would be back. That much was certain.

23

Hallie stumbled as she crossed the threshold into the house, more tired than she'd expected. She welcomed the rush of warm air. The dogs sniffed everything, frantically investigating each room, like they'd never been inside a house before, which might well be true, but Hallie had no place warm enough for them outside, so they'd just have to figure it out. She put their beds and blankets on the floor, hoped the smell would help.

The Jack Russell jumped up on the couch, sniffed carefully along the entire length, then curled up in the corner, tight up against a worn pillow. As if that was a signal, the Aussie trotted over to one of the beds and lay down on its side and the pit bull sank into a stiff straight-up down like a sphinx, like it was waiting for the bad thing, because it knew that it would come.

Hallie sighed—Jesus.

She walked into the kitchen and it just looked so . . . so normal, so like it had in the morning when she left, like everyone was still alive, like the world gave a shit about anything ever anywhere. She'd intended to take off her coat and hang it up, but she couldn't—couldn't stay, couldn't stand it.

She went back outside.

It was not quite sunset, just after five o'clock and clear, and the cold hit her like a slap in the face. Stars already sparkled in the high dome of the sky, and she could see a tiny pair of headlights on the road from town. She drew in a breath and let it out slowly, rubbed her hands hard across her face and headed toward the barn, where Boyd had gone to feed the horses while she took the dogs inside.

The first thing he said was, "Are you okay?"

"No," Hallie said. "No, I'm pissed off and I'm—I don't even know how to say it—'sad' is the easy word, but it's not the right word. He told me his luck was bad, that it was always bad. He lost his land and his family and, well, everything. And I want someone to pay for that, but even if they do, even if we figure out who it is and bring them to justice, it doesn't bring Laddie back. I feel like I did when Dell died and not at all like Dell and worse in at least one way because Dell made her own mistakes, but I feel like Laddie paid for mine or that I dragged him into this and I don't even know what this is."

She stopped because none of that was what she wanted to say and yet it was also more than she wanted to say, more than she'd ever said about anyone's death except maybe Dell's. She'd known good soldiers who died in Afghanistan, but there it had been a thing that you put aside and promised yourself you'd deal with later, though you never really did. This was right here where she lived. Dell's death had happened when Hallie was halfway around the world, but this— this had happened right in front of her. And she hadn't been able to stop it.

Boyd didn't say anything immediately, and Hallie felt a sudden regret because he'd lost half his house in a mysterious explosion, he'd seen Prue Stalking Horse shot, almost a week ago now, but still. She ought to be worrying about whether *he* was okay, not the other way around.

He reached out and pulled her close. She leaned her head on his shoulder, but the truth was she wasn't tired. They had big problems, and it wasn't like they hadn't handled big problems before—they'd handled the end of the world. But this seemed . . . more human, more like regular evil, both smaller and larger. Magic revealed itself sooner or later, at least the kind of magic they'd dealt with so far, but people, well, they were people. Whoever had killed Prue, whoever had killed Laddie could be anyone.

They went inside the house. The Jack Russell trotted into the kitchen and sniffed Boyd's pants leg. The pit bull appeared in the doorway, the short hair along its spine standing up so that it looked like a darker colored ridge. When it saw who was there, it lay down, like it understood that Hallie and Boyd were being helpful, but it was keeping an eye on them all the same.

"Are you hungry?" she asked. It seemed like all she did lately was make coffee and sandwiches, feed horses, and wait for the next shoe to drop.

Boyd took her hand and drew her to him. "I don't want to eat," he said. "I just want—"

"Shh." She kissed him. It was what she wanted too, though she didn't know the words or how to say it—to be here, to be with him, to be alive.

Hallie woke.

Had she been dreaming? She couldn't remember anything but darkness. All-encompassing, but neither comforting nor frightening. Just dark. She heard unfamiliar movement, sat up quick, and realized it was the pit bull, nails ticking on the bare floor. She put a hand on its head and it sighed, then left again, lying down on an old rag rug near the door. She looked at the clock: 4:30 A.M. She looked at Boyd sleeping on his back, one arm flung across his face. She lay back down for about ten seconds, realized she was never going back to sleep, bent over and kissed Boyd lightly on the lips, then grabbed jeans, a T-shirt, and a sweatshirt, left the room, and went downstairs.

Something bothered her beyond Prue's death and even beyond Laddie's death, which bothered her a lot. Beyond the notes someone had left her or the phone calls. Beyond Beth Hannah. Part of the reason it bothered her was because she didn't know what it was, though she thought she ought to know, something she couldn't remember or almost remembered, or hadn't understood at the time.

She went into the office and looked at maps of the Badlands. Boyd had said once that the Badlands were too chaotic, but that didn't bother Hallie. She liked chaos. And yet, she'd never spent much time there, even though it was, essentially, right there. Halfway between Taylor County and Rapid City, a place she skirted regularly, but rarely stopped for.

She thought too about the things Laddie said before he'd died. Was there anything there? She wrote down everything she could remember:

The stones. They don't just happen. It takes big magic. Big.

What did that mean? Big magic? The only big magic she knew was when Martin Weber had tried to control the weather. And he was dead.

She took Laddie's stone out of her pocket and looked at it. She didn't know a lot about rocks, though when she'd been trying to figure out what to do with her life, she considered the South Dakota School of Mines because it seemed like something hard with plenty of physical work to go with the books. Laddie's stone looked like polished granite. She went out to the living room and looked at the stone they'd put on a shelf there. It was larger, darker, but maybe granite too. A certain type of stone? From a certain place? If it was, how would they ever know? Who was left to tell them?

Around seven, when the sun was slightly more than a promise, she put her boots back on, grabbed a jacket, her hat, and gloves and went outside. On the way, she let the three dogs out, hoped they wouldn't run away, but let them out all the same, because they had to go out. As she stepped outside and the dogs tumbled ahead off the porch, Hallie spotted Laddie's ghost just outside the hex ring. The dogs raced down the shallow slope toward the old windmill. She almost whistled them back, afraid they'd keep running, but they stopped at the bottom and turned toward the house again, sniffing at bushes and rocks and grass.

Hallie walked to the barn and started up the old Ford tractor, bounced it across the iron hard ground, speared a big round hay bale, and moved it to the feeder inside the horse corral. She didn't think about Laddie or Prue or notes on posts. She didn't think about Death or harbingers or things she wanted to remember, but didn't. She concentrated on the work and what needed to be done.

She dumped the bale in the round feeder, idled the tractor, and jumped off to cut the strings and spread it so the horses could eat it. She drove the tractor back out the gate, closed it, and leaned on it as the horses wandered over to eat.

A crow dropped onto a fence post two away and cocked its head at her. The young gelding wandered away from the hay feeder when the biter laid back her ears and kicked at him. He ambled over to Hallie and pushed at her hands, like he expected her to feed him. When he saw the crow, he shied and the crow rose at the sudden movement and settled on another post a few feet farther along.

Hallie watched it, but it ignored her, pecking at something on the fence. After a moment it flew away.

"Coffee."

The voice was right in her ear and she hadn't heard anyone coming up behind her. Her arm came up as she turned, and she hit Boyd hard in the chest, which sent the coffee mug he'd been holding flying out of his hand as he stumbled back. The mug hit the ground and bounced, throwing coffee in a rising arc. Boyd stumbled, grabbed her hand, and as she felt the sharp tug of his weight, she braced herself and pulled back hard. Then he was close, so close, and she threw her arms around his neck and kissed him.

He tasted like mint toothpaste and coffee.

He grabbed her around the waist and kissed her back. She could feel the curve of his lips like he was smiling. Something huffed warm breath in her ear—the gelding, she knew it was the gelding, but she jumped anyway, tripped on Boyd's boot and stumbled. He tried to catch her, but his feet tangled in hers and they both fell. Hallie's elbow hit the ground hard; she rolled away from Boyd as he fell too, landing on one knee and his left hand. He slipped as he tried to rise and then they were both on the frozen ground on their asses. And Hallie laughed because this was the kind of thing that happened, it always happened, but this morning in the bright cold winter sunshine on cold hard ground, she was with him and the horses and a ranch—her ranch. And she knew that Laddie wouldn't fault her for this, for finding a momentary pleasure.

Laddie had known how the world went on.

24

Someone coughed.

It was a dry thin sound, like the crack of an old twig in dry mountain air, like the tear of yellowed parchment, like desiccated carapaces. Next to Boyd, Hallie spun, half-rising to a crouch. Laughter forgotten. Boyd was already on his feet, standing over her.

Just outside the hex ring, beyond the strips of old cloth fluttering in the brittle knee-high grass, stood a man, or at least something that looked like a man, wearing light-absorbing black robes, a hood, and his/her/its hands tucked into the sleeves. Looked like a man who'd appeared out of nowhere, who hadn't been there seconds before, something shaped like a man, though Boyd knew enough these days to assume nothing, especially not that something standing just outside a hex ring was what it appeared to be.

He held out his hand without looking away from the thing in black robes and offered it to Hallie. The horses wheeled and ran, even the two old mares, running like they were two-year-olds again, running like their lives depended on it.

The creature coughed again. The sound made Boyd think of parched cold desert, of barren frozen tundra. It made him thirsty, just hearing it, like he might never see water again. It made him long for oceans. He realized that there was nothing—nothing—to the creature, but black robes. The hood appeared to be empty, like there was no head at all, just the appearance of a head, a shaped hood around a stark, impenetrable blackness.

"Jesus Christ," Hallie said, her voice so quiet, she might have been remarking on the weather or a particular bit of local news.

The creature moved forward, silent. Boyd didn't quite hold his breath, but he couldn't help a quick exhale of relief when it reached the hex ring and stopped, looked to the left and the right, tried again, then huffed out another dry breath. Boyd took a step forward, Hallie grabbed his arm, but he noticed, though he was not really looking at her, just aware of her presence and the feel of her beside him, that she moved up right along with him.

"What do you want?" he asked, his voice as quiet as Hallie's own, as if they didn't want to spook it, whatever it really was, as if it would attack or run, and as if both those options—attacking or running— were equally bad. And yet, he asked, as if he'd already moved past apparition, past hallucination, into rational being of some sort, whatever sort that was.

"Death."

The voice, not dry like the cough, but more like distant thunder, like storm warnings, sounded from somewhere deep inside the hood of the robe. It rumbled in Boyd's chest, that voice, like ancient earthquakes and runaway trains. "Death talks to you."

Not to me, Boyd thought, though he knew it wasn't him the creature was talking to, might as well not have been there at all for all the notice it took of him.

"What are you?" Hallie asked. Her face looked as if it were carved from stone, as if she already knew, but wanted it to tell her something else, wanted it to *be* something else, like everyday, like both of them— Hallie and Boyd—wanted a different world, one vastly more ordinary.

"You know," the creature said.

"Unmaker." Hallie's voice was cold like midwinter and old bones.

This wasn't— Boyd both remembered and didn't remember what had happened back in November when Travis Hollowell dragged him into the under. But Hallie had told him about this.

An unmaker. Who unmade the dead. Who had tried to unmake Hallie.

"I thought—" Hallie stopped. Boyd could see her swallow hard; then she began again. "I thought you couldn't exist out here."

And yet, here it was.

"The harbinger told you," the unmaker's voice grew deeper, like the rumble of tectonic plates. "We can. Though the price." A long hiss on the end of price, "Is everything."

Boyd thought he could see smoke spiraling up in tiny wisps from the creature's robes. Or maybe it was the cold, like early morning frost. "Why are you here?" Boyd asked, even though it probably wasn't going to answer him. Maybe it was here to talk to Hallie, maybe it was here to unmake her, maybe it wouldn't go without a fight. He was ready for all that, for the fight most of all, even if he didn't know what it meant or what he'd need.

"Death," the voice said, ignoring Boyd a second time, speaking to Hallie as if Boyd weren't even there. "Death talks to you."

"Not lately," Hallie said.

"Death," it said again, more emphasis on the word this time, "talks to you."

"Okay," Hallie said, impatient. "Yeah, he has."

"That is . . ." The creature paused. "Incorrect."

"It's weird," Hallie conceded. "But I don't know what it has to do with you."

"Incorrect," the voice repeated, as if she hadn't spoken. "There is a natural order. You risk everything."

"He comes to me," Hallie said. "I didn't ask for it."

An icy breeze rose spontaneously from the west, sweeping dry grass against the paddock fence. Nothing of the unmaker's moved in the wake of that wind, not the robes, not the hood, nothing. Black smoke was more visible now, rising from the hem of the robe, the bottom of the sleeves, and the edge of the hood. The air smelled of burnt pinecones and abandoned buildings.

"You must respond," the unmaker said.

"What?"

"Death has made an offer. And you must respond. Things hang in the balance."

"The answer is no."

Boyd could hear something in Hallie's voice, though. Uncertainty? Fear? Neither one of those, he thought, but related somehow. More like resignation, like this would never end, like she was the only one standing here.

Which she wasn't.

Boyd wished he had his gun, even though it wouldn't do any good not loaded with regular bullets. He wished he still had bullets primed with blood and blessings. That was something he remembered clearly—or remembered from before he'd been dragged under— he wasn't entirely certain about the sequence. Either way, remembered or not, he didn't have them, or his gun.

"Look," Hallie began when the unmaker didn't speak.

As if it had only been waiting for the sound of Hallie's voice, the creature said, "There are . . ." Pause. ". . . Death reminds you that you already died once."

Boyd's hand reached out almost involuntarily and gripped Hallie's arm tight, like if something were going to happen right now, it would have to take them both.

"What the hell does that mean?" Hallie asked. "Is that a threat? Are you the one who's been threatening me? You know, I didn't ask for this. I didn't ask for any of this!"

But she had, in a way, Boyd knew.

She was alive.

Something happened in Afghanistan, when she'd been dead for seven minutes, when she'd come back. There was a reason that Hallie was here and not gone for good. A reason he was grateful for, but a reason nonetheless. Some offer had been accepted. Some deal had been made. There was a price. Boyd thought Hallie had done enough, had paid enough. But he didn't decide. Hallie didn't decide. It was someone else's game. And they were just the pawns.

"Hallie," he began.

"Think carefully—," the unmaker said. Smoke from its robes rose like streamers now. "There is a price for every answer."

"Look—"

Hallie stopped speaking abruptly, her head turned sharply right. Her arm wrenched from Boyd's grasp and she gripped his shoulder like a steel vise. Boyd looked that way too, but kept the unmaker in the periphery of his vision. He actually thought he saw something where Hallie was looking—a mist so light, he wouldn't have considered it anything if Hallie hadn't directed his attention that way.

"What?" he asked, his voice hushed, like speaking too loudly would precipitate disaster.

"Laddie's ghost," she said. "But it's— Oh, shit."

Boyd saw it at the same time that she did. Laddie's three dogs, which had seen sniffing around the base of the old barn when Boyd came out of the house, were now trotting briskly across the frozen ground toward that same vague mist—toward Laddie's ghost. The Jack Russell was in the lead, bouncing forward as if it were suddenly years younger.

The unmaker moved toward them.

Hallie ran. Boyd, a half second slower, ran in the opposite direction, back toward the house and his car and the iron fireplace poker he'd been carrying in the back since Travis Hollowell and the under. It took him maybe twenty seconds to cross a dozen yards, wrench open the back door, and rip the poker from the Velcro that held it in place. When he turned back, he could see that the Jack Russell hadn't stopped, though the other two dogs had. It took one step, then two, its nose outstretched to sniff. Then the ghost, or at least the mist that Boyd could see, disappeared and the Jack Russell trotted straight across the line, as if searching for it, coming to a quick stop in front of the unmaker, which was almost entirely formless now, billowing black smoke in the vague general outline of a man.

Hallie, a good twenty yards closer than Boyd, was too far away. Inches separated the Jack and the unmaker.

"No!" Hallie shouted.

"Left!" Boyd shouted, hoped she'd understand, planted his foot, and threw the iron poker like a javelin. Hallie dived hard to her left. The poker went straight through the unmaker and out the other side to land with a thump on the hard-frozen ground. The unmaker disappeared with a crack. The Jack Russell stretched its muzzle as far as it would go and sniffed the ground where the unmaker had been.

"What the hell was that?" Boyd said, even though he knew exactly what it was. Normal words used in regular conversation seemed inadequate to the situation, as if for once what he said and what he meant were unrelated.

"Damnit," Hallie said. "Goddamn."

The pit bull approached them, shoved its head into Boyd's hand, and he petted the dog without quite realizing that he was doing it.

"You know what, Boyd. I'm tired of being afraid." Boyd had no idea what she was talking about, but as he moved to retrieve the iron fireplace poker, Hallie headed toward the house, started at a walk but was running by the time she was halfway across the yard, and Boyd found himself watching her, not understanding what it was she was doing but realizing that it was more a piece of everything else that had happened than a separate mystery of its own.

The pit bull kept pace with him as he retrieved the poker, and by the time he'd put it back in his SUV, Hallie was back outside with what looked like several pieces of paper.

"It is time to face your fear." She shoved one of the notes into his hand. "Face your fear." Two more notes. "What are you afraid of—that's what they're asking."

"Dying?" Boyd asked. Not, what is this? Or, where did these notes come from? But the answer to the question. The rest would follow, had to follow. Or at least he hoped it would.

"Someone's been leaving me these notes," Hallie said.

"Leaving them?"

"On posts. Outside the hex ring."

"And you think this—that—?" He gestured toward where the un-maker had been standing moments before.

"I think . . . yeah—I think that's where the notes came from. From one of them."

"You're afraid of dying."

"Aren't you?"

Boyd didn't answer. He'd believed not so many months ago that he was going to die, had dreamed it and known it was true. Instead, Hallie had happened. And he hadn't died. Still, he believed he'd faced it, dealt with the seeming inevitability of it, and gone forward anyway. He didn't want to die. But he wasn't afraid of it.

Or at least he wasn't afraid for himself.

"Hallie—"

"I'm sorry, you know."

"What?"

"I'm sorry I sacrificed you. There was so little time, or I thought there was."

Boyd reached out and took her hand. She looked at his hand holding hers, but she didn't look at him. "You have to let that go," he said. "You didn't sacrifice me. I'm right here."

"You don't remember. It's easy to say it's not important if you don't even remember what happened."

"You took a risk," he said. "And it worked. You saved everything."

"Risks are what you do with your own life, not someone else's. You don't sacrifice your—you don't sacrifice people you love. You protect them."

"You can't protect them if you sacrifice the world." There was something about this conversation that he didn't want to have, could feel tight muscles all along his jaw, straining across his back, holding back what he really wanted to say, what they were really talking about. And he wasn't even entirely sure what they really *were* talking about, or even if they were both talking about the same thing. It felt like they weren't just talking about Hallie, like they weren't just talking about November, like the vision he'd seen, the one where Hallie died, was part and parcel of it, a price that hadn't yet been paid.

"You can," Hallie insisted. "There has to be a way that you can. Because otherwise, you can't promise anything to anyone."

"Hallie"—he spoke slowly both for himself and for her—"I forgive you. I've always forgiven you. The thing is, you have to forgive yourself."

She closed her eyes, kept them closed for a long time, like she was holding something back that she didn't want to say. When she opened them, she said, "Look, it's—it's fine. It is. What's important, really, is that there was an unmaker in my yard. In my yard, Boyd. I have to deal with that."

"*We* have to deal with it," he said.

"No." She said it calmly and quietly, but decisively. "You have Prue's murder. Laddie's murder. Your house. The stones. You have enough."

He wanted to protest. Not that he didn't have all those other problems to deal with, but he had this problem too. Because it was Hallie's problem.

"The coordinates," he asked her. "Do you know where that is?"

"I do," she said. He wondered if she was going to tell him. He felt the doubt of it like a thin stab between his ribs. But then she continued, "You have to let me—" She stopped like she was rethinking her words. "You have to give me the space to do this. It's my—" She stopped again, but for a different reason, he thought, a word she didn't want to say. "It's my fear," she said. "I have to face it. Me. I have to know that I can face it. You can't do that for me."

"But I can do it with you."

"It's in the Badlands."

"The Badlands?" Boyd had been to the Badlands only once since he moved to South Dakota, but it had always given him a bad feeling. Sometimes just driving by the edges of it on the way to Rapid City gave him a bad feeling, like someday if the apocalypse came, it would begin in the Badlands.

"I'll go with you," he said.

"Laddie said no."

"What?"

"That night everyone came for supper." She spoke very precisely, as if it were the individual words and not the sentence itself that was the problem. "Laddie said that I shouldn't take you to the Badlands with me."

"What does that mean?" He held up his hand before she could repeat it a third time. "Never mind." Because she had no more idea what it meant than he did, and if he was going to ask that she listen to him when he had a dream, he had to accept that maybe Laddie, who had told the future for a living, might have been worth listening to. He took a deep breath, let it out slow, like the instant between taking in a breath and releasing it would make the difference between hanging on tight enough to choke a person and letting go. Because he wanted to hang on, wanted to do it more than he'd ever wanted anything in his life. He couldn't forget what he'd seen in Jasper in the sleety rain. He'd seen her dead. Not dead like died-in-Afghanistan dead—dead like here, in South Dakota. Now.

But . . . he looked at her, caught again by her straightforward gaze, her determination, her willingness to act because action was necessary, and he knew that if he didn't, if he *couldn't*, step back right now, then he would lose her anyway.

This was not his choice. Because he had already made the choice. To love her as she was.

"If you go," he said. "If you insist on going by yourself," which was unnecessary, those words, because of course she did, "please be careful. You're smart as hell, and I don't care if you think you're afraid of death, you're still one of the bravest people I know, but you take chances, Hallie. You don't always think things through. And sometimes you're just really damned lucky."

Hallie clenched her jaw. But what she said was, "Sometimes luck is all you have. And sometimes you're lucky because you're pre-pared. I'll be prepared. I'll be careful. I've dealt with enemies."

"When you had an army."

"Well, now I have you," she said, and grinned.

"Hallie—" This was serious.

"I will call you if I need you," she said. Her eyes held his, sure and steady. He had to accept this. Had to let it happen this way, not be-cause he'd dreamt it, not because it was inevitable, but because what he wanted and what he cared about meant that this was how it worked.

"Yes," he finally said. "Take care. Call me if you need help. Actually, on second thought, call me even if you don't need help. Let me know you're okay." He stepped forward, kissed her quick and hard, ran a finger along her cheekbone, and said, "I mean it, Hallie, be careful."

"I'm always careful," she said.

"And see how that works out," he told her.

25

Boyd watched Hallie's truck disappear down the drive, and he knew he was both wrong and right to let her go. Or—not let her, because you didn't "let" Hallie do anything, but he hadn't insisted on going with her. She said she needed the space to do this, whatever it was. And he suspected she wasn't completely certain what it was either. But what was he going to do if she didn't return, if this was the moment when Death asked her to take his place, if this was the moment she said yes? And she would say yes, at least under the right circumstances—to save the world, to save him, to save her father or Taylor County or even possibly a stray dog. He didn't think that it was sacrifice to Hallie, more like—this thing needs to happen, okay, I'll do it. Just like that, all one thought or breath or instinct.

A contractor was coming at noon to check the flooring at his house and give him an estimate. It was just past seven and he thought, if he could concentrate on it, the best thing he could do might be to write what he knew about Prue's murder and Laddie's murder down in one of his notebooks and see if any of it made sense. Agent Gerson had said they'd identified the bones in Prue's cellar as belonging to William Packer. The name wasn't familiar to Boyd, but he hadn't been in Taylor County all that long. There had been Packers on a ranch west of Hallie's place who packed it in a few years ago. If William Packer was related, someone would know the story.

As he headed back into the house, his phone rang. It was Ole. "Patty says Tel Sigurdson's finally back in town. You want to run out this morning and talk to him about the phone call and where he was the night Prue Stalking Horse died?"

"Sure. I thought you'd reached him by phone."

Ole sounded harassed. "I been playing phone tag with him for three goddamned days. And now I got Laddie Kennedy and the DCI is apparently all over it again and wanting to know what I've got and why I don't have more, which is exactly what I've been asking them. Plus I got dead cattle and someone broke into an empty house over on Second. And Mazzolo's got the goddamned flu or something." Like Sally had done it on purpose.

"It's not a problem," Boyd said. He was happy to have something to do. "I'll go."

"Good. You can pick Gerson up at the Stalking Horse place at eight thirty."

Boyd wondered if Ole had decided not to interview Tel himself because he didn't want to take the DCI agent with him. Mostly Ole was cooperative, cooperated with Templeton police, cooperated with the state agencies and even occasionally the feds and the reservation police, but you didn't want to annoy him—and he was easy to annoy.

"That'll work," he said. Then, "Who's William Packer?"

There was a brief silence; then Ole said, "Gerson told you, did she? Well—" He drew the word out, like it was several syllables. "—it was before I was sheriff, little bit before I came. He was one of the Packers, you know who I mean?"

"The old ranch," Boyd said.

"Was a pretty decent spread at that time, as I understand it," Ole said. "Anyway, William Packer. They called him Billie. He was the second son. Jack and Billie. They were football stars, played baseball in the spring. Jack went up to SDSU got a degree in agriculture or something. Billie took classes, worked at the grain elevator for a while. Drank some. Then he disappeared."

"Disappeared."

"Took off one day is what people said. Everyone figured he left with some girl he'd been dating. His parents retired and moved to Flagstaff not long after I started here. And Jack never talked about it. At least not to me."

"Where's Jack now?"

"Bank would know," Ole said, like if he wasn't in trouble or breaking the law in Taylor County, Ole wasn't all that interested.

"This was twenty years ago?" Boyd asked.

"About then, yeah," Ole said.

"A lot of things happened twenty years ago," Boyd said. "Isn't that when Jasper was flattened? And Prue's sister disappeared then too."

"I assume Prue's sister was the girl Billie Packer left town with," Ole said. "Though I guess he didn't actually leave town, as it turns out. Huh."

Boyd didn't have his uniform with him, and he didn't have a clean one anyway; everything at his house smelled like smoke. He did have his badge and his pistol with him, and he stopped at home to get a belt holster before heading over to Prue's to meet Gerson.

She hadn't arrived, and when he looked at his watch he realized he was almost fifteen minutes early. The street was pretty much deserted. One car parked a block away and a pickup truck three driveways up. Yellow tape fluttered in the wind in front of Prue's house.

He sat for a minute, then got out and walked across the street and through the small cemetery to the frozen empty field where they

knew the shot had come from. He could see crime scene tape fluttering in the wind here too. He was glad he was wearing boots as he
made his way across the rough ground. When he stood just outside
the cordoned-off area, he stopped and looked back toward the house.

The spot was a fair distance away from the house, but perfectly
possible for someone with a high-powered rifle and a good night
scope. He could see it—what the killer had seen—the light on the
porch, the clear, cold night. The cemetery between where he stood
and the street took up the equivalent of three empty lots, with houses
to Boyd's left, but the shooter had been beyond those, beyond, in a
sense, the edge of town. Everyone asleep and waiting. Did he plan
for Boyd to come? For Prue to open the door and let Boyd in? Had
the shooter killed her like this, from far away, so he didn't have to
look her in the eye, so she wouldn't be completely real?

No one in Taylor County really knew who Prue Stalking Horse
was or what she'd done before she came to live in West Prairie City
and work at Cleary's more than twenty years ago. When people
asked, she'd smiled at them and gone back to what she was doing.
But not knowing where someone came from or what their past was,
didn't make them less real, didn't mean their heart didn't beat like
everyone else's, that blood didn't run through their veins, that they
didn't laugh or love or deserve their life. Shooting someone from
far away was still murder, still the same consequences, still just as
bloody and cruel and wrong as putting your hands around their neck
and watching them die.

Boyd walked around the cordoned-off area, but there wasn't
much to see. The only reason they'd identified it as the place the
killer had waited was the packed-down grass and the clear path
leading away, not toward the street, but behind the houses, where it
finally faded away completely in a stubble field a quarter mile farther on.

He followed the path about half its length before he noticed a second track intersecting the first. It was probably a deer trail, but he followed it anyway for a ways farther out into the prairie beyond the town's outskirts. It ended abruptly in a shallow dip where a small doe had died, its carcass partially eaten.

Boyd took a step back, studied the area. There was something odd about the deer carcass, and he couldn't figure out what it was. Something both familiar and unfamiliar. Not smell or even the look of the thing. It was the sense that something was missing, something he was expecting. He thought it might be from a dream he'd had because the feeling itself was a familiar one. He'd check his journals next time he had the chance.

He looked at his watch, realized it was time to meet Gerson, and headed back across the field.

When he reached the cordoned-off area again, a mist similar to what he saw that morning near where Laddie's ghost had been drifted between him and Prue's house, not like ground fog rising from the field, not wide and low, but a patch of something that wasn't quite even mist, more a haze, something vaguely different from the surrounding air. He walked toward it. It didn't disappear and it didn't become clearer. He hesitated, then put his hand out, foolish maybe, definitely not careful, but if he was learning anything about the world he lived in these days, it was that careful wasn't the only path.

He felt a snap, like an electric shock, then an intense cold, like he'd plunged his hand into a bucket of ice-cold water. He had a quick sense of something dark and old; then it was gone along with the mist.

When he got back to the street, Gerson was pulling up behind his car.

"Thanks for driving," she said as Boyd unlocked his SUV.

* * *

The entrance to the Sigurdson ranch was bounded by two stone pillars with bronze eagles, their wings spread a full six feet wide, perched on top of them. Arching above was a sign that read FLYING DOUBLE EAGLE with crossed branding irons: double chevrons with wingtips.

The ranch itself could be seen from the county road, a quarter mile back and to the north. The pasture in front housed a small herd of Angus steers gathered around two round bale feeders. Near the house was a big horse barn with brick running along the base and a large paddock attached. The house itself was also brick to the windows, split logs above with a massive front porch and big windows facing west. Not new, but remodeled in the last few years so it looked new with a stone chimney on the south side.

On the drive out, Boyd and Gerson had talked about what they both knew: Tel Sigurdson was in a twenty-year-old picture along with Prue Stalking Horse, Laddie Kennedy, William Packer, and a woman they hadn't identified yet, that the phone in the Sigurdson barn had been one of the numbers Prue called the night she died. Boyd told Agent Gerson what Hallie had told him, that Brett had seen Tel that same night in West Prairie City and what Meg Otis had told him, that the Sigurdsons had invested heavily in Uku-Weber and were currently having cash-flow problems.

"His hands told us he was in Pierre," Gerson said.

"Yeah," Boyd said. "I think he was in town two nights ago when my house exploded too."

Gerson looked grim. She asked Boyd what he personally knew about Tel and the Sigurdson ranch.

"Whether he's having cash problems right now, in general, he's got more money than anyone else in the county," Boyd offered. "But he's generally well liked. Goes to church on Sundays. Gives money to the volunteer fire department every year to put together a Christ-

mas party for local kids. He funds a couple of scholarships for gradu-
ating seniors. He's involved in anything of significance that happens
in West PC."

"Huh," Gerson said in a tone that implied that funding Christmas
parties or local charities or buying drinks at roadhouses didn't mean
you couldn't kill people with a long-range rifle in your spare time,
which Boyd had to agree was pretty much true.

Tel Sigurdson and a ranch hand Boyd didn't recognize came out
of the tack room as Boyd pulled into the graveled area next to the
barn. Tel was tall, probably in his early fifties, wearing a tan Stetson,
a tin cloth field jacket, leather work gloves, and blue jeans. The ranch
hand—Boyd was momentarily surprised to see that it was a woman,
then surprised that he was surprised—was wearing a hooded sweatshirt with a sheepskin-lined vest over the top, flannel-lined jeans with
turned-up cuffs, and a bright green wool cap with the earflaps turned
down. She took the coil of rope that Tel had been holding and headed
off around the near side of the barn, only casually interested in Boyd's
SUV and who might be in it.

The wind hit like the blast from a deep freeze when Boyd got out
of the car. He heard the low thunk of the passenger-side door and the
crunch of Gerson's shoes on the frozen gravel as she rounded the car.
Tel tipped his hat back when he saw who it was. "Deputy," he said,
his voice reserved, which was unusual for Tel. He was one of those
people everyone knew, everyone had a story about, and almost all
the stories were good or at least not bad.

Boyd introduced Special Agent Gerson. Tel nodded once in her
direction, then turned his attention back to Boyd, as if Gerson, coming in from outside, might be less trustworthy. "Laddie Kennedy was
shot and killed yesterday," Boyd said.

"I heard that," Tel said. "It's a damned shame. That boy never
had any luck, not his whole life. Got any idea yet who did it?"

"That's what we want to talk to you about," Boyd said.

Tel gave a quick laugh. "Don't tell me you think I had anything to do with it?"

Boyd didn't smile back. "Two deaths, both shot, and close together," he said. "It's not a laughing matter."

Tel gave him a hard, level gaze. "No," he agreed. He glanced quickly up at the house. "Let's not stand out here in the cold. We can talk in my office."

He led them through the tack room and into a small but well-furnished office with an old oak desk, two leather chairs, an expensive wool rug, and a gas fireplace, which he turned on as they entered with a switch by the door. Tel hung his hat and coat on hooks, gestured for Boyd and Gerson to do the same, then ushered them into the leather chairs by the fireplace while he perched himself on the edge of his desk. He looked relaxed, easy, but Boyd could see the way his mouth formed a thin hard line and he kept looking at the wall above the fireplace and not at Boyd or Gerson.

Boyd waited for Gerson to say something, but when he looked over, she seemed to be busying herself with her pen. He tapped his right index finger against the left cuff of his jacket, then said, "The night Prue Stalking Horse was shot."

"A week ago," Tel said, interrupting him.

"Yes," Boyd said. "Early Wednesday morning. She called you Tuesday evening."

"No," Tel said steadily. "She didn't."

"You have a phone out here."

"Oh." Boyd thought he could see something, a certain relaxation of an expression he hadn't realized was tense. "Everyone uses it." He waved a hand toward an old-fashioned wall phone near the coat hooks. "She could have been calling anyone."

"We expect she was trying to call you," Boyd said, though he didn't think any of them had any evidence that this was true, just questions layered on questions.

"I wasn't here," Tel said. "Pat and I were over in Pierre at an estate auction."

"Would she have known that?"

Tel looked amused. "Are you asking if we lived in each other's pockets, Deputy? She didn't know my cell number. Didn't have any reason to. And I don't know any reason she'd have known where I was that night."

"So she could have been trying to reach you when she called your barn number?"

"Could have been, I guess." Tel folded his arms across his chest.

"We have a witness who says you were in town the night Prue died."

"The hell you say," Tel responded, but his eyes shifted left, away from Boyd's, as he said it. "Someone says they saw me at three o'clock in the morning in West Prairie City?"

"Four."

"Four. Well, hell, they were probably drunk."

"They weren't drunk."

Tel shrugged like he didn't set much store by the witness or Boyd either. He stood and walked to the fireplace, where he opened a small panel to the left of the hearth and fiddled with the controls.

"Were you in West Prairie City on the night Prue Stalking Horse was killed?" Boyd asked.

"Pat and I went to Pierre that morning to an estate auction." Which was exactly what he'd already said.

"That's not what I asked," Boyd said.

"You think someone saw me here," Tel said. "I'm saying they were mistaken."

"We'll need to talk to your wife," Gerson said. "For verification."

"Sure," Tel said. His voice flat. "She's gone on over to Sioux Falls to visit her sister, but she'll be back the end of next week."

"If you give me the address, I'll send an agent over to talk to her," Gerson said.

Tel looked at her; then he went to his desk, scrawled something on a blue notepad, tore off the top sheet, and handed it to her.

"Thank you," she said.

Boyd said, "I understand you're having cash-flow problems."

That actually made Tel laugh. "My whole life is cash-flow problems, Deputy. I've never killed anyone over it yet. I heard you've been having some housing problems yourself," Tel said, still turned toward the fireplace.

"Heard it? Or saw it?" Boyd asked. He generally liked Tel, though he didn't know him well, but he wasn't sure what game he was playing now. If he'd been in town two nights ago or the night Prue had died, why didn't he just say so?

A ranch hand entered the room, a tall man with a dark face and big hands. A battered Stetson shaded his eyes. He didn't say anything, just came into the room, moved to one side, and closed the door behind him.

Tel turned away from the fireplace, glanced at the silent ranch hand and said with the hint of a smile. "I told you, Deputy. I went to Pierre a week ago to an estate auction. I bought a feed wagon and three sets of oak bookcases. You can check."

Boyd stood. His back deliberately to the ranch hand and the door, facing Tel square. "Stop stonewalling me," he said.

"I'm not sure what you're talking about, Deputy."

26

In the general way of things, Boyd was more patient than most men. He asked questions and gauged reactions, came back with a new set of questions or the same questions asked a different way. But not today. Today, two people were dead. He had a hole the size of Cleveland in the side of his house. Hallie had Death knocking at her door, and he couldn't even begin to do anything about that. But this? This was something he was getting to the bottom of.

"We have a photograph," he began. "We found it with Laddie Kennedy. It was a picture of—"

Again, Tel interrupted him. "Oh, I know what it's a picture of. Laddie called me about that picture last week." He rubbed the back of his neck; then he let out a long sigh, leaned back so his shoulders rested against the fireplace mantel. He looked across the room at Agent Gerson, who was sitting comfortably in her chair, somehow managing to watch Tel and the ranch hand both.

"To tell you the truth," Tel finally said. "I haven't seen that photograph in at least fifteen years. Back then . . ." He paused. "Well, back then, when that picture was taken, I'd just turned thirty-five. Laddie was maybe twenty-three, twenty-four, and he'd just gotten out of the army. Prue wasn't new in town, but something had changed recently about her, like she'd learned some basic secret about the world."

"And the other people?" Boyd asked. "There were five of you in the picture."

"Is that really important?" Tel asked. He looked at Gerson, looked back at Boyd.

"We don't know what's important," Boyd said. "Right now, everything's important."

"Laddie carries a stone," Tel said.

"I know," Boyd said. Then, he added, "Agent Gerson knows too."

Tel nodded, but didn't say anything. He pushed himself away from the fireplace and began to pace. Finally, he looked at the ranch hand by the door as if he'd just realized the man was standing there. He waved a hand, like a silent signal, and the man went back out the office door as quietly as he'd entered. Tel stopped pacing, back in front of the fireplace again.

"You say you know about Laddie's rock," he said, his voice gone two levels quieter. "Do you really know?"

"I know dead people talked to him," Boyd said evenly.

Tel huffed out something almost like a laugh. "Yeah. Lucky Laddie. That was what we called him, you know, back then. Not because he was. Lucky, I mean. Or, I mean, that was why. Because he was never lucky. Not after he got that stone."

Tel shook his head. "Crazy thing. He and Prue were dating—I bet you didn't know that. She was a little older than he was, but you wouldn't know it to look at her. Laddie'd told her about the stone— well, hell, Laddie'd tell anybody, wasn't a secret—and Prue come to me, had an idea, she told me. Told me she'd been doing some research and she thought there might be other stones, that there might be a way to make some money."

"From the stones?" Boyd asked.

Tel nodded. "I couldn't see it myself. I mean, let's say I believed what Laddie said about that stone—that he could hear the dead talk.

But saying I did, what good was it? How could you make money off it? But Prue thought she had an answer to that, said the stones would manifest—that's exactly the word she used too—that they'd manifest differently depending on the person they attached themselves to."

"What were—what are the stones? How do they—?" Boyd wasn't even sure what the question was. "How do they work? Who makes them?"

"The way it was explained to me," Tel said, like he'd learned it in a classroom, "the stones hold magic. Like a sink. A magic sink." Which Boyd already knew, but it didn't tell him much.

"Where do they come from?" Boyd asked.

Tel leaned against one of the windows and didn't answer right away. He looked down at his boots. Everything he wore fit like it had been tailored, but nothing was new, like he bought his shirts and his jeans and his boots to last, then he used them up and wore them out. Tel was a working rancher, albeit one of the few with money. He looked up.

"You don't know this, neither of you." He looked from Boyd to Gerson. "You know my son, Brian," he said to Boyd, who nodded. "I had a daughter too, would have been twenty-five the end of next month. Christmas kid. Or, just two days after. But she got her own day. We made sure she didn't feel like her birthday wasn't a big deal. She was our oldest, you know, and we thought, then, we'd have a big family—five, six kids, maybe. Ranch has got room, you know, for kids. Things to do and they keep each other company. Pat and me, we both—" He stopped, shook his head, one sharp motion, like waking himself up.

"Well, none of that matters now. Nothing gets done or undone that's already happened. Barbie—that was her name—Barbie had a brain tumor. Inoperable. We'd more or less just found out about it when Prue Stalking Horse come around talking about magic stones and there was Laddie with one of these stones and I believed Laddie because Laddie doesn't—didn't—" He corrected himself. "Didn't know how to lie. If Laddie Kennedy told you something, you could believe it. He might have been better off if he had lied." He paused, considered the man and woman in front of him, and continued. "I thought it was worth a chance, you know. Like Mayo Clinic and this place in Mexico we looked into. You try everything. I thought, what the hell."

He stared into the fireplace. "It was the money and it wasn't the money. If it worked, if something magic could cure her, then the money didn't matter. If it didn't work, then the money didn't matter either, but it was all tangled up together like somehow helping Barbie depended on helping Prue and Laddie and whatever it was they were trying to do. You understand?"

His expression held a sort of mute appeal, like he knew there was no logic, hadn't been at the time, but Boyd nodded because he did understand—sometimes you did everything you could think of precisely because you knew none of them would work.

Tel left the fireplace and went over to the window. Snow swirled, but not heavy, light enough that it might have been blowing off the ground rather than falling from the skies.

"What happened?" Boyd asked.

"I've never been entirely sure," Tel said. "The way it was explained to me, the stones have to be a certain type—granite, some particular proportion of quartz and feldspar. There's a lot of it up in the Black Hills, but it's not anything special in the regular scheme of things. If it hasn't been 'charged,' I guess you'd call it, with magic, it's just rock. So what Prue and her sister were trying to do—oh, and Billie Packer—was figure out how to charge the stones. They thought they could use Laddie's stone. Reverse engineer it, so to speak." He laughed. "That should have told me something right there. Because magic isn't something you can engineer. Think about it. If it works at all, it's not going to work like engineering."

"So, Prue and her sister figured out how to—what? Store magic?"

Tel wiped his hand down his face. "You know Jasper? The tornado?"

Boyd nodded.

"You know that happened in the fall, right? Practically winter. They said it was a freak storm, came up out of nowhere. Yeah, it wasn't natural."

Boyd leaned forward. This was a new thing, something he'd never heard talked about. And Taylor County was a place that talked about things. "That was Prue Stalking Horse?"

Tel shook his head. "She says—said—not. And I gotta say, it was right after that they took Lillian Harper Jones away—that was Martin Weber's grandmother. Always figured it was her somehow, though I didn't really know how—well, she pretty much said it was even if no one believed her. Except apparently the Weber kid. No, it was what happened after. I was out of it at that point, desperate, sure, but . . ." There was something haunted in his expression as he looked at Boyd. "You don't talk about it straight out. You get hauled away, you do that. But, people died in that tornado. They never had a chance. I figured it was past time to walk away.

"Of course, if I'm being honest, I have to say I might have gone back. Might have begged. I don't know. Prue told me they were going forward with or without me. She said she'd come back, tell me how great it worked, said I'd pay anything then. And maybe I would have. But she never did."

"Never came back?"

"Never mentioned it to me again. Her sister disappeared. Billie Packer disappeared. The Jones place burned. And it was like it never happened. We took Barbie over to Mayo about then and we were gone two months altogether and not really talking to anyone for a good while after that. So, I don't know what people were saying—whatever it was, they weren't saying it to us."

"What do you think happened?" Boyd asked.

Tel walked back to sit on the desk again. He looked Boyd straight in the eye as he spoke. "I think that tornado charged those stones. I think Prue and her sister and Billie Packer tried to use them. I think something went bad wrong out there at that old farmhouse. I think Billie Packer died and Prue killed him. Or she might as well have."

There was a long moment of silence. Tel's sequence of events was speculation at best, but it made a certain amount of sense to Boyd. The questions he was left with were: What did the events of twenty years ago have to do with Prue's and Laddie's deaths in the present, and where was Prue's sister?

"This picture," Gerson said, taking a copy of the photograph from her purse and offering it to Tel. "Can you identify the people in it?"

Tel didn't take the picture. Didn't even look at it. "There's me and Laddie Kennedy," he said, "which you already know, and Prue Stalking Horse. The big man in the back would have been Billie Packer. He wasn't the brightest kid and he never had any ambition, but that's a hell of a way to end, rotting away in someone's cellar. Prue said he had the touch, that was why they kept him around, I think."

Boyd took the picture from Gerson and looked at it again. "'All the talents,' what does that mean?" he asked.

"It was about the others, not me. I was the money guy. But it was the stone, you know. Prue would hand it to people who came in and ask them what they thought."

"What did you think?" Boyd asked.

Tel laughed. "I wouldn't touch it. I just looked at it and told her it was not something I wanted to have anything to do with. She smiled, like she already knew everything she needed just from that, like I'd only done exactly what she'd expected, and said that was fine. Wish I'd known then," he said.

"The other woman in the picture?" Gerson said. "That's Ms. Stalking Horse's sister?"

Tel nodded his head once, as if he was remembering. "Yep. Shannon. That was her name. Came over from St. Paul or Minneapolis, someplace like that, after Prue had got me to agree to front some money at that point, which was when the picture was taken. They were close back then, she and Prue. Odd gal. Intense. She had this scarf she wore winter and summer—well, you can see it in that picture." He finally took the picture and looked at it. "You can't tell in this anymore, but it was this incredibly bright blue. She'd wear it with everything—flannel shirts, fancy dress, whatever. Meant a lot to her, I guess. It's the thing I remember most about her now."

"Wait," Boyd said. "What?" He took the picture back and looked at it again. Tel was right: It was impossible to tell what colors things had been from the picture, but Boyd could see now what had looked so familiar when he'd seen this picture the first time. He hadn't seen her hair and she'd been wearing a heavy coat. "I've seen her," he said. Though he hadn't or it hadn't exactly been her, couldn't have been, because the woman he'd seen would have been about the same age as the woman in the picture.

"Excuse me," he said.

He stepped outside, called Ole on his cell phone, and asked him to check a license plate, giving him the plate number he'd noted last Friday outside Prue Stalking Horse's house. When he was finished, he went back into the office, where it looked like Tel and Gerson hadn't said one word or even looked at each other while he was gone. He picked up where he'd left off.

"Did Prue's sister have any children?" he asked.

"Shannon? I don't think so," Tel said, as if the thought hadn't ever occurred to him. "She wasn't that old when I knew her. Maybe your age, maybe a little younger. No, she didn't. I'm sure she didn't. Hell, I don't know."

Boyd looked at Gerson, but he didn't want to say more until later.

Gerson gave a small nod and took the photograph back. "Thank you for your time, Mr. Sigurdson," she said. "You've been very helpful. If you think of anything else, please call the sheriff's office. And we'll be verifying everything with your wife," she added. "Tell her to expect our call."

When they left the office, the day had turned darker, the wind strong, dry, and bitter cold.

Boyd didn't know how he knew, but the minute they walked out the door, he could feel it, not even words, just a thing that he knew in that instant.

"Get down!" he shouted, and tackled Tel, knocking him into the iron-hard ground as something thwacked into the doorjamb behind them. A startled *oof* from Tel, and Boyd was up and running, using the cover of his SUV and one of the ranch trucks parked at an angle to his own vehicle and the house.

Gerson shouted at him, "Davies!"

Careful, he told himself, the caution unnecessary, but it was the kind of thing he did tell himself. Whoever it was had a gun. Probably a good deal longer range than his service pistol. Careful. He crept around the corner of the house, not because the killer was that close; Boyd was certain whoever it was, wasn't very close at all—a thousand yards maybe, across the big field, close to the road. But he wanted to catch a glimpse of the car they were driving, and he didn't want to get shot while he was doing it. Gradually, he became aware of the sound of his own breathing, of the wind burning his face. He put his back against the rough stone wall of the house, looked at the empty road, looked back at the barn, where Gerson was helping Tel to his feet.

Prue Stalking Horse. Laddie Kennedy. And now, Tel Sigurdson.

Maybe Tel Sigurdson, he corrected himself. Tel wasn't dead, after all. It could be a setup. One of his ranch hands? To turn suspicion away from him?

But why? And how would he have done it?

Boyd listened, thought maybe he'd hear a vehicle engine even if he couldn't see one. Though where someone could conceal a vehicle within a mile or even two of Tel's ranch house, he wasn't sure. Whoever this was had parked somewhere out of sight, walked up the road, and waited. Even though it was likely that if Boyd hadn't been here, no one would have looked as he was looking now, their attention completely taken by the sight of Tel on the ground, a bullet through his brain. Even though. They'd planned for it. Prepared for it. Because they were careful.

Or it was a setup.

He heard it then, thin and clear on the wind, the sound of a car engine, somewhere west past the line of cottonwoods near the creek. Boyd waited until the sound faded; then he walked back around the house and returned to the barn.

Tel said, "What the hell was that?"

"Do you have one of the stones?" Boyd ignored his question. "If you do, you need to show it to me now."

Tel bent down and picked up his Stetson, which had been knocked off when Boyd tackled him. "No, hell no. I told you." He dusted off the crown of his hat. "I got out before things went to hell."

"Or maybe you found your own stone and didn't need Prue Stalking Horse or her sister or any of them anymore."

For the first time, Tel looked really angry. "If that were so, my daughter would still be alive."

"But she isn't. Do you blame Prue for that? Did you hate her enough to kill her?"

"What the hell are you talking about? Someone just tried to kill me."

"Or you want it to look like someone did."

"Oh, hell," Tel said.

"Mr. Sigurdson." Gerson spoke for the first time since shouting Boyd's name. She'd been watching Boyd steadily, like he was hiding something or planning something, and she didn't take her eyes off him now as she was speaking. "You've admitted that you were acquainted with both the victims and possibly with the person whose remains we found in Ms. Stalking Horse's cellar, which we've confirmed belonged to a William Packer. We have witnesses who can place you in West Prairie City on the nights in question."

Boyd looked at Gerson. Tel took a step forward and stopped, as if he didn't know exactly what to do next. Boyd could see what he was thinking written clearly on his face: Hadn't she been listening? To anything?

"Someone just tried to kill me," Tel said.

"It certainly appeared that way," Gerson said.

"I didn't just try to kill myself," Tel tried again.

"It doesn't rule out the possibility of an accomplice, however," Gerson said.

Tel looked at her, looked hard at Boyd as if he should intervene, but why? He'd just asked the same question himself.

"You know what? Talk to my goddamned lawyer," Tel said, slapped his Stetson on his head, and stalked away from them to the house.

Gerson looked at Boyd. "Sometimes anger is revealing," she said.

"I don't have an evidence kit with me," Boyd said.

"What?"

"The bullet. We're going to want that."

Gerson gave a quick nod. "Right," she said. "Of course."

27

It was a dry cold morning as Hallie headed toward the Badlands. She had her shotgun and an iron fireplace poker and the empty seat beside her. She could have let Boyd come with her; that would have been easy. She'd have liked him with her, someone she knew she could rely on, who would do the right thing, provided he could figure out what that was—and he would figure it out, because that was part of Boyd, knowing the right thing and doing it.

As she drove, she saw a dead deer on the side of the road and a dead coyote. She saw a dead Angus steer in the ditch and she stopped, grabbed the iron poker as she got out for a closer look. Roadkill wasn't unusual, was pretty common—empty roads and fast pickup trucks. It happened. Dead cattle were different, not that they didn't sometimes get hit, but it did a lot of damage, to the car and to the animal. This steer didn't look like that. And it wasn't on the road or even the edge of the road. There were no skid marks and there weren't any bits of broken glass or plastic. Hallie approached the body cautiously.

It was cold enough and dry enough that there weren't many flies—something had chewed a bit on one leg, but the corpse itself was still fresh. Not hit by a car, definitely not. Aside from the leg, the steer was unmarked, like it had fallen where it stood. There was a smell—and not the steer—that seemed familiar. Like gunpowder, but not exactly. Not quite sulfur either. Much of the grass had been trampled—deer and cattle, probably—but Hallie could see a line, less meandering, less like a place something bedded for the night and more like something traveling from one place to another. She moved farther into the field. Maker appeared at her side.

It sneezed.

"Do you smell that?" Hallie asked. "What is it?"

"Death," Maker said matter-of-factly.

"Well, you're here and there's a dead cow. So, yes. Death all over, I'd say." But then she looked more closely at the dead steer and the surrounding area. The grass and undergrowth were all dead, but that was as it should be in March in western South Dakota. She made a circle and she was out almost ten yards from the dead steer when she began to notice it. A dead hawk, three dead voles, a dead rabbit, and some mutiflora rose that looked like all the moisture had been sucked out of it. In the middle of the field now, she looked back toward the road; all of it, the dead animals, the rosebushes, the dead steer, were within a ten-foot path pointing straight through the field to the road.

Hallie remembered Travis Hollowell, how the reaper magic he wielded drew the life from living things, from birds and animals and even grass and trees, for its power.

"Is it a reaper?" Hallie asked. "What does it want?"

"Not a reaper," Maker said, and sneezed.

"Unmaker?" God.

Maker said nothing, which either meant she was right, or it wasn't going to say.

"So, unmakers in the world just kill things?"

"Unmakers *being* in the world kills things," Maker said.

"Abominations." Hallie almost laughed. In the under *she* was the abomination. "Why?" Hallie said. "I mean I know what it wants, but why does it come? How does it come?"

"You."

"I know that," she said impatiently. "Because it wants me to re-place Death."

"Because you're here."

"What?"

"It leaves a crack."

"What? Me in the world? Because I'm not dead? Is that why you're here?" she asked.

"Maybe," Maker said.

"Maybe you don't know or maybe you're not telling me?"

Maker sniffed the air. "Should go."

"Is something coming?" Maker had already gone.

Hallie turned slowly, but she didn't see anything except grass, open prairie, and the dead Angus steer. She headed back to the truck anyway.

A crack. Because she was here. What did it really mean, though? That the walls between the worlds could open up again? That saying no to Death's offer would thin the walls in the same way Martin Weber's magic had? There had been a time in her life when the world hadn't been all that complicated—do the job and get back home. Even if sometimes getting home had been difficult or even danger-ous, it was knowable. Doable. Things weren't that way anymore.

As she got back into the pickup and started it up, a coyote emerged from the tall grass maybe thirty yards in front of her. It stood on the shoulder, looking at her, like it expected something. She put the truck in gear, pulled onto the road again, and the coyote stood its ground. She slowed as she passed. She felt like it was telling or asking her something—I don't know, she wanted to say. I'm doing the best I can.

At the northeast entrance to the Badlands, Hallie pulled to the side of the road again. She told Boyd once that she'd never been to the Badlands, which wasn't strictly true, because they were close for

South Dakota definitions of close, and it was a place people drove past on their way to other places. It was hard not to go there. Though mostly Hallie didn't.

She'd been in the mountains in Afghanistan and once on leave to Switzerland and hiked in the Alps. She could acknowledge that those mountains were beautiful, particularly from a distance, and standing at the top of a mountain or the entrance to a valley could be breathtaking, everything spread out before her, like the promise of a new life. But in the pass, between the mountains, on winding roads leading up or down, everything seemed small and sharp and danger-ous, closed in until she wondered if there were something wrong with what she was seeing because her eyes kept trying to find the distant horizon and there was no horizon to find. Hallie preferred the prairie, everything right out in the open. She liked a distant horizon, big sky, big weather, and a sense of vastness and possibility.

The Badlands weren't mountains, more like prairie interrupted by great upthrust rock, the rock weathered by storms and long win-ters. But it had those same closed-in spaces, that same feeling that something was going to happen and there would be no escape. Still, it was beautiful. Even this morning, with gray sky leaching the color from everything, it was beautiful, starkly black and gray and white, no color clear to the horizon, which was foreshortened by the cha-otic expanse of rock. Tiny snowflakes, dry and light, landed on the windshield, only to be whipped away by the wind.

As Hallie put the truck in gear and eased onto the loop road, two things happened—or the same thing happened twice—Maker leaped in through the passenger window, and a ghost drifted into the pickup cab, bringing a deep cold like arctic ice.

Maker sneezed, then sat with its back against the door. "You don't have to come, you know," Hallie said. "If you're worried about being unmade or something."

"Might be interesting," Maker responded.

Hallie laughed. "It might," she agreed.

The ghost, a woman, looked old, as in died a long time ago, not old in years lived. She looked vaguely Lakota, though skin color and even subtleties of hair color were lost on ghosts. She wore a pale shirt and a long dark skirt and wore her hair in a single thick braid down her back. She wore no jewelry, which might have helped Hallie pin down her background and era, and her shirt and skirt were both plain. She was just . . . there, just floating in the middle of the seat, spilling cold and waiting, though Hallie had no idea what she was waiting for.

"Okay," Hallie said. "Okay."

A quarter mile later, Laddie's ghost drifted into the cab too. Two ghosts, a harbinger of death, and Hallie. If she didn't get to where she was going soon, she might freeze to death in her own pickup truck with the heater on high.

A car passed her going well over the speed limit. It cut back so sharply, Hallie had to hit the brakes. She got only a quick glimpse as it passed, but it looked like an old Mercury sedan with one rusted-out taillight.

Maker bared its teeth at her. "Stinks," it said.

"I wouldn't be surprised," Hallie said.

She stopped at the Big Badlands Overlook. The Mercury that had passed her earlier pulled out as she pulled in. The car had tinted windows, and she couldn't see who was inside or even whether there was more than one person.

Maker sneezed again.

Hallie looked at him. The Badlands formations held lots of fossils, lots of death, years and years of animals that had died. People had probably died here too, though not so distinctly or noticeably. Maker sneezed a third time, shook its head as though shaking off something unpleasant, then it disappeared. Lots of death, Hallie thought. Probably unmakers too. Well, that was okay. That was what she'd come for.

She sat in the truck with the engine running for several minutes as she studied the map. If she headed northwest from here for about three-quarters of a mile, she ought to end up pretty close to the coordinates the notes directed her to.

She stared out the windshield at the cold and starkly barren landscape. If Death were going to come in some way other than jumbled dreams, she thought maybe he'd do it here—in this tangled chaotic place. And he would come, sooner or later. It was time. Even if she feared what it meant and the price it demanded.

The unknown ghost drifted close to Hallie's shoulder and even through the thickness of her wool-lined barn coat, she could feel the cold, straight through to her bones. She pulled on a wool cap and gloves, turned the collar up on her coat, and buttoned it across her neck. A fierce north wind almost whipped the door out of her hand when she opened it. The ghosts drifted away from her so that, except for the biting north wind, it didn't feel all that much colder outside the truck than in it.

Hallie hesitated, but decided not to take the shotgun she carried in the saddle box in the bed of the pickup. She did grab the iron fireplace poker and struck out into the Badlands, sticking the marked-up paper map in the inside pocket of her coat. Snow, stirred up by the brisk wind, trailed across the open space between rock formations. Things changed constantly in the Badlands as the rocks eroded from wind and rain and hard dry winters. It felt desolate in a way that the open prairie never did to Hallie. The prairie was big, but it was a big that signaled promise and potential. This just felt broken and empty, like something had ripped the life from it long ago, though Hallie conceded that it might be the season. It might look different here when everything wasn't frozen and the sky wasn't battleship gray overhead.

Laddie's ghost drifted in front of her, like it had a single important destination in mind. The other ghost, the one that had floated into the truck at the entrance to the Badlands, disappeared, as if Hallie wasn't exactly what it had been waiting for, or it would wait for another time, or it would return again in that random way ghosts seemed to have—there, then not, then there again. Maker trotted beside her, sniffing at a narrow dry rivulet that ran a winding path through the dirt. It moved down the rivulet for several dozen yards, took one last deep sniff, then turned and trotted back.

"What?" Hallie asked.

"Not Death," Maker said, like that was an answer.

"Not Death the entity? Or not death, the dying?"

Maker looked at her, like it couldn't understand the question.

"Not. Death," it repeated, like, catch up, lady.

"Okay," Hallie said. "Thanks."

She needed to walk just under two miles north and west from the pull-in where she'd parked to reach the coordinates she'd been given. Simple, if she were able to walk in a straight line, but there were no straight lines. She had to climb over and around rock formations. The day was cloudy; no sun to take bearings on, and she was glad she'd grabbed an old compass before she left the house.

She came through a narrow gap between two rock formations, the ground rough underfoot, as if where she was walking had once been a rock formation too, though it had obviously worn completely down to nothing over the years. Stretching in front of her for maybe an eighth of a mile was an open expanse of short-grass prairie.

Hallie estimated that she was close now. The unknown ghost reappeared, but on the opposite side of the open space, drifting against gray rock, only visible by its movements, like ripples on water. Hallie could feel Laddie's ghost behind her, cold like winter at her back. There was no one else. Nothing moving but the ghosts and Maker and Hallie herself as far as she could see.

As she crossed into the open, a burst of wind sent dirt swirling upward along the rock face and straight toward Hallie so that she had to turn and duck her head. Particles of soil rattled against her back and scoured along her neck and face. Then the wind was gone, the dirt settled back to the hard ground. Hallie blinked and scrubbed the grit away.

Maker growled.

Hallie's hand gripped the poker. Nothing. Empty space and rock and cloud-gray sky. No sound except the far-off scream of a rabbit cut off abruptly. The poker was cold; the fingers on her hand ached. She didn't like this place—this particular spot in this particular place. She checked her map. Straight across the open and past the next rock outcropping. She pulled up the collar on her coat, tucked her chin down, and moved forward again.

A loud percussive thump, like something massive thumping onto the Earth—

"Don't," Maker said.

"What? Why? What the hell was that?" Hallie scanned the area. Rock all around. Maker stared at a broad gap between upthrust rock, the one on the left cantilevering precipitously so that the space beneath it lay in perpetual shadow.

"Magic," Maker said. "Here. Stinks."

"I should have brought a gun," Hallie said.

"Yes," Maker agreed.

"Jesus."

Another sharp rush of wind, dirt swirling around Hallie and Maker, like bitter rain. Hallie ducked her head; when she raised it again, she turned slowly so she could see everything there was to see, limited by the rock formations. It was quiet, except for the wind and the sweep of dirt and grass. When she was satisfied that they were alone, she said, "I thought magic was either small, nothing to worry about, or huge."

Maker sneezed. "You don't know," it said.

"Yeah, I *don't* know," Hallie said. "You could tell me." The unknown ghost was back, drifting at Hallie's right. Laddie's ghost was gone. "Do you still smell it? Magic? Or is it gone now?"

Maker raised its nose and sniffed the air. The clouds above their heads were so low and so thick that they felt oppressive, like they pressed her down, like they pressed the world down. The air felt damp, as if real snow were coming, though there hadn't been anything in the forecast. The sky spit snowflakes at them, but so tiny and so dry that it could snow all day and there would still be nothing on the ground.

Maker sneezed again, then trotted into the gap, right underneath the cantilevered stone. Hallie with a half shrug, because she was probably getting deeper into something she didn't want to be involved in and that would end badly, followed. Maker led her through the gap, then through a narrow crevice between two tight rock formations. Halfway through, she had to turn sideways.

It grew darker; the clouds felt as if they were sitting right on top of the rocks above her. Soft rock scraped against the back of her jacket. Maker stopped. The unknown ghost stopped. Hallie stopped. Laddie's ghost was back and it bumped against her shoulder. She didn't want to walk through a ghost, cold on cold, like the worst winter storm in the history of all storms. Then she heard Maker yelp. She plunged forward. Cold air seared through her lungs, like she'd just dived into a lake full of ice. Short, sharp breaths and then she was through, still gasping but already looking for Maker.

It was backed up against the rocks, talus scattered around its feet and a snarl on its lips, staring at a spot directly to Hallie's left. Both ghosts followed her, cold like fire along her spine.

The space widened out to her left into another flat open area, this one mostly rock, like a rock formation had crumbled but left gravel and shards of stone strewn across the resulting space. Maybe thirty yards beyond where she stood was a skeleton. Not the skeleton of a person, or of anything Hallie had ever seen before. The rib cage, which was the most readily visible portion of the skeleton, curved up from the rocky floor to nearly Hallie's height. The bones were the color of old strong tea, lines scored by wind and dirt.

She moved closer. Her hand ached and she realized that she had gripped the poker too tight again, though what use it would do here, she had no idea. She willed her fingers to relax, but it was as if they had disconnected themselves from her brain, and they remained clenched tight around the cold iron.

28

The air was filled with a low hum, like a thousand insects or a pair of high-tension electrical wires. The ever-present wind was light, though cold, like a gentle steady pressure urging her forward.

Fine particles of gray dirt drifted across the bones. The rib cage was huge, nearly two-thirds as tall as Hallie, and it wasn't even completely exposed, though judging by the curve of the bones, there was maybe only an additional two to three inches still buried. There was no skull, a few bones just above the rib cage that looked like vertebrae, some smaller bones on the side toward her that might be finger bones or part of a paw or—she wasn't close enough—they might be broken from larger bones.

She stepped forward.

"Stop."

Maker sat well back from the skeleton, almost at the curve of the rock formation, panting.

The wind died, the low hum with it.

Hallie trusted Maker. More or less. It was a black dog and a harbinger of death, but it had helped her when it didn't have to, had saved her life at least once. "What is this thing?" she asked.

Maker's mouth snapped closed and it cocked its head at her, like it was thinking about the answer. "You know," it said.

She glanced over at the ghosts, both of them drifting in the gap between rocks. Everything was still like collectively held breath—Maker and the ghosts waiting to see what she would do. Hallie herself waited, and that was—she was here because unmakers had threatened her, because they killed things simply by existing in the world. Because there was a crack in the walls between the worlds.

Because *she* was here.

She stepped up and touched the bones.

The pain knocked her to her knees, and the only thing she knew was that it wasn't her pain. Wind howled, a stormy night. She felt rain on her face. She was running, but there was something—what was wrong with the way she was running? It felt awkward and low, but she couldn't stop, it would be dangerous to stop. Lightning flashed, noonday bright, and she could see them, three of them. Their eyes glittered from the storm and something else, something that allowed them to see her. She had to run, to keep running. She could outrun them, if she didn't falter, if only she didn't falter. But the storm was getting worse; there had never been a storm like this one, never been rain like this. She would make it to the Badlands, she would lose them among the—

A sharp crack and she stumbled, righted herself, and went on, but slow, too slow.

And they were coming.

Someone shook her. What? Couldn't they—?

The wind howled. Shrieked. Like the middle of a blizzard. And maybe it was a blizzard, because something was hitting her. Snow? Was it snow? Where had it come from? Where was she?

She lurched to her feet. The world was gray. Someone in a hood shouted something at her, but she couldn't hear the words. The wind and the dirt—it was dirt, not snow—what the hell? The dirt scoured them. Hallie ducked her head and headed toward the dubious protection of the rock formations. The wind pushed her back, but she persisted. She lost sight of the other person. Her head bent low, her barn coat pulled up to cover her face, she stumbled forward.

She reached the rock face, slid along it by feel. Between the rock formations, the wind cut off so abruptly, she almost fell. Behind her it roared on, whipping up dirt like an angry god. She leaned against the rock and breathed.

Jesus.

Maker was beside her again.

"What just happened?" she asked.

But the dog didn't answer, just lay down and put its head between its paws.

After what Hallie estimated was five minutes or so, the wind swirling frantically around the skeleton died abruptly. Dirt fell, like a sudden cloudburst. Hallie waited a few more minutes, brushed one hand roughly through her hair to shake loose the dirt caught there, then reentered the open space. Something wet trickled down her face—blood from a thin cut above her eye. The palms of her hands were scraped and raw. The skeleton looked unchanged. Though dirt drifted high against the rocks behind it, the skeleton itself looked no more or less exposed than it had before Hallie touched it.

She walked around it—or as close as she could get, since the largest curve of its center rib was within inches of the rock face. She didn't touch it again. She took out her cell phone to take pictures, but the battery was completely drained.

Damnit.

"I was sure you'd be able to do it."

Well, son of a bitch.

264

Hallie turned around.

"I figured," Beth repeated, looking pretty much as she had when Hallie saw her in the cemetery, "I figured you'd be able to open it."

The clouds overhead were even thicker now, heavy and low. Snowflakes fell, larger, but still dry, still not quite sticking when they drifted to the ground, sifting into low spots, against rocks and into narrow crevices.

"This is the opening to the under? How did you find it? When?" Hallie asked.

"Just now, following you. I mean, I wasn't following you on purpose, but I know where you are, and when I realized you were headed to the Badlands, I knew. I mean, of course you knew right where it was. Because you can open it." She sounded so certain, a certainty Hallie'd probably had when she was Beth's age too.

"I had a little help getting here," Hallie said dryly.

"Of course you did," Beth said, like that was only what she'd expected.

"It's not going to open," Hallie said. "It just tried to kill me."

"It will."

Hallie turned to Maker.

"It didn't open, right? It's not going to open." Hoped more than believed. But if it were a door and it were going to open, wouldn't it just do it?

"You have to be able to see it." Which she could. "And you have to know what it is," Maker said.

"So, it's a door," she said skeptically. "Not a skeleton?"

"Both," Maker said. "It's the kind of skeleton that makes it a door."

"*What* kind of skeleton?"

Maker looked at her in that way that usually meant it wasn't going to answer, but finally it said, "Unmaker."

Well, of course.

"Let's get back out of the wind," she said. She was chill to the bone, and the wind, though not strong, was penetrating. It was a long way back to her truck and she had a feeling this was going to take a while.

They moved into the lee side of a rock outcropping that rose at a steep angle to a point at least twenty feet above their heads. Neither of the ghosts—Laddie or the one Hallie didn't know—were around, and for that Hallie was grateful. She shoved her hands as deep into her coat pockets as they would go, hunched her shoulders down, and said, "Beth, what do you see?"

"Me?" Beth asked. "Well, there's you. And that skeleton out there, if that's what you're asking. And the ghosts. And your dog."

"It's not my dog," Hallie said. But okay.

"You have to open it," Beth said.

"What makes you think I can?" Hallie asked.

"You can." Both Beth and Maker said it at the same time, one out loud and one in her head.

"You've been invited," Maker added.

Jesus.

"Okay, look," Hallie said. "Can I—?"

She heard a noise, that low hum again. In fact, she wasn't sure it was a noise at all; maybe it was something she could feel in her bones. She looked around, but she didn't see anything other than rocks and grass. And the skeleton.

"If I can open it, can I just go in, talk to Death, and come back out?"

Maker seemed to think.

"You don't need to go in," Beth said. "I'll go in."

"It sounds like *you* haven't been invited," Hallie said.

Beth bit her bottom lip. "I know where all the openings are. I can find people who've been touched by Death. I can see ghosts and reapers and that dog over there. If it takes me a while to figure out how to open a door on my own or to find someone else who can open one, I'll do it. I don't care. I won't quit." She paused again. "I thought you would understand."

"Why?" Hallie never wanted to go in there again. She turned to Maker. "If Beth goes in with me, can she come out again?"

"I don't want to come out," Beth insisted. "I know what I'm doing."

"No, you don't," Hallie said. "You don't know anything." She looked at Maker. "Can she?"

"Maybe," Maker said.

Which Hallie took to mean it didn't know.

"Look," Beth said, close now, her dark-rimmed eyes burning with intensity. "If it were you, would you want someone telling you what you meant and what you wanted?"

No. She wouldn't let anyone tell her. But this was— "You don't know," she said.

"I—I know I don't," Beth admitted. "But we don't belong here. Lily didn't and she always knew it. She died to save Boyd's life, but I don't think it was that hard, because it always feels like you're going to slip away, like you're holding on as tight as you can and you don't even know why or even that you're holding on because it's all you've got, it's all you've ever had and all you've ever felt. I never got that. I never understood. I thought it was just the way everyone felt, like the world was just this place you stayed a little while. And you stayed because that was how it worked. Not because you wanted to, but because you had to.

"But I don't belong here. Maybe I don't belong there either. I don't know. I don't know." She repeated it as if the entirety of what she didn't know demanded it. "It's not just about my father. I have an affinity for death." Which Hallie knew was true, had seen it herself in the cemetery with the ghosts. "Maybe I would have had a mostly normal life if Travis Hollowell hadn't come back, if I hadn't seen my father, if I'd never gone looking for answers. But all that happened and I'm not going back to who I was. That person doesn't exist anymore."

And Hallie knew about that too, about being someone you became and not someone you chose. She'd died once. She saw ghosts. She'd been to the underworld and returned. All of that was her. She couldn't give it back. She'd almost reached a point where she didn't want to.

With Laddie's ghost drifting against her back, it was all Hallie could do to keep her teeth from chattering. She appreciated what Beth was saying. But— "It's a sacrifice, Beth. I can't."

She wanted to. She wanted to stay here, on the ground in South Dakota, in Taylor County for a long, long time, wanted it more than she'd ever wanted anything. But she couldn't take it through someone else's sacrifice.

"Look," Beth said. "The problem for you is that Death asked you to take his place because you owe him, right? And you don't want to do it, but you do kind of owe him."

"Right," Hallie said, because she was right and it was hard to argue with it.

"On the other hand, I want to take his place, but he hasn't asked me. And you don't want me to take his place, because it lets you off the hook and feels like a cheat."

"Also right. And one more thing," Hallie added. "As long as this goes unresolved, there's a crack between the under and the world and the unmakers are coming through into this world, which is bad news and, I'm guessing, can only get worse."

Beth frowned. "I don't know what that means. The unmakers."

"They unmake things," Hallie said.

"Like the world?"

"Like reapers and harbingers. Dead things. But if they're in the world—our world—they kill everything. Just by being here. Maker says they're abominations." The word made her wince. She was an abomination too, like the inverse of an unmaker, which was something she didn't want to think too much about.

"Whoa." Beth considered. "So, okay, given that. And the whole Death invitation. Yeah. So, you're thinking you'll go in and do what? Say yes, so the world gets saved and the crack is fixed and no more unmakers and bad things?"

"Well, yes," Hallie said. It wasn't what she wanted to do. It was what she had to do.

"Well, that does seem like it might work." Beth gave a dry laugh. "If you had told me six months ago that any of this—any of this— existed, I'd have said you were nuts. But now . . . Hallie, I want to do this. You get to do what you want. I mean this is what you want. You know? It is. You don't want to lose the things you have, the people you have, the life you have. But you *want* to do this, go into the under again, talk to Death, take his place if you have to, because you think it's all obligation and duty and the right thing to do. And it is. I get that.

"But if you can do that, make that kind of decision, then so can I." She paused, rubbed her hands across her face, like she was trying to wipe things clean. "Look, look, let me go in. Let me talk to him. Just talk to him. You went in and came out. Boyd went in and came out. I can do it. I can. If he tells me no, I'll come out and it'll be between you and him again. But I want to ask. I want the chance."

"If you go in there, you'll forget. You won't be able to get back out. Boyd forgot everything."

"You didn't."

"Because I died."

DEBORAH COATES

"Well, I'm Death's daughter." And she sounded different when she said it, older and more confident, as if saying it, claiming it, especially here, made the difference. "And I got you through the ghosts, didn't I? I can do this."

"It's a big risk. I don't think you know how big."

"It's my risk. Mine. Don't take that away from me."

Shit.

"Look," Hallie said, not at all sure that what she was going to say was right or would work and was probably stupid anyway. "There's this guy I know. He's on the other side. *Should* be on the other side. Someone killed him last night and his ghost is still hanging around, so that means he hasn't passed on. This guy, I think he'll help you. I think he *can* help you. He knows more than you do and he won't forget as quickly. I mean he will forget. I think. But not as quick?" Though she had to phrase the last as a question because one trip into the under didn't mean she knew all that much, though it was possible it made her the leading expert in the field. "Laddie Kennedy. His name is Laddie Kennedy."

Beth's face lit, looking young and eager. "Really? You'll open it?"

"I think it's a mistake," Hallie said. "I think it's a *big* mistake. But it's your mistake." Which wasn't entirely true; if she opened it, it would be her mistake too. She'd be the one who made it possible. But she also believed Beth when she said she wouldn't stop, that she would eventually find a way and at least here, right now, there was a chance she'd have some help.

Maker touched her hand with its nose. She looked down. It didn't say anything, just sat and looked at her. "Can you help?" Hallie asked.

"I can watch," Maker said. "Maybe get her out."

"Okay," she said. "Thank you."

Maker turned around once and disappeared.

"Look," Hallie said to Beth, desperate now to say the one important thing that would make a difference. "You still might forget things when you go in. And when you come out, it has to be here where you went in. It has to be this way. I don't think the unmakers will bother you, because you're not dead and you're Death's daughter, which, frankly ought to count for something, but be careful. Okay?"

"Yes. Yes! Thank you." She seemed actually happy about the whole thing and it almost made Hallie change her mind about opening the door, because Beth really did have no idea.

Sometimes, though, you had to do something, and sometimes a stupid thing was the thing you had to do.

"Jesus," Hallie said. "Come on."

They walked between the rocks and over the rough ground, stopping only when they were standing between a large set of outcroppings just outside the open area where the skeleton lay. And it *was* a skeleton, still looked exactly like a skeleton.

It didn't look anything like a door.

Hallie crossed to the bones once more, studied them as closely as she could without touching them. There was something—she didn't want to say they looked too real, because that wasn't quite right—even now, even in the gray cloud-dimmed afternoon, there was something luminous about them, like a science-fictional hologram, except, of course, they were solid to the touch and, according to Maker, the actual bones of an unmaker.

Without thinking more about it, she reached out, grabbed hold of the skeleton, and pulled.

Pain, sharp and unrelenting, that was the same, but it was daytime, sun beating down and hot, so hot, too hot for people, for anyone, and there was no shade, nothing anywhere. It was sand, all sand, rising with the wind and so thick, it was impossible to see

271

through. She was on her feet, she was sure she was on her feet, but she couldn't see anything, stumbled and fell and something was hitting her, pushing at her. Go. Move. Get up now. She struggled up; something pushed her again. She could see shadows beside her, more than one. Stumbled, rose, stumbled again. And now it was cold and it was dirt, grinding against her skin, in her mouth, the cold taste of it.

Hallie crawled, the rough ground scraping her hands. When she reached a space that offered some protection from the wind and the grinding sand, it was like falling over a wall, so abrupt that it took her a minute to understand what had happened. The dust storm howled behind her, louder than thought, like the roar of jet engines. She tried to get up, couldn't do it, settled for breathing, leaned hard against a rock face, wanted to feel it against her back, something solid, something real. She tried to lift her arms, to rub her eyes, but she couldn't even feel her hands, wasn't sure they were attached to her anymore. Too hard, hard enough just to sit, to press her back against the rock, to be sure—she was sure—that she was in the world and not caught somewhere in the under.

She wasn't certain how much time passed or even if time did pass, but the next time she looked or was aware that she looked, it was dark and snow sifted across her jeans. Her hands were tucked tight in her pockets, jammed deep enough to wrap her coat hard against her ribs. She blinked, blinked again. No dust storm, everything completely silent, could almost hear her heart beat.

No Beth. No Maker. No Laddie.

It was a clear night; the low clouds from earlier had given way to a biting cold with bright white pinpricks of stars overhead. She shoved herself to her feet. Where the skeleton had been, a good twenty yards from where she now stood tucked in tight against the rocks, was a shallow basin. Light snow drifted along the edge and maybe in the center, though Hallie couldn't see it. The only light came from the moon and the stars overhead. Just enough to make out the shape of the basin, to confirm that the skeleton was gone. Hallie turned completely around. Dark everywhere, and she had to get from where she was back to the parking lot and her truck.

It couldn't have been much past noon when she'd grabbed the skeleton the second time, and it had to be nearly six now. She'd lost six hours. She was lucky she hadn't frozen to death. That she might not have been in the world for a good part of that time, she chose not to think about.

She figured she should be able to navigate by the stars and her compass, but she'd followed coordinates here, her phone was dead, she had only a vague sense of the direction she'd come in, complicated by skirting one rock formation after another. It was a mile and a half to two miles back to the truck. Great. But she wasn't going to spend the night here—she couldn't, it was too cold—she might as well start. She had hiked generally west, so she used the North Star to get her bearings and struck out east.

It was quiet, the only sound her boots crunching on the spiky vegetation.

If she kept walking, if she kept her bearings, if nothing jumped out of the shadows at her, she'd get there.

Eventually.

29

It was a good four and a half hours before Boyd and Gerson were able to leave Tel's ranch and head back to West Prairie City. Ole had asked the deputy on second shift to come in early despite overtime the night before and post a watch on Tel. He called the Sioux Falls police and asked them to drive by the house where Pat Sigurdson was staying. Tel was talking about leaving town for a while, which Ole encouraged, until Gerson said she still had questions and he couldn't leave unless he wanted to sit down right now and tell them what they wanted to know. Tel told her to go to hell.

Before Boyd and Gerson left, Boyd walked Tel back to the house. "Look," he said, "we need to know if you were in town the night Prue was shot and why."

"I didn't shoot her," Tel said.

"She called here the night she died," Boyd pointed out.

"Hell, I don't know. I hadn't really talked to her, except at Cleary's for a long time."

"Please," Boyd said. Then, "Laddie Kennedy was a friend of mine."

They were standing on the concrete patio outside Tel's back door. An automatic light on the corner of the house had come on as they'd passed it, though it wasn't dark yet, and it threw long shadows out behind them. Tel let out a long breath, like the slow leak of an old tire.

"Laddie never had many friends," he said. "Even before. He always wanted them. Always talked about things he'd do with his friends—though, you know, he never actually did them, didn't have anyone to do them with. And then, later, his brother moved away and he really didn't have anyone."

"So, thank you. For being a friend to him. He would have appreciated that." He didn't say anything else, but Boyd waited, didn't ask his questions again. He sensed, not that Tel was thinking about whether to tell him, but just thinking about events and what they meant.

Then, "I intended to be gone the whole week—that's how long we'd said we'd be in Pierre. But I got a phone call. Someone—didn't recognize the voice—told me one of my hands was in trouble. In West Prairie City. On Cemetery Street. Normally wouldn't be something I'd come all the way back here for—I'd just call my foreman, but he's been on vacation up in Fargo. Tried to call the hand in question, but she wasn't answering her phone.

"Turns out"—he rubbed a hand across the bridge of his nose—"she was at her boyfriend's house. Turned her phone off. Not any kind of trouble, though."

"You came back here to check on her? Why didn't you just say that in the first place?" Boyd asked.

"Two reasons," Tel said. "Someone wanted me back in West PC that night. Apparently, so you would come asking me questions like these, and I don't like to let someone like that win. And also," his voice dropped half a register, "Katy Kolchak—that's the hand I'm talking about—well, it's kind of her new boyfriend she's with and she's still got an old boyfriend and I know you start asking her and the foreman and her boyfriend whether they can back me up, well, it all gets real messy."

"And last night?" Boyd asked.

"I'd just gotten back to town again," Tel said. "Saw the fire trucks. I was a volunteer myself until last August when I had knee surgery. It's a habit."

"Meg Otis says you knocked on my door earlier."

Tel stared at him, then he looked away, and when he spoke he was studying the light off the glass on his back door. "Jesus," he said. "Yeah, I did. Look, it wasn't just the one phone call. I've been getting phone calls all week. Usually there's no one there. Not even someone breathing. Just . . . nothing. Then once, this voice—still can't tell you if it was a man or a woman—said, 'How much are you to blame?'"

"How much are you to blame?"

"Yeah, I don't know," Tel said. "Though you've got to think it's related to all this, whatever it is."

"Why come to me?" he asked. "Why not just talk to the sheriff?"

"Well, this seemed more like your kind of thing," Tel said.

Your kind of thing. Boyd guessed it was.

"You could have said all this," Boyd told him.

"Yeah, well, I don't explain myself to people. And I don't like that state agent—Gerson, is that her name? None of it's any of her business," Tel said, as if that were as good a reason as anyone ever needed.

"I'll check it out," Boyd told him.

"Spend your time looking at someone else," Tel said. "Prue never did me any favors, but Laddie was a friend of mine once too, and you'd be better off spending your time finding who killed him than looking at what I've been doing."

"Don't worry," Boyd said. "We'll do both."

Hell of a day off, he thought as he and Becky Gerson drove back to West Prairie City; the snow, though still not much more than a few dry flakes, flew straight at the front windshield, like driving into a tunnel. Too dry to stick, just up and over the top of the SUV.

"I wonder if someone's after the stones," Gerson said thoughtfully after they'd driven in silence for ten minutes or so. "Assuming it's not Tel Sigurdson, and while I suppose he could have an accomplice, it seems far-fetched to me. What I can't figure is why now? Why wait twenty years?"

"What I can't figure, is what your angle is," Boyd said abruptly. "Why did you give the stones to me? Why me?"

"I thought you could continue to investigate here," Gerson said mildly.

"No," Boyd said. It was a reason, but it wasn't enough, not with everything that had happened. "There's some reason that you gave them to me instead of, say, Cross. You've gotten me into the middle of this, people are dying for those stones, and I want to know what you know and what it means."

Gerson didn't pretend that she didn't know what he was talking about, though it took her a minute before she answered. "First of all," she said, sounding calm, though Boyd could hear tension too, like razor wire underneath, "you were already in the middle of this." Which Boyd had to admit was true, if they were talking about Prue's death. But it wasn't the only thing they were talking about. Not anymore. "Second, well, Ole told you that I know about these things, didn't he?"

"He said you don't know as much as you think you do or as much as you should." Boyd slowed for a turn. It was late enough in the day that the light had gone flat and landmarks were losing their dimensions. The landscape, stretching out in all directions, looked emptier than usual.

"Fair enough," said Gerson. "I don't know as much as I'd like to. No one does, though I guess it's part of my job to pretend I do. There's a—'network' isn't really the right word, it implies a structure and formality that, frankly, we don't have—but there are a few of us in law enforcement who investigate the unexplainable. Things like those stones, but also people who call in and report that ghosts have barricaded them in their houses or who claim that someone's trying to drag them to hell."

Boyd saw a shape in the waist-high dry grass, something pacing them as they drove. He couldn't make it out, just a shadow among shadows in the late afternoon light.

Gerson continued, "Usually, there's nothing to it. Someone trying to explain how they came to kill their spouse or their brother without actually implicating themselves, someone whose lost their grip on reality. But sometimes, sometimes there's something that actually can't be explained by anything we understand. I look for those things. I try to figure them out. There are a dozen others around the country who do the same. We get together once in a while. We exchange information."

"And this? The stones?"

She made a movement, maybe a shrug. It was hard to tell. She wasn't looking at Boyd as she spoke.

"There's a police captain in St. Paul I talk to on occasion and who claims that he can see ghosts—he's been telling me for years about magic sinks. He didn't tell me they were stones, just places that stored magic, magic without consequences because the price has already been paid. I don't know if he even knew exactly what they were. I mean, physically. I don't know that he knew they were stones. He says that the ghosts talk about them, though, about what someone could do if they were lucky enough to have one. Ghosts know more about magic than we do, apparently."

"Ghost don't talk," Boyd said.

He could feel Gerson's gaze on him. Two large trucks, one of them carrying half a dozen big round bales, the other empty, passed them going the opposite direction. "They talk to him," she finally said.

Boyd filed the information for later, the idea that ghosts manifested differently to different people—to the few people who saw them. It didn't make sense to him, but he was learning that if magic and death and the ways that they manifested made sense, it was in an entirely different way than anything else he knew about the world.

"I don't think they tell him much in the general way," Gerson continued, "but they're kind of obsessed with magic, at least the ones who talk to him. He and I have wanted to get hold of a sink or at least figure out what it was for years. But the dead, according to him, are forgetful and they don't always make sense." Which Boyd also knew was true. "We never discovered more than that there was a way to store magic and that we should do our damnedest to get hold of it.

"He also told me that the ghosts in St. Paul have been pretty agitated for a while. Since before the first of the year. More ghosts, talking more. Everywhere he goes lately, he says, he finds ghosts. It used to be one every month or so, and now it's dozens and all the time. They talk about this place. Taylor County. They don't call it by name, but he says it's pretty clearly South Dakota. He called me and we pieced it together from things they were saying about buildings and cemeteries. Ghosts talk a lot about cemeteries, apparently.

"When a call came in for DCI in Taylor County, you can bet I was going to be on that case."

"Hmm . . ." Boyd wasn't sure he trusted Gerson or that she was telling him her real motives. He also wasn't sure it made a difference. He had the stones. She didn't even know where they were. And she hadn't asked. "Do you talk to ghosts?" he asked. "See the future? Know what people are thinking?"

Gerson shook her head and Boyd couldn't tell if she was regretful or relieved. "No. Nothing."

"Laddie Kennedy talked to dead people."

"Ghosts?"

It was Boyd's turn to shake his head. "He said they were different. Not ghosts. Just dead."

"The photograph said, 'All the talents,'" Gerson observed. "Now Prue Stalking Horse is dead. Laddie Kennedy is dead. William Packer has apparently been dead for twenty years. And someone just tried to kill Tel Sigurdson."

Suddenly, a blast of frigid air rocketed through the car, hitting Boyd square in the side like it had suddenly become solid. He jerked the steering wheel hard to the right, recovered, took his foot off the gas, and slowed. The blast hit him again, harder and colder, like a block of ice. A hard swerve, the sound of something shattering, and the passenger window behind Boyd exploded in a thousand shards of safety glass. This time Boyd kept his foot on the gas and drove straight off the road and a hundred yards into the field, dry grass hitting the underside of the SUV with an occasional crack as something solider—the needled branches of a small cedar, an old fence post—thwacked into the undercarriage. He slammed to a stop, punched off his seat belt, leaned across Gerson to open the door, and pushed her out. To her credit, she grabbed her bag and rolled out immediately, followed quickly by Boyd, trying to stay below the windows. Boyd pulled his pistol and his phone, motioned to Gerson to work her way to the front of the vehicle as he proceeded to the back.

He couldn't see anything, didn't expect to. This was an area he knew well, drove this road at least a dozen times every time he was on duty. He knew where the shooter was, knew where they'd parked their car and where they'd taken up their position to wait for his car. Across the road, a hundred yards on, was a turn-in for semitrailers. It wasn't used much anymore, the interstate took all the traffic, but some of the ranchers used it to load out cattle for market and occasionally to park and ride with someone going to the city. At an angle to the county road, not particularly noticeable or notable. It would be perfect.

Without looking at his phone, he dialed dispatch. Ole answered again. "Shooting," he said once he'd identified himself. "On CR54 two point five miles east."

"Someone's shooting at you?" Ole said. "Why is it always you?"

Boyd didn't bother to answer. Ole didn't expect him to.

30

Boyd had just hung up from Ole when he heard a vehicle approaching along the highway. Gerson began to rise, but Boyd grabbed her jacket sleeve and pulled her back. "It could be the shooter," he said. He had an odd feeling that he'd dreamed this moment. Not the field or the SUV or Gerson next to him, but this particular time of day, the sky gone gray, the sun just at the horizon, not quite dark, still enough light for shapes and objects. And he remembered this feeling, that something was wrong, the air was wrong and the sky was wrong and even the ground was wrong. Escape was impossible. That's what he remembered.

He pointed behind them with one finger, holstered his pistol, and said in a low voice, "Go."

"You don't really think—"

"Now," Boyd said, knew that under most circumstances, she would be, should be in charge. But he knew he was right about this, knew that whoever was approaching wasn't going to help them. And they had to go now because they were in an open field filled with waist-high dry grass that would betray them in an instant if they didn't go to ground right now.

Gerson looked at him. He wasn't sure she'd listen to him, but then she nodded and slid nearly soundlessly away into the grass. Boyd followed. Up on the road, he could hear the car slow, hear the engine idling. A door opened, a brief silence, then it closed again. He urged Gerson forward. They'd have to stop soon or whoever it was would hear them. A few more yards and Boyd paused, tapped Gerson on the leg. He could hear someone moving slowly through the grass, flattened himself to the ground and hoped that the low light and the fact that they'd moved close to the ground would make their retreat—not invisible, that was nearly impossible, but unnoticeable. He stretched a hand into his inside jacket pocket and turned the volume on his phone down to mute—no sound, no vibration, nothing the shooter could sense or hear.

Boyd could hear that the person had stopped moving. Then they started again, walked slowly all the way around the vehicle, opened doors and closed them. Moving quickly, looking for something. The stones? Boyd wondered. Well, they weren't going to find them. He heard the soft rush as the back door on his SUV opened, heard the rip of Velcro as the person unfastened and refastened the things Boyd had stored back there.

"Maybe we could get the drop on them," Gerson whispered so low, it almost wasn't sound at all.

Boyd shook his head. "The grass. It would make too much noise."

Gerson breathed out a long sigh.

Boyd lay as close to the ground as he could, tried to see through the twenty feet of grass that separated them from the shooter. If he lifted his head slightly, he'd be able to see the dark shape of his electric blue SUV and maybe a shadowed figure, but he couldn't see anything from where he was lying.

The back door of the SUV closed. No footsteps. Boyd imagined the shooter scanning the landscape, looking for some sign of them. A rustle of grass, a pause. He could see something that looked like a shadow, slightly darker than the surrounding grass.

He wanted to tell Gerson to crawl farther into the grass, to get away now while there was a chance, but there wasn't a chance. The only choice they had was to hold and hope the shooter didn't spot them. Gerson presumably had her gun. He had his, but in the uncertain light and with only a pistol, it would be a tough shot. The shadow moved forward one step, paused. There was movement back and forth, as if he or she were searching. Eventually they'd pick a direction or start a sweep slowly outward from the SUV. If they were lucky, a patrol car would get here before then, but it would depend on who was available, on how fast they moved.

The shadow took another step forward. Something so cold, it felt like a piece of the Arctic blown straight down from the north rocketed past Boyd's head so clear and real, he'd have sworn it ruffled his hair on the way past. There was a choked-off exclamation followed by the sound of something smacking into the side of the SUV as if the shooter had stumbled sharply backwards.

Boyd heard the faint echo of sirens, like something blown in on the wind from a hundred miles away, but distinct and real. A quick rustle of grass, and the shadow in front of him was gone, the sound of someone moving rapidly back to the road. In a low crouch, Boyd moved forward. If he couldn't see the shooter, he hoped he'd at least be able to see their car. He reached his own SUV, heard an engine start out by the road, was rounding the rear bumper when he heard the car pull out, scattering gravel though not going particularly fast. He rose then and ran, reaching for his phone, trying to redial dispatch. He couldn't make out the model, though it was a sedan. If he could get hold of the deputy who was heading out of West PC right now to where he and Gerson had been shot at, he could ask him or her to be on the lookout for cars headed to town, but even as he watched, the car made a left turn and its lights winked out.

He still ran. Just in case he wasn't too late to see something.

Dispatch, not Ole, answered and he said, still running, "Tell them to turn onto the old Stuart Road. Car traveling without lights. Damnit." This last uttered as a car with red and blue lights flashing came screaming up the road, passed the turnoff for the old Stuart Road, kept right on past the spot where Boyd's SUV had left the road, going another full quarter mile before slamming on the brakes and reversing.

Boyd and Gerson had both reached the side of the road when the patrol car returned and stopped. Teedt and Ole climbed out.

"What the hell?" Ole said. "Was it the shooter?"

"As far as I know," Boyd said.

"Goddamn," said Ole.

They drove back over to the turn-in where Boyd was sure the shooter had waited for them.

"You can't identify them?" Ole asked on the brief drive.

"Not enough light," Boyd said and Gerson agreed. Boyd could feel an intense cold against the back of his neck. He put his hand back there, but there was nothing. It had to be a ghost, must have been a ghost that had warned them just before the shot was fired, a ghost that had shot past him in the field. But why could he feel it? He'd never felt ghosts before. Had the shooter felt it too? And if so, if he and the shooter had both felt it, why did no one else in the car right now appear to be affected?

The turn-in was lit by a single dusk-to-dawn light. There wasn't much to see, though there were tire tracks in the dirt at the entrance. "Who knows if it's worth anything, but let's get pictures," Ole said.

They spent a few minutes photographing a large portion of the bare dirt of the turn-in. Ole visited briefly with Gerson and they agreed to send a technician out in the morning and also agreed that they weren't likely to find much.

*   *   *

When Hallie finally reached her truck, it was only a few minutes after seven, but already the sky overhead was dark and clear, the quarter moon low, nearly on the horizon. The driver's seat was stiff with cold, hard and unyielding, and her fingers felt thick and useless as she fumbled with her keys. As the truck warmed up, she leaned her head against the steering wheel and did the thing she almost never did—wondered if she'd done the right thing.

She'd just sent Beth Hannah into the underworld. Sent her to hell, really. Beth had wanted it. She'd gone after it. But she had no idea.

Hallie knew she had no idea, and she'd helped her anyway. But she hadn't sacrificed her. It had been Beth's own decision. She hoped that counted for something, but she wasn't entirely sure that it did.

It wasn't that she didn't believe that people lived their own lives, that there wasn't much you could or should do to change that. It wasn't that she hadn't seen soldiers, younger and more naïve than Beth, grow up because they had to, because they owned the choices they'd made. It wasn't even that she didn't think Beth could handle it—she didn't really know whether Beth could handle it or not, just like every other person she'd ever met. It was partly that she couldn't make things okay for anyone and partly that she was thinking about Laddie and how he didn't deserve to die, and thinking of him in the under, waiting. It made his death sadder and more immediate, even, than seeing his ghost did. Finally, it was because Beth's going made things easier for her, Hallie, and that seemed like exactly what Beth herself had called it—a cheat.

She pulled out her phone, remembered the battery was dead, and shoved it back in her jacket pocket again. She hoped Boyd wasn't worried about where she was and why things had taken so long, though she was pretty sure he would be. Nothing to do about it, though, except head back to the ranch. There were horses to feed and dogs to take care of—dogs she needed to find homes for because although Laddie's dogs were fine with Laddie's ghost, she didn't think they'd be so happy with the random ghosts of strangers or with harbingers, for that matter.

She put the truck in gear, pulled out of the lot, and was surprised when a vehicle passed her on the first curve going at least twenty miles an hour faster than Hallie was herself. Flakes of snow still fell, though not quickly and not accumulating. In the taillights of the car as it accelerated away from her, she could see snow swirling up like fairy dust. The snow glowed red when the driver hit his brakes, then disappeared as the lights slipped around the next curve.

The fan in the truck was still roaring when she exited the Badlands. She was alone and it felt odd—no Maker, no ghosts. She knew the ghosts weren't really people; that had been obvious the first time she saw one. They didn't talk. And although they knew things, it was as if they were really on another plane, not quite in the world and not quite out of it. Still, having Laddie in the truck or drifting near her had held the moment at bay—just a little—the moment when she had to admit that he was gone. It wasn't the same as losing her sister, but he was someone she'd liked and he'd been killed.

When she pulled up the long drive to the ranch, it was just after seven thirty. The main yard light hadn't lit at dusk, which was odd. The house was dark, most of the yard was in shadow, the only illumination came from the clear sky and the shorter light out by the corral. The place looked cold and dark and empty.

When she opened the back door into the house, something thumped hard against her legs. She reached for the light switch and realized that it was Laddie's pit bull. The three dogs circled her, like they thought she'd forgotten them, which she had, a little. She let them out, dug the charger for her phone out of a drawer, and plugged it in. She didn't have a landline. Calling Boyd would have to wait until the phone had enough charge to turn back on. She went in the living room to find that one of the dogs had pulled all the cushions off the couch, though they didn't appear to be damaged. She made a quick run through the rest of the house, then went outside to feed the horses and check the watering troughs.

Twenty minutes later, as she was heading back to the house, figuring her phone had probably charged enough to finally make a call, she saw a set of lights turn up the driveway.

31

Halfway up the drive, the headlights seemed to pause; then they reversed all the way back down. Hallie watched as the vehicle, whatever it was, backed out onto the road and drove away in the direction of West Prairie City.

"Still stinks."

Hallie wasn't really startled anymore, hearing Maker in her head. It came and went and there wasn't a pattern or a reason, but she was learning to accept that, to miss Maker a bit when the dog was gone. She was particularly relieved this time because she hadn't been sure it would come back. If Beth offered to become Death in Hallie's place, if Death accepted, would that close the crack? And if it did, would she see Maker anymore?

It took her a moment to spot it, sitting just at the edge of the hex ring, sniffing the air.

"What happened?" she asked.

Maker cocked its head like it didn't know what she meant.

"With Beth," Hallie said. "Is she okay? Did she find her father?"

"He wants to talk to you," Maker said, then poked at the ground above the ring. "He can't get in."

"Yeah, I bet," Hallie said. Because of the ring.

"Did she find him? Is she okay?" Or as "okay" as one could be, going into the under. It wasn't a casual thing. It wasn't something Hallie ever wanted to do again, though she'd been willing to, to rid the world of unmakers. It wasn't that she felt guilty about Beth's going, though admittedly she did. But there was an obligation, and Hallie'd known it when she opened the door. If Beth wanted to get out, Hallie would find a way. That was the promise. And Hallie kept her promises.

"She forgets," Maker said.

"Forgets why she's in there? Can't you help her? Can't Laddie?" Because that was the whole idea, that Beth wouldn't be alone.

"Found Death," Maker said, unperturbed, like it knew what Hallie was going to ask and already had its responses. "Sent him to her. She'll remember." It paused, cocked its head again. One of the dogs in the house barked. Hallie heard something, wasn't even sure what she heard, not so much a sound as the sense of a sound, and it was almost—that sound she didn't hear—a sound from her past. She didn't think, dived for the ground at the same time that Maker said, "Down!"

She heard the bullet hit something behind her, was crawling and glad she was wearing dark clothes, but whoever was firing at her had a nightscope; there was no way they could fire at her otherwise. A long crawl in the dark, waiting for the next bullet and hoping the knee-high grass in the field directly past the yard blocked her from the shooter. Not much in the way of cover, hardly anything, and the shooter could already be moving, knowing she was defenseless, because why would she carry a gun here on her own property in the middle of the night?

She could hear something now, the rustle of dried grass, someone moving quickly. She sucked in her breath, got to her feet, and ran to the house. She didn't stop to figure who it was or what they wanted or why they were shooting at her. In this moment, none of that mattered.

She threw open the front door, locked it behind her, ignored Laddie's dogs, who moved back against the walls—except the pit bull, which followed her into the office while she grabbed her shotgun and a box of shells, loading it on the way back through the kitchen. She paused half a second, said, "Stay," to the pit bull, which, miraculously, it did. She stopped then with her back against the wall, trying to see through the window just to the left of the door. She could see very little, deep dark shadows only slightly different from the night itself. The merest glow from the light by the barn, enough to get her killed, but only if the killer were expecting her and only if he were set up and ready. You couldn't just point and shoot a high-powered rifle, you had to be calm, you had to be able to aim. Opening the door, even if there were no lights on in the house, might be an invitation to a bullet. She couldn't just wait, though. It wasn't what she did.

She had her hand on the door when she had a thought, turned abruptly, locked the door with the key in the lock, and went back through the house. This wasn't her house, wasn't second nature to her yet, but she was used to that, to not knowing the place or its tricks. In Afghanistan, every place she'd ever been had been a strange place, a set of walls and roads and vegetation she'd never seen before and didn't understand. It was what she associated with combat, the unfamiliarity, the sense that you could never know where the enemy was or what was just around the next corner.

In the office, she moved a wastebasket and a small wooden stool that someone had painted red and white a thousand years or so ago. The office window was loose, had a tendency to pop up when it was unlocked, and Pabby had lost the screen—and possibly the storm—for it years ago. Hallie unlocked it, popped it open, grateful that it was nearly soundless, and slipped outside, drawing the shotgun out after her.

She crept slowly around the side of the house. The moon was still low on the horizon, but it was such a clear, still night that it felt to Hallie as if someone patient and smart and with a freaking night-scope would see everything clear as day, like she had a glowing neon target painted on her back. She paused, listened. The good news, if there was any good news about all this—and why was someone shooting at her, anyway? The good news was that there was almost no wind, no rustling dry grass, no whistle around the corners of buildings, no wind itself blocking other sounds.

Still sticking close to the wall, she approached the front porch. Something moved in the field below her, not much more than a shadow, but Hallie could see a shape like an arm and the barrel of a rifle. She aimed and fired, not expecting to hit anything, more to make the shooter understand that she was ready and that she was armed. There was a sound like a hard fall and a muffled curse. The shadow disappeared. In the aftershocks, Hallie heard something on the far side of the house, moving quickly through the knee-high prairie grass. She threw caution to the wind and ran. She couldn't see anything, but she could follow the sound. It was loud, sounded panicked, like someone had gotten more than they'd bargained for and just wanted to get out any way they could.

They weren't getting away. Not if Hallie had anything to say about it.

The sound of a car engine starting up brought her to a halt nearly a quarter mile from the ranch house, the length of her driveway and hundreds of yards east.

"Maker," Hallie called. "Maker!"

She had no way to call it, had never asked if there were a way, because she'd figured Maker had had eternity to follow orders. It hadn't asked her to be its master or for anything. And it seemed wrong, not the fact that she wasn't sure whether Maker would follow a command from her—though she did wonder that. More that it was important in some way she hadn't bothered to analyze too deeply that Maker make its own way in the world, that it stick around because it wanted to stick around, not because she commanded it.

"Maker." One more try.

"Here."

"Can you follow that car? Can you find it?" The taillights disappeared once, then twice, then stayed visible for a long stretch. Maybe Hallie could get back to her truck and on the road and catch up before they disappeared completely, wouldn't be stuck at an intersection, staring long and hard in all directions, looking for some small indication that there was one car, the one particular car she desperately wanted, out there in the big open with her. But maybe Maker . . .

"Maybe," Maker said.

"Can you try?"

It disappeared without saying anything. Hallie wasn't sure if that was a yes or a "don't bother me with your petty human concerns" or whether Maker even understood what she was asking, but as soon as it disappeared, she straightened, not quite aware until that moment that she'd still been tightly coiled, anticipating attack. She shook off the tension in her shoulders and headed back to the house, the moon still rising, rendering long dark shadows like coiling tendrils, floating across the landscape.

She trotted quickly inside, turned on the light over the stove, but only after she'd pulled the narrow café curtain across the window on the kitchen door and the shade on the window.

Why her? Why had someone tried to kill her? More accurately, why had the person who killed Prue and likely Laddie tried to kill her? Because she'd known the two of them? If that were the case, they'd have to kill pretty nearly everyone in Taylor County.

She reached for her cell phone. Her right hand was shaking, from adrenaline she figured, or maybe just the cold. She wasn't afraid. And that, at least, felt familiar, felt like coming home, because it was exhausting being afraid. She thanked Beth and the unmakers and maybe even Death a little for that, though they hadn't intended it, getting her to a point beyond. There were things it was worth being afraid of or for; she understood that now. Someone who hunted in the dark without ever seeing their victims face-to-face was not one of them.

She dialed Boyd's number.

He didn't answer. She left him a message: "Call me as soon as you can."

She put the shotgun on the kitchen table, blew on her hands—so cold, they felt like the skin would flay itself at the slightest touch.

Was there one killer? Two? A gang of some kind? Not that she had any idea what any gang ever would want in Taylor County. She'd figured whoever it was wanted the stones because it all seemed to involve the stones, but why? Laddie hadn't thought it was much of a deal. Maybe Laddie's stone was worth more to someone else than it had been to Laddie.

Hallie wasn't going to say none of it made sense. It made sense. To someone. She just had to figure out what kind of sense and to whom.

She went out to the front hall closet and dug out a pair of insulated leather gloves and a dark gray wool ball cap that Brett had given her for some reason she couldn't remember anymore. She went back to the kitchen, pulled off her coat, put a Carhartt vest on then the coat again, stuffed the cap in a pocket, put on the gloves, picked up the shotgun, and stuffed the box of shells she'd left on the kitchen table in another pocket. Before she went outside, she went back into the office, opened the bottommost desk drawer, and pulled out a shell box with just twenty shells. They looked exactly like the shotgun shells she'd just put in her pocket, but they weren't. These were shells she'd loaded herself, with cast iron for the shot, dead man's blood—by which she meant her own blood—on the wadding, and a sacrament recited over each of them.

She'd made these shells, which she shoved in the breast pocket of her coat, three days after she got out of the hospital after defeating Hollowell. She told herself she'd never need them, told herself all that was done and she had the hex ring besides. But nothing was ever completely done. And it always paid to be prepared.

She checked her phone on the way out the door—20 percent charged. It would have to do.

32

Hallie waited in the cold for a good half hour before Maker reappeared. She stamped her feet and blew on her hands in spite of the insulated gloves. She cursed the hex ring, which, by its nature, meant Maker couldn't just come in the house and tell her what it found. The only way she'd know when it returned, was to wait outside.

"Done."

She heard its voice before she saw it, a dark shape on a dark night.

"Do you know? Where they went? Can you show me?"

For answer, Maker jumped through the passenger door of Hallie's truck, then looked out at her out the window.

All right. Maybe they were getting somewhere. Finally.

Hallie tried once more to call Boyd before she left. Still no answer. Damn him, anyway, what was he up to? She left a second message, then turned the phone off to preserve the charge. For the first time, basically, ever, she wished she had a car charger. She figured she'd call him one more time when she got wherever they were going—had to be somewhere within a twenty-minute drive or so. She'd even try to wait for him. If she *could* wait for him. Because sometimes things happened fast; sometimes waiting wasn't possible.

She put the truck in gear, let it roll forward, then smoothly pressed her foot on the gas, adding to the truck's momentum. "Who is it?" she asked Maker, who was already curled up on the seat with its nose touching its tail. "What do they want?"

Maker lifted its head and looked at her. Or at least she thought it was looking at her. It was dark in the truck and hard to tell. "Don't know people," it said. "Don't know."

"Well, where are they?"

"I'll show you."

Which probably meant it couldn't tell her in a way she'd understand, and Hallie was surprised that it could show her. Addresses wouldn't mean much to a harbinger of death. Still, it clearly had some way to find the people Death sent it to. It had a way to navigate in the world, even if Hallie didn't know what that way was.

"Turn," Maker said.

"Right or left?"

Maker arched its nose toward Hallie, meaning, she presumed— turn left. It was a slow, deliberate gesture, as if all new truths were contained within the gesture itself and it wasn't necessary, not now and not a year from now, to personally witness such truths. All anyone had to do—so Maker seemed to be saying, was what needed doing. Everything else took care of itself.

The tough thing with Maker, of course, was that sometimes it just looked like doing nothing.

It was a long, silent twenty minutes, Hallie driving and watching Maker out of the corner of her eye. They were in the middle of what was, even to Hallie's jaded eyes, the middle of nowhere.

She'd also been watching her rearview mirror pretty steadily as they drove and occasionally turning off onto narrow dirt roads just to see, because it seemed logical and even likely that whoever had shot at her just an hour ago outside her own house wasn't going to just give up and go home. Even though Maker had presumably followed them back to their home or lair or whatever, Hallie found it hard to accept that they hadn't just gathered more weapons and circled back. Because that's what she would have done.

She didn't see anyone behind or in front of her, but that didn't mean someone wasn't there. Her taillights would be easy to see—clear night and cold—and she would have a hard time seeing anyone following her if they were willing to drive without headlights. There wasn't enough traffic for that to be truly dangerous, though there would be some danger just in driving with the lights out—Hallie sure wasn't going to do it. But she wasn't going to sit home and wait either. The killer was in a hurry. That seemed obvious to Hallie. She was in a hurry too.

She'd forgotten about Laddie's stone stuffed into her coat pocket, but as she drove, she could feel it, warm against her hip even through the layers of coat and jeans and long underwear.

She made one last turn at Maker's cryptic directions and slowed. Damn.

She knew this place.

She parked on the side of the road.

"Here?" she asked Maker.

"Up there," it said.

Up the drive. Because "here" was Uku-Weber's test field. The place they'd set up way back—or at least it seemed like way back, though it had been only a few months—set up so that Martin Weber could demonstrate to his investors the weather control he'd promised them. He'd set up wind turbines and a fake cloud-seeding apparatus. He brought investors out and pretended that it was all scientific, though the cloud-seeding device had been a hollow shell, the whole thing powered by perverted magic and blood sacrifice. Hallie could see the bulk of the cloud seeder right now, still sitting in the open field like a particularly dark hulking shadow.

Uku-Weber.

It never went away.

"At the house?" she asked Maker. Beyond the field, up a drive lined with dying trees, was the sprawling Bolluyt ranch house where Pete Bolluyt had lived before he died. Empty as far as Hallie knew—she hadn't heard of anyone renting it out, but that also meant, on a property as rural as this one, that anyone could be up there, doing pretty much anything they wanted, and who would know.

"Where they went," Maker agreed.

Hallie pulled out her phone, turned it on, and called Boyd again. Still no answer. She called Brett, who answered on the first ring.

"I'm trying to reach Boyd," Hallie said without much preamble. "Can you try him for me?"

"What are you doing?" Brett asked. Her voice held both curiosity and resignation, like she'd given up trying to convince Hallie not to do things. Maybe she'd even given up trying to convince herself not to ignore things, though Hallie doubted it. Brett wanted science to rule the world, which wasn't a bad wish or even a bad thing. At least until ghosts and blood magic and doors to the underworld started cluttering up your life.

"Tell him I'm at the Bolluyt ranch. Tell him I think I've found the shooter."

"Hallie."

"I'm not going to do anything stupid, Brett," Hallie said. "I'll check things out a little, but otherwise I'll wait. I can wait."

"What if the shooter, whoever it is, leaves?"

"Then . . . I'll do something else," she said.

"Yeah," Brett said dryly. "What's wrong with your phone?"

"Or what's wrong with his?"

"Did you call the dispatcher?"

"No."

Because it hadn't occurred to her. Because usually, or at least lately, the things she dealt with weren't things the police could help her with. But this was a person. With a rifle. The sort of thing the police existed to handle.

"If you call Boyd, I'll call them. Thanks."

"I'd like to say anytime," Brett said. "But really I wish you'd stop finding yourself in the middle of dangerous things."

"Maybe that'll happen soon," Hallie said.

The first time Hallie dialed, it flipped over to the answering service. She hung up and called again. A man, someone Hallie didn't recognize, answered on the last possible ring before it flipped over again. "Yeah?" he said.

"Is this the Taylor County Sheriff's dispatch?" Hallie asked.

"Just a minute," the man said. A pause, then, "Okay, can you state the nature of your problem?"

"Is Boyd Davies there?"

"Is he a deputy?"

"Are you new?"

"Not *completely* new, no. Do you have a problem or emergency?"

"Would you"—Hallie spoke slowly and as carefully as she could—"tell either Deputy Boyd Davies or the sheriff that Hallie Michaels called. That I'm at the old Bolluyt ranch. They'll know where. Tell them that I need one of them—one of *them*—the sheriff or Boyd—not just any available car—out here as soon as possible. No lights. No sirens."

"No lights. No sirens. So not an emergency, correct?"

"Yes," Hallie said, her voice growing more clipped. "It's an emergency. But no lights and no sirens."

"Righty-o." The dispatcher disconnected without confirming or asking if she would wait or giving her an idea how long it might take.

Shit.

She'd done what she could. What she had to do now was wait and watch the drive. Despite the fact that she didn't like to waste time talking when there was action to be taken, Hallie was a believer in backup. That was why you had a squad or a troop or a partner. Because it was important. Because there was no reason to go in alone. Though, sometimes circumstances overtook situations. Then you just had to do the best you could.

She started her truck and moved it to the far end of the field, close to a small grouping of multiflora rose and scrub brush. She turned off the dome light, opened the door, and slipped out. She pulled the shotgun from behind the seat, checked that it was loaded and ready.

Maker was beside her, barely visible, a dark shadow that moved as she did. She slipped slowly through the field to a spot near the ersatz weather machine, where she would have some cover but could watch the drive and the road, both.

Ten minutes later, in a vast emptiness so quiet, it might have felt like the world had ended if Hallie hadn't grown up here, if she didn't know what silence was, her phone rang.

"Boyd?"

"I can feel the magic. Which means I can feel you. I know you're here."

"Who is this? How did you get my number?"

"Is that really the important question?" Hallie was certain the voice was a woman's, though it wasn't a familiar one. It was scratchy, not smooth, as if the connection wasn't particularly good. "The important thing is," the voice continued, "I know where you are. I can see you."

Hallie looked around as well as she could without rising from her crouch or moving. "Who are you? What do you want?"

"What I want is my life back. And I want that stone you're carrying in your pocket. You have them all now, don't you? They're my stones, you know."

Hallie gripped the phone so tightly, she was surprised it didn't shoot out of her hand to be lost somewhere in the tramped-down grass. Why talk to her? Why not just shoot her? Where the hell was she?

"I can give you this stone," Hallie said. "The one in my pocket. You can have it and then you can go. I won't tell anyone it was you." Which was a lie, and anyone who knew her would know it was a lie. She might give this person the stone, they might even get away, but she would find them.

"You won't do it."

"Yes," Hallie said. "I will."

"I was the most talented of all. Did you know that? Me. Laddie could talk to dead people. But what good is that? Dead people can't give you anything. They can't help you. They don't even *want* to help you. They just talk."

"I could leave it here," Hallie said. "On the device."

"Aren't you listening?" The voice rose half an octave. "I want them all, not just the one you're carrying. He'll give them to me. For you. Because he cares about you. Right?"

Shit.

It was a trap. And maybe it was a trap of opportunity and not one she'd been set up for, or maybe the whole thing had been a setup from the start. Either way, it was a trap, and she was stuck in it. Maker had disappeared, for which she didn't blame it, because what could it do except mark the time for her? She was alone, right here. And she needed to get out of this before this person, whoever she was, sucked in Boyd and Ole and anyone else who happened along.

Slowly, she started to put the shotgun down.

"Don't move." Whip-crack, a command.

Hallie didn't.

Out here, no one would hear the shot, no one would know what happened, no one would ever see her again.

33

B oyd's anger flickered all the way down in his bones. It was the kind of anger a person could use to climb mountains or ford rivers deep with spring runoff or even to send astronauts to the moon. The kind of anger that conquered the world. Today, right now, Boyd didn't care about conquering the world, but he was going to find out who'd shot at him. And when he did, they'd better be wary. Because they were never going to know what hit them.

He wasn't pacing, though even in his own mind, it felt like pacing, like there wasn't enough space to contain him and his anger and whoever else happened to be in the room. But he wasn't going to go off half-cocked, or chasing rainbows that would turn out to be puffs of cloud and smoke. He was going to solve this thing, get justice for Prue and Laddie. He was going to figure out what this person wanted, why they wanted it, and why they were willing to kill for it. Then he was going to stop them.

"What do we know?" Gerson's voice made him turn away from the thoughts in his own head and back to the matter at hand.

"Not much," he said. His voice was calm, not angry, all about the business at hand. He crossed the briefing room where they'd set up a makeshift incident room, pulled out a chair directly across from

Gerson, and sat down. "I mean, we know that someone has shot and killed both Prue Stalking Horse and Laddie Kennedy with a high-powered rifle. Someone tried to kill Tel Sigurdson earlier today, and that same someone—theoretically—tried to shoot either you or me this afternoon. Theoretically, in the sense that we're theorizing it's the same person, not whether they meant to kill someone."

"We also know or speculate," Gerson added, "that this has something to do with either the stones located in the first victim's house and the similar stone in the possession of the second victim. Or with something that happened twenty years ago."

"Or both," Boyd said.

"Or both," Gerson agreed.

"I've talked to both the forensics team and the coroner," she added. "Well, both coroners actually. Both victims were shot with the same type of bullet from the same rifle. Death for Ms. Stalking Horse was instantaneous. For Mr. Kennedy, death was attributed to blood loss and shock. The bullet nicked an artery and some of the bleeding was internal."

"What about the bullet fired at Tel Sigurdson?" Boyd asked.

"They haven't done the analysis yet, obviously," Gerson said, "but I think we can expect it will also be the same rifle. As will the one fired at your SUV."

Ole came into the room, carrying a thermos of coffee and a trio of coffee mugs, all gathered together by the handles. He set the thermos and the mugs on the table, poured himself a steaming cup, and sat in one of the two remaining chairs with a sigh that resembled the rumble of a distant train.

"I'll tell you something," he began without preamble. "This ain't the kind of thing I like to see in my county. Which probably, you're thinking, goes without saying, but the kinds of things that happen here, the kinds of things we're on the lookout for in Taylor County are always—it's always—people who know each other, spur of the moment mostly. Someone was drunk or hit someone too hard or just thought it made sense in that way things kind of maybe make sense and then don't suddenly. Since I've been sheriff there have been—until this year—," he added, "there've been six deaths by misadventure—hunting accidents and equipment mishaps mostly. Two abused spouses. Maybe—maybe—three brawls that killed one of the participants. And one, exactly one murder that someone planned out and executed.

"Well, two," he corrected himself. "That Packer fella we found in Stalking Horse's cellar. Could have been a accident, but I would say the evidence so far points in the direction of homicide."

"Everyone we've looked at so far is either dead or has an alibi," Gerson said after studying the coffee in her mug.

"That happens a lot around here," Ole said.

"Two things," Boyd said. "First, I found a fourth stone in an old foundation."

"When the hell was this?"

"Yesterday afternoon," Boyd said. "It's been kind of busy since then."

"I guess," Ole said. "I assume that's important."

"I think so," Boyd said. "I think Prue Stalking Horse buried it there not long after the tornado that flattened Jasper. It was in the old farmhouse foundation just to the west of town. You know the place."

"Yeah," Ole said. "Yeah, I do. That's real interesting. What's the second thing?"

"Where's a copy of that photograph?" Boyd asked Gerson. She pulled the one they'd taken out to the Sigurdson ranch from her purse and laid it on the table. Boyd pointed to the second woman in the picture. "Tel Sigurdson says that Shannon Shortman always wore an electric blue scarf. He says she's wearing it in this picture, though you can't tell anymore. A couple of days after Prue was shot I met a woman outside her house wearing an electric blue scarf. She looked a lot like the woman in this picture."

"Shannon Shortman. Jesus, hell of a name," Ole said. "You think it was her?"

"I don't see how it could have been," Boyd said. "She didn't look any older than me. Maybe younger. Did Shannon Shortman have a daughter?"

Ole said, "I asked Teedt to check Shortman out, back when all this started. Let me see what he's got." He heaved himself out of his chair and left the room.

Gerson's cell phone rang and she left the room too. Boyd had tried to call Hallie as they were leaving the Sigurdson ranch, but she hadn't answered. He wanted to know that she was safely back from the Badlands. He wanted to know that there were no more unmakers following her around, that she had taken suitable precautions—iron pokers and shotgun shells with iron in them. He wanted to know that she was okay. He reached for his phone to call her again, but Ole was already reentering the room. He carried a folder and a sheaf of paper that looked as if it had been torn from a steno pad. He slapped the papers down on the table, the sound sharp and brittle in the empty room. "Here we go," he said.

Boyd looked through them quickly, passing them over to Gerson when she returned.

There wasn't much. Shannon Shortman had had a driver's license registered to an address in Minneapolis, Minnesota. She'd owned a modest town house that had been sold at auction five years after she disappeared. She'd had one bank account, had made thirty thousand dollars a year working at a bank where she'd been promoted three times. No mention of husbands or children.

"Who was Prue Stalking Horse's lawyer?" Boyd asked. Maybe Prue had a daughter. One who looked uncannily like her sister.

"Henspaw," Ole said. "He's everybody's lawyer."

"Did she leave a will?"

"Leaves her bank accounts and whatever's in them, which isn't much, to some organization called New Age Weathervane."

"New Age Weathervane?" Gerson frowned. "I never heard of them."

"Some place in Oregon," Ole said. "Teedt's checking it out."

"Here's the interesting thing, though," Ole said. "Henspaw says Stalking Horse's will leaves the house and all its contents to her sister."

Boyd looked up from the written notes he'd been trying to decipher. "So, it's an old will," he said.

"I asked," Ole acknowledged. "Teedt says that Henspaw drew it up for her ten years ago. Henspaw pointed out at the time, so he says, that Shannon Shortman had been legally declared dead three years earlier. Stalking Horse had him do it anyway."

"That is interesting," Gerson said. "But what? Do we think a dead woman killed Prue Stalking Horse and Laddie Kennedy?"

"Believe me," Ole said heavily. "Stranger things have happened."

"That license plate I asked you to check earlier," Boyd said. "What did you find out?"

Ole shook his head. "It was returned to the airport five days ago. Rented to a Sam Smith."

"Man or woman?"

"Woman, but the guy I talked to couldn't describe her to save his life. I mean, Jesus, he didn't even question the name. Sam Smith. Still, the initials match. Maybe it is a daughter." He considered for a minute. "Once you'd seen her, maybe she decided to switch cars. Of course, that means we got no way to know what she's driving now."

"There's something else," Boyd said.

"Hit me," Ole said, like he had no capacity for surprise anymore, but Boyd was welcome to try.

"That explosion at my house. That was because I put all four stones in my safe. It created some sort of critical mass. Blew the safe through a wall. Blew the stones through the side of my house."

"Really," Ole said. "That's . . . I don't even know what the hell that is."

"Here's what I think." Now Boyd did pace. "I think the tornado that leveled Jasper twenty years ago was big magic, perversion magic. I think Prue Stalking Horse didn't create that magic. I think that was Martin Weber's grandmother. Prue was adamant, even back then, about not creating bad magic, though apparently she wasn't above using it if someone else created it. I think she found a way to store that magic and she planned to use it for her own purposes. Laddie Kennedy said she wanted power. Tel Sigurdson says she wanted to use the magic to heal the sick, kill people, whatever she could use it for. I think she and Billie Packer and Shannon Shortman tried to use the stones and something went wrong. Packer was killed. Shortman disappeared—vaporized? I don't know. Stalking Horse buried Packer. Buried the stones. And spent the rest of her life pretending that she didn't mess with magic."

There was silence when he finished. Ole said, "That's a real interesting theory. And I'm sure it's . . . more possible than I care to admit. But it still doesn't tell us who's been shooting people all over my county."

Boyd looked at the photograph again. "Everyone in this picture is dead, except Tel Sigurdson. And he didn't shoot at himself."

"Everyone's dead or *disappeared*," Ole said. "If you'll think back a few months, you'll remember that disappeared is not the same as dead."

Which was true, Boyd thought. But people disappeared from

Taylor County five months ago because they'd fallen through into the under. Which happened because of the magic Martin Weber had done. Perversion magic.

Which, if his theory held, was the same kind of magic that had caused the tornado in Jasper.

Son of a bitch. The same kind of magic.

Boyd felt an ice-cold breeze on the back of his neck. He looked around, but didn't see anything. He returned his gaze to the table in front of him; then out of the corner of his eye, he saw the door push open and swing closed. "Did you see that?" he asked the others. Gerson and Ole looked at him quizzically. "The door?"

Ole shook his head.

Something cold brushed against Boyd's legs. He looked under the table. Nothing. Fatigue, he told himself. Too much happening and not enough time to process it. "We need to know more about Shannon Shortman," he said. "Are there fingerprints on file? Can we circulate her picture? We need to know if she's been hiding out somewhere for twenty years, if she's actually dead, or I guess anything in between."

"Which could be a hell of a lot of things, given the circumstances," Ole said heavily.

"Then we'd better get started," Boyd said. He headed toward the door. Something yanked on his sleeve and he stumbled sideways.

34

Ole looked up sharply. "Okay?" he said to Boyd.

Boyd rubbed his arm. "Fine," he said. Something pushed against the backs of his legs, something cold, cold enough that he could feel it even through the heavy denim of his jeans, pushed against his knees hard enough to bend them.

"What the hell?" Ole said.

Boyd turned around. There was nothing behind him, just empty floor and two six-foot tables. In the corner between the window on the north side and the door at the front of the room was a shadow that didn't seem right, didn't seem as if it should be there, given where the lights and the American flag and the podium sat. But it was just a shadow. Couldn't be anything else.

"I don't know," he said. "It's fine."

Ole was still frowning and Boyd intended to say that he was fine again and that he'd head out now to talk to Teedt and help gather more information about Prue's sister, about whether she or a daughter or even some other relative might be the killer when he heard voices in the outer office. They were loud enough that it was possible to hear, ". . . Look, I don't really have time."

And, "Well, you can't just . . ."

Ole rose ponderously to his feet and opened the door. "What's going on out here?"

Brett Fowker and a new night dispatcher Boyd didn't recognize swept into the room as if Ole's words had been an invitation. Brett, dressed in a sheepskin jacket, a brown felt cowboy hat, and deerskin gloves, ignored Ole and said to Boyd, "There's something wrong with your phone."

"No, there's—" Boyd reached into his inside pocket and took out his phone. He'd used it when he and Gerson were shot at. So he knew it was fine. But when he looked at it, it said there were five voice mails.

Damn.

He'd muted it. To avoid the shooter.

"Hallie called me," Brett continued. "She says she's been trying to call you and she wanted me to try. Ordinarily, I wouldn't come all the way to town when it's fifteen degrees just to deliver a message, but my experience is that if Hallie's bothering to call, it's kind of important."

That was Boyd's experience too. "What did she say?" he asked. It would be quicker than listening to the messages.

"She said she's at the Bolluyt ranch. She thinks she's found the shooter."

"Oh yeah." The dispatcher, who'd been standing by the door, spoke. "She called a little bit ago," he said. "I got busy."

Ole looked like he might actually, literally, explode. "You got busy?" he said.

"A little busy," the dispatcher said, taking two steps backwards.

"Listen, son—"

"We need to go," Boyd said.

"She said she'd wait for you," Brett told him.

"Something will happen," Boyd said. "It always does."

"Yeah," Brett agreed glumly. "That's why I came."

"I'll come with," Gerson said.

"Take my car," Ole said. "I'll send Teedt after you. And I'll run dispatch," he said, eyeing the dispatcher with a look that made him back up another step.

"Do we know where Tel Sigurdson is?" Boyd asked.

"Deputy Peres called in about five minutes ago. He says that Mr. Sigurdson just went into the house for dinner," the dispatcher said.

"Well, hell," said Ole. "Not that I thought it was him, but it would have made things simpler."

Boyd didn't bother to point out that almost nothing the last six months had been simple, but he knew he didn't need to. He was rapidly learning that Ole understood a lot more about the last six months than he was willing to admit.

"I'll look for relatives of Stalking Horse or Shortman or whatever the hell they call themselves," Ole said. "Someone's shooting people. In my county. And we're going to figure out who that is. And stop them."

Boyd was already out the door, heard this behind him as he went. The spot of cold, whatever it was, was with him, like a circle of liquid ice just at knee level. When he looked down, something like a shadow seemed to keep pace with him. He didn't know what it was and he didn't worry about it. At least not yet. It wasn't hurting him and it wasn't stopping him, and right now that was enough.

It would take twenty minutes to get to Bolluyt's ranch. Probably take Teedt another fifteen or twenty to come in, get his gear, and follow them. Hallie was out there now, right now.

He hoped she was all right.

Hallie's left leg was cramping. She ignored it. It was harder to ignore the way the tips of her ears burned with cold, the weight of the shotgun dragging her arm down. She still had the phone to her ear.

"He'll bring everyone," she said to the voice on the other end of the line.

"I'll be ready," the voice told her.

But she couldn't watch Hallie and be ready for Boyd and the other deputies, Hallie thought. The trick was figuring out when the shooter was watching and when she wasn't. Guessing wrong would be the last mistake Hallie would make.

"I'm sorry you got involved. None of this really has to do with you," the voice said. "But I know Laddie called you before he died. I know you have a stone. And I know you can get the rest of them."

"If you let me call him," Hallie said, "I can ask him to leave the stones somewhere. I can get them for you. No one has to get hurt."

The voice laughed. "You won't come back."

"If I tell you I'll come back, I'll come back."

"No one keeps their word. No one. Ever."

"You don't know me," Hallie said.

"I don't have to," said the voice. "I'm the one with the rifle."

Boyd was a mile from the Bolluyt ranch, approaching from the east, when something hit him hard in the arm.

"Stop."

He swerved hard right and stopped. Gerson grabbed the dashboard. She looked at him, her eyes wide in the dim glow from the dash lights. "Are you all right?" she said.

"Did you hear that?" he asked.

"Hear what?"

Boyd shoved the car into park. He wasn't going any farther until he figured out what was going on, what had spoken to him, grabbed his arm back at the sheriff's office, what the cold and shadows were. Because it could be figured out.

It had to be.

He didn't have the stones with him. But he'd handled two of them. Was this related? Had the stones affected him permanently? And if this was an effect of the stones, what exactly was it?

"She's waiting," the voice said.

It didn't sound familiar. Didn't sound like a voice he'd heard before. And yet there was something familiar about it. Something he almost remembered or the sense of a place he'd been.

"I thought," Gerson said tentatively, "there was some urgency here."

"Just. Wait," Boyd said. She was right. There was urgency. A hell of a lot of urgency. But if he didn't understand this, didn't understand whether it was a good thing or a bad thing, didn't understand how it affected Hallie, they'd fail and it wouldn't matter whether they arrived on time or not.

"I can hear you," Boyd said. It felt as though he was talking to the empty air in front of him. "Who are you? What are you trying to tell me?"

The cold came again and he noticed that Gerson moved even though she'd said she couldn't see or feel anything. "Is there . . ." She hesitated, watching Boyd closely. "Is there something here?"

"Something," Boyd said, still reluctant to guess what that something was.

"You have to choose," the voice said. Like the dream he'd had right after Prue was killed.

"Choose what?"

The voice seemed to be laughing. "Choose to see," it said.

"See what?" Boyd said. Because he would do it, if he knew what it was. There was no time for games.

"See everything."

"I don't know what you mean."

"You need to remember how you died."

315

* * *

"When I say move, move."

The voice, a new one, not from the phone at all—seemed to come out of nowhere, out of nothing—almost made Hallie leap forward.

"What the hell?" She said it like something less than a whisper, like the slightest breath of air, something the person with the rifle wouldn't hear, something she hoped the disembodied voice would.

"When I say move, move."

The voice repeated the words, and she thought they might be in her head. It was so familiar, that voice, tantalizingly familiar, though she couldn't place it.

Her phone beeped. That familiar sound that said her battery was dying. "My phone's going out," she said, though she hadn't heard that other voice, the voice with the rifle, for several minutes.

No answer.

"Move now?" she said to the voice in her head, the one she knew she should recognize, but didn't.

"Not yet."

"I didn't die," Boyd began.

But he knew it was a lie. He'd chosen the lie.

"Is that what you choose?"

Was it? "You need to remember how you died." But he did. Or, Hallie had told him. Which amounted to the same thing.

"Who is this?"

"You know."

How would he know? How would he—

"Maker?"

A sound in his head like huffing laughter.

Boyd closed his eyes. He remembered the moment when he'd come back to himself, like a badly done film splice—one instant he'd been in Pabby's yard, the next in the Uku-Weber parking lot with the sound of an explosion he didn't remember ringing in his ears. He pictured the details of that moment—the burn of cold wind across his cheekbones, the ache of a bruised hip, black smoke, the smell of it like acid, like burnt oil, like the end of time. Something lurked at the edge of his memory, something white and cold, something that expanded until it hurt like a burst of flame, like dying. Like this was it, all over again.

He remembered.

At the end, when the walls between the worlds fell, Travis Hollowell had killed him. Hallie had stood there as Hollowell did it and watched. She'd stood there. And watched. And hadn't saved him.

Hallie had told him. All of it. He'd sworn it didn't matter, but he'd meant it was just words, not a real thing that had actually happened to him.

And now it wasn't. He had died. She had watched.

But he was here. He wasn't dead. And if he wasn't dead, he hadn't died. He couldn't have died.

Except. Hallie had died.

And she was here.

She had never run from it, dying or being here, either one. But then, Hallie never ran from anything. She'd died in Afghanistan and she knew it. She saw ghosts, she accepted that there were ghosts, and she accepted that she saw them.

Until this moment, Boyd would have said he didn't run from things either. He knew his duty, and it was a matter of honor to him, that he did his duty, that he didn't retreat, that he did what had to be done.

Except this time.

When he hadn't.

"Most people choose not to know," Maker said. "They don't even know they've chosen."

"I know," Boyd said. "I've always known."

"Not this."

He'd died. Not almost died. Died. He'd seen Death. He'd seen everything—ghosts and reapers and black dogs. And then he'd forgotten. Deliberately, apparently. Because he couldn't handle it? Because he didn't want to know?

No.

He knew.

"I choose," he said.

"Good idea," Maker said. And suddenly Boyd could see the harbinger, on the seat between himself and Gerson.

"I'm going to count to ten," the voice in Hallie's ear said.

"It's Laddie, isn't it?" Just like that, she knew whom that voice belonged to. "What are you doing here? What *are* you? Ghosts don't talk."

"To ten," the ghost or Laddie or something that sounded like Laddie said, ignoring Hallie's questions. "And then you move. One . . ."

Hallie took a breath and let it out slow. She was putting her faith— her life—in the hands of a disembodied voice in her head. A disembodied voice that sounded like a dead man's. It might not be the craziest thing she'd done; she'd done a lot of crazy things. But it was close.

"Five."

Something howled.

"Not yet," the voice said. "When I tell you. Eight. Nine. Ten.

"Move."

Hallie moved.

35

Hallie was cold in a way that made it seem as if it was impossible to ever be warm again. She was wrapped in a blanket, sitting in one of the sheriff's cars with the heater going full blast, and she was still cold. It wasn't shock, because she knew shock. It was cold, being in one position in below-zero temperatures for too long, and even if her body was warm enough, even if she was no longer in danger of freezing to death, she was still cold.

Laddie's ghost was gone, for which she was thankful, because that would have made her even colder. A part of her wished he were there, though, wished she could talk to him now, when she wasn't cramped and cold and trying her damnedest just to stay alive. She wanted to tell him she was sorry. She wanted to tell him his dogs were okay. She wanted to tell him good-bye.

The driver's-side door opened, and Boyd entered and sat, looking out the front windshield first and then at Hallie. Blue and red lights flashed a hundred yards away at an angle from where they were sitting so that Hallie could see the lights and Boyd's face in profile, both at the same time. One set of lights pulled away as she watched, drifting disembodied across the blackness, bouncing as the ambulance crossed uneven frozen ground.

"How is she?" Hallie asked.

Prue's sister. An impossible thing, but there it was. She'd identified herself when they arrested her, still, she looked more the age she'd been when she disappeared than that of someone twenty years older. Hallie believed her, though, even if she hadn't figured it all out yet.

Hallie still wasn't sure how Boyd and Ole had found her, how they'd managed to get a bead on Shannon Shortman without her seeing them. She'd been set up somewhere in the middle of an open empty field. How had they known?

"She'll be fine," Boyd said.

"Good," Hallie said. She thought she probably meant it.

Boyd turned in his seat to look at her. There was something in the way he looked, something more than had been there that morning even. Hallie couldn't quite identify it, couldn't even tell if it was about her or about something else.

"Are you all right?" he asked.

"I'm cold," she said.

He took her hand. He looked at it, then looked her square in the eyes. "I remember," he said.

Hallie was aware that her heart skipped half a beat. "Remember what?" Though she knew and even though they'd talked about it, even though she'd told him in as much detail as she could, she still knew that this was different, what he said now was what mattered.

"I remember that I died," he said.

"It was the only chance," she said. "I thought it was the only chance," she corrected. Maybe there were other ways to kill a reaper, but she didn't know—hadn't known—them.

"I didn't think it would make a difference," he continued. "Knowing."

Hallie waited. Before tonight, she'd been afraid of this too. And she wasn't anymore. She'd done what she had to do. The only choice she'd seen at the time. Boyd was right. Had been right all along. How he felt about it was up to him.

"But it does," she said.

He pressed her hand. "And it doesn't."

"I'm sorry." She didn't actually say that often, not to be polite or to grease the wheels of social interaction. She usually wasn't sorry. But she said it about this and probably always would. "You know that you're not less important to me than the world," she said.

That made him grin. "But not more important?"

"Well . . . no."

And yes.

In all the ways that mattered to her, just her, he was a thousand times more important than the world. And yet, he wasn't. Whom was she going to sacrifice? Her father? Brett? Taylor County? South Dakota? She couldn't sacrifice the world. But she couldn't sacrifice Boyd either. She could only do the best she could. If it came up again. Which, maybe, they would finally get lucky and it wouldn't.

They sat in silence for several minutes. Hallie wasn't actually sure they were okay. But she was too tired and too cold to ask, pretty sure it would be obvious if they weren't. "How did you find me?" she asked after a while.

"That's a funny story," Boyd said.

Before he could say more, someone tapped loudly on Hallie's window.

"Jesus!"

She said it like an explosion, half-turned and her fists raised when Ole opened the back door and climbed in. He was too big for the space and it took him a minute, three curse words and a lot of groaning, before he was finally situated to his satisfaction.

"I hope we don't transport anybody weighs more than about

seventy-five pounds in this thing," he said. Then, "You okay?" he asked Hallie.

"I'm fine," she said, which everyone in the car knew wasn't entirely true, but they accepted it because that's how you went on.

"Damnedest thing," Ole said, though not like he really thought it was the damnedest thing, more like he was sure someone somewhere would think that. "We knew where she was, but it was basically the middle of an open field and we couldn't get near her. Couldn't get a clear shot. Didn't dare get any closer. Knew where you were too, but obviously couldn't get to you. Then you moved and she stood and, well, you know, it all worked out." He nodded as if agreeing with himself. "Still. It was the damnedest thing."

"Which part?" Hallie felt compelled to ask.

"The part where you moved for no apparent reason," Ole said, like that was what he'd gotten in the car to say in the first place.

"Laddie told me to," Hallie said.

Ole nodded again as if it were just the sort of answer he'd expected.

"Correct me if I'm wrong," he said, "but Laddie Kennedy's still dead, right?"

"His ghost," Hallie said.

Boyd shifted, looking at her, his head tilted slightly to one side, like she'd surprised him. He put his hand on her knee. "I thought they didn't talk to you."

"Well, he talked to me tonight," she said. She reached into the pocket of her jeans and pulled out Laddie's stone. It was small and dull and dark. If she dropped it on the side of a gravel road, Hallie didn't think she'd ever find it again. Still, "I think it was the stone," she said. "It let Laddie talk to the dead. And I think it let his ghost talk to me." She palmed it, then opened her hand again.

"Really?" Boyd's voice was edged with something Hallie couldn't quite identify, but which she thought she understood. Another thing. Another way their lives couldn't be like other people's.

"I don't know," Hallie said. "I mean they're only supposed to work for people who have a talent for them, right? I'm not hearing random dead people. Just Laddie so far. Maybe it just lets me talk to the ghosts attached to me. Which," she added, "would be fine." And the only good supernatural thing that had ever happened to her.

Ole huffed out a breath, then said, "Yeah, listen. We still need to talk to the shooter. I *guess* it's Shortman. She says that's who she is, anyway. I need you to be there, Davies. I'm headed over to the hospital now."

"After I drive Hallie home," Boyd said, "I'll meet you there."

"My truck is here," Hallie said.

"You can get it tomorrow."

"I don't need you to drive me home," she said.

"You don't—"

"I need a statement from you too," Ole interrupted. "You might as well just come along and we can get it there."

Which effectively settled things.

At the hospital, they had to wait until the doctors were finished. The bullet had hit Prue's sister high in the right shoulder, but it was a through-and-through wound and didn't require surgery. Hallie sat in a nearly empty cafeteria with a big steaming hot cup of coffee and told Ole and Boyd everything she could about what had happened from the time she'd been shot at to now.

Ole had a notebook in front of him, but he didn't write anything in it, just listened, like this was not going to be the official story, though some of it, it seemed to Hallie, would have to be included.

When the doctor came and said that they could talk to the patient now, Hallie rose with Ole and Boyd and followed them to the room.

No one bothered to stop her. Teedt was standing outside the door, looking annoyed, but then, he usually did.

Shortman talked to them for three hours, laying out everything she did, everything she thought, and what she'd wanted.

"She killed us," she said. "Me and Billie."

"You're not dead," Ole said.

Shannon stared hard at him. The thing Hallie couldn't figure out was why she looked like she was twenty-five instead of forty-five. People aged differently, but twenty years was something you could see. Except on Shannon Shortman.

"How do we know you're really Shortman?" Ole asked.

She glared at him. "I don't have to prove myself to you," she said. "Take my fingerprints. They're on file. They'll match."

"Why do you still look twenty-five?" Hallie asked.

They all turned and looked at her as if they'd forgotten she was there.

It was Boyd who answered.

"She fell through. That's what happened in Jasper when they were experimenting with the stones. Isn't it?"

Shannon didn't say anything, and Boyd continued. "Maybe it wasn't just the stones, maybe it was a combination of the stones and experimenting in Jasper. I mean, you can see why they'd do it there, since it had been pretty much abandoned so they had shelter and privacy and a lot of space around if anything went wrong. But it was probably a bad idea because in addition to the stones, I'm guessing there was residual magic from the tornado. So they brought all the stones together and it created what? A vortex? An explosion, definitely. We've already seen that. But something else. Something that dropped Shannon into the underworld.

"She was there until the walls thinned again, until we rebuilt them, until everyone dropped back through."

"She's the third one," Hallie said.

Everyone looked at her. "Beth Hannah can sense people who've been to the underworld. She told me she could tell where I was, where Boyd was, and where one other person in Taylor County was. That other person was you," Hallie said.

Shannon shrugged. "As far as I'm concerned, I wasn't anywhere. I was in that cellar in Jasper one minute, and the next I was standing in the middle of the street in Templeton. I almost got run over. It didn't take me long to realize that it was twenty years later, that Billie was gone. And that my sister had everything."

"Why didn't you just talk to her?"

"You don't understand," Shannon said. "It was all her idea. All hers. She killed Billie. She cheated me of twenty years. She promised me power and she got rid of me instead."

Hallie didn't think that was quite what had happened, but maybe it was how Shannon had chosen to understand what had happened.

"So you wanted revenge on your sister and you wanted the stones," Boyd said.

"They were mine," Shannon said. "They had to be mine."

"Why did you have to kill Laddie?" Hallie asked. "Why did you try to kill Tel?"

"They'd have figured it out, that it was me. Especially once I had the stones. And they were talking. To you. And to you." She pointed at Boyd. "I couldn't let them keep talking or you would have figured it out too."

"We did figure it out," Boyd said.

Shannon scowled. "You should have just given me the stones."

"I still don't understand exactly how you created the stones," Boyd said. "It's not as if the rock was there and the tornado charged it. You had to know there would be a tornado. You had to put the stones there to charge, isn't that right?"

Shannon heaved a deep sigh, as if she were disappointed people hadn't gotten exponentially smarter since she'd been gone. "Billie Packer had one talent." She held up her finger. "One. He could tell you where there was magic. It's how he found Prue. How he got involved in the first place." Her face softened. "He was a big dumb idiot. He just wanted to be part of something. And look where it got him." She looked up again, glared at Boyd as if somehow he were responsible for everything, including what had happened twenty years ago. "We knew Lillian Jones was using magic. Big magic. The bad stuff, the kind we all swore we'd never use. We had these big rocks we'd gotten from up in the Hills and we put them in three or four different locations around the house and the town. And we waited."

"Big rocks?" Boyd asked.

"Oh, yes, big. Five, ten pounds. They blew apart in the tornado. I guess we should have known then. Billie only found the four afterwards. We found a few other granite rocks, but there wasn't any magic in them, not quite the right kind of stones, I guess. I don't know. Maybe Billie or Prue could have told you. All I know is Billie and I went out and found them, brought them back to the old farmhouse, where Prue would test them. We got the fourth one, brought it back . . . and I don't know what happened. I just know where I ended up. And that Prue somehow got out alive."

She smiled in some sort of grim satisfaction. "Except I guess she didn't. In the end."

Later, as they were leaving the hospital, Ole said, "I don't even know if she'll stand trial."

"It's not like she's not telling the truth," Hallie said.

"It's not like anyone will care," Ole said.

"There's something else," Hallie told Boyd as he drove her back to the ranch. Her truck was still in the field at Bolluyt's. The sun had been up for the last hour. She was so tired, she was having trouble forming words. But she couldn't skip out on this, couldn't wait for just the right time. Not after everything else.

"Can it wait?" Boyd asked. Hallie could see that he was just as tired as she was; neither of them had slept much the last couple of days. She imagined sleeping for two days, three days maybe, though neither of them would do that. There were horses and dogs to feed, Boyd's house to repair, and work. For Boyd, there was always work.

"I don't—," she began.

Before she could finish, Boyd slammed on the brakes, the patrol car skidding on the early morning frost on the road. Hallie's hand shot out to brace herself on the dash and she swore.

Something drifted out of the field to their left like old smoke and rotted forests. Unmaker. Boyd threw the car into park, reached under the front seat, and pulled out an iron fireplace poker. Hallie stared at him.

"Where did you get that?"

He grinned without humor. "When we came after you last night," he said. "I mean, I know we assumed it was a person who killed Prue and Laddie, but the way things have worked lately, it just seemed likely that I'd need it."

"Oh, yeah," Hallie said, reaching for the door handle. "Let's do this."

She couldn't tell if the unmaker was watching them as they exited the patrol car. She couldn't even tell if it was the same one they'd seen earlier. It was nearly all smoke, tendrils of dark oily black that drifted away and turned the air around it gray and sick.

Boyd held the poker like he was ready to take a swing.

"Hold," the creature said.

"What do you want?" Hallie asked.

"Thank you."

That stopped her. Because the only thing she could think of—
"It wasn't a favor," she said. "It wasn't a payoff."

"It was the right thing." The rumbly voice had an undercurrent of
decay and abandonment. "We couldn't ask. Because Death wouldn't
ask. But it is proper. Well done."

The unmaker disappeared then in a swirl of acrid smoke that
pinged sharply in Hallie's nostrils.

Boyd looked at her.

Hallie swallowed. "That's what I was going to tell you. I opened
the door to hell so Beth Hannah could go in and talk to her father,"
she said, because she was tired of long explanations and trying to
figure out the why of things or how it affected, frankly, anyone. "She
wanted to tell him that she would take his place."

"To save you?" he asked.

Hallie shook her head; this much she was sure of. "To save herself."

36

Laddie's funeral was three days later, on the coldest day of the year so far. The service was at a small Lutheran church on the edge of Templeton. Hallie invited everyone back to the ranch afterwards. She hadn't expected to, wasn't entirely sure how it had happened, but Laddie didn't have family in the area; she'd been talking to his brother, Tom, at the visitation, and it had somehow just happened.

There were more people than she'd expected, and a half inch or so of dry, powdery snow swirled through the yard as cars and pickup trucks and old Suburbans drove up the long driveway.

Hallie's father came inside and drank a cup of coffee, then put on his coat and went back outside, where he tuned up the tractor, fed and watered the horses, then left without saying good-bye, though Hallie was sure he thought he had.

Sally Mazzolo spent an hour in the side yard, throwing a stick for the Australian shepherd. The dog would have carried on for at least another hour and possibly forever, but when Hallie went outside and offered her a cup of coffee, Sally said, "I'm on duty at four, so I've got to go." She nodded at the Aussie, who had flopped to the ground and was happily chewing on the end of the stick. "She's an awesome dog. Lots of energy."

"She's looking for a home," Hallie said.

"You're not keeping her?" Mazzolo looked surprised.

"She doesn't get along with my other dog."

Yesterday, the Aussie had spent the entire morning sitting at the edge of the hex ring barking at Maker, who lay quietly a few feet beyond, looking doggishly amused. Hallie'd been glad—relieved—to see that Maker was still around. She'd asked it about the crack between the worlds, whether it was still open, since she, Hallie, was still in the world. Maker had looked at her, like the answer was obvious. "No more unmakers" was all it said, and for now she figured she'd be satisfied with that.

"I'll think about it," Mazzolo said now, looking at the Aussie with something approaching affection. Hallie was pretty sure she meant yes.

The pit bull followed Boyd from room to room, followed him when he went out to his SUV to get the paper plates and napkins he'd stopped for on the way. It ignored Maker as if the harbinger didn't even exist. When it lay in the living room so it could see Boyd in the kitchen, letting people step over it or go around, Hallie laughed and said, "That's your dog."

"I don't need a dog," Boyd said. But when he put his coat on and went outside to talk to Ole, he whistled up the dog and took her with him.

The Jack Russell yanked a pillow off the couch, moved it to a spot by the heating vent, and settled in. Two days ago, he'd gone outside, trotted over the hex ring and straight up to Maker so the two of them were nose to nose. He was the oldest of the three dogs, and Hallie wondered if that was why, if he had no fear of death or harbingers, either one. In any case, she thought it was pretty clear, he intended to stay right where he was.

Boyd returned, trailed by the pit bull and the Aussie and a swirl of snow. "It's starting to come down," he said, stamping his boots on the mat by the door. He blew on his hands to warm them. "I told Ole I was taking three days off."

"To work on your house?"

"No." He'd bent over to pet the dogs and he looked up at her now. "I think there's going to be a blizzard. I think I'm going to be stuck here."

Hallie laughed. "You think the world will leave us alone?"

He put his arms around her and she felt a chill up her spine that had nothing to do with ghosts or black dogs or anything except that he was close and she wanted him close. She wasn't going to think about tomorrow or the future or anything but this.

"I think it better," he said, and kissed her.